CW00481159

THE LAST VINTAGE

The Severn Family Saga

Lisa Absalom

To "my" Severns again.
Richard, Martin, Amanda, Emily, Katie and Wlliam

Sylvia, Alison and Anthony

SELECTED BIBLIOGRAPHY

Life on the Victorian Stage : Nell Darby

Victorian London : Liza Picard

The Memoirs of Detective Vidocq

Tales of a Victorian Detective : Jerome Caminada

The Adventures of Maud West, Lady Detective :
Susannah Stapleton

www.britishnewspaperarchive.co.uk

CONTENTS

Title Page

Copyright

Dedication

Selected bibliography

CHAPTER 1	1
CHAPTER 2	9
CHAPTER 3	16
CHAPTER 4	24
CHAPTER 5	35
CHAPTER 6	47
CHAPTER 7	57
CHAPTER 8	65
CHAPTER 9	74
CHAPTER 10	84
CHAPTER 11	92
CHAPTER 12	97
CHAPTER 13	107
CHAPTER 14	115
CHAPTER 15	122
CHAPTER 16	132
CHAPTER 17	141
CHAPTER 18	151

CHAPTER 19	161
CHAPTER 20	169
CHAPTER 21	176
CHAPTER 22	185
CHAPTER 23	195
CHAPTER 24	206
CHAPTER 25	216
CHAPTER 26	224
CHAPTER 27	232
CHAPTER 28	242
CHAPTER 29	250
CHAPTER 30	259
CHAPTER 31	267
CHAPTER 32	277
CHAPTER 33	284
CHAPTER 34	294
CHAPTER 35	302
CHAPTER 36	310
CHAPTER 37	319
CHAPTER 38	327
CHAPTER 39	335
CHAPTER 40	344
CHAPTER 41	355
CHAPTER 42	364
CHAPTER 43	373
CHAPTER 44	383

CHAPTER 45   390
CHAPTER 46   398
About The Author   409

CHAPTER 1

Powick, Worcestershire, 1881
Queen Victoria is in the 44th Year of her Reign
William Gladstone is Liberal Prime Minister

"**I** don't want anything to do with your infernal wine merchants, I'm an actor." James William Severn, eighteen years old, stormed out of the dining room slamming the door so hard behind him that the surrounds rattled and left Jane in no doubt of his views. Almost immediately the boy came back in, "For heaven's sake mother, I'm the youngest son, I shouldn't even be in the running for the family business. If cousin William doesn't want to carry on minding it, then it should be my brother Tom or at least John, they're both older than me. Why don't you insist one of them takes over?"

Jane looked at her gentle son, he was unused to showing a temper and now, close to tears, his usually quiet voice was raised and the hint of a lisp that he tried so hard to disguise, was uncontrolled as he protested so passionately.

"James darling," she spoke softly, "please be reasonable. You know Thomas has a very good position with Mr Harris's engineering company in Birmingham and John has now qualified as an accountant and is planning to emigrate to Canada as soon as he can."

"Well, I know what I want to do as well," James was petulant, "I've never made a secret of the fact that I wanted to be an actor. It's all I've dreamt of ever since I was a child and just as I'm getting somewhere you come up with this. Why do I have to give up my dreams if the others don't? It's not bloody fair."

George Wodehouse, his face purple with rage, struggled to get up from his seat, "I will not have blasphemy in this house," spraying spittle in his anger he shouted at his step son, "how dare you speak to your mother in that disrespectful way."

Jane pulled on her husband's sleeve urging him to sit back down but he shook her hand off and continued his tirade, "You have not earned a penny since you left school two years ago. You had an opportunity there for a fine education, paid for by your mother and which you squandered. You idled away your time and you have not shown any sign whatsoever of being able to support yourself since, you should be grateful to have the chance to take over the business. The business your family have built over the past hundred years, you should feel proud to be asked. Your father would be ashamed that you are behaving this way."

"How could you know what my father would think." James's eyes blazed and he snarled, "How dare you tell me that, you, you who've never worked a day in your life and think yourself a man of God, how dare you."

James spun on his heels and left the room again. This time, with his fists clenched in fury and frustration he deliberately controlled his impulse, and with an icy calm, shut the door behind him with hardly a sound.

Jane Severn sighed James William had always been different. Dreamy, often distracted, not at all like his older brothers or three older sisters. Of all her children, he was the one she worried about. She remembered him as a heart broken, seven-year old boy leaving the bedside as his father lay taking his final breaths. She had watched as James wiped his tears away and with them, it seemed to her now, his sense of belonging to the family. He had decided at that moment to distance himself from them, to bury the memory of his beloved father to save himself the pain of missing him.

James sat at the window in his childhood bedroom at Daybrook House. Now, in his privacy, he had tears on his cheeks and his anger had turned to sadness. He turned his head to look at the high, red brick wall to his right, the espaliered apricot, peach and plum just coming into leaf. His eyes travelled along to the furthest point he could see and beyond the ornate summer house with the banks of exotic rhododendrons and azalea bushes, he could picture in his mind the little stream that ran alongside the yew hedge. It was a bright, clear afternoon and he thought of taking his easel and paints down there, to sit, soothed by the sound of the water as it splashed over the deftly arranged boulders, the sun sparkling in the droplets as it trickled on under the low wooden bridge.

That scene could always calm him, even though he hated being in Powick and wanted desperately to move to London. His father had left him a house, '174 Warwick Street, Pimlico'. Even saying the address to himself made him feel more optimistic but he came straight down to earth again. It would be three more long years before the lease could be taken out of the Trust and the rents be paid directly to him. He was under no illusion that he would be able to afford to live in such a big property then, but he *would* be able to rent an apartment elsewhere.

It irked him that what Wodehouse had said was true, he had left that tedious institution of boredom, Malvern College, some two years before without much education. He had not been particularly unhappy there, he had shown quite a talent in his art classes and the master, old Chesterfield, had done his best to encourage him such that by the time James left, he had developed a decent technique and a genuine love of painting. In contrast, he had no interest in mathematics or science and would daydream of music and the theatre during those lessons, reliving in his head the Shakespeare performances he had seen on school trips to London or better still, the comic operas he'd seen locally at the Theatre Royal in Worcester. It was at school that he determined to become an actor, he was enthralled with the idea and burned with a desire to be on the stage.

He was popular, liked by masters and pupils alike. His face, even as a boy, was undeniably handsome. His thick, dark blond hair had just a sheen of the red inherited, he was told, from his great, great grandmother, and was parted on the side with a recalcitrant wave which caused a lock to fall artfully over his forehead. He insisted on wearing it a fraction longer than his peers, which together with the carefully manicured sideburns, gave him, he was told, an air of unruly difference. His deep set blue eyes, fringed with long lashes, sat under darker eyebrows and his thin, straight - he liked to think aristocratic - nose, led to wide, sensuous lips. In repose, his expression was naturally, sultry but a great deal of the time, his mouth was open, head thrown back, roaring with laughter, finding fun in life. He was a natural mimic, but not unkind, and displaying a very ready wit he managed to avoid antagonising his subjects. He was generous, kind and charming, always ready to entertain and as he matured, to sing with a pleasant, but unremarkable, baritone voice.

It was also true, that eager as he was to make his way on the stage, he was finding it hard to break into the seemingly closed circle of the theatre and the main reason for this, he had concluded, was that he was based in the country. He had taken walk on parts in a few productions in Worcester and Birmingham and had more than done his duty by the town folk who wished to sponsor amateur presentations. How many more times, he wondered would he be expected to sing Gilbert and Sullivan's 'When I was a lad' in isolation of actually playing the part of the First Lord of the Admiralty in a full production?

This week however, he was quietly optimistic as he had been granted an audition for a place in the chorus of a comic opera to be staged at a minor theatre in Leeds. Leaving his seat at the window, he picked up his pocket-book, studied the status of his funds and made the decision to leave earlier than planned. He would go the following day and spend the extra time in Leeds. He had been given the details of an agent there and wanted to introduce himself.

The decision now made, he forgot about his

painting, his mood lifted, and he pulled out from the bottom of his cupboard a brown leather suitcase. He ran his fingers over the monogram, JBS, and smiled, the gold may be fading fast, but his father was still there with him. Then he turned to the armoire to deliberate on which clothes to pack.

There was a tap at his door, "James," he heard his mother call quietly, "please can we talk?"

He opened the door and took Jane's hand, drawing her in and seating her at his desk. He bent to pick the eiderdown up from the floor where it had slid overnight, "I'm sorry Mother," he said gently, his head turned away from her, "I did not mean to be rude to you or seem ungrateful, it's just that Wodehouse really has the capacity to rile me," he now looked her in the eyes, "why ever did you marry him, you knew he was possessed by the devil, had you lost your own mind?"

"Don't be so cruel James, you know better than to echo such prejudice," Jane's voice reflected the sadness in her eyes, "epilepsy is just an illness, like typhoid or cholera, but of the brain instead of the body. Our doctors know much more about it these days and George's fits are mostly kept under control with the new drugs."

"Yes, bromide, the drug they use to treat men who have an excess of sexual desire. At least you are spared that abomination, I hope!"

"James," Jane looked at her son in horror, "never speak like that to me again, I am not one of your theatrical contacts, remember your manners and also remember, George is one of the most intelligent, educated men I have ever known. He studied theology and it is a source of great sadness to him that he is unable to take up a position anywhere. He is very kind, after your father died, I was left with all you children to raise and I was not in my first flush of youth. George gave me the protection and security of a husband."

"Yes, and got himself a full time nurse. You could have done better, I know his family are all so very important, Baron this and Colonel that, but he's a youngest son and mad to boot. You never go out anywhere, you never join in the parties and dances in the town. You must be bored to death here."

"Enough James, I came here to talk about you," Jane spoke sternly and blinked away the unbidden tears, "you have less than twenty pounds a year allowance from your father's Trust, how will you live decently if you do not have proper employment? George is right, you have not earned a penny to speak of in the past two years. Why must you insist on the acting business, it is not a proper career for a man?"

"You needn't worry about the family reputation Mother, I would not dream of plastering the name James Severn on the billboards. My stage name is Ernest Severne, my advertisements in the newspapers are under that name, you are quite safe."

"That is not my main concern James and you know it. You need money to live and, in a few years, to marry, to bring up a family and run that house of yours. Yes, I know you believe all your troubles will end when you are twenty-one, but you will find that life is tougher than that. Look at your brothers, they have both studied hard and it has paid off, Tom is established and planning to marry next year, and John is off to Manitoba. It is only you I worry about my dear, I want you to be happy, but I also want you to be secure, I can't bear to think how your poor father would be worrying about you."

"Father would be encouraging me to do what I really want in life. He used to read me those stories at bedtime where people with vision and hope always triumphed over the mob. I wish he hadn't died, Mother," James sighed, "I try hard not to think of him I miss him so much, but *he* would have understood."

CHAPTER 2

1881
The First Boer War Ends
Richard D'Oyly Carte's Savoy Theatre opens in London, the
world's first public building to be fully lit by electricity

J ames's father, James Barratt Severn, known as
Jemmy, had been required to grow up quickly, leaving his school days behind him in 1842 when his
own father, John, had suffered a debilitating apoplexy
during an uncle's eightieth birthday party. Jemmy,
John's only child, was next in line to take over running
the family firm, Severns Wine Merchants and at four-
teen, whilst a little disappointed that he was not after
all to go on to further education, he had relished the
opportunity to get started in business. With his great
uncle James still an able teacher and mentor in spite of
his advancing years, he had learned fast and over the
years had grown the merchants to become a real force,
not just in Nottingham but throughout the Midlands.
When he married a local, gentry farmer's daughter, Jane
Parr, he and his wife slotted very comfortably into the
burgeoning middle classes of England. They enjoyed a
monied life, were welcomed at all social occasions of

the elite of Nottingham and were pillars of the community, ever ready to support, with their time and money, charities and town ventures. At home, Jemmy and his wife were happy together. They produced nine children and were gratified that seven of them lived beyond childhood. They wanted the best for their three sons and Jemmy lived just long enough to see his eldest, Thomas, attend Repton Public School, the very same school he himself had been destined for had not his own father had such an untimely demise.

John Severn's untimely death at age fifty six had turned out to be less untimely than Jemmy's own death at age forty two. For three long years Jane had watched her husband as he suffered the fatigue, night sweats and general wasting of the tuberculosis victim. He had borne, stoically, the months of coughing-up thick white phlegm and blood and had fought his hardest to stay in this world but eventually left his widow Jane with seven children to guide into adulthood without him. Thomas the eldest was fifteen, Emily Jane twelve, Annie eleven, Louisa ten, John nine and his favourite child, James William, was just seven. Jane was left agreeably off financially and she enjoyed a sufficient income from her husband's various land-holdings and properties together with dividends from his shares. Her major problem had been what to do with Severns. She had become the outright owner of the business and, understanding the importance of a full education in that day and age, had no intention of removing Thomas from Repton prematurely to run the merchants. Nor would she have done so even had she been unaware of her eldest son's determination to become an engineer. Luckily, fate stepped in to resolve the matter.

Jemmy had always remained close to his many cousins and in particular to his cousin Sarah Warner. She was the daughter of his favourite aunt Mary who had married Will Warner, his great uncle Benjamin Severn's illegitimate son. Jemmy and Sarah had been very close ever since Sarah, as a five year old, had first seen him lying in his crib, eyes fixed on her and her finger held more tightly by his little hand than she could have imagined and when, she was absolutely certain, he had stuck his tongue out at her! She had laughed with him then and they had continued to laugh together as they grew up. Years later, Jemmy was delighted when Sarah chose to marry William Thorne, the son of an old friend of the family and was more than a little sad when in time, the Thorne's and their children moved away from Nottingham, first to London and then to manage the Thorne's old family drapers business in Llandstadwell, Wales.

In November 1870, Sarah, her husband and their eldest son had come up from Wales to attend her dear cousin Jemmy's funeral and after the service, when the necessary condolences had been dealt with, Sarah had taken the opportunity to admit to Jane of her frustration that their son William was adamant he would not live and work as a draper in Wales. This young man was at present lodging in Nottingham, living on a very small allowance from his father and fancying himself a gentleman. The two mothers had spoken, collaborated, planned and within a month, William Severn Thorne found himself proudly at the head of Severns Wine Merchants, Importers and Restaurateurs.

This role he had acquitted with adequate success for

the first year or two but after then there had been a slow and steady decline. The demise was not totally of his own making, both nature and the government had hastened a downturn in the specialist wine trade. Even during his own tenure, Jemmy had had his fair share of troubles. He managed to hold things together through the shortages produced when the Bordeaux wine producers dealt with a myriad of diseases in their vineyards and in particular, oidium and downy mildew. Fungal diseases, they attacked first the leaves and then the grapes and destroyed entire crops, decimating the wine trade. The growers eventually discovered that adding sulphur to the vines killed the former and 'Bordeaux soup', a mixture of copper and sulphur staved off the effects of the latter. After fighting and winning these two battles Bordeaux was ready to get back to business, but the British government determined to make the vintner's life harder again. The duty on wine was reduced to a lower rate and an act of parliament was introduced to allow, on payment of a nominal licence fee, retailers to sell wine for drinking away from their premises. Not just wine sellers but any retailer. A baker, mercer, draper, butcher, anyone, regardless of knowledge or experience could sell it and, to make matters even harder, the wine need not now be sold in the customary large quantities. An individual could purchase a single bottle. These measures hurt the established merchants badly, many of them going bust.

Just as Jemmy was already finding himself too ill to cope with the increasing fickleness of his trade, phylloxera, a tiny insect, was rampaging through the French countryside with a vengeance, feeding on and subsequently killing, yet again, the vineyards of Bordeaux. This time they thought it an insurmountable loss, thousands upon thousands of vines would have to be destroyed.

William Thorne often thought, in retrospect, his aunt Jane had inadvertently handed him a slightly tainted, if not poisoned, chalice.

Now, eleven years on from taking the reins, he had had enough. Yes, he was a direct descendant of the founder of Severns, old William who had set up in Nottingham in 1758, but there were other great grandsons too and three of them were Jemmy's own sons, now grown. If they didn't want the business, then he would have to persuade Aunt Jane to sell. After all, he now had his wife Lizzie and four children to consider and he could not continue with the millstone of an ailing merchants around his neck. He had brought in a new investor over the years who was loathe to give up, citing always how well the restaurant was performing and that it could shore up the merchants until the situation changed for the better.

William was very well aware that Severns Restaurant, housed in the fifteenth century, timber framed building on Middle Pavement next to their main shop, was successful. His great uncle John had formerly opened the restaurant in April 1842, on the very day he became paralysed from a massive stroke as the entire family were gathered there to celebrate. John had been inspired by his time in France, his experience of French ways and in particular by his visit to the great Beauvilliers restaurateur in Paris. It had taken a while for the good citizens of Nottingham to be persuaded to sit at individual tables, have their food served to them in separate courses and to appreciate the fine, white, starched linen. They were unused to the expensive silver cutlery or to accept a sommelier's recommendation of wines to drink with each food, but eventually they had become accustomed to the new ways. At first it had been the lace merchants coming for long and rowdy lunches over which they closed their deals, made and lost money. Then it became the fashion for these gentlemen to bring their wives or sweethearts to enjoy dinners together in the evening. The ladies liked to dress in their finery, see and be seen, gossip and feel part of the town society. These days it was not always easy to reserve a table, word was out that Severns was the finest place to eat in Nottingham and there was an ongoing waiting list for any other than the most important customer.

It was also true that William was not the most assiduous of owners or businessmen. He was inclined to leave the day to day running to his managers, all worthy young men with ambition if not flair, and he allowed his partner to determine the greater decisions. He was much more comfortable sitting at a table in one of the secluded window bays of Severns, watching the world go by along Middle Pavement and sampling a great deal of his fine cellar. It was not uncommon for him to be unsteady on his feet when the maitre d' bundled him into a cab and sent him home to Radcliffe on Trent where his patient wife Lizzie was waiting.

It was in the week prior to James's most recent row with his mother that William had travelled to Powick to let his aunt know that, should her sons not wish to run the business, he had no alternative but to encourage her to sell up. On learning the disappointing news that none of the three young men were willing to take over, he had gone back to Nottingham to formulate a plan, one element of which transpired to cause him to change his mind completely about selling. He made a very unwise investment with a local corn factor. He lost a significant sum of money and worse, ended up in court having gone to the factor's house one evening, drunk as a lord, where he accused the man in no uncertain terms of being a damned thief, the worst in Derby, and of ruining not only his own life, but that of his wife and children too. His parting shot, accompanied by a violent shove, was to hope that the money choked him!

William had been forced to grovel and apologise profusely to the magistrates and luckily escaped without penalty. He then came to the reluctant realisation, that now, with his finances so greatly depleted, it would be far more sensible to continue with Severns and his guaranteed income for a while longer.

CHAPTER 3

1882-1883
The Married Women's Property Act 1882 receives
royal assent in Britain; it enables women to buy, own
and sell property, and to keep their own earnings.

B y the summer of 1882 James had been in London for almost a year. He had kept in touch with only one friend from school, Martin Richards, who was now an articled clerk with Boodle Hatfield, solicitors with offices off Berkeley Square. Knowing he would struggle to live on his meagre earnings and the small income from his Trust fund, James had happily agreed when Martin invited him to share a tiny, two-bedroom, basement flat in Dover Street. The larger part of the rent was paid by Martin's father and James settled on making a contribution. His need for an affordable roof over his head was fulfilled and what the accommodation lacked in space, and indeed in light, was made up for in James's mind by the importance of an address in Mayfair.

He had come to the city immediately after what proved to be a very short spell in the chorus of the comic opera in Leeds, and stopped for less than a week at Daybrook House to say goodbye to his mother and arrange for his belongings to be sent to his new dwelling. Once in London he immediately engaged an agent, Mr Aloysius Ogden, not his real name James fancied, and was advertising regularly in *The Stage*, *The Era* and the *Morning Post*. "Ernest Severne. Unengaged, available for Comic Opera. Baritone."

These advertisements were bringing scant success but in October he was looking forward to taking a rather minor role with a previously well known actress, Miss Carlotta Leclercq, who, now well past her prime, would nonetheless be playing the leading lady in a short two act comedy, *The Little Treasure*. This was to be a single performance only at the Ladbroke Hall, Notting Hill. Miss Leclercq, newly married, had recently returned from a spell in America and her ability to attract an audience to one of the more illustrious theatres was severely diminished. James's introduction had come by word of mouth from a young actress he was friendly with, Miss Lisa Leonard. She had been engaged to play Celia in an extract from the forest scene from Shakespeare's *As You Like It,* the evening's supporting act. Excitingly for him, James was also to play Orlando. Even with these two parts, he would be on stage for just a few minutes all together, but he would be dressed in costume and in London.

"Lisa, here we are, listen to this," James had the newspapers as they sat in his tiny parlour drinking coffee and sharing a large slice of raspberry tart, bought in celebration of their performance the night before, from the Italian bakery in Piccadilly, "it's from *The Stage*," and he read, "A 'select but not very numerous audience assembled on Tuesday evening to witness a special performance given by Miss Carlotta Leclercq.'"

"I've played to a lot less," giggled Lisa, "but I have to agree, they wouldn't have filled Drury Lane!"

"Quiet, listen, 'fairly supported by those engaged ...blah, blah, blah ...the interest naturally enough was centred on Miss Leclercq's charming delineation of Lady H ... ladylike dignity consistently sustained.'"

"You do know that she's really only as French as my little finger don't you Ernest? She was born in the East End, it was her old man who went on the stage with the name Leclercq." Lisa licked her fingers, "Oh my word, that tart is good, can I have your crumbs I'm starving. Get onto us, what does the great critic have to say about me?"

"Be patient, I'm going to read it all the way through. I like this bit, he says it was a fairly good performance too by Mrs Middleton of Nellie, 'who had the good sense to make up sufficiently aged for the fascinating female with peacock's voice and parrot's nose!'"

"I thought she was like that even without the makeup," squealed Lisa with delight.

"Sssh! He says, 'Gertrude was a trifle too energetic to be natural,' I should say so, she was like a swashbuckling pirate rather than a young maid, and 'Clara a particularly pretty Jane'. Ah here we are, 'Mr Ernest Severne illustrated Walter with skill and liveliness'. Praise indeed ..."

"Is that all, didn't he say anything about your charisma or your devilish good looks," Lisa ducked as James flicked the newspaper at her head, "get to my part, hurry up."

"No, I shall finish this bit about the play. Be patient." James gave a loud laugh, "you'll like this, 'Charles committed the unpardonable sin of acknowledging applause in the middle of an act'. Then blah, blah, good Lord, this critic reckons 'the rendition' of that dreadful song, my words not his, 'by Miss Agnes Wood, was tasteful and accurate', I thought she screeched, and it was awful. Ah, now we are getting nearer to the amazing Miss Leonard," he shot her a grin across the table, "we're on to 'As I hope you Liked it'. 'Miss Nellie Jordan in the doublet and hose', oh how I enjoy dressing up…"

"You always look as if you are dressing up Ernest, look at you now, I've never seen a cravat in such an elaborate bow."

"Mind what you say minx, or I shall tear the paper up and you will never know what they thought of you. That's better, you sit still like that and I'll carry on," he beamed at her and thought how much he enjoyed this girl's company, "'Mr Ernest Severn was the Orlando and Miss Lisa Leonard, Celia'. Good God, that's it. Nothing more. The wretch, doesn't he know that we need reviews if we are to get known. Incompetent man, if he knew anything at all about acting, he'd be on the stage doing it, not making or breaking people's careers with his damned column. Tosh."

"Well what else does he say," Lisa asked, her spirits dashed, "is there nothing after that?"

"No, he goes on to praise our cockney mademoiselle for her recitation, saying she got unlimited applause."

"S'pect they were just glad it was over," grumbled Lisa, "and she took enough bows over it too."

"Then he mentions that 'Miss Fowell manipulated the piano in a most entertaining fashion' in between the acts." He threw the paper on the floor, "So

that's that little Lisa, what have we got next in the pipeline?"

"Well, I can show off my linguistic prowess there
for you. I can speak it in three languages, Nil. Nada.
Nothing."

It was to be another year before James managed to secure anything resembling a steady wage and even then,
it was little enough and for only twelve weeks. Following several months with a single, minor, performance
here and there and living very meagerly on his allowance, in October 1883 he landed a small part in a new,
six act melodrama, *The Crimes of Paris* being staged
at the Surrey Theatre. He would always remember the
thrill of entering by the Stage Door on that first day of
rehearsals. First, he was taken on a tour, starting at the
front entrance with its impressive portico and Ionic
columns. The interior was very grand, massive stone
staircases led from the front door to the lobby and
from there to the gallery. Horseshoes of elaborate, iron
balustrade supported boxes and enclosed the pit under
the huge domed ceiling. The fronts to the boxes and gallery were enriched and modelled in carton-pierre, the
papier mâché indistinguishable to James from genuine
stone or bronze and depicted medallions and wreaths
all finished with light coloured tints and gold leaf. This
decoration was continued round the base of the dome
where were also inscribed in gold letters, the names
of celebrated dramatists. James started to read, 'Shakespeare, Jonson, Vanbrugh, Dryden, Congreve, Garrick,
Byron, Sheridan ...', he could be forgiven for believing
that this, his first lucky break, was the real beginning of
his career.

The play was well reviewed 'enthralling, emotional and sensational' were words bandied about, the moral of the story was popular as virtue triumphed over vice. The performance lasted over four hours and by November the play was being released for touring the provincial theatres, its own run in London to be over by Christmas. Even though he had only half a dozen lines to speak as Captain Remy, James loved it. He was on a major London stage at last and was not unduly disappointed not to be singled out in the reviews, just grouped along with all the other minor parts as being 'played efficiently'. He had now seen his name on a proper Stage Bill, and he was elated.

He wanted to stay in London and decided not to apply to join the company set up to tour the provinces. He settled back into the routine of advertising, attending the occasional audition and bearing regular disappointments. He appeared in a charity event here and there but spent the majority of his time finding things to fill his day, an activity in which he was by no means alone. There was a growing community of out of work actors who gathered together to drink coffee or wine, commiserate, share information and occasionally celebrate a success. Lisa Leonard had moved on and one of his more constant companions now was an equally pretty and lively girl, Sophie Cousens who had played another insignificant part in *The Crimes*.

In March the following year, the day came that James had been waiting for so impatiently. His coming of age birthday. He invited Sophie to join him on the visit to his mother's, "It'll be a bit like a lamb walking into the lion's den," he warned her, "but it will help keep me from throttling my stepfather." Sophie, always willing to please her handsome beau, agreed.

They travelled down to Worcester by train the day before he came of age. His brother John had been in Canada for nearly two years now and of all his siblings, only Annie was still living at Daybrook House and she and Jane gave the couple a warm welcome. George Wodehouse offered a guarded olive branch and insisted he was very pleased to see them. Over afternoon tea Jane was animated in easy conversation about the family, the eldest son Tom, his career, his wife and her delight at a first granddaughter. She was obviously glad for Emily Jane, her husband and a first grandson, whom Jane saw regularly as they lived close by in Upton on Severn and for Louisa, who had married the previous autumn.

"It was such a shame you could not come down for the wedding," his mother said, James thought, rather pointedly, "the weather was fine, and your sister was so beautiful. She and Abraham are settled in a very nice house, just the other side of the village. Will you have time to visit?"

"I'll see Mother, but you know I couldn't leave London last October, I was in rehearsals for the play at the Surrey, it was a really good break for me, and I didn't want to upset the manager by taking two days out. Sophie, you remember, I was really torn about it, wasn't I."

The girl, in all honesty, could not recall a single conversation about it but in any event, it was George Wodehouse who responded. "Doesn't seem much of a break to me," he said sarcastically, "I understand you are still out of work."

Jane looked at her husband and James, seeing the sadness on her face, was about to lambast his stepfather when, perhaps sensing that, the man rose from his seat announcing to the room that he was retiring to his room for a rest before dinner. Jane put her hand up to James, "Please James, no, no unpleasantness today, I see so little of you. Please ignore him and tell Annie and me all about yourselves."

"Yes," echoed Annie, "you are a dreadful brother, you never write with any of the gossip."

"Your family seem very nice, well, not your stepfather, but your mother and Annie are really kind," Sophie exclaimed to James when they were left alone in the drawing room, "but Ernest, why do they all insist on calling you James, is that your real name?"

"Not any more my little duchess, do I look like a James?" He pulled her to him, hugged her fiercely and kissed her on the forehead, "No, of course I don't, and I am soon to look like Ernest, actor and man of means!" The most important information of the day as far as he was concerned having been that an appointment was arranged with Jane's solicitors in Worcester, and for James, eleven o'clock the next morning, the fifth March, his twenty first birthday, could not come soon enough.

CHAPTER 4

1884
The Third Reform Act widens the adult male
electorate in the United Kingdom to around 60%

Т he talk at dinner that first evening in Powick
was almost entirely of the two letters his
mother had received from John in Manitoba
and, even had it not been interesting in itself, James was
pleased that it kept the conversation from reverting to
the same old tired theme of pressure on him to get a
different job. As soon as the meal was finished, George
rose from the table saying, "It's been a long day. Jane
will you help me prepare my medication please."

"Yes of course dear," Jane stifled her sigh, "right
away. Do carry on James, you could read the next letter,
I can read it again at any time."

"No Mother, it can wait until tomorrow, there's
no hurry. It is nice to share it with you. It wouldn't be
the same if you are not here."

When they'd left the room Annie almost ex-
ploded, "I really need to get away from him, he is insufferable and poor mother, she is just his slave. Puts
me off looking for a husband that's for sure if marriage

is just servitude." She was striding up and down the room, "You know he has been totally ghastly to mother about you bringing Sophie here James, you not being married or even engaged and going about together 'like wanton libertines' I think were his words. He really disapproves of your lives in London, thinks you are reckless and immoral. If he had his way you would have been asked to leave the house the minute you arrived. I didn't hear what Mother promised him to make him even half civil to you, I just fear that he will be unreasonably demanding of her for weeks to come to get his revenge."

James was on cloud nine the next day after his visit to Worcester and he asked Sophie to stroll in the garden with him, "It feels so good," he grinned at her, "I'm my own man at last. It's not a lot of money, but the rent from the house will come straight to me and also, it means I am now a property owner! My entire fortunes have changed in just one day. I still have to wait until I'm twenty-five to have control of the rest of my inheritance from Father, but it's a jolly good start." He threw a tiny pebble into the stream and counted the ripples, "Oh Sophie, I could burst into song and dance I feel so happy, but not here, I wonder when the next train back to London is. I can't bear to stay in this house any longer, besides," he grasped her hand and they gave a little twirl, "I have to get these papers to my solicitor - and first I need to find one," he laughed again, "I think Martin's too grand, Boodle & Hatfield no less, I'll need a rather cheaper man."

"But you haven't read the other letter from your brother," Sophie protested, she had been absorbed with the news from Canada, "it is fascinating, and I've never known of anyone emigrating like this. Besides, your mother will be so upset. Couldn't we stay another night? It's so lovely to be in the countryside, away from the noise and bustle of the City." She thought for a moment and laughed, "Although I'm sure I shall be missing it all by tomorrow!"

"Well I suppose so, if you think we should, I'll rely on you to keep me away from Wodehouse, he really does get my goat and I don't want to upset my mother. Maybe we could visit Louisa this afternoon, her husband Abraham is a doctor at the local asylum, the big towns send all their lunatics and paupers out here to us in the country. He's jolly interesting but George is hardly civil to him, it's because he knows the asylum's where he should be locked up!"

"Ernest don't say such things. That's really unkind, your mother was telling me about the new research into, what is it? Eply... something, he can't help it and he's not mad." Sophie took James's arm, "I don't believe you mean to be cruel anyway, you are always such a gentle, kind man, it is not like you at all. Oh, look at the little bridge, can we cross over it or shall we use the stepping stones?"

"We'll go over the bridge and then there's a gate hidden in the hedge so we can go into the village. The only building worth looking at is the church, parts of it are seven hundred years old and in the autumn the creeper covering it is a glorious colour, reds, browns and gold. I often used to sit in the churchyard and paint it during the school holidays, it got me away from the house."

He closed the gate behind him, "I think Duchess, one of the first things I should do when we get home is find a larger apartment. I'll be sorry to leave Martin's, but it was only supposed to be temporary and I need more room, I would dearly like to unpack my paints. Yes, I need an attic too," he noticed her blank look, "for the light you silly goose, for painting. What did you think I meant, to lock you away like Rochester's mad wife at Thornfield?"

James and Sophie were lounging on his sofa and Martin was sprawled in an armchair crammed into the corner of the parlour at Dover Street. The couple were tired after a tedious journey back from Powick and at Martin's insistence, they were all nursing a glass of cheap red wine. Putting his glass down, James got up and went to the little table inside the front door, picked up the pile of letters the daily woman had put there, and took them back to his seat. He was sifting through the post, throwing what looked like bills to one side and ignoring Martin's advice, "That is the start of a slippery slope old chap, ignoring the demands for money. You wouldn't imagine the paperwork we have to do taking people like you to court," when one envelope in particular drew his attention.

It was from his agent and he tore it open grumbling, "Another bloody rejection I expect, or Aloysius's bill, well he can wait too … good lord Sophie, I've got the job! The seventh of May at the Gaiety Matinée, you remember I auditioned for a part in *Patience*, well I'm only in the chorus, but it's work! *Patience*, Duchess, you see, patience pays off in the end."

Sophie groaned, "That's not funny, I'm far more patient than you and I've got nothing at all at the moment. Not even a house in London and big fat funds, you poor little starving actor," she grinned up at James adoringly, "well done Darling, it looks as if this could definitely be your year."

"Come on Sophie, and you Martin, let's go and celebrate my exceeding good fortune with a slap up plate of lamb chops at the Gaiety Restaurant," James pulled her up to her feet, "it's on me, get your glad rags on, 3s 6d a plate and I'll treat us all to a good bottle of claret for a change. It's late so we should catch the after-theatre crowd, some of the actors even."

Martin declined the invitation, "I've got an exam tomorrow, contract law and there's a whole book to try and memorise before then. I'll let you two love birds go on your own, I'm sure I can find a crust and water here to eat. No, don't you worry about me ..." and he pretended to wipe away mock tears, "I'll survive."

"I'm so full up Ernest, I couldn't eat another bite. My chops were divine, it's so long since I ate this well," Sophie leaned back in her chair and stretched her arms upwards, "I've had bread and cheese for supper for what seems like weeks - except at your mother's, of course. She seems really nice, your mother, it's a pity she is tied to that horrid man, you should go to see her more often it's obvious she misses you."

"I think she misses my brothers more than me. I should imagine she's glad I'm away from Worcestershire and besmirching the family name elsewhere now!"

"Is that why you changed your name from James? That's such a lovely name and Ernest is, well, it's a bit odd really. Did she think you were lowering the family standards?"

The wine loosened his tongue and feeling more fulsome than usual, James told her, "Not really, I don't think she minds very much that I've chosen to be an actor, but she would just like me to be able to earn a decent living. No, I thought there were too many James's in my family, uncles, cousins, great uncles, great, great uncle even," he hesitated, "my father was James too. He died when I was seven and I was old enough to know that a marvellous man was gone. I could never live up to his name." Looking away, he raised his glass and took a sip, "I chose Ernest as a joke! To show that I am a very earnest fellow," he said nodding his head and grinning at Sophie, "not the wastrel my stepfather and eldest brother think I am. They are bigots, believe all actors are vagabonds at worst and decadent at best," he looked up, "aha, speaking of which Duchess, look, here comes Potty and his entourage."

Potty Sinclair was a most distinguished looking man. James had never heard his actual name, and no one knew why he was called 'Potty' other than it was a name he had been given at school which had remained with him ever since. He was both tall and broad and, this particular evening, was dressed in a perfectly turned out dinner suit with his black overcoat draped around his shoulders. Should he ever not be talking or smiling, it was apparent that his mouth, downturned at the corners, would bear an air of melancholy but Potty's face was rarely still. He had ignored the fashion for facial hair and was clean shaven, not even any bushy sideburns, and his dyed, dark brown hair was cut short, parted with precision on the left and swept back, the other side sporting a perfect curl reaching to the inner corner of his right eyebrow.

"Miss Cousens no less," he boomed approaching their table and removing his hat, added, "and the earnest Mr. Severne. How marvellous to see you both and looking so well my dears." He handed his hat, cane and coat to the hovering maitre d' who, having missed the great man's entrance, had sped through the tables to catch up with him and bowed obsequiously as he took the revered possessions. In true theatrical style Potty kissed the back of Sophie's gloved hand reverently, then as James stood up behind him, turned back to shake his. "Sit dear boy, sit, rest your weary bones. May we join you?" He gestured to the two young men with him, "May I introduce Messrs. Fuller Mellish and Teddy Loftus, both up and coming stars of the stage."

Potty lost no time in completing the introductions, arranging for chairs to be shuffled and, rather worryingly for James who thought it may go on his bill, ordered a bottle of champagne. Potty was an actor and theatre manager, although it was true to say that he was, just at present, without either premises or production, which made his good fortune at having seemingly endless private means all the more advantageous. The conversation centred of course on which plays were on where, who was playing who, good reviews, bad reviews and as much gossip as the five of them could spread.

After ordering yet another bottle of champagne, assuring James with a gentle squeeze of his arm, that he would not be passing on the cost to him, Potty said, "Let's be serious now dear boy for a moment. Fuller here is in a little clique that is performing at the great Mrs Sassoon's soirée in June and he was just telling me that one of their number, the baritone as it happens, has had to drop out. Permanently we fear on account of the fact that he died under the wheels of a horse drawn omnibus whilst in his cups last week, and whilst we are all very sad about it, I have suggested that Fuller puts your name forward as his replacement. As I happen to know Miss Helen Bruno the principal, I do not think there will be any disagreement and you may repay me in the future with much grateful thanks and fawning!"

With the possibility of the drawing room entertainment in the offing too, James was in great spirits at the rehearsals of *Patience* and if he was disappointed it was yet another single show, he was really pleased that he was to be in costume, dressed as a dragoon. He was quick to learn and by the time the date in May came, he knew not only his own part but also that of the two leading roles and, he would not admit this to anyone, not even Sophie, he dreamt at night that Bunthorne the comic poet would fail to appear and he, Ernest Severne, would be thrust into the spotlight. He could almost taste the laughter at his portrayal and the rapturous applause. In the cold light of day, he was determined to be a success in the chorus and felt, pragmatically, that this was another step forward.

Sophie joined him at the after-show party, "Darling you were wonderful," she enthused, "I hope the critics mention you, you deserve it so."

"Thank you, Duchess, it was marvellous being on such a famous stage, we must try and get you on here too. Do you think you should change agents, Aloysius seems the best of a bad bunch at the moment."

"Well, I wasn't going to tell you till tomorrow, didn't want to risk upsetting you on your big night, but I've been offered a really good deal with a touring company, we are off next week for six months to the frozen wastes of the north, Watford is first I think. Oh Ernest,

I am going to miss you so much, I know you will forget me and when I come back you will be with someone else. Please will you wait for me? I almost didn't take the job because I love being with you so much."

"Nonsense Sophie, you want to be on the London stage surely, so you have to do the other stuff too. I've played in dreadful places, Leeds, Birmingham and worse, it won't be for long and I'll be much too busy to be taking up with any other floosy! You my Duchess, are quite enough and I'll miss you too."

James found himself feeling sad that Sophie was leaving, they spent a lot of time together and he realized how much she made him laugh and kept his mood bright. Fortunately, his despondency was short lived, he was, after all, a young man and resilient. The day after she left, he received notice that Potty had been true to his word. James had been engaged for the private, evening theatricals with Fuller Mellish in June. There were to be two recitals, a one act comedietta called *A Storm in a Tea-Cup* and the famous, 'wherefore art thou' scene from *Romeo and Juliet.* In addition, he guessed there would be piano recitals and a few songs, and he looked forward to meeting his fellow artistes.

Mrs Evelyn Sassoon lived in a very grand town house in the very grand Belgrave Square. Rehearsals had been held in a scruffy hall a couple of miles away and when James arrived at her house for the show on the balmy June evening, he was not surprised to be directed to the staff entrance, down below street level! He knew exactly the order of the evening's proceedings, two piano solo recitals from a young lady, Miss Blanche St Clair whom he believed to be a niece of the hostess, two songs from Miss Beata Francis and Mr Walter

Marnoch, whom James thought rather dull and the two dramatic pieces led by Miss Helen Bruno. There were two other actresses, himself, Fuller and Teddy Loftus. He, James, was to perform only in the little comedy. Rehearsals had gone well, and he was looking forward to acting 'The Respected Parent' of the principals, Mr Felix Summerly played by Fuller and Mrs Summerly played of course by Miss Bruno. He had several lines and was extremely happy to dress up. A blue coat and white waistcoat from his own wardrobe, pale yellow, nankeen trousers borrowed from a friend and a white neckcloth, all topped by a broad brimmed hat borrowed from Potty himself.

Arriving early, the cast were responsible for setting their own stage with the help of the house servants and as his little play was to be come before the scene from Shakespeare, one end of the drawing room was set to depict a parlour in a 'villa near London'. An ornate chimney piece was central to the wall, which unfortunately meant they could not 'open onto the back garden' as the script dictated, but there was luckily a door to the right-hand side. A small round table was laid as if for breakfast and on one chair to the side sat a large, open carpet bag and on another, an open portmanteau. Round the room were a confusion of corded boxes, carpet bags and brown paper parcels.

James had to admit the plot was somewhat weak, as so many of these little plays were, but he wanted to play comedy and he was determined that his ennui with the well-rehearsed humour would not show through. For the performance, he would make it as if he was hearing the words for the first time! The crux of the story was that in the final moments before the Summerlys set off on a trip down the Rhine, a letter turns up from France, and after a servant's mishap with a bottle of ink, the name of the addressee cannot be read. Much speculation and digression follows this, until roughly five minutes from the end of the play, James's character enters and claims the letter as his own. A letter from his wine merchant in Burgundy. Sweet coincidence he thought! Mrs Sassoon's guests were suitably appreciative, they laughed in the right places and clapped generously at the conclusion.

The 'stage' was then rejigged and a raised dais, fashioned from a wooden stool, was placed behind a tall, thin table covered with a cloth and adorned with garlands of flowers to represent the balcony from behind which Miss Bruno could speak Shakespeare's famous words. Fuller was Romeo, Teddy a supporting player and all went very well for them whilst James was obliged to sit to the side of the makeshift stage, his hat on his lap, instructed to keep his eyes locked on the actors and not to scan the room and the guests. All seemed a huge success and as the review said the following day, "the players succeeded in interesting the audience." "Not much," thought James again, but it was another milestone, his name was in a revue in the *Morning Post*.

CHAPTER 5

1884
Gilbert and Sullivan's Princess Ida premières
at the Savoy Theatre, London

One advantage of performing in a patron's home was the invariable provision of a light champagne supper after the show, when the actors were expected to mingle with the audience. This practice was especially welcome to James as the major part of his income was now dispersed on the rent of a new, larger, apartment in Beauchamp Place and, when he could not find others to feed him, he was in a perpetual state of hunger. After the applause had died down and Mrs Sassoon had thanked both the company and the attendees with equally fulsome praise, they were all led through to the dining room where, French style, a long table was laden with trays of delicacies and a row of maids stood behind it, ready to serve the guests.

Not knowing what to expect, James was surprised to find most of those assembled remained standing to eat. He chose his 'first dish' and, smiling and nodding, he ate quickly moving on from guest to guest with a speed only just short of ill manners so that he could return to the table frequently without, he hoped, drawing attention to himself. Maids were circulating, holding aloft glasses of champagne on their silver salvers and spotting a particularly pretty young girl, James gave her one of his most charming, rueful, smiles and she understood immediately. She made sure to alter her route to accommodate him on each circuit, leaving him free to concentrate on accessing the food.

Soon, in spite of feeling quite full, he was edging towards the end of the table where a plate of quails eggs in aspic sat invitingly, when his hostess swept up to him and in a single, seamless, imperial action put her arm through his and pulled him away. "This will not do, I cannot have you standing here alone, you must meet people if you want to get on in this world," and demanded, "what is your name?"

"Ernest," James replied with what he hoped was a slightly vulnerable smile, "Ernest Severne."

Evelyn Sassoon ushered him towards a group comprising a gentleman and his wife and another gentleman with a young woman who, James thought, was either his mistress or his daughter.

"Mr & Mrs Farquhar, Mr Oatway and Miss Oatway, may I introduce you to Mr Ernest Severne, I'm sure you will agree he was marvellous in our little performance," and with that she was gone!

After the first awkward moments of polite small talk the gentlemen turned back to their interrupted conversation on the merits of a new silk manufacturing process and Mrs Farquar began to espouse the quality and otherwise of the evening's plays in dangerously too much detail. Whilst trying to look suitably interested in the lady, James was surreptitiously studying

Mr Oatway's daughter. He thought she was no beauty, but striking, and was about his age he supposed, maybe a year or two older. She had pleasing, fine features; high cheek bones and a straight nose and he could just see the edges of her mouth twitching with stifled amusement. Her hair was swept back severely from her face into a perfect, round bun at the back without any fashionable curls artfully arranged to soften her features, and he could tell her clothes were obviously expensive. A burgundy, velveteen dress cut in the latest mode, with square shoulders and a narrow, tailored bodice. It had the obligatory bustle, but he was sure there was something different about her, she looked less, and here he really had to think, yes, less confined, less taut. She certainly did not look as if she were wearing steel armour as so many of the other ladies did, nor, he observed when she moved a little from side to side, making way for people to pass behind her, did her bustle give her the appearance of having a shelf behind and the back legs of a horse!

Eventually Mrs Farquhar drew breath and he was able to ask, "And you, Miss Oatway, were you pleasantly entertained?"

Instead of answering the question directly, she surprised him by saying, "I am very interested in the workings of the theatre Mr Severne," and laughing at the look on his face, continued, "no, not as a performer, I am interested in all the arts and this is an area in which my knowledge is lacking. You must tell me all about the life of a young actor."

Here was a subject James was more than happy to expand on and he was beginning to get into full flow when her father finished his conversation, turned to his daughter and taking her elbow said, "Come Florence it is time to go. I promised your mother we should not be late. Good-bye Mr, er?"

"Severne," interjected James quickly.

"Severne," Oatway mumbled with the air of a man who had found an unpleasant smell under his nose, "we must take our leave of you."

"Father," Florence caught James's eye and tried not to laugh, saying brightly, "Mr Severne was telling me all about the theatre and the life of a struggling actor, it was very interesting," and to him, "I do so hope we can continue our conversation."

Just three days later, Mrs Harriett Oatway's card was delivered to Beauchamp Place, she would be 'At Home' for afternoon tea at 56, Warrington Crescent, Maida Vale, on Tuesday the seventeenth of June.

"No, that's not right," James took off the white waistcoat he'd tried on, muttering to himself, "she obviously liked the way I looked at Mrs Sassoon's," but then he thought, "mind you, I *was* in costume then!"

"No," he said out loud again to the empty room, "no, I'm going to wear father's waistcoat. She's expecting Ernest Severne actor not James, boring wine merchant."

He'd wondered if he should borrow some of Teddy's formal wear but had settled instead on his charcoal grey, cut away coat with lighter, pin striped trousers and was now convinced he should wear his treasured, jade green, brocade waistcoat. It had been his father's and James remembered as a child sitting on Papa's lap, safe in his arms, tracing the lines of the fabric with his fingers as he listened to the stories his father read to him during those precious moments before bedtime. After his death, James had sneaked into his father's closet and taken the waistcoat, hiding it in his own dresser under his clothes. It had gone to school with him and now he wore it on what he considered special occasions. The cut was a little old fashioned, buttoned too high and it still had a slight V at the waist but James loved it and as he fastened his gold watch and chain in the pocket, he imagined he could still smell his father, the mixture of tobacco and eau de cologne.

He'd made a special trip to the Post Office earlier in the week to look up Kelly's directory which confirmed that Henry Oatway was a silk merchant and now James hoped very much that the waistcoat would be appreciated by a silk merchant's family, but what tie to wear? Surely a four in hand, but should it be black or the gold silk. "If only Sophie were here," he said to the mirror, "she always had a good eye." He settled on the black, made a final comb through his hair making sure there was just the right amount of tousle left and smiled at his reflection, "Go on, you can play this part!" He grinned, "but first, you must decide on your character. Are you to be an ardent suitor or merely a provider of theatre information?" He was intrigued by Miss Oatway, he wanted to know more of her.

He picked up his perfectly brushed top hat and Malacca cane, left his flat and crossed the road to the Hackney stand opposite. There was only one coach waiting, the large, square carriage was a nameless aristocrat's cast off, painted a bilious yellow with the faded coat of arms on the panels. The two horses standing patiently in their harness had straggly manes and tails causing James to think back suddenly to Misty, the old, well ridden, rocking horse in the playroom of his childhood. As he arrived, the waterman took his hands out of his pockets, touched his cap in salute and hurried to open the door, asked for the destination needed, shut the door firmly and shouted the address loudly up to the driver.

The journey was to take the best part of an hour and James settled back on the shabby seat to enjoy the route. They left the stone and brick of the city behind for the green grass and plantations in Hyde Park with the Serpentine flowing calmly alongside. The cab followed the ancient route of Watling Street to the wealthy enclaves of Maida Vale and stopped outside a classic, red brick town house.

James stepped down from the carriage just as the first few drops of rain arrived, glanced up at the imposing façade, opened the low iron gate in the palisade and ran quickly up the eight steps to the black, panelled front door. He hardly had time to lift the shining brass knocker before the door opened and a uniformed maid ushered him inside. He was not the first guest to arrive and on being shown into the dining room, saw immediately that Florence was serving cups of tea from the end of a large table spread with a white tablecloth. In amongst vases of flowers sat dishes of tiny sandwiches, fancy biscuits and cake and, he found later, distributed around the room on smaller side tables, were little salvers holding salted almonds and sweetmeats. He stood to one side watching for a moment and recognised at once that Florence took after her mother Harriet. It wasn't simply a physical resemblance, Harriet Oatway's whole bearing was the same and she came up to James with a forthright step, her hand outstretched, "Good afternoon, you must be Ernest, do come and be introduced," she leant towards him and said conspiratorially, "I invited only a few guests today as I rather believe Florence would very much like to talk to you about the theatre. She appears terribly interested in your chosen career."

Before he could reach Florence, and just as importantly his cup of tea and cake, James was introduced to three ladies who, he was advised at length, volunteered with Mrs and Miss Oatway at The Female Aid Society based in Islington. Then he met a rather grand, middle aged lady accompanied by her husband who was the Secretary of the Midnight Meeting Movement and stood with another, younger gentleman who appeared so relieved to see James that he gushed on about the pleasure of having 'another chap to even out the petticoat rule' of the gathering. As soon as he could, James made his excuses, said that he was parched, and stepped slowly backwards to turn and face Florence. Her face a picture of mirth, she requested he take a newly poured cup of tea and help himself to a plate of their simple fare.

"Good afternoon Miss Oatway," he grinned at her, "how very pleasant to see you again. I hope your onerous duties here will not prevent us continuing our conversation, cut so cruelly short when we first met?"

As two of the three ladies left amid a flurry of farewells, "Half an hour at tea is considered polite enough," Florence whispered to him, "and oh dear, I see Mrs Farquhar and her entourage have now arrived. Please, wait one moment and I shall ask Miss Pollen, she's been left on her own over there, if she would care to serve the tea for me."

Miss Pollen gratefully took on the task, the servants bustled around topping up the tea pots and Mrs Farquhar monopolised the young man who, it transpired, was a newly qualified accountant engaged by Mr Oatway. Florence and James took their cups and moved away from the table to stand in front of the tall windows, looking down onto the now rain sodden street.

"This is a terrible way to have to meet, don't you agree?" Florence looked him straight in the eye, "we must be more inventive for the future."

James stifled a snort of surprise as she continued, "My mother will help, she is always game for testing my father to the limit," she laughed, "but right now, tell me do you have any future engagements? Were there any useful contacts made in the drawing room of Belgravia?"

"Well I'm not sure about that," James grinned, "but I have allowed myself the luxury of a little self-congratulation as I have been able to put one date in the diary. A charity evening in aid of the Great Northern Hospital. I'm not usually keen to perform at these events, but this one will be in St George's Hall which holds upwards of a thousand people."

"It's all good exposure," Florence said excitedly, "and it may well lead to bigger things. Is this how you progress from being unknown on the stage to holding the starring roles."

"If I knew that Miss Oatway, I should be holding the starring roles," laughed James, "but enough about acting, I would rather learn about you, you already appear to have the measure of me! I understand from some earlier introductions that you are involved with certain charities. Does that take up all of your time?"

"Well I play my part at the Aid Society. I find it

outrageous in this day and age that young women can be in such dire circumstances that they are drawn into the degradation and dangers of a life on the streets. The Society was founded to give guidance and what practical help we can," she added sardonically, "however, only for those women who are penitent! We have just amalgamated with the Female Mission who employ missionaries to go onto the streets at night, distribute tracts and try to persuade the fallen to follow a better life. I leave the preaching to them, but I do visit the hospitals and brothels where these young women are found and Mother and I endeavour to find them new situations, or to place them in decent homes, or restore them to their friends. It is rewarding work but distressing at the same time."

"I think it's very commendable, you must be a very good person. I see the poverty and deprivation on the streets and I'm afraid I do nothing other than tossing the odd penny into a tin cup. You will find me very shallow."

"On the contrary, I shall find you a breath of fresh air compared to the usual young men I am introduced to," she turned her gaze to the young accountant, "my father would very much like to see me married!" Changing the subject, she added, "I have been admiring your waistcoat, such a beautiful colour and fabric. Not modern I think?"

"No, it was my father's. I am glad you approve. I was worried you might think my individuality, merely passé."

"Not at all, I am hardly conventional myself. Mother is a staunch supporter of the Rational Dress Society," and seeing the look of surprise of James's face, giggled and continued, "yes, Mother loves a committee, she will be enrolling you onto one before the afternoon is over!"

"What in the name of heaven is the Rational Dress Society?" James asked.

"It is the most sensible society I know," answered Florence, "I have taken it to heart too. It has been going for some years and was set up by women who want to design and wear clothes that are more practical and comfortable than the monstrosities dictated to us by the so-called fashion of the times. We are completely opposed in particular, to tight lacing, which you will understand is the only way to force a woman's waist into such an unrealistically small size. I'm sure you are aware this comes about by crushing the body with steam moulded corsets, a practice which, disregarding the dreadful discomfort, is also dangerous. It rearranges our internal organs and ruins our health and all for the sake of vanity and foolishness. I'm pleased to say that our voice is being heard and each day more and more doctors are counselling against it."

"I could see when I first saw you that you looked more relaxed than a lot of the other ladies, and if I may be bold enough to speak as a mere, modern man, more attractive and approachable because of it." James gazed at her.

"We want to be able to wear more relaxed clothes. You will have heard of the American lady, Mrs Bloomer, and her divided skirts? They were ridiculed, regarded as too great a symbol of female emancipation, but mark my words, it will happen. Not," she added quickly, "that I would go so far as to wear such a thing. I am happy with my dressmaker's skill to keep my clothes in fashion but without the uncomfortable extremes."

They replenished their tea and James took the opportunity to help himself to a piece of seed cake which he was biting into as Florence asked, "You must tell me about yourself, your family. I am pretending we have been introduced formally but of course that is not so!"

Swallowing hastily James cleared his throat, took a sip of scalding tea which made him wince, and told her, "My father was a wine merchant in Nottingham, but he died when I was seven and a cousin runs the business now. My mother remarried and lives in Worcestershire. I have two older brothers, one an engineer in Derby and the other, an accountant and pioneer in Canada, plus three sisters, two of whom are married and Annie, the middle one, still looking. I have always wanted to be an actor, ever since I was small, and I also like to paint but I don't think I am good enough to sell."

"A very potted history Mr Ernest Severne, it tells me the facts of your life but not actually *who* you are."

Florence was interrupted by her mother who came to join them, "You two will have the tongues wagging, Florence, you must talk with Mrs Farquhar, if you don't, she will be gossiping about us throughout the town. Besides, I should like to speak with this interesting young man." As her daughter moved off, Harriet watched her go and said a little sadly, "Such a talented girl, reform for women cannot come too soon."

"Yes," said James, "she has been telling me of her good work with the charities, trying to make other's lives better."

"Did she not tell you what she really wants?

What she does every minute she can? She wants to be a writer. She has almost completed her first volume of poetry and I know she has ideas for a novel. You - and the charities - are all part of her research I suspect. Although," she smiled at James, "I think she is enjoying your company. Come, tell me of your family."

By the time James left Maida Vale he was completely enraptured by Miss Florence Oatway and was impatient for their next meeting.

CHAPTER 6

1884
In the United States, an insurance salesman,
Lewis E. Waterman, creates a fountain
pen that is not supposed to leak.

He did not have to wait long. The request for him to meet with the committee of the Female Aid Society arrived within the week, just in time for their monthly meeting. Such was James's desire for contact with Florence that he agreed immediately, wondering what kind of contribution to the organisation he would be expected to make, and, more worryingly, what kind of contribution he was qualified to make. He arrived at the headquarters in Islington on a drizzly, August morning, and was disappointed to find neither Florence nor her mother were present, just Henry Oatway at the head of the table. James was welcomed and during the course of the proceedings it became obvious that his main requirement would be to engage members of the theatrical community in fund raising and the great and good members would wholeheartedly encourage him. Business of the day over, James was wondering whether he should leave, when

Henry came up to him and with a less than friendly countenance said, "I don't expect you to be able to do much for us. You are too young and cannot possibly know the right people, but my wife was insistent. So here you are. Do try to do some good, don't show me up as a complete fool for introducing you."

He looked over James's shoulder, nodded to someone and walked off without another word. "Hmm!" James thought, "can't say I disagree with the sentiment, but he could have put it a little less harshly!" Nevertheless, he left the hall with a spring in his step, he knew this was going to bring him and Florence together.

It was a month or so later, at the beginning of September, that he was sitting in the drawing room at Warrington Crescent. Harriet Oatway was dealing with her correspondence, sitting discretely at a side table as far away from her daughter and her guest as reasonable, and James, bursting with excitement, gave Florence the news that he had been asked to join Lydia Thompson's troupe of actors in a play called *Nitouche* and they were to begin a twelve week tour, starting in Liverpool on the twenty second of that month.

"And, we end with a benefit for Miss Thompson at the Crystal Palace theatre in October," James told her, his lisp apparent as always when he was emotional. "It's a marvellous break even though I've only got a small part, but it's Lydia Thompson, and she's headline news everywhere. I just need one decent manager to see me, just one."

"I'm not sure I shall be able to persuade Father to allow me to come," Florence gave a sad smile, "the only reason I saw you at St George's Hall was because it was Mrs Burdett Coutt's charity do. You were very good in that play, I thought you made a very convincing old man," she laughed, "especially for one as young and tender as you!"

James grinned, "I'm not so young and tender that I don't know I want to marry you!" His face drained of blood and he almost fell off his chair with the shock of his words, "oh, good God! I do apologise Miss Oatway, I am acting of course, it is a line in a play I've heard," he stuttered, "I am so sorry, I really didn't mean to offend you, I just wasn't thinking. Please accept my apologies, it was stupid of me."

Florence had a mysterious smile on her face, "Maybe the idea has merit Mr Severne, it would solve several problems."

She left the sentence hanging there and rose from her seat. She moved over to her mother and James heard her ask, "Mother shall I arrange to bring Mr Severne to the hospital with us on Monday next? He has expressed a desire to become more involved in our charities."

Following his dreadful faux pas, James felt he would go anywhere and do anything for Florence and agreed more willingly than he might have done previously, to accompany her and Harriet the following week. Arriving early, he waited for them on the steps of the New London Hospital for Women, happy in the knowledge that he would be finished here and able to attend his rehearsals in good time later that day. Of course, he had heard of Dr Garrett Anderson and her hospital, run solely by women doctors for women patients only but if he was honest with himself, he was not fully committed to the role of charity member. He concurred with Henry, he *was* too young, with precious little experience of life and he should be concentrating on earning a living. As ever, he was finding it hard to exist within his means. However, he knew this was not a sentiment he should impart to Florence just yet! The visit was an education for him. He met two prostitutes, neither one barely older than a child herself who had given birth to babies, both of which had died within days and left the mothers with serious infection and damage to their bodies. Found on the street by the volunteer night workers, the girls had been brought to the hospital where, emaciated and filthy they had been cleaned up with modern antiseptics. With decent food, clean beds and tender nursing, they had a chance of recovery. James, unusually tongue tied at the sight of the listless young women, heard the harrowing stories of their young lives and listened as Harriet gave them details of where to go for help once they were obliged to leave the sanctuary of these wards. His admiration for Florence, already at a significant height, reached its zenith.

When they left the hospital, Harriet walked a little distance behind, and he and Florence were able to walk side by side. She startled him, speaking quietly, "Ernest, I have been thinking of how our conversation ended last week, if you truly meant that you would like to marry me, such an arrangement could serve us both very well." She glanced behind her and seeing her mother still out of earshot, continued, "I am keen to leave my father's governance. No," she added quickly seeing the look of alarm on James's face, "no, he is not unkind to me at all except in that he is rather old fashioned. I want to write, I have so many ideas and books full of notes for a novel but he is very much against this, he feels women should be only concerned with marrying and producing a family, and doing so with a man of his choice."

"Well I certainly would not be the man of his choice," James was bewildered, he had spent hours thinking of the last time they had spoken alone, turning her cryptic words over and over in his mind. "he made it quite plain to me when we met that he rather disliked my line of work."

"Oh, I am sure I can win him round and mother will help. She is quite beguiled by you herself. I will make her understand it is a match made with hearts rather than a bank book and on that subject, my father will be generous enough with a dowry for me. He will need to keep up appearances and I have a notion that some funds would not go amiss for you!"

"But marriage, it is such a major step to take," James managed to say just before Harriet called, "We should call a hackney coach now Florence. I have walked enough for today."

"I shall arrange an invitation for later this week," Florence smiled at him, "please, do not look so frightened."

James's head was in a turmoil. He was wanted desperately to concentrate on learning his part for *Nitouche* but all the while he was thinking of Florence. It was so hard to believe. He had realised at their very first meeting that she was unconventional, forthright even, but still, he could never have imagined her proposing marriage to him like that. It was true he was very taken with her, she was unlike the pretty, empty headed, little actresses he had spent his time with. She was educated, refined and intelligent, and clever enough not to make him feel like a blockhead himself! He was most certainly attracted to her, and he knew there was truth in his embarrassing outburst, he would like to be married to her. In the immediate future, what he didn't want was to have to ask Henry Oatway for permission, but at his next afternoon with Florence at Warrington Crescent, that is precisely what he agreed to do, and to do so before he left for Liverpool.

The full impact of James's foreboding did not strike him until that Tuesday morning when the housemaid had shown him up to Henry Oatway's private study. Now, he stood, knees shaking so violently and his heart beating so rapidly that he thought they must be heard on the other side of the door. He was dreadfully afraid that he was about to be humiliated and no amount of practicing his bravado speech in front of the mirror over the past few days was going to be of help. "Put me on the stage in front of a thousand people," he thought, "rather than this."

He heard the command, "Come," and as the maid opened the door, he went in with what he hoped was a confident stride and walked over to Oatway's desk with his arm outstretched, offering his hand in greeting.

It was refused!

"Sit," barked Henry Oatway, "my daughter has told me why you are here, and I don't mind telling you, I am not at all pleased. She is a very determined young woman and of age, so I cannot prevent her from this imprudent course of action, but whilst she sits and embroiders in the drawing room, waiting, you and I must come to an agreement for her future. She is my daughter and I will not have her abased in the eyes of our society."

Even in his discomfort James thought it very unlikely Florence was sitting attending to her embroidery, but he kept that thought to himself. Instead, he studied this future father in law. A thickset man, James thought he would soon be running to fat. His face was swathed by long side whiskers reaching below his chin, the edges turning from sandy brown to grey and he had piercing blue eyes, fixed doggedly on his adversary's face. The man's appearance and tone were doing nothing to assuage James's fears.

He heard the next command. "Give me an indication, if you can, of how you intend to support my daughter in a style at least close to resembling that to which she has become accustomed."

"Well Sir," he started to stammer, "I am, as you know, an actor and as such ..."

"As such you will always be a penniless nobody. Why Florence wishes to marry you I cannot fathom. But she does, therefore you will have to do better than that. I intend making a situation available for you in my silk factory. An under manager, you will have a lot to learn but I shall pay you adequately. I will introduce you to my chief floor manager next week and he can sort the details."

Hearing this, James immediately found his tongue, and his courage. He remembered Potty Sinclair playing a very grand general in some play or other, and copying his style, said emphatically, "I regret Sir, that is not acceptable to me. I intend continuing my career in the theatre. Florence is aware that at present I cannot attain a steady income, but it will come in time. Had

I wanted to go into business I could have taken on my own family business in Nottingham."

"Business, what business? Who are your family? How have they allowed you to follow this worthless course?"

James gave a brief account, no more information than he thought absolutely necessary, and then, his indignation at Henry Oatway's dismissal fuelling his nerve, said rather grandly, "and I own property in Pimlico from which I obtain a reasonable income, which together with an allowance from a Trust fund set up after my father's death, will, I predict, provide your daughter with a suitably fitting life style."

"Property, what property? I have made enquiries and can find nothing in this city in the name of Ernest Severne."

"It is a townhouse in Warwick Street, and it is owned in my baptismal name, James. Ernest is my stage name."

"Good God, whatever next. This Trust, when do you acquire the capital?"

"At age twenty-five, it is quite modest but will be sufficient for us." His bravado was beginning to waver, five hundred pounds was far from a King's ransom! "How old are you now?"

James hesitated, if he admitted to being barely twenty-one, he thought Henry Oatway's wrath could overwhelm him, "Twenty-four Sir," he said confidently, "the same age as your daughter."

"Hmm. This accommodation of yours in Beauchamp Place, is it fit for a lady to live in? I should like my wife to visit and make her opinion. In the meantime, as I have said, we need to arrange the finances.

I am somewhat gratified that you are not completely without assets, but I can see that Florence will depend on the dowry I had in mind and I shall require you to insure your life in her favour prior to the marriage. I will have my solicitor draw up the marriage settlement and send it to yours. You do have a solicitor I take it."

"Martin Richards at Boodle Hatfield," James was rewarded with the look of approval on Henry Oatway's face at hearing the prestigious name. "That impressed him," he thought!

In all, his interrogation lasted almost an hour and by the time James joined Florence in the drawing room and was offered a well overdue cup of tea, he was mentally exhausted. The rush of adrenaline had stopped, and he felt utterly spent. He leant back on the sofa and shut his eyes.

"Is there something you would like to ask me?" Florence teased him, "or would you like me to call for your hat and coat?"

"Oh heavens, forgive me, but I am reeling, I feel as I imagine David would have felt had he not defeated Goliath! Yes, of course I have a very important question for you," and he pushed himself up from his seat, reached into the pocket of his waistcoat and took out a little, red leather box. He sank onto one knee, extracted the ring, five fiery opals set in a band of gold and held it up to Florence. "My dear Miss Oatway, it would give me the greatest pleasure if you would accept my hand in marriage." Then he couldn't help himself, he went on with a grin, "I know this will come as a huge surprise and that nothing could be have been further from your thoughts and starving actor as I am I can offer you nothing but poverty and hunger, but I do hope you will say yes!"

"Yes, you silly boy," Florence laughed as James put the ring on her finger, "yes, it has come as a huge surprise, but I should like to become your wife, very much."

She held his hand as he stood up, "Seriously," he said, "I'm sorry the ring is not much but you know only too well the state of my funds just at the moment. I will replace it in the future when I am renowned throughout the world and commanding enormous fees."

Boldly he pulled her towards him and kissed her gently on the lips, meeting no resistance. "Now, could I please have that cup of tea, or better still a glass of wine, I thought your father was going to have my head on a platter before the meeting was over."

CHAPTER 7

1884
Dr. William Price attempts to cremate his dead
baby son in Wales. Later tried and acquitted on the
grounds that cremation is not contrary to English
law, he is thus able to carry out the first UK ceremony
in modern times and set a legal precedent.

The couple further outraged Henry Oatway by telling him they wanted to marry quickly, "Why," he had beseeched his daughter, "why do you choose to break with convention in everything you do? What monster did we breed Harriet?" But he loved his daughter and if that was what she wanted, that was what she would do.

The ceremony was to be held at All Souls church where Florence had been baptised. The marriage date, sixth of November at twelve noon, was fixed and the Banns scheduled for the preceding three Sundays. James was busy with rehearsals for his play, but before he could leave for Liverpool, he needed to write to his mother and inform her of his plans, inviting her to London, with as many of his brothers and sisters who would wish to join her. He also had to ask Martin two things. Firstly, as he was now newly qualified would he be able to act for him in respect of the marriage papers and two, would he be the principal groomsman. He asked Teddy Loftus, together with two other actors who had become good friends, Davy Mason who was to be joining him in *Nitouche*, and Frank Carlyle, to be ushers and at the last minute decided he should arrange, during his absence in the north, for his apartment to be spruced up and organised to welcome Florence. That done, he was free to spend his time and energy on becoming 'Dragoon officer Robert' and to harass Aloysius Ogden to find him more, and better, work. His final most important task he would leave until he returned to London. A visit to Garrards where Teddy's cousin, a trainee engraver, had agreed to inscribe free of charge, his and Florence's initials and wedding date on the inside of a plain gold band James had bought in the little place, barely better than a pawn shop, in Victoria Street where he had purchased the opal ring.

In the days after he proposed to Florence, a less pleasant task for him had been to reply to Sophie's most recent letter and let her know that he was planning to marry. He had tried to couch the words as kindly as possible, but he knew the news would hurt her and the day before he left London her reply had been delivered. James found himself reluctant to read it, her untidy scrawl, never a pleasure to decipher, was this time made worse with the evidence of tear stains. In the first half of the note, Sophie declared he was a heartless brute and her own broken heart would never mend. The latter part of the page however was dedicated, as previously, to the enormous pleasure she was having touring the country with her provincial troupe, tales of her 'delicious' fellow actors and her increasing hopes that this experience might land her a major part on the London stage. James felt better, it was clear her broken heart was to be easily mended.

He was in good spirits when, after the five-hour journey, he and Davy stepped down from the train at Liverpool Lime Street Station. Under the enormous iron roof of the building, they walked towards the baggage car and jostled with the crowd of passengers, all of whom were intent on engaging a porter to carry their bags. They queued with an equally large crowd at the station entrance and in time a cab whisked them away the short distance to the rooms that had been booked for them by the theatre manager.

All twelve performances of *Nitouche* were well received. Miss Thompson had very complimentary reviews, the critics declaring that age had 'not withered' her and the leading man was generally regarded as 'splendid support' playing Celestin. James was not mentioned at all which, in his rational moments, he accepted wasn't surprising but all the more galling as he felt quite sure he would have been just as good, if not better, a Celestin.

"Davy," he moaned, his frustration almost unbearable, "how the devil do we get to be noticed, I've been acting and singing now for over three years and still can't get a decent bloody part."

"Three years isn't long old chap," Davy answered morosely, "I've been at it for five. Let's go out and get drunk."

So it was with sore heads that they boarded the train and made the journey back to London the following day, James struggling to feel excited about the upcoming final performance at the Crystal Palace.

"At least I suppose we can expect a decent audience after the good reviews we had last week," he grumbled. Having been brooding over his choice of career the past couple of days he now sat with Davy, his chin resting on his hand, in the dining car as the train steamed through the countryside. They had managed to persuade the train conductor that although they had only second-class tickets, they were just the right sort of 'gentlemen' he needed to be seen in his restaurant. "That's where being an actor can help in daily life," Davy had said cheerfully, "we could always take up a new occupation, confidence tricksters!'

"I'd probably get overlooked in the papers even then," James griped, then inserted a pretend monocle in his eye, rustled an imaginary newspaper and in a terribly upper class accent, pretended to read, 'Today the two well-known swindlers, Mr Davison Smith and his accomplice, were jailed at Her Majesty's pleasure for obtaining by false pretenses, a day old steak and kidney pie, mashed potatoes and greens on the Liverpool to London express train last week!' You see, no name for me, Ernest Severn is to remain anonymous wherever I go and whatever I do!'"

"Well I'll drink to that my friend," Davy raised his glass of claret, "but whilst you do have at least one more day's work, shall we make a recce to the Crystal Palace tomorrow? It's a vast site and we don't want to be wandering around lost on Tuesday morning."

"Apparently my parents went there to the Great Exhibition in, was it '51 or '53? Anyway, it was when the Palace was in Hyde Park and the whole experience had the most profound effect on my father. He would often incorporate tales of Britain's greatness into my bedtime reading, he thought our nation the most superior in the world even then," James said wistfully, "he'd be amazed at the progress we've made since he died."

"Well the Palace is over on Sydenham Hill now and the theatre will be hidden somewhere inside," Davy brought him back to the present with a start, "and I've been told there's some sort of trade exhibition on so we don't want to get caught up in the wrong hordes."

"Good idea, but after we've done that, I have a few errands to do for my forthcoming nuptials," James brightened up, "I need to firm up with the agent about our wedding trip. November weather is too dire to go to the Lake District, or even the south coast, so I think it will have to be the continent. I'd be a bit more excited if it didn't mean my entire savings gone in one fell swoop, but girls today expect a decent holiday."

Whilst James had been away, Florence and her mother had been making the majority of the arrangements for the wedding.

"It's not very much time at all Florence," Harriett had also been surprised at the haste, "and I'm very busy with the Society at the moment. Those girls we saw the other week are out of hospital and I'm pleased to say the older one turned up at our centre. We're hoping we can find her a place on a training course for domestic service because if she has to go to a public laundry or the like, she will feel it's far better to be back on the streets. We need money Florence, money."

"Well, I don't need such a fancy wedding Mother, you could save some here and use it for the girls." Florence was finding a lot of the protocol a little tiresome,

"Why do I need four bridesmaids? That's four dresses, presents and whatever. I could just do with Edith, she's quite capable."

"We cannot disappoint your father yet again," Harriet had agreed with her husband that they should give their daughter a day befitting his standing in the community, "he's been very good reconciling your choice of groom, he needs it to be seen that you have his consent and endorsement of the match, let's not make things any more difficult."

"Of course," Florence sighed, "I'm sorry. We've got a fitting for the dresses tomorrow and I have to admit, it may be regulation bridal attire, but I look quite handsome in white, and pale blue manages to suit Edith, Alice and Etta. I'm not sure about Annie, Ernest's sister, but I believe she is fair so it should be perfect. It will be lovely to meet her tomorrow Ernest is very fond of her so I am sure I shall like her too. Mrs Gay is very skilled with her needle, we have hardly any padding and no whalebones, but the robes still have a very good, fashionable shape. I shall dye mine a deep blue afterwards, it will make a very good afternoon dress. Oh, Mrs Gay wants to embroider my veil with tiny flowers, white, not coloured, and the bridesmaids will have white bonnets with marabou feathers and white pardessus."

"Has Ernest engaged his groomsman and ushers? He needs four in all and hopefully, if they are actors, they will be perfectly dressed with manners to match!"

"Yes, you met Martin Richards once at a Society reception, Ernest brought him along, and being a solicitor, he seems to be perfectly capable of organising the church and the ushers. The others are actors," Florence picked up a notebook from her escritoire and read, "Davy Mason who has just been to Liverpool with him, Frank Carlyle and Kit Smith. I've not met them but I'm sure they will acquit themselves with glory - and hopefully, the girls will not all fall in love with them!"

"Have you got the guest list up to date dear? Mrs Wodehouse has confirmed that her husband will be unable to attend, I understand he does not enjoy good health?"

Florence sat and picked up her pen, dipped it in the glass inkwell and scratched out George Wodehouse's name. "Therefore," she informed her mother, "those of Ernest's family who will be coming are, his brother Thomas Parr Severn and his wife Sarah; his sister Emily and her husband Thomas Barney; his sister Louisa and her husband Abraham Sherlock and his sister Annie of course. Apart from the friends I have mentioned, that will be all."

"Well, we have a few more guests on your side, but not so many that it will be obvious. I see your trousseau is almost finalised, your dress and coat for going away?" Harriett was running her finger down her own list, "Cook has all the information regarding the catering and the cakes, and she will organise the staff to arrange the drawing room for the breakfast. What about your list for the Cards, has Ernest given you his and have you given them to Edith? You will want people to call on you as soon as you are home from your honeymoon."

"I've completed mine and I hope to have Ernest's names just as soon as he is free next week."

"Well that seems to be all for now," Harriet got up to leave the room, "I must go and check that the room is ready for Annie tomorrow. Did you say Ernest would be joining us for dinner?"

CHAPTER 8

1884
Mark Twain's Adventures of Huckleberry
Finn is first published, in London

The wedding day dawned on a cold but dry November morning and the sun peeped through the clouds as the two greys pulled the last carriage of the cortege, carrying Florence and her father, to All Souls. James and Martin had been waiting in the vestry since a little after eleven o'clock, James constantly fidgeting with his collar and tie. He would have liked to have worn his father's waistcoat but had been persuaded to stay with convention and was wearing a white, silk waistcoat under his mid blue coat and light grey trousers but had managed to purchase the brightest, royal blue, paisley, ascot tie. Florence would expect a dash of exuberance in his dress and James thought this worked well. As they stood, Martin was trying hard to break the nervous tension with general, idle, chit chat and, at James's request, removed his white glove to check, more than once, in the groom's left-hand waistcoat pocket to feel the ring tucked into the corner.

His stomach was fluttering with nerves, "She will come won't she Martin," he asked, more of himself than his friend, "I have an awful feeling this is some kind of charade and we will all disappear in a puff of smoke, like a genie from the Arabian Nights."

"Now is not the time to be so theatrical James, she will be here. It's only a quarter to twelve, just stay calm and be patient."

He looked out into the church itself, "It's filling up and oh, Potty and the others have just arrived. I wouldn't say they've brought chaos with them but there's quite a lot of shuffling going on in spite of Davy and Frank trying to seat them all. I can see Katy Warren, she's in fits of giggles, the other side are frowning a bit! I think the breakfast is going to be fun!"

"I thought my wedding would not be complete without them," James finally smiled, "I see you noticed Katy, I rather thought you had a soft spot for her?"

Martin had no time to confirm or deny, the first of the carriages were arriving and James received the bridesmaids and his mother Jane. Annie had loved Edith, Alice and Etta as soon as they met and was perfectly at ease with them, arranging Alice's bonnet and then hugging her brother. Jane looked very grand, her increasingly stout figure looking even more so as it was encased in drapes and a bustle of deep crimson velvet. Her bonnet was festooned with huge ostrich feathers to match. Harriett arrived, elegant and far less stiff, in deep cream brocade and having greeted James was at pains to look after Jane.

At last the bride arrived with her father and James greeted her with a mixture of relief and admiration. Florence looked superb. He could only glimpse her face behind the short veil which fell from the orange blossom coronet, but he could see she was smiling and immediately she and Henry took their places at the door of the vestry to begin the bridal procession up the aisle. James came next with Harriett, Jane was accompanied by an elderly Oatway uncle and they were followed closely by his groomsmen paired with the bridesmaids.

Florence stood at the altar and James moved to her right, glanced at her again and then turned his attention to the vicar. It all seemed to happen in double fast time. Henry publicly and willingly 'gave' his daughter to James, thankfully there was only silence when the words 'just cause and impediment' were reached and the bride and groom both spoke "I will" in loud, unwavering voices. Miraculously, the ring was in his pocket when James went to retrieve it and in spite of his shaking hands, he was able to place it on Florence's finger without mishap. He shook hands with the clergymen, walked proudly back to the vestry with his wife on his arm where he signed the register urging the tremor in his hand to stop; and watched Florence sign her name, Oatway, for the very last time. He smiled as her father and his mother signed the book as witnesses and to the sound of the church bells ringing out loudly, he and Mrs James William Severn emerged into the pale sunshine to be showered with rice and reach their carriage and the four white horses that would take them back to Maida Vale. In just thirty short minutes, his life had changed completely, and he felt utterly blessed.

He wasn't sure if he spoke a single word on the journey home, other than when he drew Florence into his arms and kissed her gently on the lips, "Hello, Mrs Ernest

Severne, I am very pleased to meet you!"

The house was a picture. The doorways, balustrades, windows and fireplaces were adorned with garlands of beautiful, white gardenias and roses intertwined with silver leaves, sequins, tendrils of silver ribbon and juniper boughs. The couple stood towards the corner of the drawing room with Henry, Harriett and Jane to their side as the ushers guided guests towards them, all eager to give James their congratulations and tell him how honoured he was to have such a bride. Some two hours later, the meal over, the cake cut and eaten, and the toasts drawn to a close, Florence slipped quietly out of the room to prepare for the journey to come. She had no idea where they were going, it was a closely guarded secret between James and Martin, and she was excited as Edith came to help her dress in the new russet brown travelling outfit.

James began to say goodbye to his friends, waiting as Potty gave a short, but apposite and immensely funny address on the perils of marriage, to which he stumbled a response, and then he too withdrew. Florence came downstairs and made her farewells, surprised that tears came to her eyes as she took a last look around the house she had lived in for almost her whole life, and moved by the humble congratulations of the servants. Finally, she hugged her mother and hearing a soft cough, she watched her father summoning up resolution and, not trusting his voice, she went to him as he held out his hand and he gave her a single kiss. Henry led her down the stairs, through the hall and to the door where he delivered his daughter to her new guardian. James helped her quickly into the carriage, jumped up after her and waved his hand to the guests watching from the windows. He smiled at the group around the door, shouted to the coachman and they were off. Then he leant back in the seat, put his arm around his wife and breathed an enormous sigh of relief.

"Let's just hope Martin is already at the station and has got the tickets and the bags!"

Jane Severn's first reaction on receiving the invitation to James's wedding had been one of huge concern. She thought him far too young, not at all settled in career or finances and, she was slightly ashamed of herself, worried he was marrying an actress. When she received a subsequent letter from Harriet Oatway introducing herself and learned that Florence was a well-educated lady from a perfectly respectable family, she relaxed a little and to James's enormous relief, wrote immediately to say she was delighted at his news. More importantly she wished to give him a wedding present of one hundred pounds and with these funds swelling his account, James had seconded Martin to assist in arranging their wedding trip to the French Riviera. The least of his problems was taking a month away from work, as after the flurry of performances in the summer, James's diary was disappointingly empty and by the time he and Florence were on their way to Victoria to catch the first class express train to Paris, he was feeling carefree and merry.

His mood was infectious, and Florence soon recovered from her earlier sadness at leaving her home, "Ernest dear when will you tell me where we are going?" she laughed, "I am mad with curiosity. It will be rather cold and wet in the Lake District or Scotland. Let me guess, are we going to Italy?"

"You can keep guessing, I shall not say. Our destination is to be a surprise, so do not let go of my arm or you may get lost and never know! All I can tell you now, is that we are to take the overnight steamer to Calais."

Martin had done well. He handed over to James the tickets bought from Thomas Cook for the train to Dover, the boat to Calais and the onward train to Paris where he had procured Cook's hotel coupons for two rooms for one night only at the Hotel D'Anglais. Safe now in James's pocket were also the tickets for the following days travel, reserving a sleeping car on the train from Paris to Nice on the Côte d'Azur.

"Your bags are checked all the way through from here to Paris," he told James quietly as they arrived at their carriage, "but you will need to collect them there. The porters and hotel staff are very used to visitors travelling through the city on their way to the south so you will be looked after and shouldn't get lost trying to find the right station! Now's the time to dredge up the bit of French you learned at school!"

He kissed Florence's hand, shook James's fiercely and bade them farewell. "Have a marvellous time," he called as he turned and walked away quickly. James grinned at his wife and handed her up into the railway car.

In little more than ten hours they arrived in Paris and, baggage located and inspected, were whisked away to the hotel. After a very light supper they retired to their single rooms where fatigue overcame them both and they slept. The next morning, they rose early and ate breakfast together before the concierge came to take them to their waiting cab. At the Gare de Lyon, their tickets were stamped, the baggage registered, and they boarded the train to find the seats in their compartment already drawn out to form a comfortable couch. To gain this comfort and privacy, James had paid the additional cost of the two sacrificed places in this four-person carriage and there would be, he reflected, a huge dent in his hundred pounds by the time the couple returned to England!

By now Florence knew they were on their way to Nice and she was thrilled, "I feel as if I am a migrating swallow going south for the warmth," she said excitedly, "I have read that the Rivera is a beautiful place with sunshine, fruit and flowers and we may be able to bathe in the sea Ernest. I hear the water is an ultramarine blue. I have only been to the seaside once in England, Father took us on the train to Southend and the water there was far from blue, as I recall it was a muddy brown."

She clasped James's arm tighter, "I am so happy, I never expected such an extravagant trip, thank you Ernest. I'm not going to sleep I don't want to miss a single minute of the journey."

"Now that the secret is out, here is Cook's handbook," James handed the little volume to her, "he'll tell you all about the route we are taking and what to expect in Nice. Plus, it gives other important bits of information, like one franc is worth nine pence ha'penny, and ten centimes is a penny, but look here, I have written down the value of five, ten francs and so on. I don't want to tip the porter a sovereign by mistake, that's for sure!"

"We are off," Florence was peering out of the window watching the grime of the station pass by, "it should take just over twenty hours it says here so we will be in Nice in good time for 'dejeuner' tomorrow.

Does this booklet have a French dictionary? I cannot remember many words, not many more than 's'il vous plâit' and 'merci'. Look Ernest, we are crossing a river and it says here we shall soon cross two viaducts over the 'wooded valley of the river Yeres'. Oh, it is too thrilling."

James was just as enthusiastic, and sitting arm in arm, they were engrossed with the scenery, rivers and towns that they sped through. Florence wanted to read every little detail, "Listen Ernest, we are about to cross the river Seine near a town called Melun which 'was besieged and taken by Henry V in 1420, but only remained in the possession of the English ten years' and then we go through the Forest of Fontainebleau 'which is about fifty miles in circumference and comprises …'."

James stopped her talking with a kiss, "My dear wife, you cannot recite the entire contents of Mr Cook's guide to me. Just a snippet now and then please."

"Don't you want to learn everything Ernest? I had no idea I had married such a dullard, oh," she said, her face wreathed in smiles, "we are coming into our first stop, 'Montereau at the junction of the rivers Seine and Yonne', it says there is a buffet here. Are you hungry my love, should we buy something?"

"I am happy enough with the wine and bread we have with us if you are my dear? We are scheduled to stop at one or two other stations that have a buffet, so maybe some meat and cheese later. Then at Lyons this evening we stay long enough to have proper refreshments, so we will eat dinner there."

It was late when they sat down to a superb meal in the restaurant at Lyon-Perrache station. A fine salad of chicken livers and green leaves, followed by chicken in a Burgundy wine sauce with herbs and vegetables which they were told was very popular in Lyon, accompanied by delicious sliced potatoes, sautéed in butter with caramelised onions and finished with fresh chopped parsley. A dish they learned, that was invented in Lyon as were the sweet Angel Wings, tiny fritters dusted with icing sugar that were served with their coffee. Pillows and blankets had appeared in their carriage whilst they were eating and the lateness of the hour, the comfort of the food and wine and the soporific motion of the train, all combined to lull Florence to sleep in spite of herself. They woke the next day to the warmth of the sun and the sound of the conductor calling that they were now arriving in the south, at Marseilles.

"Good morning Mrs Severne," smiled James, "welcome to the French Riviera. I am going to suggest that we do not get down here but wait until we reach Cannes to find a pastry or two and coffee. This is France's chief port and I have been following the spread of cholera here in the newspaper, the number of deaths is rising so I think we should stay safe inside our carriage. The time is still very early and we will reach Cannes at the perfect hour for the buffet and very soon after, we shall be in Nice."

CHAPTER 9

1884

*Greenwich Mean Time (GMT) was universally
adopted at the International Meridian Conference
in Washington, DC, and the International Date
Line was drawn up with 24 time zones created*

T he front of the Grand Hotel on the Quai St Jean
was bathed in bright sunlight as the hotel's
omnibus drew up. The hotel manager was there
to greet them, "Bienvenue Monsieur, Madame Sevairne,
bienvenue à Nice," and with handshakes all round they
followed him up the marble steps to the front door
whilst commands were given in clipped tones to the
waiting porters. Florence stumbled and turned, startled by the frightened whinny of a horse which she saw
had been spooked by a man, almost invisible beneath
the quantity of baskets he was carrying, calling deaf-
eningly, 'paniers à vendre' and the concierge shouting,
equally loudly, for him to move along. James tightened his hand on her arm, "It is just as noisy as London
I think, but it sounds so exotic in a foreign language
doesn't it?" He guided her through the door, laughing.

Inside all was calm and cool. Standing beneath

an enormous chandelier in the foyer, Florence looked around her whilst James followed the manager to the elaborate reception desk set as a half-moon in the corner. She admired the paintings of local scenes hung on the walls, the curving, marble staircase with ornate, iron balustrades, and then walking over to him, took James's arm, smiled broadly and said, "Yes, I shall like staying here very much and I shall be able to observe so much life. I cannot wait to unpack my notebooks and pens I have a head full of ideas already to write about."

"And I want to paint," James replied, "it is a long time since I was inspired and there is an amazing light here. Did you notice all the artists sitting along the streets as we drove from the station? It will be perfect. I am really looking forward to our month here."

"Let me read to you what Mr Cook has to say about Nice, Ernest." They had gone immediately to lunch leaving the hotel staff to unpack their cases and settle them into their room. "It's not too long I promise, 'Nice is the centre of fashion and gaiety during the season, which commences in November and lasts until about Easter. Life in Nice is one perpetual round of balls, horse races, regattas, concerts, parties and fetes. Bands play on the promenades daily at certain hours and the whole of the fashionable world turns out en masse, clad in gayest toilettes, to see and be seen on the Promenade des Anglais.' It sounds wonderful, we shall have plenty to do."

"And we can take the train to the neighbouring towns. I particularly want to visit Monte Carlo and there's Menton where Queen Victoria stayed, or we could always hire a carriage if you would prefer not to use the train?"

Florence nodded her head, "But first, this afternoon and evening, we must explore round here. We are very close to the banks of the river Paillon and I should like to see the Bay of Angels as soon as possible. Maybe we could stroll by the sea, that is, of course, if we can find our 'gayest toilettes' to wear!"

A few days later, after breakfast, James got up from the table and looking out of the window said, "I thought I would take my paints this morning and try my best with the women doing their washing in the river. I spotted the exact place to sit when we passed by on Monday. Shall I ask for another chair for you, or would you prefer to go to the Promenade with your notebook?"

"The Promenade I think," Florence answered thoughtfully, "I like to make notes as people stroll by, I am looking for the image of a man with inner evil - quite the opposite of you my dear husband."

"Why not try writing a light romance Florence, I find your taste for sinister themes a bit unsettling. You don't divulge much but I'm slightly worried you may be plotting a murder!"

"Ah, but *you* will not be my victim," his wife gave James a devious look, "you do not *deserve* it!"

The steps down to the river were only a hundred yards from the hotel and a porter carried his chair and easel there for him. James shifted the seat into position, fixed a new sheet of water colour paper in place and turned the key in the tiny lock of his paints box. This was made of beautiful mahogany and a present to him from his mother on his sixteenth birthday. Designed for travelling, the top layer held thirty paint blocks in different stages of use, some hardly touched, others almost worn away and, on the reverse, each was embossed with the name Reeves. From the drawer at the bottom, he took out a flat, china palette and laid it to one side, checked that his large brush, small quill brush, drawing pens and the box of nibs were present, filled the little glass dishes with water from the stoppered bottle he had brought and set the box on the ground. He sat back, his eyes drinking in the scene before him.

The stream ran slowly down the centre of the river-bed and there were more than two dozen women, their full brown skirts protected by aprons, kneeling on the stones at the edge of the lapping water. Their large, flat brimmed, straw hats protected their faces from the sun when they looked up from their task in hand from time to time to speak with their friends around them. They pummelled and rinsed, the soap bubbling up and making a current of foam. Resting behind them were huge piles of washing, neatly wrapped up in yellow sheeted bundles, tied with long tailed knots. Dark wicker baskets were dotted across the pebbles, overflowing with what James recognised to be shirts and pantaloons amongst the bed sheets. Makeshift stands were covered in fresh laundry drying rapidly in the sun and the sound of the women gossiping was like the twittering of a tree full of birds settling down to roost for the night.

He looked up at the brick bridge, two symmetrical arches and white iron railings spanned the water and his eyes were drawn to the other bank where the same scene was playing out, another little ribbon of foam lapping on that shore. Behind this, rose the walls of a row of tall town houses, the Old Town and the skyline broken by the tower of the church of St John the Baptist.

James took a long, slow breath, picked up his broad brush, dipped it in the little dish of water and, totally absorbed, wetted the paper.

Meanwhile, Florence was immersed in her own world. The cab had dropped her on the Promenade des Anglais some way west from the pier where the blackened dome of the recently, fire damaged casino dominated the view. She chose a seat a little distanced from a cluster of ladies who were sitting, chattering together and facing the sea, she took time to watch a fisherman as he heaved his small boat up onto the shingle and settled down to mend his nets. A steamer was on the horizon, too far out to be making for Nice Port she thought to herself, maybe on its way to Monaco or Italy.

The sun on the water deepened the azure blue and the warmth soaked into her bones. Florence was not an avid follower of fashion, but today she was feeling good, wearing a new costume from her trousseau, a deep green, velvet walking dress which she wore with a matching, dark green plush, Gainsborough hat sporting an abundance of dyed green feathers. She looked every inch à la mode. Raising her face to the sky, she decided to close the umbrella protecting her from the sun and rely on the shade from the palm trees. She then opened her leather travelling handbag and took out a notebook and a pencil.

Those passing by might have thought she was daydreaming, but Florence was wide awake studying her surroundings and, covertly, the promenaders. She watched how they moved, heeded their expressions and listened for snippets of their conversations. It was to be her lucky day. Two gentlemen stopped in their tracks before her, engaged in a heated debate, the subject of which did not interest Florence, she was transfixed by the appearance of the more belligerent of the two.

"That's my 'Mr Ralston'," she said to herself and after a few moments of observation, began to write. 'He was a rather short, thick set man, about sixty-five, with grey hair, pent-house eyebrows, deep set, piercing eyes and strongly marked but rather regular features.' "He's ideal for my murder victim," she thought excitedly and carried on writing, 'There was considerable power in the forehead and shape of his head, and iron will in the compressed mouth and strong jaw. The characteristic expression of his face was hardness and resolution'.

The men moved on and she was smiling to herself, the notebook resting in her lap and gazing out at the ocean when she was startled by a voice, "Would you mind awfully if I share your bench? The others are all taken up by babbling matrons!"

Florence looked up into the face of a dignified, statuesque, young woman, whose dark, velvety soft eyes reminded her immediately of the ripe loveliness of one of the artist Lely's, beauties.

"I shall not disturb you I have a book I wish to continue reading, I could not help but notice you like to watch the world go by."

It had often occurred to Florence that she could, with just a single glance, discern whether she and a stranger would become friends. As she had anticipated with James that evening in Belgrave Square, so she now took the same view of Miss Sylvia Quinn and after the briefest of introductions they sat in companionable silence. It was not long though, before Florence finding her intense curiosity almost impossible to bear, took the first opportunity to speak when her intriguing companion closed her book and looked up at the sea in front of her.

"Are you staying long in Nice?" Florence asked.

"Three months. I am with my elderly mother and I fear I may well go completely mad with boredom."

Florence was unsure whether to commiserate and so responded, "I see from the title of your book that you may be more interested in exotic places further afield, but I am assured the Côte d'Azur has plenty of diversions to offer. Three months should not destroy your sanity completely!"

Miss Quinn lifted the book up, "Yes, this is the account of Isabella Bird's travels in Japan and I make no secret of the fact that I am determined to travel the world. Miss Bird is my heroine, she has explored so many places, America, Australia and the Sandwich Islands and she lived for a year in the Rocky Mountains. Such a determined lady, her health has never been good you know?" Florence shook her head, bemused at the enthusiasm as Sylvia spoke rapidly, "On this latest trip she went to China, Korea, Singapore, Vietnam and Japan. They'd only just opened their doors to the West and Isabella travelled through regions unknown to many of the Japanese themselves. She covered well over a thousand miles by pack horse, rickshaw or on foot and followed mountain trails, crossed countless rivers to meet villagers in their remote communities and peasant farmers in their fields. The book comprises her vivid letters to her sister and friends and describes in awful detail the discomforts and dangers as well as the pleasures and excitement."

"I'm not sure I should be brave enough," Florence managed to say, "but you obviously are?"

"I spend my days planning my future, but I owe it to Mother to stay with her for now. My father died some years ago and she would be on her own if not for me, I have no brothers or sisters, and this winter might well be the last time she can make this journey. She loves France very much, but I have been here so many times and fear the diversions you mention are of little interest to me. However, I do enjoy the weather, it is so much more agreeable than the cold and wet of London."

The Quinns were staying at the Hotel d'Angleterre and having arrived only the day before, Mrs Quinn was feeling tired and her daughter had taken advantage of her keeping to her room for the day, to take the air. Having enjoyed a late breakfast Sylvia had promised to return to the hotel in time for afternoon tea.

The new friends talked as if they had known each other all their lives. Sylvia was, Florence thought, a more determined version of the woman she thought of as herself, a kindred spirit in whom she had no hesitation in confiding her innermost thoughts. She admitted she had chosen to marry James quite deliberately in the knowledge that their union would provide relief from the current stumbling blocks they both faced to their lives.

"It seemed to me that my father's money could be put to our good use and I was confident that I should have more freedom to do as I wish as Ernest's wife, rather than remaining under my parental roof. If I was courageous like Miss Bird, things may have been different, but I have chosen an easier way I hope."

"But he is a good man, Ernest? He will be a kind husband?" Sylvia questioned, "I must say he sounds thoroughly modern I'm surprised your father gave his blessing to such a marriage. An actor and an out of work one too by the sounds of it!" Sylvia laughed, "For you to choose such a marriage of expediency, shows either great courage on your part, or foolhardiness!"

Florence smiled broadly, "Please don't get the wrong impression. I am very fond of Ernest and I am sure he feels the same about me. He is divinely handsome you know and has a great sense of fun. He is still very young, only twenty one but he pretends to be older, he doesn't know his mother told me his true age. I haven't said anything, it is not important, oh, and his real name is James, but he prefers to be known by his stage name Ernest! An unconventional man I would say, and in my opinion a moderately good actor, but it is a very difficult profession to make one's way in. However, he is determined and what is marvellous is that, as an artist himself, whether it's acting, singing or painting, he understands completely my great ambition to write. So yes, he is very modern I suppose!"

"Oh Florence, I am so pleased we have met, we must remain friends when we are home in London. I feel our lives are in parallel."

They stood, linked arms and as they began to stroll towards the road and the cab rank, Sylvia said seriously, "We do have one major difference, marriage. Before my father died and even before I came of age, I always hated to be told I should not be able to follow my own life or travel the world without a husband to facilitate it." Seeing Florence raise her eyebrows, she continued quickly and kindly, "Of course I have no reason to disagree with marriage for others, I am sure it is a wonderful state should you be lucky enough to find a man you find tolerable enough to share your life with and I quite understand and applaud your own actions. It is just not a state for me, and especially it is not for me as I have no desire whatsoever to procreate. I absolutely do not want any children."

CHAPTER 10

1884

The phylloxera epidemic was devastating most of the European grape growing industry. In France, total wine production fell from 84.5 million hectolitres in 1875 to only 23.4 million hectolitres in 1889. Some estimates hold that between two-thirds and nine-tenths of all European vineyards were destroyed.

Sylvia's words were dwelling on Florence's mind as she retired for the night, and it dawned on her fully, the awful certainty that she too, absolutely did not want a child. She stood at the marble washstand, poured some water from the pitcher into the basin, rubbed her cloth over the bar of Castile soap and wiped her face carefully. She patted herself dry then took the cloth again and with a glance to check the door was firmly shut, quickly washed her intimate parts. From her grooming bag she took out a small yellow sponge and bottle, soaked the sponge with the vinegar and squatting, she pushed it as deep inside herself as she could, making sure to hold onto the ends of the twisted threads that were tied to it. She hastily slipped her linen nightshift over her head, rinsed her hands again and began to take out the multitude of fine pins holding her hair in place. That done she picked up her brush and gently pulled it through her waves until they shone, dark and glossy.

She slipped under the covers of the hotel's matrimonial bed, picked up her book to read and waited for James's knock at the door.

"Florence, my love, what is wrong?" He had turned in bed, taken her in his arms and was running his fingers down the length of her spine, "are you unwell? Would you prefer not to have my attention tonight?" He moved away, she was lying rigidly on her side and the look on his wife's face was so different. This was not the woman he was getting to know, confident and forthright, she looked worried, scared even. "Florence, is there something the matter, have I offended you, please tell me."

It was such a relief that she spoke rapidly, "Ernest, I'm so sorry, it is not that I dislike the ... the act of love itself, but I am frightened I might conceive a baby and I was reminded starkly today that I just cannot contemplate that happening. I have absolutely no desire to be a mother at this time of my life. I know I cannot refuse you your rights but my head rules my heart and I hoped you might understand, our marriage was a way for both of us to further our ambitions, yours as an actor, mine as a writer. I feel guilty that we did not have this conversation before we married, I'm not sure I had grasped the reality of the situation," and then it seemed that once she had started to speak she could not stop, "I know what religion has to say, that motherhood is the most valuable contribution a woman can make to both her husband and society, but I really do not want it." She paused just long enough to take a breath and seeing James open his mouth to speak, rushed on, "The American campaign for voluntary motherhood says that women should have control over their own bodies and they advocate a woman just refuse her husband's advances but I cannot completely agree with that, but now ..." she stopped abruptly and, to her complete mortification, began to cry.

James was stunned. He wasn't angry, it was as if he too just that minute realised the importance of her words, "Good God Florence, no, I really don't wish to have a child either, well, as you say, not yet anyway." He pulled his arm away completely, "please, don't worry, please, don't cry like this."

Over the previous week he had not given a thought to this problem, he had found Florence passive but accepting of his advances and had missed only the spontaneity he and Sophie had enjoyed, the laughter and teasing. He and his wife had coupled in silence at a duration of his own choosing and whilst he was well aware of the common assumption that a married woman was not designed to enjoy intercourse, he really could not detect any such feelings of distaste on Florence's part. He knew what the pink silk threads were. Sophie had explained and James, not wishing to trouble with any method of his own to safeguard themselves, had been happy to accept what he thought to be a trustworthy method of preventing a pregnancy.

"But, the ... the pink silk," he hesitated, blushing, "surely they will prevent a baby?"

Mrs Quinn invited James and Florence to tea at her hotel later that week and it was arranged that the four of them would take a carriage ride to Monaco the following Monday. The journey took about two hours, the ladies sheltering from the hazy sun under parasols and Mrs Quinn acting as their guide.

"My husband loved the Côte d'Azur," she told them, "and now since he's gone, I am so lucky that Sylvia can accompany me. Look," she pointed to a grand, castellated villa as they reached the top of the road leading up from the Port, "that's Smith's Folly. Built by the late Colonel Smith of the East India Company. By all accounts a little bit mad, as you can see from his house!"

They travelled along a rough road, high up on the side of the hill, overlooking the sea.

"Oh, what a charming little town down there, the houses all pell mell, one on top of the other and so many boats in the harbour? What a glorious bay," Florence turned to Sylvia, "there are bathing machines on the beach. Do you bathe in the sea?"

"No," Sylvia made a face, "I'm aware that it is supposed to be very good for your health, but to my mind it is thoroughly cold and unpleasant! I was persuaded to try it once some years ago, and never again, not even down there in glorious Villefranche sur Mer." The two young women laughed and chatted and Mrs Quinn named the places they passed. The peninsular of St Hospice, the beach at Beaulieu sur Mer, Eza with its medieval town perched high above on the mountain peak and Turbia with its Roman tower. They descended to sea level and arrived at Monte Carlo just after one where Mrs Quinn suggested they went straight away to lunch at the Café de Paris following which they might take a tour of the town and the Palace. The Place du Casino was thronged and the mâitre d' hurried towards them, smiling and calling, "Ma chère Madame Kin, Mademoiselle Kin. Please, come this way, I shall find you a seat with fine sightings of the peoples." He led them to a table on the perimeter with a perfect view of the famed Casino and the Hôtel de Paris, took James's order for a bottle of champagne and bustled away.

Florence looked around, "What magnificent buildings, you should paint them Ernest."

"I'm not so sure," James said absently, "I've no real architect's eye, I prefer landscapes," and then smiling ruefully he added, "and I regret we shan't be playing the tables in the Casino, the stakes are far too high for a struggling actor!"

"And only a fool would lose their money there," Florence struggled to disguise her indignation, "for that one man who so called, 'broke the bank' there are hundreds who have lost everything. A fool's game indeed."

"Well, when we've eaten, we *could* have a tour of the interior if you like, it is very beautiful, or maybe in view of what you have just said, we should go straight away to the Palace?" Mrs Quinn raised her eyebrows at her daughter, "I should like the confit duck please Sylvia, with the vegetables."

Some days later, Mrs Quinn chose to stay in Nice and Sylvia accompanied James and Florence to Menton. They travelled on the train along the coast and hired a cab from the station. James, keen to take his sketch books into the old town, was dropped at the foot of the hill where he set off on foot up the steep, narrow streets. His eyes moving from side to side, each step unveiled a subject for his pencil!

The ladies were set down later on the promenade and strolled arm in arm before taking a seat facing the mountain sides in the distance, flanked by aloes, olive, orange and lemon trees.

"It is nearly the end of November and yet the weather is so warm," Florence held her parasol over her, "it is easy to see why people come here in the winter but I'm told the south of France is not quite so desirable in the summer, dust and scorching sun so I am very lucky to be here, I have not travelled before and I rather hope I shall come again."

"Maybe you can understand my longing for exotic places now?" Sylvia looked around wistfully, "but I must be patient." Changing the subject, she said, "What are you writing at the moment? I have been wondering since we first met but you have not mentioned it and I have not wanted to pry. You appear to have stopped these past days, I do hope I have not taken away your inspiration."

"Oh no, never! No, my mind keeps working," Florence, feeling quite shy, opened her bag and tucked the notebook she had just retrieved, away inside again, "I dabble in poetry as all women writer's are expected to do, I have a little collection forming, but I am also working on a novel. It is still in the early stages, but I have the makings of a story and am building my characters at present."

"Who inspires you most? Miss Austen perhaps?"

"Well no, of course I admire her work, but I have a rather more macabre disposition. I am plotting a murder and I can tell you, on that morning we met, I saw my victim right there in front of me! He had the perfect appearance, but that is all I shall say at present, there is still a long way to go."

"I understand, I like to keep my own plans to myself until I am sure they are ready for consumption. We are very alike Florence, I feel we shall stay friends forever and for now, if your husband is agreeable, I am looking forward to spending more time with you before you go back to London."

The night before they were due to leave Nice, James obtained tickets for a comedy at the Theatre Français.

"We will not be able to understand all the words," he had said, "but I'm sure we'll be able to follow the essence of the plot. Let's face it, they are never very complicated," he started to laugh, "as I've found out by my own experiences!"

"How lovely Ernest, and you must be missing the stage," Florence took his hand, "and I know it's rather shocking to say this, but I am glad the Italian Opera is not open, I much prefer lighthearted operetta. I will have to nudge you with my elbow though if you sing along too loudly," she squeezed his hand, "we cannot have you upsetting our Gallic companions!" She took from the table behind her a little packet and handed it to him. "Here is a little thank you for your kindness, I found it in one of the tiny shops along the Paillon."

He untied the string and inside was a white, satin handkerchief with a design representing an artist's palette and brushes.

"It will be ideal with your evening dress," she said shyly, "I hope you like it."

James took her in his arms and hugged her. "Thank you, Florence, it is perfect."

It had not been Florence's express intention, but the beribboned sponge had not been required again whilst they were in Nice. Without ever raising the subject again, it appeared that both James and his wife were content with the removal of bedtime anxieties and James had taken the opportunity to remain in the hotel lounge enjoying an extra post prandial brandy and his wife, that of reading undisturbed. The days had passed very happily. When they married, they had no understanding of each other at all, but now, following their conversation that night they had made a new beginning. With a fundamental compatibility, they shared many ideas, interests and the same humour. Their conversations flowed, their laughter wrinkled their eyes and their fondness for each other grew to a true friendship.

CHAPTER 11

1886
July, Robert Cecil, 3rd Marquess of Salisbury, Conservative,
becomes Great Britain's 30th Prime Minister

Back in London, James carried out the final marriage custom required of him and carried Florence over the threshold of Beauchamp Place. Florence had set the two 'at home' days for the twentieth and twenty first of December, thinking it best to make the dates before Christmas rather than wait the customary five weeks. Edith had sent the cards out whilst they were away and in the little time they had before then, Florence enjoyed unpacking her personal belongings into the smallest bedchamber which had been transformed into a sitting room and boudoir for her. "You will need somewhere quiet and private to write," James had said, "and I think this will do nicely. It is light and airy even though it is small and your bureau from home fits perfectly under the window." He was pleased with the work done in their absence, "you should be comfortable here my dear."

Whilst James got straight back into the routine of visiting his agent, monitoring the stage press and meeting up with his fellow resting actors, Florence got to know Mrs Cox their cook and Biddy the general servant. She checked the necessary accounts were open with the butcher and grocer of her choice, arranged for the replacing of the old brown curtains in the large drawing room with ones of crimson brocade, dealt with the rearrangement of the linen presses to accommodate her own clothes, ordered further china and glassware and generally took control of the household. She also found time to explore her new area and staggered James one evening when she told him, "Beauchamp Place is all well and good my dear but the area around is well known for its brothels and boarding houses, there are many unfortunate young women here. As soon as I am settled, Mother and I are going to start our visits and try to help."

The days arrived for Florence to sit at home each afternoon from two until four, arrayed in her wedding dress and with James awkwardly hovering, patiently receiving her visitors. Her bridesmaids, Edith, Alice and Etta were there to serve wedding cake and wine and Florence greeted everyone cordially, accepting graciously as each visitor drank her health.

"Well, it was not as tedious as I thought, and it was good to meet your friends again," she sighed at the end of the second day, "I thought Davy Mason was so amusing, and Teddy of course, and Martin is such a good man. How did you like meeting the Farquhars again?" She giggled, "they don't get any easier, do they? I'm sure they think I am a fallen woman. It's such a pity Sylvia could not be here. I really want her to meet Edith, but I don't think she and her mother come home until April."

"What did her latest letter say, are they still in Nice or have they moved on?" James picked up a last piece of cake just as Biddy was about to clear the plate, "thank you Biddy, I think Mrs Severne has left you and cook some cake in the pantry." He turned back to Florence, "I'm hoping you don't catch Sylvia's wanderlust."

"I did enjoy our time in France Ernest, I enjoyed it so much and it is a pity we didn't have the chance to visit all of the towns Mrs Quinn recommended, I do hope we will have the opportunity to travel again."

"In that case, I had better get on and find someone to put me top of the Bill," James said, not all together light heartedly, "I'd better get on with it now."

It was not proving easy for James to gain a foothold in the theatre, the entire year had yielded very few opportunities for him, the odd appearance at a charity gala, one or two single performance operettas where he played minor parts and even changing agents brought him no more success. He spent more and more time in his studio which, his enthusiasm for painting rekindled in France, he had set up in the attic. Alas, making an income from his art was not proving easy either and he was beginning to despise meeting with gallery owners, none of whom had, in his view, the judgement to spot talent when they saw it in front of them.

Finances were just about holding up, Warwick Street provided a modest regular income, he had the balance of the wedding gift from his mother, the twenty pounds a year from his Trust and the generous dowry Henry Oatway had settled on his daughter for the year. He and Florence were managing to live moderately comfortably, but he was impatient for more.

Early in 1886 James received a letter from his

mother telling him there was no alternative but to sell Severns in Nottingham. Reluctantly, he had agreed with Florence that they should visit Powick but he would stay only one night for the family dinner where Tom, his sisters and cousin William Thorne would also be present. William had found a buyer for the wine merchants and the restaurant and had agreed a fair deal for both the businesses and the properties in Middle Pavement where they were housed. Thomas was quick to make his disapproval of James very clear, his already jaundiced view of an actor's life not changed on learning his brother was habitually out of work. His mother was kinder, her disappointment however, almost palpable. When she heard that the new owners had agreed to continue trading under the Severn name, it had softened the blow for her a little, she was pleased her husband's name would continue to mean something in Nottingham. The houses had always remained in Jane's ownership too and the proceeds were hers to be distributed as, and when, she saw fit. James had been disappointed that she did not see fit to distribute some right then. Thomas had taken her aside and made her swear not to.

She did however have one treat for him. "The stock has of course been sold, but I told William I want you and Thomas to each receive fifty cases of wine. Let me know the name of a wine merchant who can store it all properly for you."

Whilst James found it very difficult to be patient back in London, Florence's days had settled into a contented routine. Her morning dealings with the staff concluded, she would wait for James to leave the house and if she had no committee meetings to attend early, would go to her own room, sit at her writing desk, open her notebooks and study the last words she had written. Most days she would sit writing, oblivious to the world around her until Biddy tapped quietly on her door at one o'clock and advised her that a luncheon had been prepared in the dining room. Following her meal, she would go about her charity work, meet with her mother or take tea with her friends. Especially with Sylvia when she was at home.

She and her mother also began to introduce themselves, in their capacity as ambassadors for the Female Aid Society, to some of the madams of the local brothels. Initially they were viewed with great suspicion. They well knew the two most commonly held attitudes by reformers towards the social evil of prostitution, were condemnation and reformation, the latter often offered in the guise of the former. However, Harriett and Florence did not preach, did not judge and nor did they harangue and because of this, they gradually became welcomed by some and hoped the information and advice they left would be distributed to the working women and would be of use to them. Over time they were able to talk with some of the prostitutes themselves and were often moved to anger or tears by the stories they heard, tales of how sad lives had led, often decent girls, down this path.

CHAPTER 12

1886
Yorkshire Tea is established in Harrogate, England
American pharmacist Dr. John Pemberton invents a
carbonated beverage that will be named 'Coca-Cola'

In December, Biddy came to Florence to announce timidly that she wished to hand in her notice, she was to be married to the young market porter she had been walking out with for some months. She admitted to Florence that she was 'in the family way' and the slight irritation she felt at having to find and train a new servant was dispelled by the knowledge that, Biddy at least, would have the protection and security of a husband. Florence thought of the number of tragic women she had met, those who had been abandoned by the fathers of their children. It was Biddy's leaving that made her decide to do some real good, she knew a few girls who, if only they had the means, would give up their sordid lives in the brothels. She could offer one of these her servant's job. She took the bull by the horns and discussed the proposition with James who, preoccupied with his own matters did not give it much thought and needed little persuasion to agree. It was then a case of who Florence should approach.

Her first thought was of a girl whom she thought to be about seventeen years old and at present under what was euphemistically called, the protection, of a house in the next street. Lottie was an open and friendly girl who seemed to Florence to be intelligent, always ready to listen and played a large part in encouraging the other girls in her house to be careful. She nagged and berated them to have their regular medical checkups, "It's for your own sake," she would shout when one or another said they were too tired, or they didn't have the time, "you ever seen someone with the pox or worse. Well I have, covered in sores and going mad in the head." She argued with her madam demanding she should ban any customers who took delight in hurting the girls. This was a losing battle, the bigger money being there for flagellation, so instead she pleaded that only girls prepared to be beaten should be assigned to those perpetrators and certainly not any new, young recruits. Florence was convinced Lottie was an ideal candidate to be rescued and made up her mind to approach Mrs Robbins the brothel keeper, who was not pleasant, but at least not openly hostile.

"Good heavens no," Lottie was aghast when Florence asked her, "why ever would I want to give up this life for one of domestic slavery? No offence to you of course, I'm sure … well, you know what I mean. It's just that I get much better pay here for shorter hours and the work's quite easy once you've learned the ropes," she laughed, "no, not me. I'm putting my money away to buy a little coffee house like my friend Agnes, she's up the King's Road and doing fine."

"But the conditions here are dreadful," Florence

said as she looked around the dingy, sad room. There was a threadbare carpet and curtains, a chipped wardrobe with one door hanging slightly loose, the chair she was sitting on sagged badly and the bed Lottie was lounging on, had only the thinnest veneer of cleanliness, "surely you would prefer a clean and comfortable room to yourself and, more importantly, what about the harm this work is doing to your body?"

"Well, as I looks at it, it's my body and I can do with it what I like. I go for my checks and at least I choose to let a man have his way with me, not like a wife who has no say at all."

This took Florence aback and she swallowed heavily, "Yes, of course Lottie and I admire you for wanting to take control of your own life, I just feel there are better ways."

"I'd never get to have me own business if I worked for you though would I? No offence meant again, and I like most of my gentlemen. Some of 'em give me extra tips now they know I'm saving up and there's one, won't mention no names, said he'd help me when I'm ready to set up shop. I'm sorry Mrs S., I don't mean to be ungrateful, but it's not for me, I like my life just as it is at the moment. Old Robbins is not too bad, she takes her cut but leaves us alright. Except when's she's drinking of course, but she's got a happy house, the girls here are all quite content."

"That's good to hear," said Florence guardedly, "but maybe I could speak with Bessie, she told me how badly she was treated by her employer and left destitute when they threw her out of the house. She may well want to become respectable again."

"I don't think so. Her kid died and she's angry

about it all underneath, don't think she'd settle down in your house Mrs S, no matter how kind you are." Lottie picked at her finger nail and in between evening up the edges with her teeth said, "You could try one of the girls at the Blue House on Walton Street, I've talked to one or two from there and one, calls herself Hope, I'm pretty certain she's desperate to get out. She hates the work but can't escape. I've given her your leaflets, but I reckon that old bag in charge takes 'em off 'er. She's not after having you lot take her income away, is she? I could help you get to have a word with the girl."

Florence thanked Lottie and suggested they both try to come up with a plan and that she would be in touch again at the end of the week.

It was not until the following week that Florence's visit to Mrs Robbins's coincided with Lottie being 'unengaged' at the same time and the two women were allowed to sit in the shabby parlour where they were provided with a pot of tea to share. Incongruously for such faded surroundings, the tea service was a fine example of Royal Doulton china and Florence had to wonder after all at the extent of the madam's income.

"I've rather drawn a blank," she admitted to Lottie, "I called at the Blue House with my usual Society hat on and the dreadful harridan there was even ruder and more aggressive than usual. I did manage to get a glimpse inside the house though and it is a disgrace. If the keeper and the premises are *so* bad, goodness knows what sort of men frequent it. I'm certain she has girls there who are underage too."

"I don't think Hope is sixteen yet and she's been there a few years now so she would certainly have been underage then, before they put it up from thirteen.

Poor kid, she needs looking after and I've got a plan. You'll have to kidnap her!"

"What? I can't do that."

"I'll get Mrs R to agree that I can walk out down Walton Street early one evening and wait for the girl to come out. That bitch will be keeping an eye on her, so I'll say loudly that there's a bloke just up the road, a real gent, too shy to come forward, who wants a young 'un and I'm too old. I'll say he won't go into the house, just wants a quick one behind the wall on the corner with Beauchamp."

"Will the madam let her go? Out of her sight I mean?"

"I'll tell her that he told me he's not a regular, just wants to try it out and that she's got to be young and that he'll pay her five shillings for it. That'll get the greedy old bag's attention and I can offer to 'supervise' her girl if she likes. I'll bring her up the road to you and you can whisk her away."

"What about you Lottie, what if she catches you?"

"I can look after meself don't worry, and she don't know me, I hardly ever go up that way. My regulars know I'm always up Pont Street."

When the strategy was explained to James, he reacted with horror. "You cannot be serious, you cannot possibly do this, it could be a disaster. You know nothing about the girl and I'm not sure it's even legal. You could be accused of false imprisonment, it's too risky. Find a girl who's willing and whose controller agrees to let her go."

"But Ernest, isn't this exactly the sort of child I should be saving? Lottie says she has been under the control of this brothel keeper since she was a child. If I am to go around saying I am trying to help, surely I should use actions rather than words when the opportunity arises."

James realised that, as usual, Florence would have her own way. "I shall come with you then, no argument, you are not going alone."

The operation, executed that Saturday evening, did not go entirely according to plan. Lottie played her part perfectly, the madam's avarice got the better of her, and Hope, recognising and trusting the older girl, walked away with her from the Blue House. Unfortunately, there was not sufficient time for the child to completely understand what was happening so when confronted with a well-dressed, affluent couple, Florence quickly throwing a cape around her shoulders to cover her bare skin, she began to scream. She kicked and scratched at Lottie, yelling to be let go, and Lottie, holding onto her valiantly, tried to drown out the screams with shouting of her own. It was a very anxious few minutes and James in particular was terrified of the constable being called to the disturbance, but Lottie took charge, her hand over Hope's mouth, she pushed and pulled the girl forward and pleaded with her to believe what she was saying. She painted Florence as a saint sent specifically to save her, and when this still did nothing to sway opinion, she threatened the girl. "If you don't go with this nice lady and gentleman, I'm going to tell that old hag that you tried to run away. That'll be the end of you!"

All four were stunned by these words but Hope went quiet, head bowed she allowed herself to be hurried to the door, she walked silently up the steps and, with goodness knows what thoughts running through her traumatised mind, let Biddy take her upstairs to the small room in the attic, undress and wash her.

After a while, Biddy brought the girl back downstairs to the drawing room, her hair was tied back neatly and she wore an old, but clean, brown dress and apron. Watching the child, she could be no more than fifteen, wringing her hands in her lap and nervously picking at her apron, Florence started speaking gently, "Lottie told me how unhappy you were at the brothel and how you were not allowed the information we brought around explaining where you could go to get help. We need a new servant and she thought you would be pleased to leave the Blue House and come and live here with us. But we had to come up with a plan for you to leave, the woman in charge at your house would never let you go, and I am sorry if we frightened you on the street. You will be quite safe here, there is nothing now for you to worry about. Can you tell me about yourself, what is your name? Do you have any family we could contact?"

The words did not even appear to register, Hope's only response was to open her eyes even wider in fear.

"You will be expected to carry out the duties of a general maid," Florence pressed on, "Biddy here will help you learn what you have to do, the work is hard but I shall make sure the hours are not too long for you and you will have a clean, comfortable room and as much food as you like. Mrs Cox, the cook, will see to that. I shall pay you twelve pounds a year and you may have Wednesday afternoons to yourself."

There was still only agonised fear on Hope's face, "Please, my dear, you will be perfectly safe here, Mr

LISA ABSALOM

Severne and I will not let anything bad happen to you. There will be no more men, no one to hurt you again." There was still no word of response, but Florence noticed the girl shrink back into the chair as she glanced over to James, "My husband and I want only for you to be safe and happy."

It soon transpired that Hope couldn't seem to grasp even the simplest of tasks quickly, "Either you are stupid or you are just not trying you ungrateful girl," Biddy's tongue sharpened with frustration, "for heaven's sake, cover those ashes or you'll sprinkle them all over the carpet." Mrs Cox, made no disguise of her contempt for the new girl, "she may be young and had problems in her life but haven't we all and we didn't turn out to be common whores. I don't know what the mistress was thinking of, taking her on."

Biddy had left and Hope was still desperately unhappy. Only the terror of recriminations prevented her from walking out and returning to Walton Street and she spent her days working, taking no pleasure or pride in trying to do the tasks properly, eating sullenly in the corner of the kitchen and refusing point blank to take a step outside the house. She crept around the rooms, shrinking into the shadows whenever she saw James coming towards her, unwittingly causing disquiet throughout the house.

"I shall have to speak with Mrs Cox, insist that she shows more compassion," Florence told James after the first few weeks, "we cannot go on like this. I cannot concentrate on my writing and I hardly like to go out and leave them alone."

The turning point came quite by chance. Hope was alone in the kitchen, Mrs Cox having an urgent need for the privy had slipped out to the back yard, when she noticed the pan of pea soup begin to boil. Unsure of whether to incur the cook's wrath for not preventing it from spilling and burning on the range or for interfering, she chose in that split second, the latter. Moving the pot to the side of the heat, she took up the large, wooden spoon and stirred slowly and it was at the very moment that she had put the spoon to her mouth that her adversary came back in.

"What do you think you are doing, you little devil. How dare you touch the food. Get out of my way, give me that spoon." As if to check Hope had not curdled the soup, she tasted it herself, "Think yourself very lucky," she snapped, "it's is still perfect."

"No it's not," her fear wiped away by her resentment, Hope spoke up, "it needs a spoon of sugar. Mrs Beeton says to add that if the peas are old."

"What do you know about these things, you're nothing but a little slut. Get out of my kitchen, the scullery floor needs cleaning. I dropped some flour earlier."

When she'd gone, Mrs Cox was thoughtful, maybe the sugar wasn't such a bad idea. "Of course, I knew that would take away that sharpness," she said to herself, "the little upstart."

Nevertheless, Hope had intrigued her and over the following days her manner softened a little and she prised the girl's story from her. As far as she was aware, her parents were both dead and the orphanage she'd grown up in had placed her in service at a modest house in Chelsea at about the age of eleven. The motherly cook of the house had taken a shine to the quiet little child and began teaching her some basic cooking skills, allowing her to help when she had the odd moment. Over their evening meals, Hope listened and learned as the kindly woman spoke of recipes and dishes. Unfortunately for Hope, her employer too had taken a shine to the pretty, quiet little girl and, bewildered and scared, she had been constantly at the mercy of his unwanted, sexual attentions. This in itself was bad enough and the cook could do nothing to help but inevitably, the mistress of the house saw what was happening. She could not confront her husband, so in a fit of jealous rage, she accused Hope of stealing two silver spoons and threw her out onto the street with only the clothes she stood up in.

"I were ruined," she sobbed to Mrs Cox, "no reference, no nothing. It was raining and I was so cold I went to the train station, they always has a coal fire going in the waiting room and all I could think of was to get warm. Anyway, this man come up to me and said he'd find me a bed for the night. In my heart I knew this was trouble, but I didn't know what else I could do, and he spoke nice and seemed kind. He wasn't though and that's how I ended up at Old Granny's," she raised her head defiantly, sniffed loudly and wiped her eyes, "I hated it there, I was never there 'cos I wanted to be and the men, the men were disgusting. If I'd had a knife, I'd 'ave killed most of them."

"Mind your language Hope, this is a respectable house," Mrs Cox said really quite kindly, "well, you are safe here. The mistress is a very good woman and you should be thankful to her, not moping around with a face like a wet blanket. Now, tell me about this sauce. What do you think? Nutmeg or not, you have a very good sense of taste my girl."

CHAPTER 13

1887
*The British Empire celebrates Queen Victoria's Golden
Jubilee, marking the 50th year of her reign*

From then on there was a gradual change at home and the days became happier and well ordered. When Florence finally managed to convince Hope she would not be recognised, she left the house or garden and ventured to the high street once or twice. Thankfully, Florence felt she could now return undisturbed to her writing, everything was as it should be - except that her husband was still not earning a living!

It therefore came as a surprise, when only a week or so after Florence breathed her sighs of relief, they were disturbed one morning by a local constable coming to the door. By chance James was still at home and took control as Hope, shaking like a leaf, showed the policeman into the morning room.

"Charles Arrow, Sir," he said holding out his hand, "I'm sorry to disturb you. It's a strange matter, this, we've had a complaint that you are running a house of ill repute, but I can see immediately that it is all a nonsense."

"Absolutely ridiculous!" James snorted, "wherever did that come from, I can assure you there is nothing of the sort going on here. My wife is a tireless supporter of the Female Aid Society and even I am on their committee. Who gave you this information?"

"An anonymous member of the public told us that you had kidnapped an underage girl and were keeping her here for prostitution purposes and," he said with resignation, "since the criminal law act came in a couple of years ago, my boss is keen to be seen upholding it, protection of the women and all that."

"What!" Florence could not believe her ears, "I think I know exactly what has happened."

When she and James had finished telling the whole story, Charles Arrow relaxed, "I didn't think for one moment it was true," he smiled, "and especially when I found out who lived here. I really couldn't imagine Mr Ernest Severne the actor could be involved. I saw you at the Royalty in *Hoop-La* not so long ago, I thought you were splendid! Good voice too."

"Well what a coincidence," James grinned, "so few people did come to see it, and," his grin changed to a rueful smile, "apparently not all them appreciated it!"

"Well I thought Miss Barry was uninspiring in the other play, the one about the Americans, and I usually love her, it was all a bit of an anticlimax, but I did like yours, much more my style," he turned to Florence, "made me laugh out loud and I enjoyed your song."

"Well that's proof indeed that the critics know nothing," James rummaged through a pile of newspaper cuttings on the side table, "listen to what the man said in the *Sporting News*, 'the interpolation of a song for

Miss Dysart who sings a great deal better than she acts, was easy to understand, but why Mr Ernest Severne should have attempted a ditty passed our comprehension!'"

There was a slight apprehensive silence, and then as James began to roar with laughter, Florence and Charles joined in.

"I can laugh about it now," James calmed down, "but it was jolly hurtful at the time. Still, it helped me make up my mind, I'm going to take the plunge and set up my own company, become an actor manager. My judgement on what makes a good show can't be any worse than these others." The three of them laughed again.

"Back to the matter in hand," Florence said seriously, "will you have a cup of coffee Constable? Hope can bring it and you can see for yourself that she is here of her own free will, not at all abused and moderately happy. I am sure one part of the story is right though, she is not yet sixteen and I would suggest your Inspector sends you to investigate the brothel in the Blue House, it has a bright blue door, in Walton Street. The woman there guards her girls like a jailer and will not allow them to have any contact with those of us trying to help."

"And," added James, "as you seem to be a fan of the theatre, you might like to come along sometime to The Albion with me. I can introduce you to members of the acting fraternity, a lot of us gather there to share the news, drink and generally gossip about the business."

When Charles had left, James was about to leave the house himself when Florence called him back, "Ernest, what do you mean you are going to become a manager? You haven't mentioned it before."

"I was waiting until everything was in place, but it was reading that review again that made me absolutely sure. I've found a play, I'll tell you all about it when it's mine, but it's early days and I need to get the paperwork sorted. I didn't want to raise any hopes that your husband might soon be in a position to support you properly," he said slightly shamefaced, "until it's signed and sealed.

He made his way to The Albion in Great Russell Street and was hoping James Meade the author and owner of the play he was interested in, would be there. Meade had been introduced to him two weeks before by Potty Sinclair and had tempted James with a proposition that he both bought a share in his new and original drama, and also, produced it.

The bar was crowded when he walked in. Through the smoke he could see a group he recognised, sitting in what they all called cuckoo corner. A gruesome stuffed cuckoo, once blue grey but now predominantly tobacco brown and dusty, sat calling it's last from the shelf behind the scrubbed deal table and chairs.

"Welcome Ernest," Teddy Loftus sprang to his feet, "come on you lot," he spoke to his companions, "shove up and make room for another chair."

"Have you heard," asked a pale faced young man whom James knew only by sight, "they are auditioning for a tour with Helen Barry in August, you need to get your agent onto it."

"Miss Barry knows you, doesn't she?" Teddy looked at him, "so you'd have a good chance of a part."

"To be honest Teddy, I'm in the middle of fixing

something else up," James answered quietly, "can't say anything yet but hoping to have it all sorted out later this week. In fact," he said, spotting Meade's reflection in the huge, etched glass mirror at the end of the room, "I just need to go over and speak to that chap over there. Get me a jug of claret in, I'll not be long."

"Who James Meade?" Teddy looked across the room, "I know you're thinking of buying his play?" He laughed, "Don't look so surprised, you can't keep a secret amongst this bunch, we all know about it!"

Meade was a tall, rather thin man in his fifties and the achievement of having still abundant dark hair, albeit the sides tinged with grey, was by virtue of Messrs. Thomas Gibbons, wig maker. His beard, James thought, would bear an abundance of grey too had it not been dyed a most unconvincing black.

"Mr Severne, how good to see you. Are we ready to do business?" His voice boomed out, disembodied from such a slight frame, "you'll need to get cracking if you are to tour *The Oath* in the autumn."

"Good morning to you too, yes, I was hoping to find you here for that very reason. The papers are ready and if we could meet to sign them tomorrow, they can be lodged at Stationers Hall, can you meet me there at ten? My legal friend will deal with the formalities."

The meeting arranged, James wrestled his eyes away from the hair piece and returned in high spirits to sit with his friends. This time he stepped over Teddy's legs and plonked himself down in the space Kate Warren had made for him next to her on the banquette. She put her arm through his and squeezing it, purred, "Where've you been Ernest? I thought you said you'd be here early today."

"Business my little poppet, but I'm done now, so we could have a sixpenny plate to eat here and then I'm all yours for the afternoon."

James and Florence had never returned to sharing a bed after those first few days of their marriage. At home James had never presumed to bother Florence in the huge, carved, walnut four poster in the bedroom, he took to a more modest brass bedstead in his smaller dressing room. Not another word about sex had been uttered by either of them and James had gradually slipped back into his previous ways with the young actresses. He was always discreet, he would not wish to embarrass his wife and as he was found to be enticingly attractive, he was never without a girl for company. He and Kate had appeared together, both taking very minor roles, in a short lived play the previous December and although James found her company pleasant enough, he did not care for her rather proprietary, possessive air. In his serious moments he knew that he should finish the relationship before it became too well established, but as with most things in life, he found the status quo easier to maintain and right now he was so preoccupied with his career that he did not relish expending the inevitable energy and emotion that breaking up with Kate would bring.

On April 30th, James handed over sixty pounds, the purchase was lodged at the publisher's livery company, Stationers Hall, and he became the proud co-owner with Meade of the rights to the play, *The Oath*. Importantly, he and Meade were to share the provision of future capital needed to produce it.

Later that day he visited Henry Jubb at Jubb & Larkin, wine merchants in Mark Lane and checked that his fifty cases of wine had arrived from Severns in Nottingham. Surprised and delighted with the selection, he agreed which of the wines should be laid down and which would be sent to him as and when he made an order. Slightly staggered by the cellarage costs he immediately consoled himself by arranging an immediate delivery of a quality claret from Chateau Lagrange, a St Julien he thought most appropriate to toast his new path in life.

"Ernest, you've told me about Mr Meade's wig and his beard, please tell me about his play! You are so excited I should like to share in it with you." Florence was eating dinner with her husband and he, as jovial as she had ever seen him, regaled her with the detail of his dealings with the playwright.

"You'll like the story Florence, it's a melodrama, set in Ireland and knowing your love of ghoulish plots, you'll like the fact that the main protagonist is a murderer. He gives his confession to the priest - hence the name, *The Oath*, but the lord of the manor is accused of the murder and is sentenced to be executed. I'm not going to tell you any more, I hope you will come and see it to learn what happens."

"You say Mr Meade is an actor too, will he be performing?"

"Yes, we have agreed that he will play the lead part of the murderer, Mr Byng and all together there are twenty characters for me to cast and with several songs I need the actors to be able to sing too. Meade has already arranged to put it on at Manchester and Worcester and I need to concentrate on organising a bigger tour for the autumn.

"Tour?" Florence raised her eyebrows, "where do

you intend going?"

"I think the midlands and the north. Birmingham, Leeds, Blackburn and maybe Newcastle. I'm really confident Florence, it's a good play."

"I'm so thrilled for you, let's drink to your success." They lifted their glasses and Florence pronounced, "With this delicious wine, I should like to raise a toast to Ernest Severne, Impresario!"

CHAPTER 14

1887
The Theatre Royal, Exeter, England, burns
down, killing 186 people

I t was now barely three months since that celebratory evening when he and his wife had toasted his new life. It had taken only twelve short weeks for the whole business to turn sour. Things had begun to go wrong within the first month. Following positive reviews of the play in Manchester and Worcester, James, feeling bullish had agreed to buy out Meade's half share of the play and then, as proud sole proprietor, he arranged a matinée at the Strand theatre in June. He also engaged Meade on a salary of twelve pounds a week to be stage manager for his newly arranged ten-week tour to follow and also to continue to star as Stephen Byng.

Meade immediately began to upset the cast in rehearsals, his language was vulgar, and he reduced most of the actresses to tears with his aggressive manner. After the Strand matinée, matters took a turn for the worse and the next morning Florence had hugged her husband a little longer than usual as he left the house. The reviews of his play at the London premier had been brutally scathing and now he was having to pick himself up and arrange rehearsals for a week's engagement in Shoreditch in July.

"Hardly a fashionable quarter," he had grumbled to Florence, but I'm lucky to have that, given the awful critiques we've had. The papers have laid the blame firmly at Meade's door, called the production amateurish and said the acting management was chaotic. One critic even found fault with the look of the auditorium because we'd provided extra chairs, but the stalls weren't full. He criticised how the story, which he thought was fine, had too much padding and was too drawn out. Nor did he have a good word to say about most of the actors, Meade included. I'm not particularly surprised, they were all demoralised by that man's behaviour. I can't believe he'd even refused to let the prompter have a copy of the script to help out. That man is a charlatan, how he's managed all these years heaven alone knows."

"Do you have to keep him on?" asked Florence.

"He's refusing to let even me have a copy of the manuscript. The cheek of it, I bought it, it's mine. So at the moment I'm completely confounded. I'm going to see Martin, ask for some advice.

Later that morning Martin had told him, "James, I'm sorry old chap, there's no way Boodle will let me take this on, it's not respectable enough for us and anyway, I'd be way too expensive for you. There's a good man, Robert Bartlett in Queen Street. Mention my name. He'll do a good job for you, take out a summons against Meade for an order to pay the cost of you obtaining a copy of the script from the Lord Chamberlain."

"That's about ten pounds."

"And you should get your own court costs paid, but not Bartlett's fees alas."

James could not move ahead, he could not risk keeping Meade on as stage manager and he therefore had to have a copy of the script for himself. The summons for this was not to be heard until the 29 June. He cancelled Shoreditch and told Meade his services were no longer required. He was not up to the job. When the two men appeared that following week at Bow Street police court, Meade paid up the ten pounds for a copy of the script without a quibble. The reason for this acquiescence, his solicitor went on to dumfounded James by announcing that, as far as they were concerned, there were a number of matters in dispute and as such they would form the subject of a further action in the High Court of Chancery.

"It seems the whole world is out to thwart me Florence!" James sat with his head in his hands, elbows on the table, staring into space, "what have I done to deserve this. I bought that play in good faith and Meade has turned it into a nightmare? Any money I might have thought of making will all go on solicitor's fees, and you can't trust the courts to get to the truth of the matter, that's evident."

"But he's paid the ten pounds, hasn't he? The court thought you were in the right then." Florence's heart went out to him as she saw the pain in her gentle, kind husband's eyes. His face was unshaved, and his normally tousled hair was now quite untidy, left unbrushed that morning. He was dressed but without his usual panache. No silk handkerchief in his top pocket, no colourful waistcoat. He looked an unhappy, worried boy, and she just wanted to take him in her arms and comfort him as a mother would her child.

"They didn't have to actually make a judgement on that, the solicitor agreed to pay for the script pending the bigger court case," he lisped and Florence reached out to take his hand across the table as James almost cried, "Do you know what that rogue has gone round saying? That I've not paid the company *and* that I forged a cheque."

"Well surely that cannot be allowed. That he can say such untrue things about you?"

James ran his fingers through his hair again, and sighed, "Robert is putting in a counter claim. Meade is suing me for breach of contract, and we'll sue him for slander. My reputation will be ruined with this going on." Angrily he added, "I want the shirt off his back."

"Do you have a date for court?" Florence asked as she poured James another cup of coffee, added cream and sugar and pushed the cup towards him.

"It could be months, Robert is dealing with it and will act for me, he's proving to be a very good friend, and in the meantime, I'll just have to carry on."

There was a light tap at the door and Hope slipped in quietly, "Here's the post Sir," she said and looking at Florence, smiled and asked, "is there anything else I can do for you M'am?"

"No thank you Hope, but you could tell Mrs Cox I shall not be in for lunch and …"

"What the devil! How the hell can the man do this?" James leapt up startling Hope such that she jumped behind Florence's chair and his wife looked up anxiously. "I must go, I have to see Robert," and as he moved to the door, he shouted, "he's sold the damned play to someone else as well now!"

"We'll put an immediate denial in the papers," Robert Bartlett tried to calm his client down, "this will go against him in court, that's good for us."

"Look, he says this agreement with Rollo Balmain - I know him, I always thought him a decent sort, he can't know the whole story - anyway, he says the papers were signed on the 29th June, that's the day we were at Bow Street. The day he paid up the ten pounds. The audacity of the man, the bare faced brass. How can he sell what isn't his to sell? That's all in the certificate at Stationer's Hall."

"I'll write to Balmain today to inform him of our proofs," Robert stood, shook James's hand, "try not to worry James, we'll have our day in court, and all will be well."

Unbelievably, it was only a few days later that James was back in Robert's office.

"You know, if I made this story up and tried to put it on as a play, it wouldn't be believed," James was saying, "I really don't know what to make of this chap in Australia, but one thing's for sure, I most certainly cannot trust a word Meade says."

In the past days there had been a flurry of letters printed in *The Era* starting with one from a George Darrell claiming Meade had stolen the play which he himself had written and performed in Sydney, with Meade renaming it *The Oath*. Meade had written back immediately with a rebuttal, denying that it was in fact the same play, that he had found the story in a rare book and admitting that it may have a few similarities, but that was all. He asserted further that yet another individual, a Mr Finn, had already been in dispute with

Darrell, laying claim to the idea of the very same story himself.

"The effrontery of the man," James had refused to take a seat and was striding up and down the room, "what shall I do? I'm supposed to be in Birmingham, we're rehearsing, and the opening night is in two days. I need to be there."

"Please, try and calm down. This is aside from our court case so we can deal with it separately. If I understood rightly, you are not due to pay any author's fees just yet?"

"That's right."

"So, I suggest we draft a letter to *The Era* saying that you have decided to withhold making any payments until the ownership of the play is established. It's quite reasonable, we'll make absolutely clear that you are willing to pay, it's just that you do not know as yet who is the legitimate recipient. We don't know who actually wrote the play. However, James, I would suggest this is the least of your problems, you still need more capital don't you? Now that Meade's not going to stump up his share?"

"Be that as it may, I have to go ahead. I've already paid out, booked the theatres, engaged the actors, I need this to be a success, but you're right, we'll run out of money."

His troubles magnified. Florence's mother Harriett died suddenly on the day he left for Birmingham. He wrestled with his conscience, his wife needed him and his company needed him. Sylvia went to the funeral in his place.

In spite of the omens, the tour was successful, Birmingham, Leeds, Burnley, Bradford, Newcastle and Blackburn. Universally the reviews were glowing, everything from the play itself, the actors, the scenery and the props, they all received glowing praise. James could not remember a happier six weeks, if only the nagging doubt of the finances had not been in his mind. He had loved taking on the role of stage manager, arranging the rehearsals formally, ten in the morning until four in the afternoon. The tour had not been without drama on and off the stage. At Burnley, the actor playing the excitable Irish victim, fell and cracked his head open minutes before he was due to be murdered leaving James a very fast decision to make. The chosen understudy of course was secretly pleased. As manager he was called on to intercede in a potentially tricky situation of an over ardent fan of the leading lady, his worshipping behaviour at the stage door each evening becoming intolerable and he was also called on to find and arrange alternative lodgings for more than one member of the cast when they found those previously booked to be quite unsatisfactory. Vermin and bad or no food being the major problems. All his own rooms thankfully had turned out to be superb homes from home. His landladies had loved having the handsome, gentle, well mannered 'boy' in their homes.

But this success just wasn't enough. By the end of the tour, James ran out of money. He could not afford to continue his company. He could not afford to bring the show back to the London stage. He returned to London, dejected and broke, visited his agent, advertised for acting work for himself as he always had done and waited for his court case. If he won and was awarded the one thousand pounds damages for slander, he could set up again.

CHAPTER 15

1888

*William Lever builds Port Sunlight as a model village
for workers in his Sunlight Soap factory*

"I'm just not sure this is a good time to tell him."
Florence was sitting in Sylvia's Bloomsbury
drawing room, the enormous mahogany table
covered with travel papers in neat, regimented piles,
each with a label announcing the topic. Her mind was
not on her friend's plans.

"Well I think it's superb news and would give Ernest a bit of a lift. It will at least show him that there
will be some extra income," Sylvia leant over, reached
out but her hand falling short asked, "pass me that pile
labelled 'Honshu' could you please, it's in the wrong
order."

Florence had been offered a publishing contract
with a major London house for her first novel, *The Pillar House*, the culmination of almost three years work,
everything she had dreamed of.

"But I don't want to appear as if I'm bragging,"
Florence said anxiously, "you know he writes as well?
For journals and the newspapers but he's not had any

success yet. Anyway, it will be some months before they actually publish the book, first I have an editor assigned me and I have to practically rewrite the whole thing. Maybe I could leave it a bit longer. See if he gets back on his feet by then."

"Florence!" Sylvia looked up from her sorting task and looked sternly at her friend, "Tell your husband your splendid news. You are a clever woman, and this is a major achievement. Ernest has never struck me as mean spirited, he will be happy for you and you most definitely deserve to celebrate. Now just help me put these away in the right places and we can get going."

Mrs Quinn had died in the winter of '87 and now that spring had arrived, Sylvia was putting the finishing touches to her plans for an expedition to Japan, following in the footsteps of her idol, Isabella Bird. With her departure expected in September, the two friends were spending as much time together as possible and this particular morning, Sylvia was accompanying Florence to a meeting at the Female Aid headquarters in Red Lion Square. As it was not far from the Quinn's house, the ladies chose to walk. The weather was warm, and the sun was breaking through high, scudding clouds. They strolled arm in arm.

"I shall miss you so much," Florence sighed, "it was a long enough time apart when you stayed in France, but this trip will be even longer." She smiled at the exotic lady next to her, "Not that I am not excited for you my dearest. What an adventure! I'm almost sorry I shall not be coming with you. But only *almost* sorry!"

"Miss Bird wrote letters to her sister whilst she was travelling and I thought I would regard you, my dear friend, as *my* sister and write to you constantly," Sylvia squeezed Florence's arm tightly, "maybe I shall give you some ideas for your next plot even?"

"I should be honoured to be your sister and I shall look forward to your letters immensely."

Florence's business at the Society done, she asked Sylvia, "I have a favour to ask of you. Will you come with me to St Giles? You remember the girl, well, woman really, who suggested Hope came to us and helped her escape? I might have told you her great ambition was to save enough money to open a little coffee house, and now she has. It's on Lewknor Lane, which I think is a respectable enough area, it's off Drury Lane, but it might be nicer with you?"

"Of course. Perhaps we could have chocolate and cake for our lunch there, very decadent! I'd be interested to see how she is managing, it's quite a different way of life for her."

The cab dropped them outside a well-kept, smart shop. The window had six large, glass panes and behind them they could see trays of bakery on the shelf inside. High above the closed wooden door hung an ornate, square lamp, the shade of which was inscribed in purple with the lettering, "Lottie's Coffee House."

Florence pushed open the door, a bell tinkled their arrival and the sweet scent of fresh baking and coffee filled their nostrils. They scanned the room. Framed prints of the countryside almost covered the walls and Lottie herself was behind a polished wood counter pouring milk into a plain white jug. She placed it on a tin tray already holding a pewter coffee pot and two white cups. Looking up at the sound of the door, her face lit up with a surprised smile, "Good heavens. I never thought you would come out 'ere. Give me two secs and I'll be with you." She walked round and unloaded the tray for a couple sitting at one of the dozen small, round tables placed against the walls. Each had a tablecloth of printed, floral cotton and held a tiny jar of violets in the centre. Lottie was wearing a pale purple dress with a crisp white apron, her hair was piled on the top of her head and held in place neatly with two purple combs. Her only flaw, the slightest smudge of flour on her cheekbone.

"Mrs S., how good to see you," she said walking back to them, her pleasure showing on her face, "and your friend. Please will you take a table, this one here in the window is the best, I think. Can I bring you something to drink? On the house of course, it won't be too often I have such illustrious customers!"

"This is Miss Quinn, Lottie. She is interested to see how you are doing and is looking forward to hot chocolate and a cake. Which would you recommend?"

"I made 'em all myself, so they're all good," Lottie giggled, "maybe a currant bun? No, that's too ordinary, what about a slice of ginger cake. That's very popular with *my* ladies," and she giggled again as she made her way back behind her counter.

"You have a beautiful café here Lottie," Sylvia told her when she returned, "you have an artistic eye and oh," her eyes lit up at the sight of the cake, "you look as if you are an expert baker too. Where did you learn?"

Florence gestured to her to sit with them and she answered, "My Ma taught me, she worked in a bakery when I was little, and it seems I've not forgot. I'm really happy here Mrs S. Really happy. Not that I don't worry too, I need to sell a lot of macaroons to pay the rent," she laughed, "always looking for new customers. Being here near the theatre helps, lots of actors pop in. Not seen your husband though, s'pect he's too grand for the likes of Lottie's."

James wasn't too grand he just did not know about the coffee house until Florence told him that evening.

"She has done a wonderful job with it already, such a success story. She's intelligent all right, it is just such a shame that in our society she felt the only way to get the money to start her business was by selling her body. She was lucky to be in a reasonable house, look how that other one was with Hope. No, it's high time we were treated equally. Time the Banks made loans available to women as well as men."

"Mmm." James assented, his mind only half on the conversation, but he did think to ask Florence for the exact whereabouts of Lottie's, "I'll call in when I leave The Albion tomorrow, and if it's as good as you say, I'll put in a word for her with Potty and the others."

"Thank you, Ernest. Oh, speaking of good words, I almost forgot to tell you. Sylvia was at Lady Wilde's last Saturday afternoon and have you heard of a young woman, Romola Tynte Potter? I think that's right. Well she is looking to put on a drawing room entertainment and is wanting a manager. Sylvia suggested you and Miss Potter said to leave a note at the Wilde's in Chelsea."

"I do know *Miss Romola Tynte Potter*," he answered in a theatrical voice, then reverted to his own, "otherwise known as Mary Potter, daughter of that Irish clergyman who's always hitting the headlines. She wouldn't marry the man of his choice so he cast her out. Yes, I've met her a couple of times, she does recitals and the like. She's a bit strange but I will get in touch, a drawing room event is better than nothing and it will be useful to remind Lady Jane of my existence too. Why don't you go along to her Saturday afternoons Florence? Mix with other writers and artists, even the odd actor. Could be useful for you?"

Florence felt this could be the right moment to tell James of her contract. He was, as Sylvia predicted, completely thrilled for her. "Thank goodness one of us is going to achieve their ambition," he said as he got up and placed a kiss on his wife's forehead, "well done Florence. I mean it, you've worked so hard and you have talent, you deserve this. Now, I'll away and write a note to Miss R.T.P. and also to Miss Q. to thank her for the introduction. What it is to have a wife with contacts, how fortuitous for me."

He *was* delighted for Florence of course, but he had a great feeling of despondency when he met Potty Sinclair, Teddy and Davy, at The Albion the next day.

"I really hoped I'd reached a turning point with *The Oath*," he despaired, "but it turned into the biggest debacle yet and I've nothing but the prospect of managing a drawing room event on the horizon, how the mighty have fallen, eh?"

"Do not give up hope, remember you are the 'earnest Mr Severne', alas, our profession is an uneasy one, full of trials and tribulations, speaking of which," Potty waved his cigar in the air, "come over here Mr Arrow, your friend is in need of direction from one such as you, practiced in dealing with trials and tribulations!"

Only James did not smile at the joke, "Morning

Charles, off duty again then? You're becoming quite a fixture here, good to see you."

Since the day he called at the house checking on Hope, Charles Arrow had become good friends with James. He was always keen to talk of the theatre, but James also liked the occasional conversations which dealt with matters entirely removed from his own sphere of life.

"Morning Ernest, Potty, all not well today I take it?"

"When the only thing I have to look forward to is my case in the High Court next week, you know it's not a good day. In fact, could I talk with you about that before you go?"

"Of course, by the way, I managed to find out from the lists that you'll be heard in front of Justice Hawkins. He's fair and you'll stand a good chance of winning, but he's very stingy on damages. The courts are packed to the gunwales these days with actors or their managers suing for breach of contract or libel. You thespians are a very sensitive lot you know," he smiled, "nothing new in the world of the stage for you then?"

After about an hour the subdued gathering ended, Charles advised him on a few points for the following week and James got up to leave. He stood outside the door, breathed heavily, wondering if he should go over to Clapham to see his agent face to face. He began walking down Great Russell Street and the warmth from the sun lightened his mood somewhat. Remembering his promise to Florence, he set off more purposefully towards where he thought Lewknor Lane was.

He was fascinated when he saw Lottie. He had met her only that once on the night of the kidnapping and taken scant notice of her other than as, in the drama of the moment, a screaming, cloaked figure intent on engineering his arrest for abduction. He would never have known her again. In contrast, she knew exactly who he was the minute he stepped inside 'Lottie's'.

"Good afternoon Sir," she curtseyed, "your wife told you about my little shop then?"

James ordered coffee and brandy and as she prepared it, he watched her. That November night, all he had noticed in the dull streetlight and under the hood of a woollen cape, was an over powdered white face, with bright red lips and cheeks, and thin, black, arched eyebrows. Now, without the make-up and with her light brown hair neatly dressed with purple combs, he could see she was very attractive. He was idly wondering what circumstances had brought her to become a prostitute when she brought his tray to him and, at his invitation, she sat down at his table. Glancing round to make sure her customers did not need anything she said, "I'm pleased that young Hope is working out, Mrs S. says she's a good worker and pleasant with it. I thought she'd be right for you, well," she stammered, "not *you*, of course, I haven't ever met you prop'ly, but thought if Mrs S. was married to you, you had to be a good 'un."

James laughed, "Yes, all is well at home, but tell me how you managed all this," he looked round the room, "it's very impressive. Must have cost a pretty penny?"

"I saved up Sir and I was lucky," she lowered her voice, "one of my regular gentlemen helped me find the place and, bless him, sorted the paperwork. He paid the first month's rent, for you know," she turned again to check no-one was listening, "for services rendered, and he promised to stop by from time to time. Although," she curled her lip, "I ain't seen him yet."

"It must be a lot of work my wife says you do all your own baking. Do you have anyone to help you?"

"Good grief no! Pardon my language Sir, I'm sorry. No, I do everything myself, couldn't possibly pay someone and I don't have no family to help. Nor do I want any neither mind you. Makes it a long day though, I'm up before dawn to cook the cakes and I like to do some breakfast stuff and toast of course for my early birds. Then I stays open for the pre theatre crowds in the evening so it's late when I finish. I'm fair knackered, oh sorry, there goes my language again, but I'm fair knackered by the time I get to bed of a night."

"You need to take on a girl as soon as your funds allow."

"It's a pity my gentleman doesn't seem to have come good," she looked James directly in the eye, "I was banking on a little extra from him."

He understood immediately, "Well if that's the case, maybe I could take his place? I have a requirement that I think you could fill admirably."

Lottie looked at the handsome, young gentleman sitting opposite her, thought of the wrinkly, fat, old man who had let her down and not believing her luck, smiled coquettishly and murmured, "I would be more than pleased to fulfil your requirements Sir and I'm confident you will find it done 'admirably'!"

James became very pleased with this new arrangement. He and Kate had gone their separate ways during the summer when he was so occupied with his tour. Amid recriminations, tears and hysterics she had left London and as far as he knew, had left acting too. He had not wanted a situation like that again, an agreement where emotions played no part was ideal, and of course, he could rely completely on Lottie's silence.

CHAPTER 16

1888 – 1889
An undetected murderer who slits the throats
of seven London prostitutes, becomes known
by the public as Jack the Ripper

C harles Arrow was right. Judge Hawkins was very
parsimonious when it came to awarding damages to James for the slander Meade had committed against him.

"Ten pounds! I knew when we sued for a thousand that it wouldn't wash, but I hoped for more than ten," James was furiously stirring the contents of the sugar bowl as they sat together in Lottie's, "the law's an ass, as our friend Dickens reminded us, ten pounds for trying to ruin my reputation."

"Disappointing I know," commiserated Charles pulling the bowl away and brushing the spilt sugar onto the floor, "but it could have been worse, Hawkins might have found for Meade and you'd be paying him for breach of contract. I'm sorry I couldn't be in court I've read the report in today's paper and it makes interesting reading!"

"It had its lighter moments," James conceded

with a small chuckle, "when Meade's counsel suggested that his client's use of profane language was just the 'idiom of his vocation', strong language being habitually used in stage management, I thought the Judge would clear the court there was so much laughter."

"What did Meade have to say to that?"

"It was totally bizarre. The whole proceedings seemed to concentrate on whether he said 'Damn' with a capital D, or 'damn' with a little d. Apparently trying to make a distinction between the former, profanity, and the latter, harmless."

"Did you see the headline in *The Era*?" Charles opened it and pointed to the top of page four, "look, 'The Oath and the Big Big D', its priceless."

"It was a bit tricky when I was cross examined on my own language," James could not help but laugh, "I was asked if I had ever used the D word!"

"And …," queried Charles, "however did you answer that?"

"Fudged it a bit but could honestly say I'd never used a big D or a little d in rehearsals and that I do have an objection to swearing, particularly in front of ladies." He stopped to thank Lottie for the extra jug of coffee she put on their table, smiled at her and watched her as she swayed back to her counter, "um, oh yes, then I was asked what was my particular swear word. Quite outrageous question, so I said it was so long ago that I'd used one that it had completely slipped my recollection."

"Did your counsel manage to get it back to the serious matters, the fact that Meade was incompetent and had slandered you?"

"Eventually, that damned Meade …," the two

men guffawed so loudly that all of Lottie's customers stopped their own conversations and turned to watch them, whereupon James took it upon himself to apologise profusely, and lowered his voice to finish, "Luckily the Judge believed our witnesses and took exception to the lies Meade had told about me. Counsel did a good job addressing the jury and Hawkins directed them in my favour too. I think they were completely bewildered to have sat through so many hours discussing the use of one little word!"

"What do you plan on doing now Ernest?" Charles asked, worried for his friend, "you've won the case but are no better off financially. Will you go bankrupt?"

"Not if I can avoid it, I'll try to keep my creditors at bay, but I'll have to stick to auditioning for acting parts, can't afford another foray into management at the moment."

"I'm sure you don't want to, but have you thought of a complete change of career? I think you'd make an excellent private investigator. I've seen many of them in my line of work and I reckon you'd enjoy sleuthing. It could be a bit like acting, disguises and different voices whilst you uncover the hidden truths. You've got a keen eye for observation and detail, you'd be good at it and I could push business your way from time to time, we often use a private man when we need extra information on a case.

"That's a bit out of the blue Charles. I've often agonized over whether to give up trying to make it on the stage, but I've never given investigating a thought, it would never have occurred to me. I'll bear it in mind though. If I can't make a go of this, I'll have to do something else and Lord knows, I'm not qualified to do anything."

"Come along to court with me when there's a PI going to present his evidence. You can see what it's all about, I'll send you a message. But now I have to go," he got up, picked up his hat, shook James's hand and calling, "Farewell Miss Lottie, the coffee was delicious as ever," he left.

Miss Potters drawing room entertainment was duly held and proved to be unremarkable. Recitations and various musical pieces, James would rather have been singing than managing but the bonus of the event was that he renewed his brief acquaintance with Lady Jane Wilde.

"We've been invited to the Wilde's Saturday salon next month." He had stopped Florence dead in her tracks as she left Mrs Cox in the kitchen and handed over the card received that morning in the post. "I know you've never wanted to go with Sylvia but this time her son Oscar and his wife are going to be there, holding court I should imagine, and it should be interesting for you."

"I do sometimes read his reviews in the Gazette and he can be very entertaining," Florence chivvied James out of her way and went back to the morning room with him in tow, "but did you say his wife Constance will be there? Now *she* I would like to meet. She is a great advocate for dress reform, and she wrote a charming book for children last year. So yes, please, will you accept on my behalf? I thought you were not disposed too kindly towards Mr Wilde?"

"I admit he's not my cup of tea and it's nothing to do with the rumours that go around about his personal life, no, it's his endorsement of what I've heard called 'anarchistic socialism' that I can't stomach, that and so much talk of Ireland," he finished buttoning his waistcoat and ran his hands over his hair, "but all the same, being present at Merrion Square could be very useful."

"Sylvia says there are often some of the most popular playwrights there, as well as authors and artists."

"I wasn't actually thinking of that, it was more keeping in with the high and mighty. I've been mulling over Charles's idea that I become an investigator and if I do, I'd prefer to be working for the upper echelons of society rather than the dregs! I need my face to be known." He drained his cup of, now cold, coffee and made as if to leave when he noticed Florence's face was lit up with a huge smile.

"I shall be a published author myself by then," he turned back when he heard the words, "you will be coming with me to Kegan Paul on the twenty fourth won't you?"

"I wouldn't miss publication day for all the world," James kissed her lightly on the cheek, "I am so proud of you."

"Thank you, Ernest, it is everything I have been working towards these past years. Imagine, my book in the shops. People, strangers, reading the words I have written. I don't know whether to be ecstatic or terrified."

"Ecstatic, Florence my dear. Kegan Paul would not have paid you had your work not been good enough, so you have nothing to worry about and I look forward to being with you to share the moment. Also, we should arrange a proper celebration at home, friends and family to toast your success."

"How kind of you Ernest, but low key please, maybe just a few friends at dinner?"

"Certainly not," James said with his eyebrows raised to heaven, "whatever next! This calls for major jollifications. You make a list and I'll make one too, we shall send the invitations today."

Florence peered through the square window-panes of the book shop and could see the red covers of *The Pillar House* on a table inside the window. She thought her heart would burst her pulse was racing so fast with excitement. Inside, a warren of green panelled walls were covered with shelves of books on every topic, all in regimented lines. Florence's editor came hurrying over, his footsteps echoing softly on the wooden floor, "Come in, come in Mrs Severne and this must be Mr Severne," he nodded to James and ushered them past the sombre bust of a man James assumed was some long dead author, towards a large, oak desk placed to the side of this first chamber. He bade them take a seat behind the impressive pile of red bound books and he handed Florence the top copy, "How do you like your book?"

"I am thrilled, we agreed it would be in red and I like the black frieze at the top and bottom and I love the gold sword," Florence held the volume in her hand and caressed the words, beaming to see her name in gold lettering.

Looking at James, the editor said, "It will sell at six shillings, the usual price for this type of edition. Advertisements of its publication will be in all the major newspapers and magazines and copies of the book have been sent to them in the hopes of a written review."

Florence opened the cover, "Here Ernest, see the frontispiece. It is perfect, just as I had imagined."

James looked at the picture, a black and white drawing of a common place, substantial, brick house, the portico at the front door supported by two tall Doric pillars. He almost shuddered, the artist had conveyed an air of malevolence with the towering trees surrounding it and a lowering, ominous sky. "Sets the scene alright, you can sense nothing good is going to happen in there, quite eerie."

"I'll keep the other illustrations as a surprise for you when you read it," Florence said gleefully, "this is your copy my dear, the finished article."

Her elation was still evident when the guests arrived at Beauchamp Place that Saturday evening for the celebratory dinner. The guest lists had been reduced at Florence's insistence, she was adamant there was insufficient space in their dining room for more than twelve and that in any case, there was no way the likes of Lady Wilde would ever contemplate dining with them. They had finally agreed. Privately, it suited James not to invite their families and to choose only ten close friends, his finances were not at all healthy, he would have to rely on credit and that, he was finding, was becoming more and more difficult to obtain.

Mrs Cox had initially been overwhelmed at the prospect of preparing the food for the party but Hope's enthusiasm won her over and together, with Mrs Cox reading aloud to the girl, the recipes were chosen from Mrs Beeton's book and then limited on Florence's instructions, to soup, fish, meat and desserts. A girl was engaged for the occasion to help with the serving and James arranged for a 'resting' baritone to act as their butler for the evening and at the end of the night, to transform into a kitchen boy!

Champagne and canapés were served. Florence's bridesmaids, Edith and Alice arrived with their husbands, the five children they now had between them left at home with nannies. Etta was heavily pregnant with her first child and was holding the arm of her new husband as if her life depended on it. James's fellow actor Teddy Loftus had no wife to bring, nor did Charles or Martin who found much in common to discuss. Sylvia, vivacious, with her glamorous looks and imminent adventure to Japan charmed and entertained.

They moved through to the dining room, now decorated to Florence's taste with muted salmon pink walls and Pompeiian red curtains at the windows, where the table looked glorious thanks to the linens and china which had come to Florence on her mother's death. The centre piece was a stunning French majolica bowl in shades of red and brown, holding two dozen deep pink roses. This was placed on a bevelled, oval mirror, the reflections adding to the abundance. There was more silver cutlery than Hope, who had helped to lay the places, had ever seen, and gold rimmed plates, tiny silver salt cellars and fine, crystal goblets and glasses. The buffet to the side held two tall vases of green foliage, decanters, cake stands and dishes of berries. Everything was ready for the feast.

Dinner was a triumph! Clear mock turtle soup followed by roast turbot with horseradish sauce and tiny smelts. There was a gasp of pleasure as the saddle of mutton, aromatic with thyme and rosemary was brought in, and finally, when it seemed impossible to eat more, the guests tucked in heartily to a curaçao soufflé and a marbled jelly. The wines, brought from James's stock at Jubb & Larkin flowed and when coffee was served, before the ladies withdrew for the men to smoke their cigars and drown in vintage port, James stood, and the guests became silent.

"Thank you all for coming here this evening to celebrate my wife's superb achievement. Her first novel, the first of many I suspect," he smiled down at her, "published by a major house and now on sale. This considerable feat is the result of her hard work, dedication and remarkable talent and I am very proud to be her husband." He smiled at her again, then continued, "Join me please in raising your glasses in a toast to her success, may *The Pillar House* be read the length and breadth of the country and achieve literary acclaim." He reached down and picked up his goblet of wine, raising it high he pronounced, "To Florence and *The Pillar House*."

CHAPTER 17

1889
During a bout of mental illness Vincent van Gogh infamously cuts off the lower part of his own left ear, taking it to a brothel, and is removed to the local hospital in Arles

J ames pushed his shoulder against the door of The Albion and backed in slowly, shaking the September rain from his hat and banging the drops off the skirt of his coat. He was soaked. He felt the steam rise from the wet fabric as the warmth of the room reached him, he took off his gloves and pushed his hair back from his face, peering round the bar looking for Charles. It was early, a deliberate move on his part, he wanted to talk privately before the acting fraternity turned up, before, he thought, they might even have woken up, actors preferring late nights to mornings. He spotted the policeman in the corner, sitting by the roaring fire.

"Charles, I can't thank you enough for coming this early," they shook hands, "and in this filthy weather too." He shucked off his coat, hung it on a convenient nearby hook and sat at the little table, opposite his friend. He looked up and caught the barman's eye, "A jug of ale here please," looking at Charles, "unless you'd prefer port?"

"Not for me Ernest, I'm on duty later on and," he hesitated a moment, "isn't it a bit early for you? Wouldn't it be better to drink coffee?"

"No, I need a drink. I've got serious matters to discuss with you and the beer will make me think clearer."

His friend raised his eyebrows but thought better of saying the words on the tip of his tongue. They had not met up for some weeks, Charles had been preoccupied with work, undergoing interviews and training to join London's specialist criminal investigation department and he was shocked at James's appearance. His friend did not look well, his eyes, already deep set, had a haggard look, the sockets unnaturally dark and there was not a hint of the usual smile on his tired face. He looked old, worn down, and Charles said, "Serious matters? That sounds ominous."

"Ominous and tragic," James replied, "I have come to the painful conclusion that I cannot make a living in the theatre. I'm almost stony-broke Charles, my capital's all but gone and I'm reduced to living on the rent from Warwick Street and my wife's earnings. It's enough to crucify a man. Florence doesn't say anything much about it, but I see how she looks at me. With pity. It wasn't supposed to be like this, I'm nearly twenty-six, I should be able to support her."

He called for a whisky chaser, "Thank goodness we don't have a child," and he said, unguardedly, "just as well Florence dealt with that, left to me we'd probably have had a brood by now and I can't even support a wife."

"Do you have a plan for what you will do? Have

you thought over my idea of investigating? As I said before, you can use your acting talents and you've always liked dressing up in disguise."

"I'm serious Charles, I had such hopes of being a successful actor, I've lived and breathed the stage all my life. It's a bitter pill to swallow, I can just hear my family saying, 'I told you so, I told you to get a regular job.' Thomas will be insufferable, he already blames me for losing the family business." He downed his whisky in one and continued, "I have been thinking about your suggestion, in fact I've thought about nothing else these past weeks. I've had plenty of time," he added sourly, "that's why I wanted to talk to you today, I need to come along with you to court as you suggested, get a better idea of what's involved."

Before that could happen, Florence accompanied James to Powick. George Wodehouse had died of meningitis. Six days of high fever and unrelenting seizures which, James had to concede, was an end he would not have wished on anyone, not even his step-father. Jane, now widowed twice in her life, dealt with the situation in a matter of fact way and then turned her attention to her youngest son's future. The relief she had felt on hearing the news that her worrisome boy was to give up the stage and start his own business was short lived, but she put aside all misgivings of the nature of his intended enterprise and offered him a small advance on his future expectations from her estate. His elder brother Thomas arranged all her financial matters and it was made quite clear to James that the money he was to receive once probate was granted, was entirely against his advice. The disapproval he felt for his wastrel younger brother was almost tangible on the papers he produced for signature.

On the third Sunday of January '89, James and Florence, bundled up in their winter coats and hats, walked home from church in the weak sunshine, their feet making a satisfying, gentle, crunch on the still thick, frost covered path.

"Charles will be here any minute," James clapped his hands together, willing the blood to return to his icy fingers and cast an envious glance at Florence's hands warmly ensconced in both gloves and a beaver fur muff, "you can join us if you like," he said, "I want to bring him up to date with my plans."

They were in the morning room at Beauchamp Place when Hope showed the visitor in. Charles was a big man, taller than James and stout with it, he had dark hair parted in the middle and oiled back, piercing, honest brown eyes and, a relatively new addition, a neatly trimmed, downturned moustache. He was wearing an obviously new, mid-brown worsted suit but he could not disguise his bobby on the beat, large feet. His presence was in danger of filling the room.

"Charles, how lovely to see you," Florence greeted him first, "we hope you don't mind being in here, it's small but far cosier than the drawing room on such a cold day. Ernest rather grandly calls it the morning room, but I often think of it as the snug!"

"Come in Charles, take a seat, it's good of you to come over on your day off," James indicated for him to take the deep green, velvet covered armchair by the fireside, "will you stay for luncheon? I've told Florence that congratulations are in order!"

"Yes, *Detective* Constable, that is marvellous news," Florence beamed at him, "no more uniform for you?"

"No, and no more standing for hours at the hackney stand outside the Marylebone Gardens! I shall be at Scotland Yard and there should be less night duty I'm pleased to say. Most of my time used to be spent out at night when the burglars choose to go burgling and the arsonists come out. The pity of being over at Whitehall though is that I'll not be able to pop into The Albion so often - unless I can combine it with making enquiries," he laughed. "it is going to be very different, but I am looking forward to it. I start tomorrow and I've got a decent boss and my training these past weeks has been pretty comprehensive, so I'm feeling confident."

"I can picture you now, you'll have exchanged your truncheon and whistle for a grubby trench coat!" James laughed, "Not forgetting, you'll be puffing away on a pipe."

"Now that you are in this new career it's time you found yourself a wife," Florence said boldly, "one that will feed you properly, keep you away from the pie stalls every day!"

Charles looked wistful, "There's not many women want to take on a policeman," he admitted, "and now I'll probably be working even more hours, I've a feeling I'll never be off duty. There is a young lady though," he said mysteriously, "Ernest has met her, I'm hopeful it may come to something. Won't say any more about it, just that she's in the theatre, not an actress mind, she helps with the costumes, and you will be the first to know if we start walking out together."

Florence was a little surprised, she thought Charles had been very taken with Sylvia and a seamstress was most definitely a rather different sort, but she had to admit, a rather better bet for him! Sylvia had left England at the end of the previous September and Florence missed her dreadfully. She had received a letter a month later from the Oriental Hotel in Tokyo with a beautifully written description of the ocean voyage and her friend's first impressions of the coast of Japan but she was now eagerly awaiting more news, wondering if Sylvia had left the capital and started on her adventure to the north. She considered for a moment whether she should give Charles this latest news. She chose not to.

Once they were seated at the dining table James directed his attention to reason he'd asked Charles over, "I need to pick your brains again on my new career. Since October I've been in funds, not enough to clear my debts, but enough to set up as an investigator. I've done a huge amount of research and can't see any more stumbling blocks. I could be ready to set up next month."

"Did your trips to the courts help make up your mind? Listening in and hearing what the investigators actually do?" Charles watched as James turned his nose up.

"Not really," he said, "I'm grateful to you of course for your help but I want to set my sights a bit higher than petty crime and character assessments for common thieves. Whilst I am establishing the business and getting my name known, I think there is better money to be made in the civil sector. Divorce. It's expensive so only the well-off can afford it and as you know, since they introduced the Matrimonial Causes Act, every case requires proof of the wife's infidelity. Dates, times, places and of course the other man's identity."

"Yes, of course," answered Florence, a slightly bitter edge to her voice, "the other man! Women cannot divorce a husband for *his* adultery, the law endorses all our indoctrination. It is just 'the way of men', it is only 'natural' for them to take a mistress or two, a man's marriage vows it seems, do not count, only the wife's promises."

James jerked his head to look at Florence with a surprised stare, but she quickly smiled at him and shook her head imperceptibly, "Of course," she added, "there will be plenty of wives for whom that arrangement suits, but for those it doesn't, they have to prove there has been cruelty too, and how do you prove mental cruelty?"

Charles felt uncomfortable, he had witnessed the look between them, but Florence quickly changed the subject.

She said gaily, "So, my dear Ernest, tell us how far you are with your plans."

James relaxed, "I have chosen my name. I cannot be Ernest Severne, he was the actor and I don't think I want to revert to James. No, I thought of the name Justin Chevassat. He is a character in a detective novel I read. How do you think that sounds?"

"I like it. Justin, that's excellent, conjures up the idea of just, upright, righteous even, and Chevassat is good too, makes me think of chivalry," enthused Charles, "all good attributes for an investigator."

"What do you think Florence, would that name instill confidence in you? As a woman of words," James asked.

"Yes, my love, I agree, Justin is absolutely right, but I think Chevassat is a little difficult, too many syllables for our English tongues? People might stumble trying to say it. It is subjective of course," she added, "but could you shorten it? Cheval maybe?"

"I don't think so," James said roaring with laughter, "that's 'horse' in French. A righteous horse is not quite the message I wished to convey."

"And there's a cheval mirror too," Florence giggled, "so no, not Cheval."

"What about Chevasse," Charles asked, "still sounds suitably chivalrous and it certainly sounds exotic. The two roll off the tongue nicely together."

"Justin Chevasse," James tried it out, "Justin Chevasse, Private Investigator. Yes, yes, that has the perfect ring to it."

By the time they had finished dessert he had described the premises in York Buildings he was looking at, explained his intention of advertising regularly in the classified sections of all the major London papers and mentioned his possible programme of personal introductions.

"You know Charles that Potty Sinclair introduced me to his Lodge? Royal Somerset House. My initiation is this week and I shall be meeting with as many new people as possible, making sure I don't insinuate that *they* need my services of course," he roared with laughter again, "but should they hear of a friend who might! Justin Chevasse, I think that name will stand out from the crowd," he savoured it again, he could not stop grinning, "Justin Chevasse."

Charles thought he had not seen or heard James so happy and enthusiastic for a long time, "I hoped I was not being premature for your venture," he picked up a brown paper packet which he'd placed under his chair when they took their seats, "and it seems not, you have everything well in hand. I have brought you a good luck gift. It should be entertaining and, hopefully, informative too."

He handed James a set of *Memoirs of Vidoqc*, "These are the English translations, I guessed your French may not be up to the originals," he joked and looked at Florence, "Vidoqc is regarded as the first ever private investigator."

"Thank you, my friend," James said warmly, "I'm sure I shall learn a lot from these autobiographies. Vidoqc had a very colourful life before turning from convict to crime solver, and," he added mischievously, "in any case, they will go towards filling my empty book-shelves!"

Lunch over, Florence looked out of the window, "The sun has gone, I rather wish I had not arranged to go out this afternoon," she crossed her arms and rubbed them, "just looking outside has made me shiver, but Miss Pollen," she looked at James and chuckled, "you remember her Ernest? She is very eager to accompany me visiting what she insists on calling, 'the fallen women', and now that Sylvia is gone, I find it hard to dissuade her."

"What is on your agenda today? Sunday?"

"Illness takes no notice of the day of the week I'm afraid Charles, we are to visit a very sick girl who was showing signs of wanting to give up the life before she got ill. The doctors say she has contracted a disease from one of her customers, so we must speak with her whilst her resolve to escape is still there."

"There is a lot of fear on the streets," Charles said guardedly, "since the Whitechapel murders started, I hope you will not be going in that direction?'

"No, quite the opposite thankfully, and afterwards," she told James, "I thought we would take a cab to Lewknor Lane and I will introduce Miss Pollen to Lottie, show her a success story at first hand so that that she will be able to encourage others more believably."

"Well the more women you can get off the streets, the safer they'll be. You do good work Florence."

Smiling at Charles's compliment she said her goodbyes and left the men to carry on putting the world to rights over their coffee and cigars.

CHAPTER 18

1889

The Eiffel Tower is inaugurated in Paris. At 300 m, its height exceeds the previous tallest structure in the world by 130 m. Contemporary critics regard it as aesthetically displeasing.

He pushed open the doors of 13A York Buildings, walked across the tiled lobby and climbed the stone stairs, glanced out of the semi-circular headed window on the first landing and carried on up to the second floor. Taking the keyring from his coat pocket, he examined each key until his fingers grasped the solid brass one that would open the lock of the door on his left. He stopped and took time to look at the door. The bottom third was of mahogany with a single panel and above that a large, frosted glass pane, a Greek fret etched around the edge, an inner etched frame with ornamental corners and above the centre, a design of elaborate swirls and curls and below, the identical design inverted. In the centre itself, in bold, gold script was:

JUSTIN CHEVASSE
Private Investigator

He could not hide his pleasure and with a huge grin on his face, unlocked the door, strode across the room and opened the polished wooden shutters. Light flooded in through the window and he turned, pulled back the deep-buttoned, leather, revolving chair and sat behind his desk, surveying the room. The walls were panelled with dark wood to chair rail height and above that, were covered in a Sienna brown, flock wallpaper. To his right was a large, plain, oak fireplace. James approved of the simple design, no unnecessary ornate, organic decoration. The iron grate was laid ready to light with kindling and coal as it was January and, James thought, the room was unlikely to get the sun and would need a fire most of the year. In the chimney recess to the right, were floor to ceiling bookshelves, largely empty but the fourth shelf down held a full set of brown, leather bound books, their subject matter immaterial and chosen only for their aesthetic value. On the mantlepiece sat a brass, reeded column, oil lamp and an old-fashioned ink pot with a quill pen rising from it. Above hung a large, framed portrait of the Queen, marginally discoloured, it had been left by the previous tenants and in the absence of a replacement print, James was loathe to remove it.

The fireplace was guarded by a black, iron fender and an old, black coal scuttle was positioned to its left, on the wall above which, was a fine William Burch mahogany drop dial clock brought from Beauchamp Place where it was not required. In the corner of the room, to the side of the door, stood a pile of dark, cardboard storage boxes topped, incongruously, by a pink, floral, hat box. On the left-hand wall was an old oak chest of drawers and next to that, an equally shabby table and rickety wooden chair. In front of his desk were two, straight backed, visitor chairs, the red leather worn and shabby, but again a useful legacy from the outgoing solicitors.

James looked down. Whilst at his mother's house, Jane had insisted that he take, from Powick, his father's old desk. The history of it made James more than happy to accept. Made of a beautiful mahogany, the top was inlaid with burnished leather, the rich burgundy colour now faded to a light brown. It had been a gift to his great, great uncle James, the founder of Severns, from his mistress Livy Martin a wealthy mercer. It had then been used by John, James's grandfather, before being handed down to his own father James Barratt. For some sentimental reason, Jane had removed it from Nottingham to Powick on his death.

In pride of place was a silver pen tray with dual ink wells on which lay a solid silver pen with beautifully engraved scrolling, a present from Florence, and several pencils. There was a silver letter opener, a wooden rocking ink blotter, wooden stamps and ink pad, a large leather-bound notebook, two board covered notebooks with patterned covers, an accounting daybook- no need as yet for a ledger, and another plain, brass oil lamp. He took from a small wooden box one of his trade cards and read.

'Justin Chevasse. Specialist and Expert in Confidential Investigation for the Aristocracy. Dispatch, secrecy, reliability and absolute integrity. 13A York Buildings, Adelphi, W.C.'

Here he was, day one! It had taken a lot of research and preparation, but this was his own office, his own business, and through a solicitor friend who had become a Free Mason on the very same day as himself, he had his very first potential client coming to see him here later that morning.

He had been quite nervous, he told Lottie that evening when he'd called into the coffee house before going home for a late supper with his wife.

"Oooh, tell me all about 'im," she said wrapping her pale blue, lace trimmed robe round her naked body and tying the ribbon, "what was he like? 'Nother glass of wine whilst we talk, have you got time?"

"Yes, to the wine, but I haven't got long, I promised Florence I'd be back in time to tell her all about today too," he pulled himself up, plumped the pillows behind his head, and leant back. Taking the glass, he began, "He's German, a Baron. I can't tell you his name," then looking worried he said, "oh, God, I shouldn't have even told you that should I. Forget what I said. It's a man, that's all, and he has become suspicious of his wife with ... no, I can't tell you that either. Let's just leave it that he's a man who wants me to follow his wife. He thinks she's having an affair with a friend of his."

"It sounds ever so exciting. Will you be able to follow her in disguise? Who will you be? Will you wear a false moustache, or a wig? You could dress in a shabby coat and hold a walking stick, walk doubled over like an old tramp?" Lottie was laughing so much James joined in, "I don't think I'll have to dress up at the beginning, but I might have to if she sees me, because then she'd know me another time."

"If she clocks such a good-looking man following her, she might get the wrong idea, I'd watch your step Mr Chevasse! She'll be after *you* too!"

His potential indiscretion with Lottie was a

salutary lesson and when he told Florence later that night, he made no mention of his client's nationality or social status. He was determined to be professional and that meant secrecy was paramount.

James learnt a lot from this first case. The first day, he had stood on the pavement diagonally opposite the lady's house, from eleven in the morning until five in the afternoon. He stood in the cold, his nose turning blue and his feet becoming lumps of ice. The strap holding his monocular made his neck ache and he had waited, waited in vain for her to come out or for the suspected lover to call. He had stamped his feet, strolled up and down, endlessly fingered the little note-pad and pencil in his pocket, and finally giving up, had gone to the public house at the end of the road to warm himself, have a pint of ale and a steak pie to eat.

   The second day, not long after he had taken up his position, a servant came out of the house and hailed a hackney cab. The lady hurried down the path, climbed into the carriage and was whisked away. Whilst she was absent, James made sure he knew exactly where the nearest cab stand was! The third day he had a lucky break, the weather was fine and his sub-ject, as he thought of her, decided to walk from her house. He followed, maybe fifty, sixty, yards behind, ready to crouch and attend to a problem with his shoe should she stop and turn round to look, but she didn't and he tracked her to a house about half a mile away, where, with a quick look up and down the road, she ran up the steps, pulled the bell rope and almost immedi-ately slipped inside. It was not the address the Baron had given him of the suspected lover. There being noth-ing for James to see from the road, he made his way to the Post Office and looking through the Directory found the name of the occupant of the dwelling. It was an elderly widow. Day four, nothing.

The following day was Saturday and James was feeling fed up and bored, he was also feeling very conspicuous. He had been loitering on this road for a week and it was quite likely that he himself was looking suspicious. He just beginning to wonder if he should change tactics and move areas to watch the other party, when a hackney carriage with a gentleman inside, drew up and stopped outside. A servant came out, went to the cab and spoke to the occupant. James had to make a split-second decision. He ran away from the house, rushed around the corner to the hackney stand, hired the first one and, feeling very pleased with himself, instructed the driver to 'follow that cab'! Peering as hard as he could, he thought he could detect two passengers in front of him and became more and more convinced of that as they led him to Waterloo Station. Staying at a discrete distance, he paid off his driver and followed his subjects, both of whom were carrying carpet bags, into the station. He stood close enough, his collar turned up and his hat pulled low, to overhear their destination and then he, in turn, bought a return ticket to Guildford.

Sitting in the next-door compartment, he took the time to consider his own predicament. It was four o'clock on a Saturday afternoon in March, he was on his way to a provincial Surrey town where, he thought it did not take a detective to work out, the couple he was investigating intended to stay the night, and he had neither bag nor overnight equipment with him. There was nothing he could do now, he was, he thought excitedly on the scent and his previous days of uncomfortable boredom were paying off. Alighting at Guildford, he again hired a cab and this time tracked them to the Hut Hotel at Wisley, a village some eight miles north of the town. Waiting what he hoped was a sufficient lapse of time, he went into the foyer just as the couple moved to the stairs together. James booked his single room, bluffed about his lack of luggage, words to the effect that he had been separated from his bag at the station and he was hopeful it would arrive some-time later that evening, and retired to his room to fill in the details of his afternoon in impeccably neat handwriting, in his note book.

The rest was easy. He sat at dinner watching the lovers at their table towards the back of the restaurant and when they left, so did he. He was able to give his report in court some weeks later and swear that they had stayed at the hotel until the Monday, occupying the same room as man and wife.

The two most important lessons James learnt from this case was that he needed to have an overnight bag, packed and close to hand at all times when on surveillance, and more importantly, to move as quickly as possible away from the tedium of having to gather evidence for petty divorces himself. What he wanted, what he was intent on having, was an international, aristocratic clientele with interesting, thought provoking problems for him to solve.

A real bonus was that he gained a faithful companion from this first case. The Baron, when settling James's fee, half admitted to a temporary shortage of funds and being, it transpired, well respected in the world of dogs, offered him a beautiful, sable and white,

Collie puppy in part payment. He could, the Baron assured him, command towards a thousand pounds, he had a perfect pedigree, but this mattered little to James, he took one look at the bundle of fur and fell in love. From that moment on, Montague was rarely away from his side.

The reality of the early days in the business was quite different from his future ideal. The inquiry work did not come flooding in as he thought it might and James still found himself with plenty of free time. He rarely painted, his easel and paints gathering dust in the attic after the flurry of enthusiasm when he and Florence had returned from their holiday in France. He accepted that his art was unlikely to be a commercial success and he was now, when not dining with contacts, or researching a client, or teaching himself poker and baccarat should they be necessary in the course of his investigations, concentrating on writing. He had managed to get several reviews he'd written into the *Music Hall and Theatre Review* magazine. That the performances he had written about were in his opinion, third class, did not have him turning up over eagerly to the music halls or theatres and nor did the remuneration swell his bank balance. What it did do, was ensure he kept up his friendships with the acting crowd who frequented The Albion, and his visits there, when he closed up his office, were frequent.

"Are you writing a regular column in that rag now?" Potty enquired rather loftily, "pity you can't write for a proper paper."

"Beggars can't be choosers Potty, and at least I am in print," James had joined Sinclair and his followers on a sultry, late summer evening, Monty sitting obediently at his feet as usual, "I don't have a regular column as such, but most of what you read on the 'Babbles' pages is mine. Did you see my review of the variety at the Alhambra last week? The report was a good deal better than the show!"

Laughing, the group made way for three girls who'd just arrived, "Come in my dears," Potty gushed, "always room for the young and beautiful at my table - and beautiful, not so young, men," he added with a smirk and show of his hand to James. "Have you met the earnest Mr Severne, lately of the theatre and now, when not investigating the nocturnal antics of the adulterous, writes reviews for a terrible publication."

James was introduced. It was not unusual for him to meet aspiring actresses, but one of these caught his attention more than most. She was ravishing. Her black hair, with waves that reached almost to her shoulders, shone with blue lights and she had piercing sapphire blue eyes set in a delicate pale face and a laugh that made him tingle. He dragged his eyes away from her, he felt sure she was no more than sixteen and feeling every one of his own twenty-eight years, he thought it wise to keep his mind on conversation with Teddy and Frank. By the time he had visited Lottie later that evening and arrived home, inebriated, as was becoming the norm these days, all thoughts of the dazzling Miss Emily Drake had disappeared. He had far weightier matters on his mind.

James's had a bankruptcy hearing scheduled for the first week of October. It had been a fruitless struggle over the past four years since his disaster with *The Oath*, trying to pay off his creditors and at the same time provide a home for himself and his wife. The constant worry over money had been weighing down on his shoulders for months and now he had finally given in. Charles had been a constant support to him but even he had eventually agreed, "Enough is enough Ernest, get it over and done with and you can get on with your new life. You're trading as Justin Chevasse, you're not a company, being bankrupt won't hurt you there and you'll be able to give the business your undivided attention."

Over that year and a half, Justin Chevasse had managed to secure contracts to act for a handful more gentlemen who wished to divest themselves of their wives. Cases where he had been obliged to lurk in the shadows watching the comings and goings of the wayward women and provide the prurient details to their husbands. In one case he was certain the evidence he was to gather was contrived. A middle aged man, the co-respondent, looked completely uncomfortable in his role and, when the couple were viewed on a bed together through the most conveniently, open curtained, ground floor bedroom of a seedy house in Shoreditch, James saw that the poor chap had neither taken off his coat nor lifted one of his feet from the floor. James made no judgements, who was he to prevent what was presumably the wishes of both parties, the dissolution of an unhappy alliance.

These engagements had brought in welcome fees, but it was not enough and even with additional payments earned by taking on some background work for the police ascertaining suspect's characters, together with his writing, his finances remained in a perpetual, hapless state.

CHAPTER 19

1892
The Conservative and Liberal Unionist coalition government loses its majority in the House of Commons, leading to Prime Minister Lord Salisbury's resignation. William Gladstone, Liberal, takes over with Irish Nationalist Party support.

Not unsurprisingly, Florence having her second book published at the end of 1891 did nothing to lessen James's feeling of inadequacy in his own life. In the cold light of day, he knew that what he felt was plain and simple jealousy. An ugly, unwarranted and unwanted, emotion. One his wife did not, and had never, deserved, but on the nights he returned to Beauchamp Place and to his dressing room to sleep alone, he could not rein in his feelings and he smouldered with irrational resentment. When Uneven Ground was launched and he saw copies in the window of Hatchards, he thought it was more than he could bear. As he had convinced himself when younger, that he could not be successful in the theatre whilst he lived in the country, now he convinced himself that it was his marriage that was denying him his own success. The constant, overwhelming feeling that he should provide financially when he was unable to do so, and saw his wife's growing success. He began to believe that he had been tricked into marriage and the pressure was making it impossible for him to flourish and like many negative, self-destructive reactions, it was becoming a self-fulfilling prophecy.

Whilst James spent more and more evenings at The Albion where he could continue to act the part of the charming, congenial fellow, always popular and entertaining and sleeping more and more nights at Lottie's from where he would rise in the morning with a dry mouth and throbbing head to go directly to his office, Florence retreated to her own desk, directing her energies into her writing and charity work. The hurt she felt by James's behaviour was eased a little when Sylvia was home from her long expedition to Japan and the two friends spent many hours together, Sylvia's new, smaller home overlooking Hyde Park becoming Florence's sanctuary. Her friend becoming her confidante and saviour.

By the beginning of the following year, strengthened by Sylvia's support and encouragement, Florence had made her decision. She missed the laughter and merry companionship she had enjoyed with James when they were first married but at the same time, she was realistic, she knew those times would not return and that the advantages of their marriage alliance, no longer applied. She was still very fond of her husband and had thought long and hard. She was a self-sufficient woman, but even so, it had not been an easy resolution to make.

On one dark, dreary night in February they were sitting in silence together in front of the fire in the drawing room, James's legs stretched out in front of him, a whisky in his hand, morose and unsuspecting. Then, as it had been Florence who had persuaded him of the mutual benefits to be gained from their marriage some seven years before, so it was Florence who extolled to James, the virtues of their separation.

She made no demands on him, she asked for no support, she even apologised for not being in a sufficiently buoyant position to help him financially herself. She was, she told him, going to live in Bayswater with Sylvia who would be travelling again soon and had kindly offered her the property whilst she was away. Florence would not however, acquiesce to James's rather timid request that she might like a divorce. She had not, she reminded him firmly, ever had or made the slightest improper thought, word or deed during their marriage. She had never put a foot wrong and had only ever supported him. She was sorry, but she would not have her reputation tarnished, and her future damaged, by fabricating her own moral demise. He was her husband, it was through no fault of hers that the marriage had broken down and she was sure he would agree, on reflection, that it was unkind of him to ask her to do so.

She had brought him to tears with her final words, "Stop and take time to be yourself Ernest, the self I knew when we first met. When you are yourself you have a great generosity of spirit and a depth of kindness unknown to most. I am truly sad for the part I have played in your unhappiness and I hope with all my heart that by leaving I shall be helping you to achieve your own goals in life."

He had met with Charles the very next day and this

time, Charles judged that the time was right for some plain talking to his friend. They were sitting in James's office, late that morning in February.

"Florence is being more than reasonable," he had said, "more so than you deserve in my view. Ernest, you have behaved atrociously towards her at times, your manner unbecoming of a gentleman. None of your perceived problems are your wife's fault." James had such a look of stunned surprise on his face that exasperated, Charles went on, "For goodness sake, grow up, stop behaving like a spoilt child who cannot have everything his own way." He saw in his mind's eye how James must have appeared all these years to his estranged family, petulant, thinking only of himself. Charles could understand how his mother would have made allowances, feeling guilty that he had lost his father when so young she had let him hold her to ransom. She saw in his behaviour, the sad, frightened little seven-year old, running away from the truth, wanting to blame someone, anyone close to him, for his own flaws. "You have relied too much on your ability to charm everyone Ernest, your innate seductive nature. But it's time to face up to your shortcomings. Yes, you wanted to be a good actor and I know you tried hard, but that was not to be. Now you can put things right. You need to make a success of your business so stop wasting time on theatrical matters, buckle down, put in the effort required and go out of your way to find new inquiry clients. It is up to you, no-one else."

He looked up at James who was rubbing his face in his hands, Charles could see traces of tears wiped from his eyes, "Florence is a good woman and just now, even though you are my friend, I'm not sure you ever deserved her. Turn your life around, make her proud of you. Better still, make yourself proud of you."

It was with a feeling of relief for James, as well as regret, that events moved forward from that night, exactly as Florence had determined. By the end of March, he had settled the lease on Beauchamp Place and rented a basement flat in a house in Milner Street, Chelsea. Charles's words had been difficult to hear, but he had now taken them to heart and began dedicating his time productively to Justin Chevasse, unhampered, as if a large load had lifted from his shoulders. Then it happened very quickly that the separation from his wife was not to be the only major change in his life. He had gone to see Lottie a few days after his conversation with Florence and was rocked back on his heels by her news.

"He's been calling in early evening for the best part of a year now," she told him, "It's not so busy then and we've taken to talking, he's a clerk over at Simpsons and now he's asked me if I would care to be his girl. So, you see, I can't go on with our arrangement Ernest, it wouldn't be right, would it?"

"That's good news Lottie," James said, his disappointment injecting a degree of insincerity in his words, "but, well, does he know about your life before?"

"Yes, I told Raymond, that's his name, everything. He didn't seem to mind, he said he admired me for making some 'at of myself with such a bad start in life. Fancy that, someone saying they admired me. He's really easy to talk to, not like you of course, he's not clever and funny," and she gave James a coquettish grin, "and he certainly ain't handsome and sexy like you. But he's nice. Nice and steady and he'll be kind and he wants to marry me."

"Does he know about me?" James wondered out loud.

"I told him I have a gentleman, just the one, who's helped me keep the shop when times have been hard, and who reads the papers for me," she giggled, "but I"ve not told him no names. He don't know it's you, but I want to do this right. I don't want to lose this chance, he even said what did I think about having kids. Me, Lottie, a mother! I like the sound of it, I never thought I'd have that sort of life. Mind you, I'm going to keep on with the shop, I've got ideas for it, thinking about Frenchifying it and calling it Lottie's Café!"

"Well Lottie, I can't pretend I'll not miss you but I'm happy for you. You know, I admire you too, I admire you very much, you deserve to take happiness when it comes along."

It may have been pure coincidence, but James put it down to his new found freedom that within the month, a well-heeled hotel owner from Jersey engaged him to watch his wife. It was to be his most lucrative case to date.

It necessitated him going to the Channel Islands and he decided it was a good moment to bring forward his intention to employ an assistant. Someone to man the office in his absence, to fetch and carry, learn how to manage James's paperwork and, eventually, be trained to carry out the mundane, simple surveillance tasks, releasing James for the bigger and better things he hoped were around the corner.

His old school friend, Martin Richards, was now a senior solicitor and married with, what seemed, a handful of children. James did not see him as often as he would like but tried to catch up now and then over a lunchtime pie and pint of ale. They had spent an hour together only a few days before, so Martin had been curious when he received a note asking to meet again so soon.

James got straight to the point, "Last time we met, you were telling me about a young clerk that you couldn't help with a position at your firm, but who you thought really had something about him. Something special. You'd told him you would keep your ears to the ground. Well do you think he'd like to work for me, as my assistant, it's not that much different from being a clerk and in time, a damn sight more exciting!"

"I couldn't possibly say but I have his address. It may be that he is fixed up already. Like I said, he's very bright. Very personable, but no money and a bit of an unfortunate family background. I'll let him tell you about that though if it comes to anything." Martin took out a small notebook from his pocket, wrote on a page which he then tore out and handed to James, "See if he's here."

James was in a hurry and took a cab rather than the omnibus, and within the hour, knocked on the door of a shabby house in Clerkenwell where he met fifteen year old Mr Peregrine Danvers. He had been somewhat amazed at the sight of a smartly groomed, moderately well-dressed young man who answered the call from the grubby urchin who had opened the door to him. Peregrine had run down the stairs quickly from his attic rooms, taken one look at his visitor and suggested they walk along the street to a coffee shop. He said, "It's not much to look at, but the coffee won't poison us!"

Perry, as he was known, struck an immediate

chord with James. Not quite an orphan, his mother was long dead and his father, who had at one time been employed by the Sun Loan & Deposit company, was currently passing a few months at Her Majesty's pleasure in Newgate Prison, convicted of uttering a forged promissory note. The details were appearing rather involved and James stopped Perry in his tracks, "So you are on your own? Your father will be ruined with no chance of further employment. Tell me, what is your opinion of him?"

"I truly believe he was persuaded by his superiors as he has only a little education and his main fault lies in being gullible. I will not excuse him though. He broke the law and deserves his punishment. The pity of it is that I had just taken up my position in the same company as a junior clerk and very fortunate I was too the city is awash with ever hopefuls even though we earn a pittance. Anyway, they sacked me there and then, guilty by association I suppose. I did not, I assure you, have any idea of what was going on and as you will have noticed in my narrative, even now I do not quite understand it all either." He risked a low laugh, "I want only to work and try to restore my reputation. I am living on next to nothing at present and by this time next week, it will be completely nothing. Mr Richards said no reputable firm would take me on, sins of the father he said."

It made James smile, he could detect what Martin had seen in the young lad, "It seems I am not classed as reputable then? I think we will get along together very well."

CHAPTER 20

1893
The Independent Labour Party has its first meeting,
in Bradford under Chairman Keir Hardie
Elementary Education (School Attendance) Act
leads to raising of school leaving age in England
and Wales to eleven years

J ames left for Jersey the second week of May. Travelling from Paddington to Weymouth and then on the steam packet, Ibex, to St Helier. He arrived to warm blue skies and made his way to the Pomme d'Or Hotel from where he would organise his vigilance. The Hotel was very fine indeed, Justin Chevasse was aiming at the aristocracy and he was happy to be setting his standards. His first port of call was to be the lobby of the Royal Yacht Club Hotel where his client, Mr Parkinson the owner, would be sure to parade his wife for James's recognition.

He had foregone sideburns long ago and chosen to remain clean shaven during the current fashion for a more hirsute appearance, but today, at Perry's suggestion, he attached with spirit gum, a false, brown, neatly trimmed moustache to his upper lip. It tickled and he wriggled his face and mouth constantly to begin with, but looking in the mirror he agreed, it certainly added a little gravitas, he no longer looked quite such the handsome, *young*, man. Picking up his cane he left his room and strolled along the quiet streets, feeling unusually anonymous in a dark grey suit and bowler hat, only his crimson tie testament to his aversion to complete invisibility. Arriving at the Royal, he went smartly up the steps, nodded to the doorman as if to say, 'of course you know me, I have just returned from a walk', entered the plush, marble lobby and sat on a gold fringed sofa, his back to the wall, with a perfect view of the foyer.

He had to wait only a few minutes and at the agreed time, the cuckold and his wife descended the stairs and walked past. She stood gazing dreamily around whilst her husband spoke with the staff on duty at the reception desk and then the couple left the building. James did not know what he had been expecting, but it wasn't the rather short, plump, motherly woman that he'd just seen. Why he wondered did adultery only produce mental images of tall, sophisticated, glamorous sirens? Next he made his way to Museum Street, where he waited, and waited, outside number twenty-two. He waited two hours before he was able to identify Mr Frank Cabot, the suspected lover.

Over the next two days James quite enjoyed his watching and waiting and this was because he was able to spend the better part of the time on the terrace of the Royal hotel, sipping the odd cognac, smoking his cigars and soaking up the warmth, safe in the knowledge that he would be alerted should his subject be leaving the building. The newspapers he held in front of his face invariably went unread, but provided him with necessary camouflage, the overheard conversations and tidbits of gossip were entertainment enough. On the third day his luck was in, he followed the lady out of the front door, through the gap in the low, stone wall onto the pavement where she turned right, walked past the Elephant & Castle hotel and along the Weighbridge. His luck continued, she met up with Mr Cabot after only a hundred yards and they walked together, stopping to look in the shop windows, talking but not touching.

The details of the liaison carefully noted in his pocketbook, when she was safely back with her husband, James was able to enjoy his evening. The food at the Pomme d'Or was excellent, the wines eminently drinkable and there were a few convivial characters who lingered on in the bar with him until it was time to retire for the night. The next day he pursued the couple as they took a cab and drove out into the countryside. When they stopped along a quiet lane, he instructed his own driver to pull up a decent distance past them and went back along the path by foot to observe his quarry sitting on a blanket, leaning back against an old oak tree in a field to the side of the road. Careful not to be seen, he mentally checked all the details, their appearance, their manner and their physical contact. He worried about remaining there at the field gate and decided to make his way back to his transport and linger in the next gateway until they were ready to leave. This was some half an hour later, and happy that he had noted everything of import, James sat back in his cab. He listened to the singing of the birds, gazed at the blue sky dotted with fluffy clouds above and looked forward to his evening at the hotel. It just remained for him to serve Mrs Parkinson with her citation which he was able to do on his sixth day on the island and he then returned to London, his client completely satisfied with his evidence.

"All very straight forward so far," he told Perry, "and Jersey is a beautiful place. Caught a glimpse of a sandy beach or two. It's not England but not France either, quite unique."

"And full of very rich, hopefully unhappy, husbands!" Perry laughed, "let's hope there are some referrals."

"Next step is to wait for my client to send a telegram to let me know he has told his wife to leave. He's sure she will follow Cabot to London. He'll tell me the date to expect her. The co-respondent," seeing Perry frown, "the co-respondent Perry, come on, tell me, give me the names."

"Oh sorry, Mr Chevasse. I know this, your client will be the plaintiff, the one suing for divorce, his wife is the respondent and the other man is the co-respondent. Meaning they were in it together."

"Right. He's already here in town, he lost his job as a centenier," he didn't wait for Perry to frown, "that's a kind of policeman, and left for England suddenly. Apparently, there was a bit of a fracas between the parties, but I didn't see that. I need to hand Mr. Co-respondent his citation too, so I need to find him."

James had used much of his time over the past months building contacts with as many of the hotel doormen as possible. They were mines of information and inexpensive sources, whereas the managers he approached had an inflated sense of their worth! He also, through an introduction by Lottie to a girl who had come good and was now a chambermaid at a second rate, but central, hotel, managed to encourage a network of maids across the city willing to provide information for cash. This tactic paid off almost immediately as on enquiring at Andersons Hotel in Fleet Street, he found his man. The papers were served to Mr Cabot on the sixth of June and a telegram from Jersey told him Mrs Parkinson would arrive in Paddington, on the Jersey train, on the eighth.

It could not have been easier, this time without the moustache but with a pair of dark, horn rimmed, clear glass spectacles, James was waiting at the station and witnessed the couple meeting. He was able to shadow them to a hotel where a room had been reserved for Mrs Parkinson, masquerading as her sister, and the two of them disappeared to her room together. With their further, frequent, meetings documented, and the information dispatched to Jersey, Justin Chevasse submitted his fee note for the balance owed. The daily retainer, including expenses, which had been paid in advance, having covered only five of his six days.

"The case probably won't come to court for months," he told Perry, "I'll have to give evidence but hopefully there'll not be too big a splash in the newspapers. Hearing divorces in open court means publicity which is bound to bring out prurient curiosity and it's a fine line between my advocating secrecy and the need to get my name mentioned to bring in more business. In the meantime, what's come in from the advertisements, if anything?"

The enquiries for divorce evidence came into the office in a steady trickle, both from the advertisements and word of mouth but mostly from requests from solicitors. Martin, not dealing with matrimonial matters himself, had introduced James to those of his colleagues who did, and they were a welcome source of income. Perry was deployed to carry out much of the mundane surveillance on what James thought of as ordinary cases, and he kept himself free for matters that had a potentially more lucrative outcome. He very much wanted two things, top notch clients and more interesting cases to investigate and this was happening a little too slowly for his impatient nature.

"I have been working out how to operate more along the lines of French espionage Perry, I need a proper network of what we might call, spies. Not just here in England and not just hotel staff either, I need contacts all over the world. I'm looking at America and France first. It really hurt that I had to turn down that Rosenberg divorce, but it was impossible for me to travel to America with all my commitments here. If I'd had a man in New York, they could have done the ground-work for me and I would have kept the contract."

"How're you going to do that then?" Perry looked at his boss with admiration. In his eyes, Justin Chevasse was his hero, "has Sherlock Holmes done it?"

"The difference dear Perry, is that Mr Holmes is very much a fiction and I am dealing in facts. I think the first thing I can do, now that my reputation is becoming better known, is to approach Pinkertons in New York to suggest a reciprocal arrangement with one of their operatives." He looked up at the clock, took out his pocket watch and compared the two, put down the pencil he had been idly nibbling and stood up, "I'm off to Kensington Gardens now. Sorry Monty, not this time, back to your bed." He bent and stroked the dog's head, "I'll not be long, and we'll walk home, how about that?"

Perry leapt up from the chair at his little table in the corner and took the frock coat off the stand, helped James into it, handed him his top hat and cane and stood back, "It's good to see you looking the gentleman again Sir, you're too often in your bowler!"

A friend of Lady Wilde's had engaged him to elicit certain facts of his wife's behaviour with an officer in the Guards and this Saturday morning he had reason to believe they would be strolling together in the Park, rendezvousing at the Round Pond at half past midday. Completely anonymous among the throng of gentlemen, many accompanied by fashionably dressed ladies sheltering from the springtime sun under their pastel parasols, he found his targets. The crowd of promenaders provided excellent cover and he was able to monitor the meeting with ease, even getting close enough to overhear their intimate conversation. When the lovers had gone their separate ways, James decided, the day being so warm, to linger for a while and he sat on a bench overlooking the Long Water. He took out a little pack of notecards from his pocket and began to write down the salient points of the encounter. That finished, he turned his face to the sinking sun and contemplated his life at present and his plans for the future.

CHAPTER 21

1893 - 1894

William Gladstone resigns as British Prime Minister and Archibald Primrose, 5th Earl of Rosebery takes over

H is visits to The Albion had dwindled significantly since his separation from Florence but he did his best to keep in sporadic touch with his acting friends. He would spend the occasional evening enjoying their company, astonished at the youth of the many newcomers before. Charles had to remind him that he had been no older himself when he first came to London some twelve years before. Potty Sinclair had asked for his help not long ago to sort out an unfortunately all too common case when one of his actresses was being coerced to pay a man who threatened to disrupt her performances with loud heckling, cat calls and cause a general disturbance in the theatre. She had paid once, and the man was due to collect again. James had to advise Potty to go to the police, in this instance, he as a private investigator could do nothing, only the threat of prison would work.

Florence had stayed in contact, two letters with all her news to which he had responded at length, his heart faltering just the tiniest bit as he remembered how well they had once understood each other. On a less cerebral level, he missed Lottie and having declined her invitation to fix him up with a highly recommended ex-colleague of hers back in Knightsbridge, he found himself from time to time weakening and having short lived, unsatisfactory flings with ever willing young actresses. He was not proud of his actions but neither was he so repelled by it that he stopped.

Sitting on his bench, lost in thought, smiling to himself at the thought that if girls made such a play for him he must still be regarded as a desirable catch, he became aware of a woman, dressed in a green bloomer suit with voluminous, plaid pantaloons, stopping by his bench. An oversize, cream bow billowed at her neck and a brown, straw boater hat was anchored to her head with a green ribbon tied, in another large bow, under the chin. Dismounting from her bicycle she propped it up, leaning it against the back of the seat, and sat down next to him.

"Mr Chevasse?" She asked, "Well, actually I know it's you, my name is Augusta Bourne and I have a proposition for you!"

"How intriguing, Miss? Mrs? Bourne", James replied, raising his eyebrows and employing his most charming smile.

"The Hon. actually, my father is Gordon Bourne, Lord Moreton, but I'd rather you called me Gussie like my friends do. I've heard quite a bit about you, Sylvia Quinn and I seem to frequent the same soirées when she's in the country, she lives with your wife Florence doesn't she?"

Trying to hide his surprise, James said, "You

have the advantage of me, Miss Bourne, I regret to say I have not heard your name, nor indeed, I might add, that of your father. Perhaps you could enlighten me?"

"Of course, sorry, I always get a bit carried away," she smiled a bit ruefully, "in everything!"

"Perhaps you could start at the beginning and work up to the proposal?"

As she spoke, James studied the woman's face. She was older than him, maybe as much as thirty-five, but the premature steel grey hair scraped back, the severe face with its pointed nose, prominent cheek bones and thin, wide lips, all unsullied by any artifice, might have exaggerated the years. What he found immediately beguiling was her frank brown eyes, obvious enthusiasm and genuine friendliness.

"I'm a private investigator too. Father, much against his wishes, but worn down by Mother and me, set me up with an office in Oxford Street and I'm doing nicely, but, and I hate to admit this, there are times when I need a man on a case and not yet being in a position to employ one, I was rather hoping it could be you."

"Why me? You could have an arrangement with Slaters or Clarkes?"

"That would not be so much fun! Like I said, I've heard about you and anyway, I don't like either of those companies, Father made me approach them in the first place and they had the temerity to turn me down. Not so much because of *me,* more because they had their token woman on the books and wouldn't take on more. Did me favour though, Father coughed up and I'm much happier being Bourne Detectives."

"Whatever possessed you to want to be a detective? Even as a man I have to put up with at best condescension and worse, vilification, of our profession. Ironically, this comes mainly from the snooty members of society who are also my main clientele. Not the done thing to poke around in a gentleman's private life is it, unless of course he asks you to! It must be worse for you?"

"Oh, water off a duck's back, I don't let it bother me. I can't remember a time when I wasn't off sleuthing somewhere, although my brother always said it was more like sneaking. I couldn't bear a secret, if I thought someone in the family was hiding something, I had to uncover it. Got very good at not being found out and I was reading a lot of the adventure stories in *Girls Own*, then I found Conan Doyle and I was determined. You're right though, they think it's fine for women to be employed as security staff in the shops, catching women stuffing bolts of satin under their skirts, but when it comes to private work, it's quite unseemly."

She gave a little shiver. The sun had gone behind the clouds and the evening temperature was dropping. She stood up. "Well, what do you think Mr Chevasse? Could we help each other out?"

"It sounds promising. Perhaps we could go back to my office and draw up a piece of paper? But tell me first, how did you know where to find me this afternoon?"

"Your young man in the office told me you'd be in the Gardens, nice rooms by the way. No, please, I can see by the look on your face that you're going to give him a piece of your mind, but it wasn't his fault. Don't forget, I'm a detective and a jolly good one at that, I'm practised at finding out information, and besides,

I might have frightened him a bit. I can be a little bit scary."

"Yes, I can see that!" James laughed.

They walked back slowly, Gussie pushing her bicycle by her side and she looked for a suitable railing against which to abandon it again. Perry brought tea for them and they sat side by side in the shabby visitor chairs. That Monty immediately made a friend of her was another reason James felt he could trust the woman and besides, he was enjoying her company. The case she had been investigating for some months involved tracing a certain gentleman, who may or may not, she was in no position to confirm or deny, owe another certain gentleman in America, a great deal of money. She had checked the passenger lists and the possible suspect was arriving in England on the SS Marquette the following Tuesday, where, she had reason to believe he would be staying at The Reform Club.

"He could well have altered his appearance so it will be impossible for me to identify him from the ship, but he's a member at the Club and will have to use his real name, there's no way he'll be allowed in otherwise." Her problem was that the doormen of the London Clubs were as tight lipped as clam shells.

"They pride themselves on their utter discretion and I've not been able to make any progress in the past," she sighed, "I even tried a disguise as a plumber once, but they saw through that. Goodness knows what they think will happen to them all if they allow a woman to so much as step into their hallowed halls. Maybe I'm not as good an actor as you?"

James was impressed, "Is there anything you don't know about me? Although I can tell you one thing you've overlooked, I am not a member of the Reform, nor am I likely to become one yet, so I don't see how I can help."

"You'll go along as Pa's guest, he's a member and will be happy to oblige. I'd ask him to do a bit of asking around but that wouldn't work on two counts, one, he'd make a huge fuss about betrayal of trust and two, more importantly, he'd be useless!" They laughed together and she carried on, "Don't get me wrong, the old duffer is a good sort, just not really of this modern world. Will you do it if we can agree a financial arrangement? Don't forget, I can help you when you want someone to infiltrate the ladies' inner sanctums."

They did agree terms and when she left, James settled down and wrote up his report on the mornings work. He also wrote a letter to Pinkertons in New York.

Lord Moreton was almost a caricature of himself so like was he to the illustrations in Punch, but he was also, as Gussie had assured him, good and interesting company for the evening. James had arrived at Pall Mall in top hat and tails at six on the dot. He was expected and taken to meet his host who was ready and waiting for him in the library. Moreton put down the book he was reading, fussed with his waistcoat and stood, "Chevasse I presume?"

At his suggestion they moved to take a low table in the gallery overlooking the grand staircase and the lobby below. James sank into the deep leather chesterfield and accepted the offer to take a glass of Madeira before dinner.

"My family were wine merchants," he said by way of opening the conversation, "three generations, four if you count my great, great, great grandfather. I was supposed to be the next but never wanted it, so it's out of the family now and I'm the black sheep."

"Trade is not to everyone's ilk," Moreton managed to raise just his left eyebrow, "but has a rather better reputation these days than the path you and my daughter have chosen to follow."

James, for once, was lost for words.

"I don't understand Augusta," Moreton went on, "she had every advantage in life but got this notion in her head and well, she's me daughter and her mother and I are very fond of her, so we help where we can. With luck she'll tire of it soon, but she's a bit long in the tooth now to find a husband. I don't know what the world is coming to, working women, riding bicycles in those unbecoming trousers, they'll be getting the vote before we know it. Ah, here we are," he looked up at the waiter, "leave the decanter and we'll let you know when we are ready to dine."

He picked up his glass and raised it silently to James, "Good health. Now tell me what our subterfuge is this evening."

Gussie had calculated the likely time Mr Dennis Roper would arrive in London on the Southampton train. Unable to properly identify him, she was to watch and if moderately confident she had found her quarry, would cycle to Pall Mall, which she reckoned would take her less than fifteen minutes. Barring accidents, she would arrive before him, always supposing her assumptions as to his destination were correct and that it took the customary wait of quite some minutes for him to reach the head of the cab queue, and hand a note to this effect to the concierge for passing to her father. James was to keep a close eye on the entrance looking for a gentleman in travelling clothes and with at least one large portmanteau.

It was going to plan! Such a gentleman had arrived, the formalities had been dealt with and the new arrival followed the porter away towards the bedrooms. James slipped quickly down the stairs and up to the reception desk. Putting on an air of breathlessness he panted, "Confound it, I'm just too late," looking anxiously at the young man behind the desk he said, "I was sitting up in the gallery and couldn't believe my eyes, that was George Rutherford just checked in wasn't it. I thought he was still in America, haven't seen him in five years. I'm married to his sister," he put on a slightly vacant look, "she's not heard from him either. Thought the devil was dead." Looking alert again, "Rutherford, can you get a message to him?"

The desk clerk looked abashed, "I'm terribly sorry Sir, there's no gentleman by that name here."

"Rutherford," James employed the age-old tactic of raising his voice to guarantee further understanding, "he just checked in. I saw him with my own eyes."

Flustered, the clerk stuttered, "I'm afraid you were mistaken Sir, that gentleman is Mr Roper, Mr Dennis Roper."

"Good Lord, I'm sorry. I could've sworn it was Georgie. Well," he said brightly, smiling, "I'll not need to tell him how much he's upset my wife then," and he turned away, crossed the hall, joined Moreton and they made their way to the dining room.

"Do you know if he is dining here tonight," Moreton asked, "the chef's damn good so he will if he's got any sense."

The food was delicious, and Dennis Roper

showed he did have good culinary taste. James excused himself from the table, went over to confront him and served the necessary papers directly into his hands.

CHAPTER 22

1894
London's Tower Bridge raises its roadway for the
first time to allow a ship to pass up the Thames

"Observation. The most important weapon in your armoury. You need abnormal patience, sometimes we'll have to watch a person for weeks or have our eyes glued to a doorway for hours. No good our turning away at just the moment the subject leaves the building. We cannot lose heart and we must not make blunders. A mistake can have dire consequences and lives can be ruined, and our livelihood gone too. Facts must be checked, and double checked. All those notes," James nodded towards a polished, oak card index box with little brass drawer pulls that stood on his desk, "need to be labelled and dated exactly. They form the basis of our reports and how do you think we can get a lot of that detail."

"By following and observing?" Perry answered.

"Yes of course, but I also mean by listening. Listening is the next most important skill. Whether you are speaking with the subject themselves or you've managed to sit next to an acquaintance and take tea with them. Or you've gone to an office to talk with the clerk, or you've called at the house and are talking to the housemaid or the porter. Listen. You cannot be seen to be interrogating anyone, the best way to make people say more than they might wish to, is to listen attentively and give the occasional little nod of encouragement. It makes them feel important, but you must also be genuine, if you are not sincere, they will see through you, you cannot fake it if you wish to be successful."

Perry was writing furiously, making notes. It was one of their regular lessons when James taught him the finer points and subtleties of becoming a detective. "You have to develop a good memory Perry. Imagine I was your subject and you were watching me, we are in the street," he said, "you couldn't be taking your notes right now, you'd have to remember. Try it, put your pencil down and just listen but always heed this, the memory is fallible, you must write it all down as soon as possible." The boy looked worried but did as he was told, clasped his hands in front of him, leant forward on his chair and looked at James intently.

"Let's go back to *seeing,* and I mean *seeing* not just looking. It takes a lot of concentration, you should note the atmosphere around your subject as well as their appearance, note the weather as you never know when that will be important, note the people and activity going on around them and obviously eavesdrop if you can on their conversations." James stood to stretch his legs, Monty jumped up too, thinking it was time for a walk and James bent down to stroke him, "It's possible to tell a huge amount about people by the clothes they wear," he continued, "give me an example."

"Yes, if they wear a uniform, you'd know if they were a soldier or sailor. A woman might have a nurse's cape," Perry was about to list many more but James gently interrupted, "No, not purely uniforms. The characteristics and individuality of a man will show through his clothes. Say you put a valet in his master's clothes. What would you expect? How might you discern he is a copy of his master and not the real thing?

Perry thought, "His speech?"

"Yes, but he could have practiced."

"His bearing, how he holds himself. He would have to give off a confident air, one that would not be usual for him?"

"Exactly, it's the details and if you train yourself to be observant, you will notice them. I believe I can identify an ex-army officer, whatever he is wearing. He has a way of dressing that is precise, a way of holding himself, a way of commanding others even though he no longer has the rank."

"You mean, he still bosses people about," Perry made them laugh, "once in charge, always in charge."

"You could be right. We'll go out walking later, Monty is eager to get going, and we'll see if you can single out say, a physician. Sleek appearance, an impeccably cut coat and silk hat, but a man mainly aware of his superiority of knowledge and self-assured because of it. And," James grinned at his young apprentice, "what about an actor?"

"Dressed in mismatched bits and pieces I should think," Perry answered cheekily, "left-overs from the parts he acted."

"Yes, but think about it, instead of disguising

who he is, this would alert us to his profession. We should know who he was!"

Towards the end of the year, Potty Sinclair died, and James found himself desperately upset, he felt this marked the end of an era. The funeral was a huge, expensive occasion, with the ambience of a Final Performance rather than a solemn affair. At one point, the circular vestibule at All Souls in Langham Place looked like the final curtain call of a particularly successful production, and sitting amongst the more prominent members of the profession, he also found the regular coterie from The Albion.

Charles Arrow came up to James outside the church later, "We'll miss Potty, they don't make them like that anymore. Fancy a pint?"

They made their way to the Masons Arms in Maddox Street, "I'm not sure I want to go to The Albion," James had said, "let's find neutral ground. It was quite a happy gathering back there, but I feel unaccountably sad."

The dark, wooden interior of the public house was welcoming, and the friends sat, drank and talked. Charles and his wife Fanny had kept in touch with Florence and learning that she had another novel about to be published, James decided to take a chance and call on her that afternoon. Not for the first time, he was aware that he missed her.

"You were lucky to catch me in," Florence said moving quickly across the room to take James's hand when Hope showed him into the Bayswater drawing room, "I am invited to tea at the Farquhars," she chuckled, "not a prospect I relish as you can imagine, but there is money for the Society in the offing, so I must make sure I take advantage of it."

"Still working away on behalf of the fallen?" James let her hand go, "I'm pleased there are good people like you in the world, I'm seeing rather a lot of an all together different sort. Selfish, cheating and not particularly nice."

"How is business? Do you enjoy it? You always thought you might and if you can thwart some of these unpleasant characters, you should be glad?" She glanced at the clock, "I still have an hour before I must leave, so shall we have tea here? It's good timing on your part to call, I've had a letter from your mother, it seems she does not have your address?"

"Oh good Lord, it's not that I've deliberately kept my whereabouts from her, I just didn't get round to writing. How did her letter find you?"

"I took the precaution of giving a forwarding address to the porter at Beauchamp Place of course, I cannot imagine what might have gone astray for you!"

"Nothing of importance I'm sure, I informed my wine merchant, the most essential man!"

"Ernest, you are incorrigible. Sit here and I will fetch the letter."

He sat and looked around the room. It was very elegant with expensive furnishings and a wealth of strange, eastern looking curiosities. Threatening, ornate handled, crossed swords were on one wall, a beautiful but strangely erotic Japanese print on another and every surface appeared to hold an eclectic array of colourful, enormous pots or round, gold, or stone, Buddhas. His eyes nearly popped out of his head, when he noticed the life size samurai warrior in the corner. Florence came back in, "It's rather like living in an oriental emporium," she beamed, "but I am very used to it now and Sylvia of course, adores them all. She regards Junichi," she said, gesturing to the figure in the corner, "as her ideal man, his name means 'obedient one'!"

Jane Wodehouse had written with news of the family, more nieces and nephews for James, his brother Thomas now engineering in Manchester and interestingly, his cousin William Thorne, late of Severns wine merchants, was running a pub in London, at Newington Butts.

"How the mighty have fallen," James said rather unkindly, "I always thought him inadequate, but he did me a favour I suppose, took the heat off when I refused to take on the business. I've no regrets there at all, I'm much happier being a disreputable inquiry agent than I could ever have been as a provincial merchant." He pulled a face, "I'd have been even more inadequate than Mr Severn Thorne!"

They spoke about Florence's new book, "I think the title is always so important, don't you?" Florence asked, "this one's called *In the Meshes*, I have an orphan girl caught up in the meshes of an unscrupulous doctor, a querulous old woman and a poisoned wife! I hope you'll read it?"

"Most certainly, especially as you have your usual macabre plot, whatever is wrong with a gentle romance? Is that too far from real life for you?"

He had not meant to sound wistful, but Florence noticed, "Absolutely too far, Ernest, I fear I am a sceptic on such matters. But tell me about Justin Chevasse, is he working on any interesting cases?"

"Divorces, a fraud or two and serving papers to

errant gentlemen. Still searching for compelling problems to solve but I'm making a web of international
contacts now and am very hopeful that I shall travel to
Paris on a matter shortly. A planned trip I'm happy to
say rather than the frequent train journeys taken at the
eleventh hour without any notice at all. I am gathering
quite a collection of new shirts and ties and even shoes
bought from the strangest of stores, in the strangest of
places. Oh, and I could open my own toothbrush shop
I have so many now!" He looked at her smiling at him,
"You are better off with your life here my dear."

It was a happy hour spent together and James
left, his mood pensive. Then he gave himself a mental
shake and set off back to the office thinking of work.
The Knight of the Realm and his missing wife, where
the only lead he had at present was that her best friend
was last heard of in Paris. He would accept the terms of
engagement tomorrow.

"I could come with you?" James had gone to discuss his imminent investigations in Paris with Gussie,
"my French is fluent, and I know my way around."

"Good of you to offer, but I'll get by with the language and I can read a map," James said smiling at her,
"also Sir is not likely to pay for two of us to go, although
I'm happy to say at the moment that there's no sign of
any expense being spared."

"Well, I've written and introduced you to Monsieur Barreau, he will help if he can. He's been my contact for two years now and he seems quite competent.
He can at least point you in the right direction and his
charges are more than reasonable."

"It should not be too difficult to track down an
aristocratic English woman, but whether she will tell

me anything helpful about my Lady, I'm not so sure. If she's run away from Sir, the friend isn't likely to tell me, is she?"

"I'm sure you'll be able to charm her in no time," Gussie smiled wickedly, "one look from your seductive eyes and she'll melt in your arms!"

"I shall take that thought with me," laughed James. "I'm hoping whilst I'm there to explore the city a bit, I've an idea for an article for *The Spectator*, I happened to meet the owner Mr Strachey the other week when I was a guest at Brooks."

"Brooks no less, you're moving in high circles now Justin."

"Yes, all down to my old friend the actor Gilbert Sinclair for proposing me as a Freemason. You know, I only found out his name was Gilbert at his funeral the other week, he was always known as Potty. I still don't know why."

James's sleuthing in Paris turned out to be interesting and enjoyable. He had been right to think that tracking down the friend of his ultimate quarry would be relatively easy and acting as Ernest Severne, journalist, he bluffed and tricked her into revealing the name of a hotel on the south coast of England, where a certain Mrs Smith could be found.

He tried not to think too long and hard about the methods he used to gather information. On the face of it, an investigator was often as deceitful as those he chose to expose. It usually required him to act a part and he disliked acknowledging that he was actually lying, to peruse a subject's private life. What cheques had been cashed, told to him by an unwitting bank teller. Credit checks, outstanding debts, current state of finances and living arrangements. Their sobriety or otherwise, their vulnerabilities, gambling, horses, women. There were of course legitimate and public repositories of facts, the street directories, Club membership lists and *Who's Who* to tell you if his interests were golf or hunting, billiards or play going, but the information was usually found by subterfuge, engaging the servants, friends or colleagues in conversation. The suggestions or insinuations, the questions that don't appear to be questions, that would lead them into betraying confidences. James had to reconcile his conscience with the belief that he was, generally at least, doing good.

More challenging and ultimately satisfying for him, was that his time spent roaming the streets of Paris produced what he considered to be one of his best articles yet for the press. It had been accepted by the *Saturday Review* rather than the *Spectator* and had subsequently been taken up by other papers at home and abroad. He was particularly delighted when Al Grayson, his new Pinkerton's man, telegraphed to say he'd seen Justin Chevasse mentioned in a marvellous piece about the Slums of Paris in the *Boston Sunday Post*. In fact, it wasn't just a mention, James had written the piece as a third party. The well-known detective Justin Chevasse had accompanied the author on a tour of the underworld of Paris.

James had seen the paupers and the misery for himself and was outraged, "That a city of two million can have a whole 'lower' city inside of a hundred and twenty five thousand beggars is beyond belief," he was telling Charles, whilst they waited together outside the police courts not long after he had returned home, "I've never seen such filth and degradation and the numbers are increasing. People coming in from the provinces and ordinary people unable to cope with rising prices and the struggle to survive in what they call the 'upper world'."

"Isn't it the same in London," Charles asked.

"I'm afraid you're right, but the numbers in France are bigger. I saw people living in cellars, overrun with rats. There's a whole community of these souls. You should read my article, two and a half thousand of my most erudite words, philosophy included."

"It will have to wait, I'm up," Charles was called into court, "yet another pickpocket. We'll meet up properly soon, catch up on things."

CHAPTER 23

1897
Robert Gascoyne-Cecil, 3rd Marquess of Salisbury
has been Prime Minister since 1895
The Diamond Jubilee of Queen Victoria is celebrated

W ork came in steadily and James found himself recommended both within the private world and that of business. His great friend Teddy Loftus found himself so often without acting work, that he joined James and Perry and the office moved to slightly larger premises still within York Buildings.

He adjusted his advertisements to read, 'Justin Chevasse. Private Investigator for the Aristocracy. Divorce. French and Russian system of espionage. Secrecy guaranteed: Specially retained by many high-class Firms'. The business was making money, but it seemed, never enough and it was not his intention to take on cases that would result in a lurid court case. He found his clients preferred to keep incidences of blackmail, embezzlement or fraud very quiet and the perpetrators, mostly of the higher classes themselves, when caught out, found the resulting social exclusion punishment enough.

James received a message early one spring morning in 1897 from his friend Paolo Bertini, the manager of the Cecil Hotel, to call by when he had a moment. He strolled slowly along the Strand, in no hurry, needing to get things straight in his head. He was deep in thought, worried as ever about money and whether or not he would have to let his latest employee, another out of work actor, go. The work was never consistent, it came in as feast or famine.

He arrived and looked up at the soaring red brick facade of what was being heralded as the largest, most luxurious hotel in Europe, possibly in the world. Finished only last year, it had eight hundred bedrooms, a vast Palm Court ballroom and three top class restaurants. James had met Paolo at the grand opening when he had been invited as a guest of one of the architects for whom he had quietly averted a scandal the year before, and James had taken an instant liking to the little, clever, quick eyed Italian. He greeted the doorman who gave him a semi-salute and walked through under the imposing archway into the bright, airy courtyard, a popular meeting spot particularly for Americans, and already christened The Beach. In spite of the cool April temperature, the place was packed, guests, wrapped in their winter coats and hats, sitting in the dozens of cane chairs, waiters darting back and forth with drinks, skirting piles of luggage and rocking chairs. He made his way past the newspaper stall to the main door and walked across the foyer to the porter's desk.

"Good morning Auguste, beautiful day isn't it. The sun has brought everyone out I see."

"Good morning Sir, Signor Bertini is waiting for

you, he is in his office," Auguste clicked his fingers and a young boy in hotel livery rushed up, "take Mr Chevasse to the manager's office and arrange for coffee to be sent in."

"Justin my friend, it is good to see you. You are well I hope?" Paolo met James with a hearty slap on the back, and leaving no time for protracted greetings, said, "sit, sit. I'll get straight to the point, I need your help."

"Well, if I can help, I shall. Is this as a friend or business?"

"Business. The man I employed as head of security has shown himself to be inadequate for the job. I think he was honest enough but lacking in the perspicacity necessary for such a position. I blame myself, I chose him, but he has let me down and leaves me in need of a replacement. It is a difficult job in the normal way to protect our many guests, you know as well as I do that hotels attract thieves and fraudsters like honey pots attract bees, and this year will be harder. The Queen's Jubilee celebrations are being held in June and London is expecting to be overrun with visitors from home and abroad for the occasion. We will be fully booked for weeks and this is bound to bring more than our fair share of problems. Could you, Justin Chevasse my dear friend, run my security team? At least for this one year?"

"I have my own business Paolo, we've ongoing cases, I cannot just abandon my offices and staff, much as I'd like to help."

"I should pay you well, you would be able to employ another man perhaps? Of course I would accept that you must attend to your own matters too. I was hopeful you could arrange to take on both responsibilities? We have a splendid suite on the first floor you could occupy?"

James thought it over and came to the conclusion it was too good an opportunity to miss. He thought it quite likely to lead, in time, to more investigations than petty theft from bedrooms. He set about coordinating his staff to divide their time and duties and soon there was a constant exchange of visits and information between York Buildings and the 'Mr Chevasse, Head of Security' office in the lobby of the Cecil Hotel. Perry, at twenty years of age, brimmed with pride at taking on the authority of office manager and a senior operative.

The arrangement was working well, and Paolo had been right to anticipate a spate of incidents in the lead up to the national celebrations during June of that year. The city was crowded with people intent on wishing Her Majesty well. The usual soot coated streets had been transformed into a sea of patriotic colour with Union Jacks draped from balconies, flowers and rainbows of bunting festooned overhead and on the eve of the grand parade, James had gathered together a party of friends for dinner in the Cecil restaurant. It was a spacious, lofty room with imposing pillars of deep blue, and they were seated at a large round table by the window which gave a feeling of light and air not felt elsewhere amongst the walnut panelling. The bonus was a glorious view of Westminster. The food was superb and waiting for the post dinner coffee and liqueurs, James sat back contentedly in his chair listening to the happy conversations, watching his friend's smiling faces. It had been a long time since he had entertained and he felt a hint of sadness. His friend Martin was here with a wife, Charles with a wife, Teddy was with a young man about whom James enquired little but knew they were close. Even Davy Mason was now married. Either side of James sat Gussie and her friend Constance, the woman Gussie lived and worked with, Connie, who, it was plain to see, adored her. Only he was alone, if you didn't count Monty sitting as usual quietly at his feet. This rarely bothered him but tonight it was making him think.

"Mr Chevasse," Guido the maître d' spoke softly in his ear, "please could you come with me."

James dabbed his lips with his napkin, scrunched it onto the table and stood up, "Please excuse me one moment," he said as his friends looked towards him enquiringly, "I am never off duty it seems and I have a small matter to attend to, I shall be back as soon as possible. In the meantime, please enjoy yourselves, finish your dinner and join the dancing in the ballroom when you are ready."

He followed Guido to the Palm Court and slipped past the chairs and sofas arranged around the sides of the ballroom filled with chattering, laughing, gawping guests. There, centre stage was a perpetual thorn in his side, Miss Cordelia Lamond, her gown unfastened at the front, eyes shut, head thrown back and her arms above her head, whirling like a dervish. Taking his own jacket off, he walked over and grabbed hold of her flailing hands with one of his, and with the other, covered her shoulders. He gripped her so tightly that she whimpered, and accompanied by her screams and spitting, he frog-marched her out of the room.

"All in a night's work," he was laughing later,

"lucky for me she is only tiny, she fights like an alley cat." Looking at Charles he said, "We'll have to bar her from the hotel now, she's been trouble for about eight months, and we gave her notice to quit long ago. Several times in fact, she just won't go and she's done this elsewhere, a hotel in Brighton I think. She's paid up, all but a few pounds, but that doesn't matter, we'll just be glad to see the back of her, I have a nasty feeling if she comes back for her belongings, she'll not leave again."

He was right to think Miss Lamond would be back and only two days later she had tried to sneak into the hotel through the Prince's entrance near Savoy gardens. Auguste the porter had put his arm out to bar her way and she had struck him three times in the face. As a result, on the first of July, James was waiting at Bow Street Police Court to give his evidence against her. He sat on a bench in the waiting hall reading, his attention fully taken up with Perry's report of a vicar looking for their help to put an end to a blackmail situation, when the sound of a slight commotion caused him to look up and see the flamboyant entrance of an exquisite creature, a swirl of blue black curls, feathers, velvet and perfume. She looked around the hallway, smiled a smile that lit up the entire dismal room and then came rushing up to him.

"Ernest darling, what in the world are you doing here? It's a positive age since I saw you, it was Potty Sinclair's send off wasn't it?"

James was almost knocked over by her exuberant embrace and as she held him back at arms-length, looking him up and down he started to speak, but before he had chance to gather his wits about him, the black robed usher called 'Miss Emily Drake to court two please'.

"Darling, I have to go," she said breathlessly, "please wait for me here or I'll wait for you. We *must* talk, we must catch up," and with that she pirouetted after the usher and disappeared through the courtroom door.

When James's case was over, intrigued, he did wait for her. She came flouncing back into the lobby and straight up to him, "Ernest darling, you would save my life if you could take me for a little champagne, just one coupe, my nerves are jangling. A horrid little man tried to swindle me out of ten pounds, but I was too clever for him, he's going to prison I'm pleased to say. Please, Ernest, just a little glass of champagne at Café Royal. We have so much to talk about."

James was mesmerised and feeling powerless to refuse, he followed her out of the building. Emily stood at the edge of the pavement looking up and down the road, she pouted, "The wretch has gone. I told him to wait for me," seeing James's face she explained, "my driver. He's done a bunk."

"Your driver?"

"Never mind, I'll tell you all later. You'll have to hail a hansom."

They arrived at Regent Street and James found himself entering through the pillared door into the famous Café in Emily's wake. He followed as she swanned down the passage to the grill room and followed again as a uniformed steward greeted her fulsomely and led them to a table which commanded an excellent view of the already busy dining room.

"I'm ravenous," she purred at James, "let us order champagne first and then perhaps we can order luncheon?"

"Of course," James answered, almost in a trance, and as the sommelier arrived, concurred with him that a bottle of the Clicquot vin rosé would be perfect and "Yes of course, a little caviar to accompany it." Emily spoke almost non-stop, the questions she asked of him went largely unanswered as he listened, hypnotised and tongue tied at the heady, enchantress opposite him. No longer was she a pretty young girl, she was an elegant, confident, beautiful woman. Over a light lunch of noisettes of lamb, green beans and foie gras accompanied by a fresh green salad, James fell in love with Miss Emily Drake. By the time they had finished their fresh fruits and cream, coffee and crème de menthe, for Emily, cognac, for James, he was certain she was a damsel in distress and was determined to help her escape her situation.

She was, she told him, under the patronage of Freddie Matravers, "You must have heard of him darling, he's an MP and quite a favourite of the Prime Minister. Well, he saw me in *Mrs Tanqueray* at St James in '95, I played only a small part and I was disappointed Mrs Campbell wasn't playing the lead, but Ernest, it was wonderful. I'd been so lucky, if Mr Wilde hadn't been arrested *his* play would have been on all season, but they put these short runs on instead and there were a lot of us unknowns got a real chance. I had a lot of lines, I thought it would take me to stardom." She took a sip of her champagne, "It didn't of course but, where was I? Oh yes, Freddie. He tipped the usher to let him come backstage and my, he was so charming. Asked if he could hire me for private theatricals and I looked at this tall, handsome man in his immaculate evening attire and I was so flattered." She looked into James's face, "I had no idea what he meant Ernest, of course I didn't, or I should have said 'no' straight away."

"I am not judging you Emily," James spluttered, "I am not judging you at all. Please, go on."

"Well, he rather bowled me over and after the run finished and nothing else came in for me, he set me up in the sweetest little flat in Gordon Street. It's all gone horribly wrong now. Freddie says it's over and that I must make my own way. He's not giving me a penny more after the end of August and I have to vacate my home. He must have called my driver away today too and that is just petty." She pulled a lace edged handkerchief from the sleeve of her velvet jacket and held it to the corners of her eyes, "Oh Ernest, it is such a mess. All I can do is hope he will change his mind when he learns I have nowhere to go."

"What happened to make him act like this? It is hardly gentlemanly."

"Oh, he's being thoroughly unreasonable. He got to hear of an unimportant little dalliance I had with a divinely pretty young actor I met a Gaiety party. It was just a flirtation, I was lonely. Freddie only managed to get away from the House, or his wife and children, twice a month and I was not working. The days were very long. There are only so many girl friends to lunch with and the evenings could become very dreary. It's because of Freddie that I got caught up with that dreadful business this morning, that man assured me he held shares in the Theatre Royal and that my ten pounds would obtain me a meeting with the manager. I thought I could get back on the stage."

"I'm glad that rogue has been caught of course,

but I still don't understand why..., why your benefactor, would not assure your financial security for some time to come? Would he risk his reputation? You could make his spiteful treatment of you public."

"Well, my dear Ernest, there is a little more to it. I thought I'd found myself enceinté and Freddie refused to believe it was his child and was therefore not prepared to own it nor to pay for its removal," she gave a coquettish look, "my pretty little actor was in no position to do so either. When, shall we say, my circumstances righted themselves of their own accord, Freddie was adamant that he would not keep me any longer. So, you can see my dilemma. I'm twenty-four now," she paused and looked vacantly at the ceiling, "I rather liked the idea of a child."

James saw her wistful look disappear just as quickly as it had come as she sat back allowing the waiter to remove her last dish and place a coffee cup in front of her.   "Do you have family you can go to? Who will support you until you find work?"

"No, I've not seen my parents for an age, not since I left Ireland to come to London."

That explained her beauty, the dark hair, alabaster skin and deep blue eyes. "I had not thought you were Irish," James gazed at her anew, "you have no trace of an accent."

"Ah, but to be sure I have, if I so want," she replied in a thick brogue, "but you'll only have to be asking me to use it on the stage."

They laughed and he asked, seriously, "Do you want to start acting again? I still have a few contacts in the business."

"Shame on me Ernest. I haven't asked a single

thing about you. I heard you've given up treading the boards but what are you doing?"

CHAPTER 24

1897 - 1898
The British government arranges a 99-year rent of Hong Kong from China

J ames would never really understand why, on that first afternoon, he failed to tell Emily he was married and then as the days went by, it seemed the moment to tell had passed. She was like a drug, he could not keep away from her and he visited Gordon Street as often as he could over those first intoxicating weeks. At the end of August, James arranged for her to have a very pleasant room at the Cecil.

As he showed her in, he said, "Paolo regrets this will only be a temporary arrangement," he smiled, "he's still smarting about the long-term lady we took to court!"

"Well I for one *love* Miss, what was it, Lamond? Without her I would not have run into you at the court house," Emily put her arms around James, "but I shall do my utmost to keep my clothes on in the hotel my darling, unless," she smiled seductively, "you'd like to come in my room and shut the door?"

James was bewitched, he tried hard to concentrate on his daily life but his thoughts were full of her, he saw her in every glance, he longed to be close to her and he believed that when she was in his arms as they lay, spent with love, in her big, soft, hotel bed each night, that he could die of happiness. He even ignored his bell-wether, Monty did not like her. His low throaty growl whenever she came near unnerved Emily, "I'm just not an animal person and it knows it," she complained, "I do not like dogs very much at all, I wish you would keep the beast away from me." James agreed and Monty was banished to his office when Emily was with him.

This state of euphoria had, of course, to come to an end and there were many outside influences hastening this. Wanting to stay near to his love at all times, James delegated more and more of his private investigative work to his staff and even called on Gussie to assist. He advertised less and when the enquiries began to dry up, let his most recent recruit go. Worse, at the back of his mind, even breaking through all the heart racing, deliciously exciting throes of love, he knew his position as head of security at the hotel was not sufficient, it was not fulfilling, it was not what he had set out to do and by the time the year ended, this awakening brought him to his senses.

"Emily sweetheart, I cannot continue working here at the hotel, it was only ever meant to be a short-term arrangement and I need to get back to my own office and my own work. Gussie thinks she may have found a complicated fraud case that would suit me down to the ground. It's likely to take some time and I want to take it. It will mean leaving the Cecil."

"But where does that leave me Ernest? Whatever

do you expect me to do? I thought you loved me, how could *you* abandon me too," and she drew out her handkerchief to wipe her eyes, "how could you be so cruel."

"I thought you wanted only to get back into the theatre my love," James said bewildered, "I arranged for you to meet with three managers and you must have made new contacts at the Gaiety." James had had to contend with many evenings hiding his raw jealousy as Emily went, bedecked in jewels, wearing her finest gowns or furs to meet with acting friends for dinner. "Darling Ernest" she had assured him, murmuring as she covered him in kisses and petted him, "I love only you. These people are just trying to help my career." Still, he had spent his time left behind at the hotel on duty, battling the urge to run after her and would breathe a huge sigh of relief when she returned, not too late, promising she had drunk only 'the one glass of champagne to steady my nerves'.

Now, at this very moment, he was in turmoil. What could he say, what should he do, how could he ask her to live with him in his basement flat in Chelsea. She solved the dilemma for him, "Darling Ernest, marry me then we can be together always."

James knew he was completely lost, he could not bear the thought of losing her, he gazed at Emily's beautiful face and in a husky voice he did not quite think belonged to him, said, "Of course my sweetheart, yes. Will you give me the greatest pleasure and become my wife."

He was desperate, he could not, he would not, ask Florence for a divorce. James knew well the expression 'set a thief to catch a thief' and like it or not, his mind had become practiced in the art of deception, at discerning the devious. His education was extensive. The answer came to him, he would need to pay a visit to the disgraced vicar in Spitalfields.

The Reverend Gervase Maddock had served his apprenticeship as curate at St. Andrew's in Puckington, a village in Somerset and when the incumbent had moved on to that higher authority, they all aspired to, Maddock moved up the ladder to become the vicar. However, he had two distinct disadvantages for a man of the cloth, a propensity to live a more extravagant lifestyle than his miserable stipend would secure and a rather healthy taste for the pleasures of the female body. Both these desires got the better of him and when he was found out, he was fortunate that the desire of the church to avoid scandals at all costs resulted in him being quietly removed from his country living and placed in a parish in the east end of London. His married lover and her baby son had made the move with him and lived, to the outside world, as his housekeeper in their shabby terraced house. Maddock had called in Justin Chevasse after a parishioner from his village, now in London, stony broke and looking unsuccessfully for work, had attended the Sunday service seeking comfort and succour for his soul. He had recognised the exiled vicar and his first anonymous request for two shillings to refrain from advising the new congregation of his history had been paid, the coins left at a certain tree in a local park, but Maddock was not prepared to pay the second demand but was also unwilling to approach the police.

In the course of Perry and James's investigations it was found that the pub landlord's wife and child was not the only property stolen from Puckington, a proportion of fees paid by honest men to wed their beloveds had also found their way into Maddock's personal possession. Still, James had tracked down the extortionist, a sorry wretch for whom he might have felt sympathy at another time and threatened him with the police and prison. No more was heard of him and whilst James thought Maddock was left free to continue his theft of wedding fees in London, his conscience did not bother him unduly. In order to carry out many of the jobs he was paid to do he forced himself to ignore the morality of the situation. It was not his to worry about.

Now, having asked Emily to marry him, James went to Spitalfields the following Sunday morning. He attended the service and then lingered outside the church door until all the worshippers had dispersed, waiting to speak privately with Maddock about his requirements. It was obvious this would not be the first sham marriage he had arranged as Gervase Maddock was most helpful in providing the necessary details.

"I shall ensure we call the Banns for the three weeks before the date and I am confident I have a loose certificate for you to sign afterwards. What about witnesses," he asked smirking, "I can provide them for you should you not wish to involve your own guests?"

It was when Maddock raised the question of his fees that James knew he could not go through with it. "Of course, Mr Chevasse, there will be only minimal remuneration due, I am grateful for your help in," he lowered his voice even more, "that other matter. Your discretion is part payment enough."

The bile rose in James's throat. The sight of this creature with his popping eyes, receding, greasy hair and breath that told of rotten teeth brought him to his senses. He knew in that instant that he could not cross that line, the line between turning a blind eye to this odious man's dishonesty and becoming a criminal himself. He could not go through with it. He could not commit bigamy. Ashamed of himself, beads of sweat broke out on his forehead despite the bitter cold day and he turned on his heels, leaving without another word. Maddock was left staring after him, an amused and scornful look on his face.

The journey back to the Strand had been a blur for James, his mind was reeling and his resolve to tell Emily the truth ebbing and flowing as his destination drew nearer. He had delayed going to see her immediately and instead, gone straight to his office, where, with the door firmly closed, he had discussed the situation in depth with Monty and rehearsed his speech. Finally, he could put the moment off no longer, he stroked the dog's head, told him he would not be long, and went, his heart beating rapidly, his hands damp with perspiration, secure in the knowledge that this was the end, to knock on his sweetheart's door.

He had expected hysterics and tears, tantrums and recriminations. He was primed to beg, to plead, to promise anything at all other than marriage, in order to keep her but the look of utter shock on her face and her complete silence was a thousand times worse to bear.

"Sweetheart, please say something," he went to take her hand as she walked to the window and stood looking out into the street, "please, my love, I cannot bear to have hurt you so badly."

She withdrew her hand and he could hear her breathing, fast and shallow. He studied her impassive face, no tears, no trembling lips. "Please my love, tell me what I can do to make this right for us?"

After what seemed to James a lifetime, Emily's face broke into a huge smile, she turned to him, took his hands in hers and said, "Let's pretend that we are married then! I should so like to live with you as your wife and what does a piece of paper matter anyway? This will be so much fun Ernest, but we must make sure your wife does not get to hear of us. Your friends will need to keep our secret too don't you think?"

When James stopped shaking, he took her in his arms and held her tightly, "My dear, sweet Emily, I adore you, you are without doubt the loveliest woman in the world and I shall make you happy, I will love you forever."

When it came down to it, James had never been one to talk of his private life and so there were very few people that he mixed with who knew of Florence and those that did, Charles, Martin and Gussie, made no judgements. James would not be the first of their acquaintances by any means, to be living with someone other than their spouse. On a Friday morning at the end of April 1898, James and Emily packed their overnight bags and took the train out of London to stay for the weekend in Brighton. It was only when they sat with their hands clasped together, as the train chugged out of the station, the steam spewing from the funnel, the sound of metal wheels screeching on the rails that James drew a deep breath, leant his face close to Emily's and addressed his latest dilemma.

"Ernest is not my real name," he watched her closely, "it is James William and I have not wanted to be called that since I was a child. I am not a James William, I don't feel like a James William. I chose Ernest as my stage name, but I think I should change it now that we are to be together and I'd like to be called Eric. The same initials will be helpful, but I'm not associated with the stage now and my business name, which most people call me anyway, is Justin Chevasse."

Speechless for only a moment, she asked, "Well my darling, what name shall I call you or shall I stick with 'darling'?" She laughed loudly, "I really don't mind what your name is, I'm happy with Eric! When we get back to London after our *wedding* this weekend, I wish to put an announcement in the Irish Times, so we'll call you Eric in that. My family will not be surprised that I have not invited them to our marriage, they will think we have married in a protestant church, they will wish to disown me completely then for breaking the faith."

"Does that make you sad my sweetheart?"

"Good Lord no, I was never close to my mother or my father, I always disliked my sister and my young brother was just a nuisance to me. I do not mind at all and we are so alike my darling, you have no family either. It will be just the two of us together, alone in the world, how romantic."

It was true, James had not been in touch with his mother or sisters for years and now, without meaning to, he had lost touch with Florence, and as far as he knew, so had Charles. He had heard that she moved from Bayswater and had published another book as he had seen it in the bookseller's window and bought it with every intention of writing a note of congratulations, but somehow, he never got round to it. He assumed that if anyone wished to contact him, they would write to his house in Warwick Street and his agent there would let him know.

Mr and Mrs Eric Severne had a wonderful time in Brighton, they strolled under the cliffs along the walled esplanade with raised terraces and elegant wrought iron arcades, all designed in a mock oriental style inspired by the Royal Pavilion and they braved the strong breeze to walk out onto the pier. In the evening they sat in the concert hall, the waves beneath them, listening to a performance of Strauss. On Saturday night they dined at the Grand Hotel and at every opportunity, Emily raised her gloved, left hand and displayed the magnificent, deep blue sapphire and diamond ring on the third finger.

James had given her the ring on their first evening there. She had looked ravishing, her hair swept up in the very latest plumped out chignon, carefully placed curls framing her face, her small, brimless hat a concoction of deep, sapphire blue feathers, ruffles and netting which formed a delicate veil over her face and matched exactly the deep blue, silk gown, trimmed in lace, with the waist cinched in so tightly James felt he could circle it with just one hand. She had taken his breath away and her delight at the beauty of the ring, matched his delight at the beauty before him. The days at the seaside had been magical, James had never thought he could be so happy, and he prayed, as they journeyed home to London, that the feelings would last for eternity.

"Well my darling, we may not have had an actual wedding, but we are having a perfect honeymoon." It was later that week and Emily was stretched out on the bed in one of the superior suites on the top floor of the Cecil, a wedding gift from Paolo Bertini who had insisted his friend, the famous detective, must have a week of luxury for his bride. Her hair was unpinned, held as one long, loose braid which draped over her left shoulder as she rested on her right elbow amongst the downy pillows. James refilled the two coupes on the bedside table and stood holding the champagne bottle, gazing down at her. He loved to look at her, the way the little curls cradled her ear, her slender neck, the slightest upturn at the end of her nose, the perfect, long, dark lashes framing those deep blue eyes. She was wearing a cream satin negligée, her flawless face the colour of alabaster with a hint of rouge high on her cheekbones and the faint remains of a touch of red stain on her lips. She smiled at him and picked up a magazine, "I'm glad we have a little time before I have to dress for dinner, I feel so comfortable and *so* relaxed," she giggled softly, "I think I'll stay here and finish my bubbles. What about you?"

James wrenched his eyes away and took the bottle back to the small table by the window. He stood, naked, looking without really seeing, down at the street below, still feeling the bliss of her fingers caressing his body, the trust, hopes and dreams and the promise for their future that they had just shared in their lovemaking. He looked back at the bed and sensing his eyes on her again, Emily glanced up from her reading. They smiled, that sweet and lazy smile of lovers and he went back, lay beside her, one arm behind his head, the other resting on her hip, his fingers idly stroking the curve of her waist.

CHAPTER 25

1898 - 1899
*The Second Boer War between the United Kingdom
and the Boers in South Africa begins*

J ames did not, after all, leave his position as the
hotel's head of security, but Emily did give up all in-
tentions of returning to acting. James did not want
to be parted from her for a moment, they lived together in his suite on the first floor of the hotel and his
heart thrilled whenever, from his office, he caught sight
of her in the foyer. Emily was thoroughly happy, she
would while away the late morning on The Beach, there
were always people there to join for drinks, people to
talk to. She would shop endlessly and entertain ladies
to afternoon tea in the restaurant. She cajoled James to
invite her new friends, many of them Americans, to join
them for dinner most nights. She could charm the birds
from the trees, and she could especially charm James
who watched her, adoringly. He was under the spell of
her beauty and her effervescence, he was hopelessly in
love. Monty had learned too, that much as he disliked
her, if he left her alone and did not growl, she would
ignore him, and he could stay by his master's side with-

out reproach.

Perry and Teddy continued to work from York Buildings, their cases often confined to basic, dull, divorce work, the income barely covering expenses, but James put this to the back of his mind. He concentrated on his lovely wife and for several blissful months, he strived and succeeded, in doing everything within his power to please her. It was on the eve of the new year, 1900, when, he understood, a few years later, that everything changed.

"I don't give two hoots whether it is the end of the century this year or next," Emily was saying rather peevishly, "it is the end of the year and I was so looking forward to celebrating and I cannot believe that you are to stay on duty until so late. You had agreed we would meet early with the usual crowd at Limmers. Beth and I are completely addicted to their Tom Collin's punch, it will be perfect to start the evening. Then we thought afterwards we would carry on to the Palm Court at The Carlton before coming back here for a late supper. Guido has reserved us tables. It's just too bad if you cannot come, I am very upset."

"Please don't be cross with me my sweet, I will join you all here for dinner. I am sorry but Auguste is unwell, and I cannot leave the hotel in the hands of a junior. I have a job to do. We shall be together at midnight my love, when the new year begins."

He made to take her in his arms, but she pulled away.

"I shall have to punish you if you cannot put your wife first," she gave a pout and then sighed, "oh well, it cannot be helped. I suppose," and looking him in the eye with a grin, told him, "I shall have to rely on

Matthew, or Benjamin or maybe Edward to chaperone me."

She walked away into the bedroom and it took James several minutes to calm his heart rate, he knew she was deliberately provoking him, but it did not stop the unwelcome beast of jealousy appearing on his shoulder again, whispering in his ear. It would be a long evening for him.

It was gone ten when the revellers arrived back at the Cecil and Emily was flushed and skittish. James met them in the courtyard where she linked her arm in his and pulled him along, "Darling, we are having such a wonderful evening and now I am so hungry, I could eat a horse. Have you had a beastly time? I wish you could have been with us. Limmers was crammed and The Carlton was devine, full of people deserting the Savoy, so just everybody was there. Come along, quick, let's catch up with Beth and Peter, I'm dying for a glass of champagne."

She gave him a kiss on the cheek and James hurried along, happy now that she was back, back with him. They dined well, fresh caviar, crevettes and bortsch à la Russe. Suprêmes de soles in a creamy, tomato sauce. Poulardes, fat tasty chicken stuffed with sweetbreads, livers and mushrooms, truffles with champagne and shrimp mousse. Before dessert, the band quietened, the leader headed the count down, the glasses had been charged and as midnight struck on the huge clock above, everyone raised a toast to the year 1900. The church bells rang out and as the band struck up again, James held Emily close and they kissed.

"Thank you, my sweetheart," he whispered in her ear, "thank you for making me so happy, I look forward to this new year with you, this next year and all the rest of my life."

The dinner finished, the dancing ended at three in the morning and James held her tightly as they went back to their suite. Emily was relaxed, more than a little drunk, and playful. As soon as they had closed the door behind them, she left a trail of James's clothes across the floor, his jacket, his tie, his shirt, his shoes, his socks, his trousers and, as they reached their bed, his undershirt. Their lovemaking was passionate, urgent, delicious and afterwards they slept soundly, Emily still in her shift and stockings, her arms wound around James in their sleep.

On a grey morning at the end of May that year, they were standing outside a handsome block of Mansion flats in Foley Street, "Number twelve," said James, "if you like it, it's ours." The doorman took them up to the fourth floor and let them in. Emily walked quickly into the large drawing room. "I love it. Such wonderful high ceilings darling, and it is so much nicer to be up high than on the ground floor don't you think?"

"Through here," she beckoned him, "the dining room is splendid too. Plenty of room for our friends to come."

"Let's look at the bedrooms," James called as he walked along the passageway, "ah, this is the main one here and," as he moved next door, "yes, this will be perfect for the nursery. Look sweetheart, it is an ideal size, the nurse can set up a little bed whilst baby is tiny and then look here, this small room next door can be her room later. My love, it is ideal, we shall be entirely happy here." He pulled her into his arms and leant to kiss her, but she pushed him away. "Please don't, and please do stop being so very jolly about all this. It is not you who will become fat and ugly over the next few months, it is not you who will have to endure untold agony. It is me, and I cannot say that I am as pleased as you are."

"Emily my love, you will never be fat and ugly. You are a beautiful woman and you are already looking even more ... I think they use the word 'blooming' and you are more enchanting than ever. We shall be a real family, I am so proud of you my sweet, I know we are going to be happy here. I shall tell the agent to prepare the paperwork today, you will love going shopping! You shall have everything the exact way you want it and our home will then be as perfect as you."

"What time are you meeting your brother?"

"His train arrives from Birmingham about two, he's not staying at the Cecil but he's coming over about five. Depending on how it goes, and I'm not anticipating a friendly meeting, he might stay for dinner. If he does, will you join us?"

"I can't see him wanting to meet me," Emily made a face, "any more than I want to meet him. He does sound a righteous prig, not at all like you my darling, and no doubt he'll be even worse as you didn't go to your mother's funeral."

"Well that was his doing entirely, he gave me no notice. Did not even tell me that she was so ill."

"Had you arranged to get the mail from Warwick Street earlier, you would have found the letter from your sister. I think you *will* be blamed my dear," Emily smoothed the backs of her gloves and straightened the front of her jacket, "anyway, I think I'm done here, shall we go?"

"You're a thorough disgrace James. How you could have left your mother to wonder how you were all these years I don't know. That was cruel, you are perfectly aware that she worried about you. You are still as selfish as you were as a boy. It broke her heart that Father's wine merchants left the family, all you had to do was the decent thing and take over. It's not as if you have made a success of your life, you do not appear to be a star of the stage after all. You don't have the talent, nor for your painting, nor writing. All the things you gave up a decent business for, none of them have worked and now, a private investigator? So called head of security for a hotel, a disreputable career and it's no better than you deserve." Thomas Severn stopped to draw a breath his anger palpable on his red face. "You've ignored your sisters. You caused our mother untold heartache and now you just expect to have her money. God knows what Father would have thought of you."

It was the reference to his father that made James flip, "Father? What would Father think? How dare you, how could you know what he would think, he saw something in me that you don't have, you with your narrow-minded outlook on life, your smug complacent view of a conventional life. At least John upped and got away, he did something exciting and different. What have you done, a safe apprenticeship in a boring industry, a wife and children, don't you have dreams Thomas, don't you wish you had experienced something, anything, different or brave in your life?"

"How dare *I* mention Father, you didn't know him, you were only a child when he died and ..." Thomas stopped suddenly as the door had opened and Emily came in.

"My word, there was no much shouting you did not hear me knock my love," she said gaily, smiling at James as she approached his brother her arm outstretched, "good afternoon, you must be Thomas, I'm very pleased to meet you," she thought his eyes would pop out of his head, "I am James's wife and," she smoothed her hands over her swelling belly, "soon to be the mother of his child!"

"When I thought you could not stoop any lower," Thomas glared at his brother and fought for breath, "this!"

James's shrank back under his murderous gaze, but then looked with incredulity at Emily as she spoke, "Will you stay for dinner Thomas?" She was outrageous, she was really having fun, "I'm sure you will find our chef here every bit as good as those in, where was it, oh yes, Birmingham."

James spluttered, "Emily, I don't think that's a good idea, Thomas has some papers for me and then I'm sure he would like to leave."

"You're damned right James, I'll not stay a moment longer. Here, here are the papers for your signature. If it was up to me, I would make sure you never laid a hand on a penny of this. Think yourself lucky, you and your ...," he just stopped himself, "the solicitor's name is on there, sort it out yourself. I shall never be in touch with you again. You are no brother of mine."

He stormed out of the office, the wall of tension with him. "Well, that could have gone better," Emily giggled, "oh, my darling, don't let it upset you, he is an insufferable prude. Have you looked at the papers he brought?" She picked them up, a thin sheaf with the name Edwards & Bell at the top, "we could call into Lincolns Inn Fields tomorrow?"

He kept it to himself but the whole episode had upset James dreadfully. That he was estranged from his family, almost by default rather than design, had been one thing. For his family to deliberately disown him, was quite another. The silver lining to the cloud, as Emily pointed out to him more than once, was the five hundred pounds now in his bank account.

CHAPTER 26

1900 - 1901
1901, Queen Victoria dies at age 81 after more than 63 years on the throne, and her eldest son, the Prince of Wales, formally succeeds her as King Edward VII

"**A**re you sure you shouldn't stay in bed my love, the baby is only two weeks old and Dr Fry says if you get up too soon it can cause all sorts of complications," James looked tenderly at Emily as she lay back in her bed, "I cannot bear the thought of you becoming unwell, you were so clever bringing our daughter into the world, another few days of rest is not too hard to endure is it? For all our sakes, little Victoria needs you strong and healthy and I do too," he pleaded.

"Nonsense, I feel fit as a flea and I am bored here. I've been locked away far too long, confinement is certainly the right word, I would have had more freedom had I been sentenced to hard labour in Brixton. If I am to stay here can I have a few drops of that remarkable chloroform," she winced as she shuffled position, "my back is aching such that I think it is broken, I should be much better walking around."

"This is hardly a prison my love," James ignored the question of chloroform. He had been terrified when the doctor had given into Emily's pleas for something to reduce her pain, it may have been as she said, commonplace, these days, but it had scared him badly when she got her way. He looked around the sumptuously decorated room. The legacy from his mother had given Emily a free hand furnishing the apartment in Foley Street, the wardrobe, table and bed were all of finest walnut in the latest curved, design. The carvings were of flowers and leaves and the wardrobe and drawers had beautiful, floral, bronze handles, locks and keys. They had cost a fortune! The curtains were of gold damask and at the foot of the bed was a lovely Aubusson rug with intricate detailing of roses, acanthus leaves and scrolls.

"Darling, don't take things so literally, please could you pass me my scents box, I think I'm beginning to smell like a dairy. Dr Fry assured me that this dreadful business would be over by now," she looked down at her strapped bosom, "I need a splash of Jicky."

James passed her the ornate wooden box with its etched silver trim and from the satin lined interior, she took out the little Guerlain vial, removed the stopper and dabbed her wrists with the magical fragrance. "That is so much better, it reminds me I am a woman after all."

James had always known Emily was not a conventional woman and he loved her as much because of that fact as in spite of it. She was living with him as man and wife which went against all her teaching and upbringing. In one of her more thoughtful moments, she had talked to James of her indoctrination as a child which she now scorned, the notion that women were the heart and men the mind and only together could they create the whole. She had been more than scathing that in spite of this, a man was able to survive on his own, but a woman was not. She ignored the premise that she was born to be controlled and guided by a husband and it had come therefore as no surprise to James that Emily was not about to become a traditional mother either.

He helped her out of the bed and wrapped her negligée around her. She agreed that she would sit for a while in the chair placed by the window and watch the world pass by. She looked pale, James thought too pale, and she sighed, "Eric my love, I have been taught all my life that being a mother is my basic mission in life, my profession even, that motherhood is a totally inseparable part of a woman's nature. Well you must be well aware that I do not agree, I have always gone my own way, I left my family to follow my own path and much as I am sure to love our daughter and maybe even give up my life to protect her, I refuse to give up my own self for the sake of this child."

James knelt in front of her and encircled her with his arms, "My sweetheart, I would never ask you to lose your self. It is who you are inside that I adore, the very essence of you, far more even than the beauty I see on the surface. I will love you forever and I will love our little Victoria as much as I love you."

There was a tap on the door and the nurse, Lizzie, a plump young woman from Norfolk with a kind, smiling face, her cheeks perpetually rosy, came in holding the little bundle swathed in a fine, woollen shawl.

"Here you are Mrs Severne, baby is fed and clean and looking forward to a cuddle with her Mama." She placed her in Emily's outstretched arms, "She took nearly the whole bottle this morning, such a healthy little girl. I shall come back for her when you call."

James got off his knees and drew a chair up, he leaned across and pulled the shawl away from his daughter's face, "She is beautiful," his voice was choked with emotion when he spoke, "as beautiful as her mother."

"Well I think that is a little fanciful darling. With those wisps of gingery hair and that tiny round, red face she looks more like her name, a Victoria plum!"

James laughed out loud, "That's perfect," he said running his finger down the soft baby cheek, "I shall call you Plum, you will always be my little Plum."

"Norton, you say. Let me check Auguste's register, yes, here he is *Captain* Norton." James pointed to the entry on the porter's desk at the Cecil, "he's the fellow that booked the rooms for Mr Rockefeller and his party last week, they're arriving later today and the entire hotel staff's in a spin, everyone's very excited."

Charles Arrow made a note of the details in his notebook, "Well, I hate to disappoint you but I think it's all a hoax, we're hot on the trail of an American who's been swindling hotels, shops and gullible women for the past two or three weeks. False cheques, ordering expensive clothes for himself and lady friends without paying. In fact, that's why I'm here, Asprey and Buller's say that they've sent an old suit of his here after he walked out in a new one, he had a Cecil card and room number. Calls himself Colonel Hay too, has sent some ladies' hats to you to hold onto?"

"Let me call Auguste," James had a very uneasy feeling in his stomach, "he mentioned some parcels to me yesterday. Had them sitting waiting for the Americans."

The parcels had gone and when Auguste told them that 'Captain Norton' had ordered a carriage to collect the Rockefellers from Victoria Station earlier that morning and had not yet returned, it was obvious to James that they had been duped.

"Dammit Charles, there was no way I could have caught on. I'd heard of Rockefeller of course and even said to Emily, who by the way was very keen to meet him, that it seemed unusual he was visiting London, but I only got to know a fraction of the story, there was nothing to make me particularly suspicious. Did you use a private agent to help catch him?"

"Yes, with you out of the running and Perry busy on a divorce, I gave the assignment to one of Slater's men, he did a good job. I miss coming to you though, are you ever going to get back to being a proper detective? You must prefer that to being shut up in here sorting out problems for over privileged guests and catching the odd pickpocket. It hardly taxes the brain does it?"

"You've hit a raw nerve my friend, I'm torn between doing this where I'm able to see Emily and Plum so easily, sometimes I run over twice during the day just to say hello and I'm always at home eventually at night, and going back to private work where I have to be away, often days at a time. I hate the thought that Plum will grow up without me but you're right, the tedium of being head of security is getting me down."

"You'll be losing the reputation you'd built up and losing your contacts too if you're not careful. I wouldn't leave it much longer and don't worry so much about Plum, in my experience babies, and I have four of them, have no idea about their fathers. As long as they have their mothers, that's all that matters to them."

"I think Plum relies on her nurse more than on her mother, I'm not sure Emily has quite grasped the maternal instinct idea. It's not an easy decision for me to make Charles, but you're right, it needs to be taken sooner rather than later. I must say I'd have liked to have been the one to find your American for you."

"Right, yes, back to Norton or Hay or whatever his name is, we've got a tail on him, so we'll pick him up in the next day or two. You'll be called as a witness in due course, I'll see you then."

James went back into his office, sank into his chair, put his elbows on his desk and rested his head in his hands. It was true, he needed a change.

By September 1901, Paolo Bertini had found a new head of security for the hotel and James was back, firmly established, in his offices in York Buildings.

"It's so good to have you back full time Mr Chevasse Sir," Perry had been overcome with pleasure to have his hero return, "it's not been the same here without you and I don't just mean the work has been routine and boring. I've missed Monty so much too," he bent down to stroke and pet him, "can I take him for his walk in the afternoons again, like I used to?"

"Of course, Perry, he'll be glad to be out of the Cecil I expect, although there were always a lot of people making a fuss of him and feeding him treats, so I expect he'll sulk a bit now they've stopped," he laughed. "Yes, it's good to be back."

"Teddy's not coming in until much later today Sir, he's out on surveillance for the Bennett case and expects to be over in Penge until late afternoon."

James looked down at the papers Perry had spaced out neatly on his desk, dismayed at how few enquiries there were, he said enthusiastically, "We must get the regular advertisements back into the Morning Post. I want to make some changes so let me see the old one." Perry quickly found a copy and James scanned it, "Make a note of this and get the wording over to their offices this morning. I still think it sounds right so leave the text exactly the same as before but add, *'Specially retained by solicitors, bankers & Co.'*, we need to beef up our importance, there's a lot of competition out there and also, put in we're open from ten until four, I don't want to have one of us always here outside those hours, the advertisements are going to allow us to expand, get us all out in the field, earning fees!"

"Is there anything in the pipeline Sir? We could certainly take on more cases at the present. It's been very quiet recently."

"There soon will be Perry and I'm going to form us into a proper company, Justin Chevasse & Co., we'll take on more operatives," and seeing the shadow of a frown cross the young man's face, added quickly, "no need to worry, you'll still be my principal man, I'll have you taking on some of the more complicated matters as soon as you can."

"I've done a lot of reading and learning about accounting Mr Chevasse, in my own time of course, you told me there's a lot of investigating to be done in company accounts and I'm quick with figures. I find it interesting too which Teddy doesn't, he'd rather trail people, ducking into doorways, standing outside with the rain running down his neck," Perry grinned, "I like working out the hidden numbers."

"That's excellent," James smiled back, "but in the meantime, all I've got for you this week is a summons to serve on," he looked at his note, "Oscar Treadaway. You'll have to track him down in Clapham please."

The assignments rolled in and by the end of the year, Justin Chevasse & Co. employed three new investigators. Two more men and, from Gussie Bourne, a young woman she had trained up but felt was one member of her own staff too many. "It's Connie's decision really," she had confided in James, "she's a bit jealous of Agnes, thinks she's too much 'my type'! She's not of course," Gussie laughed, "but I can't convince her of that, so my loss in your gain."

Teddy excelled at following travelling salesmen around the country, noting their spending patterns, determining if they lived within their means, the employers fearful that they were stealing from them. Perry was expert at wheedling out information on suspected parties, his subterfuge could unlock doors to financial records James had seldom been able to gain without considerable expenses of his own. Agnes was an affable young woman with endless tact, invaluable at gleaning intelligence from ladies' hairdressers, manicurists and dressmakers. The company acted for more and more prestigious clients, living up to their marketing, they were retained by leading solicitors and bankers. James increased his network of informers and watchers not just in London but in other major cities and he began a concentrated drive to find more agents across the world and take on international frauds and scandals.

CHAPTER 27

1901 - 1902
1902, Coronation of Edward VII at Westminster Abbey
1902, Lord Salisbury retires as Prime Minister
and is succeeded by Arthur Balfour

James was elated, here he was at last beginning to feel successful. He juggled his time, desperate to spend some of it each day with Plum, he was besotted with her and his heart melted each time she smiled at him and knew he was her Papa. He worshipped Emily, prepared to spend every extra penny he now earned in fulfilling as well as he could, her needs and desires but he did not see just how restless she was becoming.

Still wholly dependent on Lizzie for Plum's daily routine, Emily had found that first summer and autumn, wheeling the little girl into The Beach at the Cecil, had provided her with a new-found kudos and fascination. At one year old the baby was adorable and acted as a small magnet for attracting men and women alike to stop and sit at her table with her crowd. Plum's little face had changed from round and red to a flawless, translucent oval and was framed with blond curls,

tinged with red. Propped up in her splendid baby carriage, it's deep aquamarine coach work decorated with
fine gold detailing, and dressed in exquisite, expensive
little gowns and petticoats, Plum's eyes, the blue of
lapis lazuli, followed the goings on with great concentration. Her solemn expression elicited both comment
and laughter from her Mama's gay, mingling friends. At
the first sign of baby's fractiousness, Lizzie was summoned from her solitary station inside the arched entrance to the hotel and Plum was returned to her safe
custody, leaving Emily free to idle away her time. She
was bored, and by the time the colder, wetter weather
arrived, she left Plum with nurse more and more to
take lunches and teas with other equally bored, distraction seeking wives and mothers, all of them looking for new and amusing pastimes to fill their days.

Emily introduced them to a new distraction
in the spring. In the post one morning there was,
tucked in amongst the envelopes, a pamphlet advertising "Madam Tantzy. Unexcelled Reader of Fortunes. Recently arrived in Hampstead and Willing upon receipt
of Five Shillings to give Readings to Ladies of Quality."
She immediately contacted her friends in her crowd
and a message was sent to make an appointment later
that week. The first James got to know of this, however,
was after the event, late in the afternoon when he arrived home to find Emily in an unusually agitated state,
immediately launching into an account of her day.

The ladies had taken a carriage out to Hampstead and arriving at the row of bay fronted, terraced
houses, had opened the low wooden gate in the box
hedge, walked up the short path and rung the bell
of number thirteen. Giggling a little nervously, they

introduced themselves to an ancient, ugly woman, dressed entirely in black, who shuffled them inside and directed them to a room on the right of the hallway. The door closed behind them, the curtains were drawn keeping out the daylight and as their eyes became accustomed to the gloom provided only from the light of two candles, they could just make out an oval table covered with a lace cloth and four empty chairs. A slightly accented voice requesting them to be seated, appeared at first to be disembodied but gradually Emily could discern a hugely fat woman seated at the top of the table, her head covered in a multi coloured turban, wearing an enormous iridescent green robe which also covered much of the surrounding floor. Large leafed plants filled the corners of the room and the air was heavy with the scent of incense and herbs. They could hear soft, jangling music in the background.

"Welcome dear friends, I am Madam Tantzy, please sit, relax and free your inner minds. The spirits are happy to greet you, we shall have a most successful afternoon. But first I am afraid I must raise the ugly matter of remuneration. If you would all be so kind as to pass five shillings to my assistant, we can commence."

As they handed over the money to the old crone who had shown them in and she had left the parlour, Madam Tantzy slowly pulled back the large, black cloth covering a glass crystal ball which stood on an ornate, brass stand. She cupped her hands around it.

"I should like you to think, think very hard of the questions you wish to ask, but the spirits may only wish to tell us that which may be helpful to you at this time," she intoned and began to pass her right hand over the ball, again and again. Breathing noisily and deeply she gazed into the glass, her eyes staring, unblinking.

Emily too stared at the crystal ball, her mind was a blank, she couldn't think of a single question! She reached her hands out to hold Lydia's on one side and Beth on the other and sensed Olivia take Lydia's other hand. The silence seemed to last forever but eventually Madam Tantzy spoke, "I see an old woman, she is to be my spirit guide, she wants to be remembered to her daughter. She passed only recently," Lydia nudged Beth and raised her eyebrows excitedly. Tantzy looked directly at Beth, "She wishes you to know you were a good daughter and she thanks you." There was another short silence and as Olivia whispered something to Lydia, the medium wailed, "I see a child, they are looking for their Mama."

Emily heard Olivia give a gasp and the medium continued, "The child says they are happy in the spirit world, they have many toys to play with," she glanced up to where the gasp had come from, "many people to love them."

"Is it a little boy?" Olivia asked anxiously, "about three years old?"

"Yes, yes, a little boy, he has a toy train in his hand, he says he loves his Mama, he has not forgotten you. He has gone now he has run to meet his friends."

Olivia took her handkerchief and wiped her eyes, little sobs escaping her lips.

Madam Tantzy ran her hands back and forth again over the glass ball, and spoke in an eerie voice, "Ah, the mist is clearing again. I can see a figure it is a man. He is coming to say here what he was unable to say in the real world. He is not tall, but not short. Fair haired I think, but not too fair, nor too dark. He is holding out his hand, he wants to take yours," she looked up secretly from under her eyelashes, all four guests were spellbound, eyes fixed on her, no obvious signs, and she looked down again, "he is saying he is sorry. He wants your forgiveness for his sins, he knows he has deceived, he has hurt his family. He has done wrong."

"Is he still living?" Lydia asked in a small voice, "or has he passed over?"

"I shall ask him," Madam Tantzy answered slyly, "he is worried only for you and those around you, not for himself. He is saying ... I cannot hear him, alas, he is fading, I cannot see him anymore, he is gone." Slumping back into her chair, Madam Tantzy closed her eyes and within seconds she made a soft snoring noise. The door opened, the crone reappeared and showed the friends out.

Emily was almost beside herself with panic, how on earth could this stranger know that James tormented himself with guilt that they were not married, that his precious daughter Plum was illegitimate, a bastard child. She had never told a living soul. Her mind was in such turmoil as they climbed back into their carriage that she didn't notice Lydia was also flustered, her face drained, her mind in parallel to Emily's wondering how this stranger could possibly know of her clandestine, married lover. Beth commented briefly, only to express disappointment that her question, 'will I ever be free of my odious husband' was not answered, but the void was filled with Olivia, who was openly crying and talking, overcome with joy that her baby boy was happy, that he remembered his Mama and loved her. She had no reason to wonder how this stranger could have known, she was convinced she had concentrated so hard on asking her question, that her child had appeared in Madam's crystal ball.

Having listened to Emily's detailed description of the afternoon James did his best to comfort and assure her that she was giving it all far more credibility than the episode deserved. He was angry, "There are far too many of these charlatans around, preying on the fears and anxieties of trusting women like you," he soothed her, stroking her cheek with his hand, "you cannot believe them. They take a general idea and leave the rest up to you to interpret, to imagine. You chose to think the man saying sorry and asking forgiveness was me. Well I can assure you it was not, I've been hard at work all afternoon, not conjuring myself up into a glass ball in Hampstead!"

He was pleased that brought a little smile to his beloved's face, "It's all a trick my sweetheart, you must not be upset about it. These pretenders are clever, they learn how people think, they know how to prey on someone's fears and hopes. There is no truth in any of it, not crystal balls, cards or palm reading, they are all tricks and a way to steal your money. This phoney was undoubtedly a good actress. She would have to be to convince *you* my love, you are not a silly woman, you could not be easily tricked. Promise me you will stay away from all this nonsense from now on. Please, I cannot bear to think of you being upset like this, we are a proper, secure family. You, me and Plum, we are invincible, and no harm will come to any of us, I shall make sure of that."

The next day in his office, still outraged, he was

discussing the matter with Agnes and Perry, "How can we deal with this vile cheat? It is not as easy to prove as with the conmen who hold seances and levitate a body by means of wires and a pulley, this is all deceiving the mind. But it's dangerous deception and a damnable dishonest way to make a living. It's not just the gullible they prey on, they deceive ordinary, sensible women too."

"From what I remember, they can be prosecuted under the vagrancy act. Why that act I don't know but let me look it up." Perry left James's office and returned a few minutes later with a fat, leather bound book which he was leafing through. "Yes, here it is, and he read, 'Every person pretending or professing to tell fortunes, or using any subtle craft, means, or device, by palmistry or otherwise, to deceive and impose on any of his Majesty's subjects, shall be deemed a rogue and vagabond. Excerpt from The Vagrancy Act of 1824'. Well, she fits that bill. How shall we go about it?"

"I can go along," Agnes said, "Perry can pretend to be my husband, we can make encouraging noises when she says something about, what? What will our problem be? I know, we are desperate for a child, let's pretend it's that. From what you've told us Mr Chevasse, your wife or one of her friends must have inadvertently given the woman a clue or two along the way, certainly to centre on a dead child. It is so cruel to do that to the poor woman."

"Although that did seem to give her some comfort," Perry wasn't necessarily playing devil's advocate, "but the friend, the one who believed it to mean her husband is a bigamist," James had adapted Emily's story of course, "that's downright, unkind deception and this so called medium needs to be stopped." He looked at Agnes, "Yes, 'Mrs Danvers', let's go get our fortune told, if she buys into our false story, we can tell Mr Arrow and will be able to give our evidence in court. But," he grinned, "when we go, could you possibly wear a dress instead of those bloomers, no wife of mine would be seen dead in 'em!"

The matter was concluded some weeks later when Elsie White, alias Madam Tantzy, was taken to court, charged under the vagrancy act, found guilty and sentenced to three months with labour.

After the visit to Hampstead, James watched Emily spend a difficult time, her mind full of worry about her and Plum's legal status. She and James had from the very beginning slipped into an unspoken understanding that this would never be mentioned, that love would conquer all, but during those few weeks it festered on her mind. Her Catholic qualms, long since relegated to the very back of her conscience, reawakened and disturbed her. When summer arrived, she pretended her anxiety had faded and she chose to mock the whole cult of fortune telling with her friends, maintaining that it was all a sham, a dishonest money making fraud, but deep down the little niggle that there just might be some truth in it, stayed with her.

There was a definite change in the air since the old Queen had died the previous year and the country was looking forward to the Coronation of King Edward VII in August. It had been postponed from the original date at the end of June when the King had suddenly been taken into hospital with appendicitis, but the arrangements were now in full swing. The streets were decked with flags and flowers, visitors flocked into the city and the Cecil Hotel finalised arrangements for the coronation celebrations taking place on the ninth. Emily loved a party, and this was one she was determined not to miss nor was she prepared to spare any expense for such an auspicious occasion.

The evening was to be the highlight of the proceedings, but James was insistent that they go during the morning, as a family, to watch the Procession in State. They were lucky to have an invitation from a Swiss industrialist to watch from the balcony of his rented rooms in a magnificent house in Great George Street. From here, the assembled guests would be afforded a superb view without the indignities of standing in bustling, noisy crowds at the side of the road. As Justin Chevasse, James was Herr Gerber's current saviour, he had, only a month before, prevented a very unseemly scandal involving his daughter, Rosa.

Whilst dressing early that morning and in response to yet another anxious remark, James reassured Emily, "Plum is quite old enough to be with us, it is a great occasion for us all. There has not been a coronation in the whole of my lifetime."

"Well I'm sure there will be more in hers," Emily raised her eyebrows and made a face, "I can't see Edward reigning for sixty-four years like his mother did, he's sixty already!"

They had been obliged to arrive at their host's well before the crowds blocked the streets, and for the long wait ahead, the dozen guests were in festive mood. The weather was fine, most fortunately it was dry, and they all settled down in the spacious drawing room enjoying coffee and cakes. Lizzie was in another room with Plum, comparing her child's prowess with three other nurses and their charges. Finally, the sound of the fanfares reached them and crowding to the balcony and the windows, Plum held tightly in James's arms, they saw the first of the coaches pass by. The little girl was thrilled by the sights and sounds of the horses, their harnesses jangling and their hooves clattering on the road. She loved the roar of the crowd and the music of the bands playing as the carriages moved slowly along the street bordered by sailors standing straight as ram rods.

Questions and cries filled the air, "Who is who? Can you see who is in that carriage?". "Is that the new Prince and Princess of Wales and their sons?". "Is that the King of Denmark?". "No, he's not coming, that's Queen Alexandra's brother I should think.". "I heard most of the foreign delegations went home after the cancellation in June?". "That's right, they've not come back. We've more of our own soldiers, marines and sailors out instead.". "So many Dukes and Duchesses". "Oh, how beautiful the Royal Coach is, can you see the King?". "Can you see the Queen?" All too soon the entourage had passed by and their faces wreathed in smiles, James and Emily returned Plum to Nurse and joined their fellow revellers for Herr Gerber's celebratory luncheon.

CHAPTER 28

1902
Britain has crushed Boer resistance and the Treaty of
Vereeniging, officially ends the second Boer War

L ater that afternoon, James sat in the rocking
chair in the little nursery, Plum was sleeping
peacefully in the crook of his arm and Monty
lying by his feet. He had been telling the baby a tale involving the family of kittens he had painted as a frieze
around the centre of the room, pretty little creatures
all dressed in tiny, detailed dresses, hats, trousers and
jackets, some enjoying a picnic on lush green grass,
with hills and lakes in the distance, or playing on
swings, with fluffy balls or hoops. Perfect scenes of a
perfect childhood and the childhood James was promising his own sweet daughter. He kissed her gently on
the forehead and handed the soft, warm bundle to Lizzie, then tip toed out of the room and went to find
Emily. Monty stayed behind, he had adored this tiny
person since the first time she had crawled to him on
the floor, put her plump little fingers in his ears, probed
his eyes and nose and joyfully held onto handfuls of his
fur. He had inhaled her unique scent and she became

an equal first and most important person in his life. He would defend her forever as he would defend his master.

Emily was still in her boudoir and called for James to come in when he tapped on the door. He stopped in his tracks and looked at the woman he regarded, absolutely and completely, as his wife. Her slender body curved like a letter S, he had thought she could not look any more beautiful than she had earlier in the day, but looking at her now, she took his breath away. She stood looking at her reflection in the long mirror, her vibrant, forest green, silk gown hugging her figure and falling gracefully to the floor where it fanned out, her silk shoes peeping out from underneath. The décolletage was daringly low, edged with a froth of palest apricot organza which also formed two thin straps over her shoulders. From the bodice, draped around her upper arms as if it were a stole, were two garlands of matching green silk roses with apricot centres, placed exactly above the tops of her long, apricot silk gloves. Her hair was swept up on top of her head in an elaborate, pompadour style with a single apricot organza rose pinned into one side. Emily smoothed the dress over her tight, flat stomach, smiled at herself satisfied with the image and without looking at him, said to James, "I thought my emeralds? Do you?"

Overcome with desire, James fastened the simple, diamond and emerald drop pendant round her neck and bent to kiss the nape, nuzzling into the warmth and sensuous softness of her skin. His arms enfolded her tiny waist and he moved to turn her, to pull her close, to drink in her heady perfume but was pushed calmly, but firmly away.

"Now, now Eric," she laughed, "I haven't spent all this time dressing to please you, for you to mess it all up before we go out! No, no, not even just a little kiss, you'll smudge my powder," she wriggled out of his reach, "you'll have to be patient, I cannot turn up to the ball with my hair bedraggled and my gown awry, whatever would people think? That's no way for a respectable *wife* to act is it?" She took his hand and pulled him to the door, come along downstairs, it's almost time for our carriage."

The Palm Court at the Cecil was decorated with red, white and blue bunting and already buzzing when they arrived. It took quite some half an hour to walk across the room, there were so many acquaintances to stop and speak with on the way, but eventually they reached the cluster of tables reserved for them and greeted the group of friends they were to share the evening with. They made three sets of twelve and James and Emily had a very jolly table, sitting with Charles and Fanny Arrow, Gussie and Connie - who had taken the place of Martin Richards and his wife who had cried off at the last minute, scarlet fever in the house - and from the crowd, Beth and Lydia with their husbands. The sixth couple were unknown to James, friends of Lydia's, Johnny Rollinson and his sister, Alice, and they proved to be the couple with the most tantalising gossip of the day.

Johnny Rollinson was a one-time schoolteacher who had given up what he referred to as 'the thankless task of trying to instil knowledge into the brains of unwilling savages', to take up the less noble calling of hotel management. He was at present one of several under managers at The Savoy. Alice taught piano to private pupils from their home and the father of one of her more talented protégées, was a chorister seconded to boost the numbers singing at Westminster Abbey that very morning. They had met up during the afternoon and the Rollinson's heard first-hand of the minor fiascos that had occurred during the coronation service. These mostly involved the Archbishop of Canterbury who had refused to delegate any part of his duties even though he was extremely elderly, infirm and with failing eyesight, in fact, not far off blind.

The meal was well under way and Johnny was in full flow, "The poor old boy had to be supported by two other bishops and when he knelt down to pay homage," he convulsed with laughter, "when he knelt down, he couldn't ...couldn't get back up and the King, yes the King himself had to help him up!"

As the friends joined in howling with laughter, Alice broke in, "That wasn't the worst of it, Johnny, tell them about the crown!"

"Oh, the crown," he controlled his face, "the crown! When he put it on the King's head, ... he put it on back to front."

James thought Gussie would fall off her chair she was laughing so much, Emily was holding her sides squealing, "Oh stop, stop. It hurts too much. How embarrassing, did he take it off again or did he leave it?"

"He turned it round and one of the other bishops asked him if he was alright and the Archbishop practically shouted 'go away' at him. Everyone could hear."

"Poor man," said Fanny kindly, "I feel a little sorry for him - but I would love to have been there," she giggled, "must be a first for the crown to be put on the wrong way around."

"It wasn't just Archbishop Temple who made a mess of things," Alice grinned, "apparently Princess Beatrice dropped her service book from the Royal gallery, and it landed on a gold-plated table. Made the devil of a clatter and caused more hilarity I expect. How people didn't laugh out loud in the Abbey I don't know, I'm sure I would have found it hard not to."

Calming down, the conversation moved on and flowed as freely as the wine but James was waiting for the evening to end, he wanted to take his gorgeous wife home. He wanted to take her away from the intense gaze of Johnny Rollinson.

"Justin, you're not listening to me," Gussie said a little exasperated, "I asked if you knew where Sylvia and Florence had moved to."

"What, oh, sorry Gussie, I was miles away," he took his eyes away from Emily, "Sylvia you say? No, I didn't know they had moved, thought they were still in Bayswater? I haven't been in touch since before I met Emily ... I'm sure you understand why?"

"Of course, I just thought you might have known. Sylvia must be travelling again. I haven't seen hide nor hair of her for months. I suppose as a private detective I should be able to track her down," she guffawed and Constance looked at her and frowned, "sorry Connie, didn't mean to be so loud!" She turned again to James, "Let me know if you hear anything and you can take your eyes off your wife you know, she's not going anywhere!"

"Do you know anything about Rollinson?" He asked her, "not sure I care much for the fellow, too damned handsome and ... precise."

It was true, Johnny Rollinson was immaculate. Tall and well built, his short, dark brown hair was parted perfectly to the side and combed neatly. His dark eyes were warm and open and beneath his perfectly proportioned straight nose sat a flawlessly trimmed moustache. This was teamed perfectly with an equally well groomed, pointed, goatee beard. The total impression was of precision rather than passion, but undeniably attractive. Without a grey hair in sight, James guessed him to be about ten years younger than him, Emily's age.

The orchestra was about to play a tune he recognised and thinking he could muster a passable waltz to this, he stood and asked Emily to join him on the dance floor. His own appearance was the antithesis of the other man, his hair was slightly longer and casual, his face clean-shaven with a sultry, sensual demeanour. Together with Emily's undoubted beauty they made a striking couple and the admiring glances drawn from men and women alike, wiped away his insecurities for a moment, only for them to return four-fold when they returned to their table. Alice was talking of her new-found interest in modern music and whether or not she could dare to teach it to her pupils.

"Eric my darling, you are such a dinosaur, rag-time is *the* music of the times." Emily rebuked him when he admitted his ignorance, "It's all the rage, especially in America, and they've got new dances for it too. Johnny, you explain it to him, I know you can play Scott Joplin on the piano."

"Better than that," he answered, "the band are about to play the *Maple Leaf Rag*," he looked at James, "if I may be allowed to borrow your wife, we could show you how to dance to it?"

Emily's lovely face was lit up with pleasure and she began to rise from her chair. At James's polite acquiescence, she put her hand on Johnny's arm and they walked to the centre of the dance floor.

The orchestra struck up, the dancers clapped with delight, Johnny Rollinson put his arm around Emily's back and James felt a cramp of panic in the pit of his stomach and thought for a moment he would collapse. He felt Gussie shaking his arm, "Justin, are you ill? You look white as a sheet. Would you like to get some air, I could do with some myself."

The rest of the party had become a blur for James, the cool, night air had cleared his head a little and he had gone through the motions of polite conversation, had partaken of more brandy than was wise and had been greatly relieved at two in the morning when word came that their carriages awaited them. Emily was in wonderful high spirits and chattering incessantly. She had had a 'heavenly' time and thanked James over and over for being so good to her, for taking her to such a marvellous party, but when he went with her to the door of her bedroom, she sighed, "Darling, I'm exhausted, I cannot keep my eyes open another second." She kissed his cheek, "I really must sleep, it has been such a long, incredible day."

He could not let go of her hand and he battled with the voice inside his head. He knew he should not say anything, but the demon won, "Emily I love you with all my heart, do you still love me? I could not bear to see you dancing with that ... boy ... do you really think me a dinosaur? I am not that many years older than you, please don't say you have tired of me." He was practically sobbing, "My dearest love, you mean the world to me, I only want to make you and our beautiful daughter happy."

Emily hesitated, then smiled broadly, "Whatever has brought this on! I have no feelings for that 'boy' although I might add that he is twenty-nine, the same age as me, so hardly a youngster! It is just that he is a splendid dancer, I was enjoying the new craze and you have to agree, he and his sister were particularly entertaining at dinner. His account of the coronation was hilarious." She shook her hand free of James's grasp and brought both her hands up to cup his face, "You are a silly goose, there is no need for jealousy. You are my love, you and that poppet asleep in her crib in the nursery. You are my family, now please off you go, I am exhausted. No more of this nonsense."

CHAPTER 29

1902
Discovery Expedition: British explorers Scott,
Shackleton and Wilson reach the furthest southern
point reached thus far by man, south of 82°S

Blackmail would presumably always be unexpected, but when it confronted James, after Emily had, if not come to terms with the irregularities of their relationship, at least stopped fretting about it on a daily basis, it came as a huge bolt out of the blue. One cold but dry December afternoon, he had taken Monty for a walk along the Thames Embankment and was coming through the Watergate into the public gardens on his way back towards the office when he was confronted by a large, middle aged woman, dressed in fine but plain clothes which had seen better days, and who looked a little familiar.

"Mr Chevasse?" She was tall enough to look him directly in the eye, and ignoring Monty's warning growl, she continued, "You don't recognise me then? You ruin my life and then I am forgotten, you don't care a jot what happens to me?"

"Madam," he replied and tried to move forward,

but she stood directly in front of him, blocking his way, "I would ask you to step aside. I do not know you and more to the point, I do not wish to know you." He made as if to brush her aside with his walking cane, but she stood her ground.

"Well I know you Mr Justin Chevasse and I know a great deal about you, facts I'm sure your *so-called wife* would not want broadcast amongst her circle of snobbish friends."

Immediately, she had James's attention. His heart beginning to beat a little faster, he studied her face closely but still had no recollection of her. "Who are you and what do you want?"

"Perhaps we could go to the Ship and Shovell, I could do with a drop of brandy to warm my bones, it's cold down by the river today. We can have a nice talk there and I can remind you of the errors of your ways."

James's first instinct had been to push the woman aside and ignore her but here was someone threatening to harm his family, he put his cane back on the ground. Then, taking a deep breath to calm himself he said, "You can talk here if you have something to say but first, I demand to know who you are."

"I'll tell you who I am and then I think we should go and have that brandy, you'll not want to conduct our business here in the street, all these listening ears around us. My name is Elsie White, I'm surprised you don't recognise me, but maybe four months hard labour at His Majesty's pleasure has changed my appearance more than I thought." She saw the blank look still on James's face, "Madame Tantzy, now you remember? But I have not used my psychic powers to learn your secrets, so, shall we go to the hostelry for sustenance?"

It was only a few minutes' walk to the public house and James's mind was in turmoil. He remembered only too well Emily's distress after that afternoon in Hampstead, she had believed this charlatan knew all about their lives and although he never thought for one moment it was through a crystal ball, he needed to find out what this harridan did know. They sat at a table in the corner of the smallest bar, a feeble fire smouldering in the hearth, brandy in front of them both, and she told him.

"We have a mutual acquaintance Mr Chevasse. You know him, he is a man of the cloth, in Spitalfields. Ring a bell?" She leered.

"The vicar? That degenerate? You know him?"

"Yes, Gervase Maddock is my brother. I took the opportunity to leave my no-good husband and came up to London at the same time when the parish asked him, oh, ever so nicely, to leave Puckington. The landlord's wife used to be a good friend of mine, not now though." She poured some water from a jug into her brandy and took a long slug from the rummer, "Gervase was very helpful to me in my line of work until you put a stop to it. I've been hounded by your policeman ever since I got out of prison even though I've changed my name and rented different rooms. They know where I am. I can't earn a living no more. My brother used to tip me off if he heard of anyone up to no good. You'd be surprised," she drank again, wiped her mouth on the back of a grubby hand, and smiled unpleasantly, "or perhaps *you* wouldn't be, at the number of bigamists there are out there these days. I would make sure to send them all one of my leaflets, come and have your fortune told I'd say and when they knew I had their secrets, they paid

well for my silence. I sent an invitation to your dear
wife, but your interference put a stop to my little plan
there, so I had no alternative, I've come direct to you
instead."

James had drained his glass and stood up to go, "I
am no bigamist, you are misinformed."

"A bigamist no! But I am aware you almost were.
But that is not the point, the matter at hand is the best
interests of your child. A daughter I believe. The one
your, what shall we call her, your *harlot*," she raised her
eyebrows, "the child your unmarried harlot has borne
you, not your legal wife."

James sat down heavily, as if his legs had been
whipped from under him, "My daughter is of no concern to you. How dare you mention her from your filthy
mouth."

"So sorry if I've offended you Mr Chevasse, but
you see, she is just a general *bastard.* Such ugly words, I
much prefer to say, illegitimate. You see, I am not a sav-
age, I have standards. No matter, whichever word we
want to use," she was taunting James, "the *shame* will
be the same for Emily Drake. The *scandal,* the *ignominy*
when all her fancy, *respectable,* friends find out you are
not married, that the child is not your lawful daughter? And the poor girl herself, growing up knowing her
shame. How will she find a suitable husband?"

James was speechless, he poured himself more
brandy from the bottle, added no water and drank the
glassful in one go, "What do you want?"

"That's better Mr Chevasse, I was sure you would
see reason. I think five nice sovereigns would help clear
my memory, yes, I'm sure I could become very forget-
ful for that amount. Shall we say, here again, tomorrow,

same time, same table?"

When she had gone, James sat and thought. He could not, he would not, allow himself to be blackmailed. He understood how it worked, this would be the first of many demands, the woman would return again and again. However, it would take time to gather his own defence on the matter and in the meantime, he could not take the chance that this information would be made public. This time, he would have to pay the wretch her gold.

"Sweetheart I'm sorry, but I will only be gone a few days, five at the most. It is an important case and I cannot leave it all up to Perry. Besides, he is busy on another delicate matter and I cannot let him delay his enquiries there, the fee will be substantial if we can finish ahead of schedule." Even at this stressful time it was foremost in James's mind that income was desperately needed, Emily was enslaved to shopping, he never knew what would arrive each day in the Harrods or Fortnum & Mason's bags. "No," he said softly, taking her hands and kissing her lightly, "I must do this myself and I promise, I shall make it up to you."

"That's what you always say when you go away," she answered rather sulkily, "it is very tiresome being left alone here, with only Plum to talk to."

"I'm sure you will find entertainment with your crowd, it seems to me you are playing bridge everyday. You will be impossible to partner when I get back, you will be so advanced. But for now, I have packed my bag, I leave first thing in the morning."

The previous day James had paid a visit to Willy Clarkson's theatrical costumiers in Wellington Street. When he was struggling to become an actor, he had known Willy's father, a skilled perruquier and from time to time he had borrowed costumes and wigs from his shop. He had not met Willy junior before and was amused by the tiny, pompous man who greeted him. He had lush, red, wavy hair, which James guessed was a toupée, a curly moustache, a fully dyed and crimped beard and his face was patently powdered and rouged. However, Willy listened to his customer's requirements and Justin Chevasse left an hour or so later carrying a parcel of clergyman's robes and collar, a sparse, grey hair wig, two little tufts of grey hair for his cheek bones, a black kohl pencil to fabricate blackened eyebrows and the instruction to collect a few small stones to put inside his shoe should he think the addition of a credible limp would be helpful. He had declined the suggestion of putty, moulded to a bulbous nose shape and covered in make-up, he was not likely to be recognised where he was going, he just would not want to be remembered as he really was.

He took the morning train from Paddington to Taunton where, tired and hungry from the journey with its frequent stops and incessant passengers, he took a room, initially for two nights, at the Great Western Hotel. Here he ate a late supper and retired for the night, only to lie in his bed and rehearse again his 'performance' for the next day. He was up for an early breakfast and then dressed in his disguise, carrying a small leather bag containing an essential repair kit of glue and eyebrow pencil together with his notebook and pen, the 'Reverend Joseph Adams' boarded a train on the local Chard branch line, alighted at Ilminster late morning and took the only transport available, a horse and cart, for the last two and a half miles to

Puckington. Here, he went straight to St Andrews to keep his appointment with the incumbent, the Reverend Cole, who immediately took him to the vicarage for a very passable lunch prepared by his wife.

James's cover story was that as a vicar, presently stationed in the north of England he was on his way to Exeter to stay with an acquaintance and realising he would pass so close to the parish of South Bradon, next door to Puckington, where he was told he might have ancestors graves, he had decided to make this small diversion to come and pay his respects.

"I am grateful to you for your hospitality, my interest is particularly in the family of Joseph Adams who left here for London almost a hundred years ago."

"I'm afraid you may need more specific information than that, we have several branches of the Adams family, they reach all over Somerset now. It would be difficult to say which of them are your relatives," Reverend Cole chuckled, "I wish you luck, there must be twenty Joseph Adams still within a ten-mile radius!"

"Maybe it would narrow it down to say my branch is connected to the Maddock family? I should like to walk in the graveyard, tread on the same ground as my forefathers. I was rather intrigued to do this when I crossed paths with the Reverend Gervase Maddock, now vicar in a poor parish in London"

Cole remained silent, he looked at James uncertainly, "That's a name I haven't heard for a few years, nor, I am afraid would I wish to hear it," he said eventually, "Is your interest in fact in him rather than your ancestors?"

Fortunately for James, the pre luncheon schooner of sherry together with the generous quantity of claret consumed with the meal, loosened his host's tongue and the whole sorry tale came flooding out. Cole had been moved into St Andrew's when Maddock had been ousted. Thinking he was speaking with a fellow clergyman, he furnished James with all the damning information and he, professing outrage, asked if he might speak with some of the parishioners so badly wronged. Cole told him the name and whereabouts of the abandoned wife and family, the abandoned husband of the woman now living as Maddock's wife in London and, as a bonus, some of those innocent bystanders who had been swindled by him.

He needed to speak with them and realising there would not be enough time that afternoon, he enquired if there was a local inn where he could stay the night.

"My dear fellow, you must stay here with us, my wife will be delighted to have company other than her old husband, and then you can continue your visit to South Bradon early tomorrow." Cole got up and bustled to call his wife, "No, I'll not take no for an answer, your room and dinner will be ready for you when you return later. No, I insist."

That evening, after a very convivial dinner, James retired to his comfortable but draughty bedroom and before getting into bed, transformed the rough scribbles from his notebook into detailed notes. Each item written on a new index card, each one, in his usual thorough manner, headed and dated. The next day he would interview more victims and add the information to the stack of cards, ready to be filed away. Later that month, back in London, he added to his bundle. The cards procured from his clandestine enquiries in the Spitalfield's parish. This time, he had allowed Willy Clarkson to transform him into a bulbous nosed, red headed, penny a week insurance policy salesman. He found out most of the necessary, damaging intelligence from a disenchanted, bitter, mother of six children who rued the day she had left Somerset with the local vicar! She had pocketed James's sovereign greedily, she would not be mentioning the visit to Maddock when he returned home.

Back in his office James compiled a file with all the evidence gathered from Somerset and Spitalfields, together with records of Elsie White's conviction. He wrote a detailed account of her blackmail demands, time, place and money received. He put the file, labelled 'Victoria Severne - Insurance' in his cabinet and turned the key. He didn't know when the next demand for money would come, but he knew it would and he would be ready to squash it with his own threats of exposure and without the danger of his own secrets coming to light.

CHAPTER 30

1903
England's conservatives, opposed to autonomy
for the Irish, pass a land reform law for Ireland,
hoping this will delay or prevent the Irish acquiring
anything like independence.

When Elsie White came back to him next spring demanding another payment, James took the time to explain in detail all the evidence he had gathered on the Maddock family and ensure she understood the drastic penalties that awaited her, her brother and their entire family should she breathe a word of his business to anyone. She left without money but with the certain knowledge, and prospect, of a long prison sentence should she speak out.

James kept the whole episode to himself, certain it was over and content that his office held sufficient information to prevent a scandal. He could tell that Emily had long ago stopped thinking or worrying about Madame Tantzy's revelation and was, as was her wont, concentrating on enjoying life. Plum was an enchanting little girl, pretty and clever, a little chatterbox who still loved nothing more than sitting on her Papa's lap, reading together before bedtime. Every time, it brought back the soft, faint memories for James and he hoped fervently that he and Plum would share their close bond for ever. It was plain to him that Emily did not share his desire for a cosy, domestic, family life. She was determined to remain her old self, a fun loving, bright young thing and she was lucky enough to have several friends who felt the same way, her crowd provided her with the excitement and stimulation she craved. James began to feel more and more insecure and increasingly he could not stop these feelings manifest themselves in jealous questions, outbursts and pleadings. He convinced himself the only way to keep her was to find entertainment to please her and that autumn he was able to combine work with what he anticipated would be a highlight in Emily's year.

The gentleman sitting bolt upright in one of the soft leather visitor chairs opposite Justin Chevasse, was tall and thin, with ebony hair groomed with Macassar oil, parted in the middle and slicked back either side. He sported a precise, black moustache above his small, thin lips and peered at James with a slightly superior air, from time to time tapping the end of his fat cigar onto the edge of the large, round, black marble ashtray.

"You understand the problem, my dear fellow," he said, "I really must have those letters returned to me. They're not what you might call in popular parlance, love letters, don't think I am that naive, just notes of when and where we were to meet. I never thought she would wish to keep them, but she did, and they could land me in all sorts of hot water if the," he lowered his voice a notch, "lady in question, were to allow them to fall into the wrong hands." He gave James what he meant to be a knowing grin, "Seems my little kitten is decidedly upset at me ending our little dalliance and has become a tiger, but I'm sure you understand, it all became far more serious in her pretty little head than I ever meant it to." He puffed on his cigar, and blowing the smoke towards the ceiling, looking up he said, "She has assured me she will sing like a canary if I withdraw my attentions from her and I am, I'm afraid to say, rather reliant on her husband's investments in my company. It will spell disaster for me if he were to have proof of my indiscretion with his wife."

From the first glance, James did not care for this boor, but he disliked blackmailers with a vengeance and assured the gentleman that he would devise a plan to retrieve the careless notes. He warned that this could take some time and advised him not to be too hasty in his retreat from the lady. When his visitor had left, he headed up a new series of index cards: Mr Malcolm Harrington - Scottish Banker, Mrs Venetia Harrington and Harrington Manor, Marlow, Buckinghamshire. He had a lot of research to carry out, Perry could help.

The necessity for James to maximise his income to allow Emily to lead the life she wished for, had led to a pleasant revival of his love of journalism and writing. Over the preceding few years he had managed to build a minor reputation with some of the better publications, whilst at the same time providing less erudite, fictional pieces for the popular, sensation loving masses. He enjoyed writing theatre reviews but these were few and far between as, since Emily had made the decision to give up acting, she was reluctant to attend the theatre or music hall and James not wishing to be away from her for any time more than totally necessary, sacrificed his love of the stage to stay with her.

He mulled over how he could gain access to the home of Mr and Mrs Harrington to find the offending letters and the plan he came up with involved an assignment for Country Life. He had been introduced to the owner of the magazine at his Masonic Lodge a couple of years before, and through this overture, one or two articles he had written on racing, the sport of kings, had been accepted and printed. Now, he needed two things. Firstly, a personal introduction to the Harringtons and secondly, in order to provide a credible reason should it be checked, an interest by the magazine editor for an article on Harrington Manor for their popular property section.

The late July day being fine and not too warm, James had arranged to meet Gussie, "For the sake of tradition," she had laughed, at the bench in Kensington Gardens where they had first met ten years before. The beginning of their great friendship.

"As the Hon. Augusta Bourne," he feigned a bow, "you do, I am well aware, know everybody who's anybody in this land."

"And you want my help I suppose, as usual!" She grinned widely as James raised his eyebrows with indignation, "When you want something done, ask a woman!'

They laughed, Gussie was petting Monty behind his ears, her bicycle parked behind them as on that first meeting.

"Not something *done* this time, I need to pick your 'who's who' brain. Do you happen to know Malcolm Harrington or his wife? Banker with Willis Perceval in Lombard Street or his wife Venetia? Their country seat is Harrington Manor, on the Thames at Marlow."

She thought, gazing blankly out at the Long Water, "Hm. I know the name, but I don't think I've ever met them. How long have they been at Marlow?"

"Not long I suppose, couple of hundred years, upstarts really!" James and Gussie laughed together, "I need to get Eric Severne an introduction. I want to write about their Manor for Country Life. Thought you'd have them on your list."

"Leave it with me Justin, I'll put out some feelers, someone told me it only takes six friends of a friend to make a connection. I'll be able to test the theory. In the meantime, how is life in Foley Street?"

James didn't so much as confide in Gussie over the years, he reacted to her uncanny perceptions of situations and she had sensed for some time Emily's restlessness, her constant searching for something. Something, the nature of which, Gussie thought, Emily did not know herself. "How's that gorgeous child of yours? I saw her a couple of weeks ago, she is delightful and very forward. Shouldn't you be looking for a governess rather than that dull-witted nurse?"

"Nurse is just fine for now she loves Plum and Plum adores her. We think we will make the change next year, when she's four. That's plenty soon enough."

"I daresay the Norfolk girl will be happy to stay with you, but you have to be careful your daughter doesn't become too fond of her, it will be more upsetting when she has to leave." Gussie saw James's face, "That's the end of my parenting advice. What would

I know? Except, I remember being heartbroken when my Nursie left! Has the lustrous Emily found a new interest to keep her busy?"

"Is it so obvious she is not content being a wife and mother Gussie? She loves Plum, I know she does, but she's not happy with her own company, she needs people around her to feel alive. She has no interest in embroidery or scrap booking any more but is obsessed with playing bridge and so she does meet new people, although she has a regular partner," James's voice dropped away and he made a fuss of Monty, "and she plays the piano. She learnt when she was young of course but is having lessons again, from her card partner, Alice Rollinson."

Gussie's heart went out to him. She had heard the rumours about Emily and John Rollinson, "It may be a short-lived interest, your lovely girl is like a butterfly, flitting from one passion to another. Don't worry." She got up to go and patted him on the shoulder, "I will be in touch as soon as I can on the other matter and notice how restrained I have been, I have not asked why you need this introduction!"

"That's professionalism Miss Bourne, I would expect nothing less from you, a Hon!"

Within the week James had in his possession, an offer from the editor of Country Life inviting him to submit, with no obligation on their part to print, a two-thousand-word article on Harrington Manor and an introduction to Venetia Harrington. Venetia Beynon as she had been then, was an old school chum of one of Gussie's cousins who had been delighted to help. The cousin had written immediately to introduce Eric Severne, her praise of his character and integrity such that she might have known him intimately herself, and tantalised Venetia with the prospect of their beautiful home featuring in the prestigious magazine.

James was expecting a note to which, in reply, he would write and ask permission to visit the Manor one afternoon, to gently interview one or other of the owners and make notes on the history of the house, the architecture and gardens. He was therefore surprised to receive in the very first instance, a fulsome letter, written in large round letters on pale blue notepaper, from Mrs Harrington warmly inviting him and his wife to attend a Saturday to Monday shooting party on the nineteenth of September. Not absolutely sure in his mind that this was a sensible idea, he nonetheless persuaded himself to accept in the certain knowledge that Emily would be overjoyed at the prospect of the occasion, and his overriding motivation, as always, was to please her.

He was right, she was incredibly excited at the invitation and he loved seeing her beautiful face so happy. He listened to the lists of clothes she must buy in order 'not to look out of place', the beauty regime she must step up and the need to find one of her crowd to quiz on etiquette for the event. James on the other hand was apprehensive. He had learned to handle a gun at school and, on a handful of occasions, had joined a local farmer's shoot near Powick, but he had never been a guest at a country house shooting party and was rather unsure of his ability. Therefore, learning that it was usual for there to be more ladies in a weekend party than Guns, he had written to Mrs Harrington to plead the necessity for him to write his article during the day and therefore be allowed to relinquish his place to a more enthusiastic participant, leaving him to be only the necessary boost to the male numbers for dinner. What he didn't mention was that he also had to plot his strategy to recover the offending letters from a bureau inside a lady's private boudoir during her house party. He had to admit both matters dulled his sense of excitement!

CHAPTER 31

1903
The first Tour de France bicycle race is
held; Maurice Garin wins
The Ford Motor Company is founded by Henry Ford
with $28,000 in cash from twelve investors

James had toyed with the idea of hiring a private carriage to make the journey to Marlow, but he quickly came to the conclusion that the railway to Maidenhead and the Harrington's coach onwards from there, would make for a faster and more comfortable journey. They had made an extremely early start on the Saturday morning and as they crossed Brunel's bridge over the Thames and caught their first glimpse of Maidenhead, Emily stood to peer out of the window hoping for a glimpse of the notorious Skindles Hotel, "Darling, it would be marvellous to stay there don't you think? Who knows who we might meet."

"Dudes and ballet girls most likely, according to something I read the other day," replied James unduly sourly.

"Don't be so stuffy Eric," Emily started to complain but just then they pulled into the station and she began to gather her belongings together, as thrilled as a young girl, waiting for the fun to begin.

James rather pitied the porters, between them they had several heavy, leather portmanteaux and other, smartly dressed passengers alighting, had even more. Emily, she had assured him, could not possibly wear the same outfit twice and as different clothes could be expected at least at lunch and dinner, if not afternoon tea, this three-day visit required an extensive wardrobe and explained the excessive luggage. The question as to whether any of the other people leaving the station had the same destination was answered by the coachman when they learned they were to share the Harrington's double brougham with Mr and Mrs Edmond Dantes, and they sat, a little too snugly for James's comfort, for the short journey to Marlow. Harrington Manor's driveway snaked through perfect parkland with a small copse of trees on a rise to the east. As they travelled further there was another wooded rise to the west and as the Thames came into view, the carriage swept to the right, encircled the rotunda and came to a stop outside the front of a small but imposing, Palladian style, red brick house.

"It was designed by Sir Robert Taylor a hundred and fifty years ago, he was also the architect for the Bank of England," James announced, "and the park, woodlands and these beautiful gardens you can just see were laid out by Lancelot Brown. It's a very handsome example of a Thames side villa."

"Enough Eric," Emily half laughed but she was alarmed, "you are sounding like the article you are to write for the magazine. Mr and Mrs Dantes have been here many times before, you will bore them."

Two footmen and a butler came to lead them up the left-hand flight of stone steps to the huge central arch and the wide open, welcoming, double doors. They stepped inside to a black and white tiled entrance loggia and with hardly time to notice the elaborate decor, they moved straight into an airy vestibule, the domed roof allowing the light to flood in. There was no one waiting to greet them, they were taken instead directly to the dining room where their hosts waited and introduced them to Sir Desmond and Lady Napier, Mr and Mrs Herbert Pocket, a single lady, Isabella Giles and a cousin of Venetia, Henry Ozgood. They had met, of course, the Dantes and that comprised the party. They also learned that breakfast would be served for another hour and James was to make sure to eat heartily as he would be going out with the Guns later that morning. His host had politely disregarded James's request to allocate his gun to another, deeming it unnecessary. As it was already late, he was told they would shoot through, there would be no lunch and, whilst not relishing his day to come, he managed to tuck into a substantial meal from the vast selection of meats, fish, pies, eggs, breads and fruit laid out. He was offered tea or coffee but chose, in keeping with the other Guns and wisely or not, a tankard of cherry brandy.

The group all knew each other well and their curiosity at the addition of, quite obviously, a couple who were very unused to this circuit, was amply satisfied on learning that Eric Severne was there to write for the prestigious Country Life. They expected him to extoll the virtues of not only Harrington Manor, it's owners and hosts but to also confirm the serious matter of acknowledging that the society present, with their roots in the countryside, formed the backbone of England.

Breakfast over, a servant showed them up the grand, central staircase to their splendid bedroom, the window overlooking deep, green lawns as smooth as a croquet ground. It was politely suggested they change and freshen themselves up after their journey and, in James's case, to present himself to the gun-room in thirty minutes. Their bags had been unpacked and Emily guessed some of her dresses had been taken to be pressed. In no hurry herself, she watched James put on his unfamiliar, and on loan from Alfred and George Moss for ten shillings, tweed knickerbockers, long woollen stockings and ankle boots, shirt, tie and Norfolk jacket. The final touch, which was greatly approved of by Emily, his tweed flat cap.

"You look perfect darling," she said and kissed him lightly on the nose, "now all you need is a gun!"

Leaving Emily, he found the other men, was furnished with a shotgun and joined them, gun broken and hooked over his arm, as they all walked out to pile together with four dogs, into an old wooden cart with seating around the edge that Malcolm Harrington delightedly called the tumbril. This was their transport through the grounds to where the estate workers and local men, beaters for the day, would be driving with their big, wooden sticks, the unsuspecting pheasant out of their hiding places and over the assembled guns.

By the late afternoon, James was pleased to have got through the day without calling too much attention to himself and more importantly, without shooting anybody. He had, he was quick to acknowledge more by accident than design, bagged just three, low flying and slower birds, but thankfully not a forbidden white pheasant or wood snipe. He felt ambivalent, the thrill of the sport and his admiration for the skill of the better Guns, was very severely dampened by the unsavoury sight of these beautiful birds thudding to the ground, spewing blood, to be picked up by the retrievers. On balance, he thought he really would rather not go out the next day.

As they changed for dinner Emily was reciting her day and it was plain that she could not have spent a more enjoyable time. She had loved wearing her new clothes, had been thrilled to have a maid come to help her dress, and having been warned that her hostess would not appear again until luncheon, happily amused herself in her room until it was time to go down. After lunch, they had taken the carriages into Marlow, "Such a pretty little town darling," Emily trilled at James, "I tried hard not to shop, but I could not resist this beautiful dorothy bag," and she showed him the little draw string purse, a confection of blue velvet, satin and lace, "don't you love it too?"

"It is nearly as beautiful as you my love." It was at times like this, seeing her so happy that he felt he too would burst with happiness, "I'm glad you could not resist. Did you have tea?"

"Yes, the sweetest little tea shop in the High Street, and I do so like the ladies, but especially Venetia who is very kind to me. She guessed I was not used to house parties and Isabella, the lady on her own, is great fun too and we got on very well, the conversation never stopped all afternoon. Lady Napier is a bit severe, she's a lot older and I thought for a moment that she disapproved of me, but Harriet Pocket assured me she is like that with everyone! The other two, Diana Dantes and Cecily Ozgood are very friendly. Oh Eric, I'm so looking forward to tonight. We shall play bridge after dinner. Venetia is very keen like me."

He looked at her smiling face and decided not to mention that his own afternoon had been rather less pleasant. The Guns had been full of bonhomie, maybe due to the flasks of cherry brandy passed around, and were friendly enough, but James knew he didn't fit in. It did not help that he knew he was here to act in a thoroughly underhand way, to abuse his hosts hospitality, and that was not sitting well with him either. He determined to absolve his guilt by writing a precise, informative and glowing account of the house, the family and their whole life-style. To be featured in Country Life would certainly be a feather in the Harrington's cap.

He was unable to relinquish his gun on Sunday, "My dear fellow, it's the best of the days," Malcolm had said, completely unable to understand anyone not wishing to shoot, and slapping James on the back as they had left the gunroom the previous evening. "We shall be out longer, and the bag will be bigger. Besides, your loader told me you were just getting your eye in when it was time to finish up today. You must come out with us, you'll not miss the cream of the birds, but on my wife's instructions, I have asked a neighbour of ours to take your place on Monday. You can do your scribbling then. We won't disband till after a late luncheon at the house with the fillies."

So, James went out again. It was a beautiful estate, the tumbril made its way along a track parallel to the river and looking back at the house, Harrington told him the secret of its handsome facade, "There are two storeys below ground level, all the domestic offices are perfectly hidden away, a great benefit to the look of the place don't you think? And there's an underground passage leading to the basement so none of the staff need ever be seen," he said proudly, "we have rooms in the attic for essential house servants, my valet and Venetia's maid, but the rest live in the village."

James thought of the long walk they would have to take before dawn each day, whatever the weather, and the long walk home after sunset. In winter, most of them would never see the light of day and he wondered what the servants thought about being invisible. But, he told himself, I can't write about that aspect of fine country house living, it's not at all a fashionable view. No, a servant must never be seen or heard. He concentrated on the lie of the land as they passed through the sweeping lawns, the rise with stately trees to the north until they reached the lodge at the East Gate and then continued on their way to the neighbouring farm-land and the waiting beaters.

They took their lunch in the rough. The respite from banging guns and the rustic, delicious food more than welcome, whereas the tipple of choice for the day, 'Kings Ginger', a potent liqueur supposedly created for the king, James found quite unpleasant but which, in the absence of a personal hip flask of brandy, he drank. The day passed quickly enough and in spite of the Ginger, his shooting aim improved. He made a friend of a beautiful, soft mouthed, golden retriever who reminded him how much he missed having Monty with him and his amicable companions provided him with much food for thought to write about.

Emily was still having one of the best times of her life. She had again spent the morning in her own room. She wrote notes to Lydia, Alice and Beth, telling them all about her adventure, letters which were whisked away by a maid and would reach her friends before night fall. Her hostess took her on a tour of the rooms which all led off the central square hall, the library, dining room and drawing room looked out onto the river and rushes growing in the meadow. She thought the library the most pleasing room she had ever been in, splendid plaster panels showing hunting and fishing scenes, and scenes of painting and music. The afternoon passed far too quickly for her when they went to play bridge and take tea some forty minutes carriage drive away with Venetia's great friend Mrs Ponsonby, at her equally grand house on the Thames.

"How I wish we could live like this always Eric," she said with a dreamy, far-away look in her eyes, "I'm sure I was born to have this life."

"Well, my love, if this was every day, you would tire of it," he answered sadly, "it is because it is different that it is so good. Um, when you had your tour of the house, did you look in the rooms upstairs as well?"

"There was no need, there are only the five bedrooms on this floor with their shared dressing rooms and of course that splendid bathroom and the lavatory. Not that you can use that," Emily giggled, "It's as well Venetia told us," she adopted a stern voice, "that 'the gentlemen use only the lavatory downstairs' or you might have made a huge mistake! I haven't used the bathroom, but I had a peek and it has a beautifully decorated bath but no system of hot water which means the servants have to carry the hot water up. Venetia didn't actually say I couldn't use it, but neither did she say I could. So that's a pity."

Trying to sound casual, James asked, "Did you see the Harrington's room? Do they have dressing rooms and a boudoir?"

"No, I haven't been in, but I do know that it is an oval suite that looks out directly over the river and the little island. How wonderful it would be to wake up to that view every morning. We had time to have a short stroll in the flower garden around the house earlier and there's a walled kitchen garden and greenhouses. They grow their own produce for the house. I think I could be persuaded to give up London you know." She wrapped her arms around James and kissed him, but first, I must get dressed for dinner, I want you to be proud of me."

"I'll always be proud of you", he said, his heart full, and sat at the desk by the window, opened his notebook and wrote quickly about the architecture of the house, the grounds he'd seen that morning and a little of his daytime company. His thoughts strayed. He knew he would have to retrieve his client's letters tomorrow and he needed to check where the boudoir was and then find out where the occupant would be. If the routine was to stay in her room until lunchtime, he would have a very short window of opportunity to carry out his break in. He also needed one of the servants to drive him around the estate, there was a gothic dairy, a temple and a shell shaped grotto that his host was adamant should be written about.

James didn't sleep well that night. Emily had chattered away, everything had been 'divine', the candle sticks 'sublime', the people so 'riveting', so 'refined', the food 'exceptional', the chandeliers 'perfect' and playing bridge with Venetia as her partner, the pinnacle of the evening. They had won two rubbers which, she explained to James, "Is nearly impossible with a partner you do not know. I had no inkling of how she might bid, I just know we could be friends."

James held her close to him, he knew it was all a sham, they were not real guests, they had been invited purely to provide something the hosts wanted. Their behaviour was a perfect example of perfect manners but after tomorrow, Emily would be forgotten, or if remembered at all, just as that pretty little woman, wife of the journalist. He caressed her, listening to her breathing slow, and realising she had suddenly fallen asleep, silently wished her happy dreams.

CHAPTER 32

1903 - 1904
Britain and France end almost a thousand
years of intermittent conflict with the signing
of a treaty, The Entente Cordiale

H e had a restless night, dropping off to sleep it seemed only minutes before a housemaid knocked on the door, greeted them with a cheery 'Good morning,' pulled back the curtains, filled the ewer and basin with hot water and scuttled away to deal with her other charges. Emily was unable to tell him of the ladies' timetable, she herself did not know, and his anxiety robbed him of his appetite for the sumptuous breakfast. At last the Guns left and the ladies remained in their rooms as on previous mornings. James sought out the butler who assigned an estate worker to drive him around in an old horse and cart. They stopped at intervals, looking at the house from all angles and he made notes in his small, neat writing. They drove up onto The Grove to see the gothic dairy, out into the parkland to view the 'artistically ruined' Grecian temple, the seat in the shell grotto, even the ice-house and the lodges at all three entrances. Eventually he could put his mission off no longer and returned to the house.

To his relief he saw that the ladies were in the drawing room and his excuse ready for anyone who might ask, that he must go immediately to his room to write, he decided to strike whilst the coast was clear. Running quickly up the stairs, he listened outside the central door leading off the landing, due south. There wasn't a sound, but he tapped quietly, if a maid was inside, he would say he had been told there was a stunning view and he thought it would be best to see it in order to describe its beauty properly. There was no answer and, holding his breath, he turned the large brass knob. The door opened and he let out his pent-up breath and slipped inside closing it quietly behind him. It was a magnificent bedroom, dominated by a fine four poster bed with chintz hangings and topped by a frieze of golden crowns and shells. A huge oriental rug almost covered the floor, the walls were covered with landscapes and paintings of horses or dogs, and a fine black marble fireplace stood to the right-hand side. He took all this in whilst considering which of the internal doors led to the boudoir and which to either a bathroom or dressing room. He took a chance and turned to his left, opened the door and went through into an equally finely furnished ladies' sanctuary.

His eyes were drawn immediately to a superb, walnut inlaid bonheur du jour. A cupboard at the centre, its door had fine brass moulding and was flanked either side by three little drawers, all with ornate brass handles. The curved edges of the desk-top had a frieze, below which was a centre drawer decorated with a mask mount. James's first thought was, 'If I had a secret it would be locked away and there's only one keyhole, the cupboard door'. He put out his hand tentatively, touched the delicate brass key and the relief surged through him. Inside was just one shelf, little notebooks but no letters. He carefully opened each of the side drawers, no letters. Finally, he pulled the little ring in the centre of the mask and drew out the wide drawer underneath the writing surface. He crouched to look to the very back where he saw a small packet knotted with a length of black cord, it held a few cream envelopes. This was it. He took them out carefully, put them into an inside pocket of his jacket, gently closed the drawer and froze.

The bedroom door had opened, and he could hear voices. Appalled, he recognised Emily's, "What a divine room Venetia, I adore it and what a remarkable bed, how romantic it looks."

"Come and see the view from these windows," he heard Venetia say, "perfect views of the river. Oh look, there are two skiffs. I wonder if they are landing here, I hope not, I'm not expecting anyone."

Emily watched as the two small boats, each holding two ladies with beautiful hats and two gentlemen at the oars, turned and went back the way they had come.

"That's good," said her hostess, "frightfully bad manners to turn up unannounced. Now, that copy of the engraving of the house should be in my desk, the original is really quite important, by William-Bernard Cooke, I'm sure your husband will find it helpful. Where is he by the way?"

As Emily replied that she was unaware of Eric's whereabouts she would have been alarmed to know that he had done the only thing he could think of, stereotyped or not, he had slipped behind the curtains. He stood holding his breath, desperate to calm his rapidly beating heart, when he sensed the ladies come into the boudoir.

"I must have a word with the maid again, she should never leave this door open. I will have a lock put on it I think."

Venetia went straight to the desk and Emily made straight for the window. She looked downstream, "The skiffs have gone now," she called over her shoulder and then turned to look the other way, "Er..." she squeaked seeing him standing there, his finger to his lips, his face imploring her to silence, she finished, "Er..verybody has gone."

"Are you alright my dear? You have gone white as a sheet." Venetia made to move towards the window, but Emily darted over to the desk, "Yes, quite alright, I'm sorry to have startled you. I suddenly thought how dangerous it might be, rowing on the river I mean. Oh, is that the engraving. May I take it downstairs with me, the others must have finished their game by now and you and I can play the victors."

She moved over to the door and Venetia followed laughing softly, "You are as keen on bridge as I am my dear, a kindred spirit indeed. Here take this," she held out the paper copy of the engraving, "I am expecting an ideal write up in Country Life."

The rest of the day was an agony for James, he avoided Emily before dinner, which was an informal affair, the Guns coming straight from the shoot, and he endured the meal ignoring her hostile looks and feeling absolutely certain everyone could see he was a fake. The letters were hidden away at the bottom of his leather Gladstone bag, covered with his notebooks and on top of that, for extra security, his personal grooming kit and washing bag. Even so, he was waiting for a servant to burst into the room and point an accusing finger at him.

They did not of course and it was with a sense of unparalleled relief that, farewells concluded, they took possession of the two brace of pheasant that the gamekeeper had put up for him and stepped into the Harrington's carriage to travel, in stony silence, back to Maidenhead station. Emily kept her tongue all the while James fiddled with pockets and tickets, whilst the porter whisked away their bags, whilst another porter showed them to their carriage, whilst she settled into her seat and whilst the door remained open. When the whistle blew, the steam billowed and hissed and the train pulled slowly away from the platform and began to gather speed, she looked at James and between gritted teeth, bordering on hysteria, wailed, "What on earth were you were doing?"

He explained and was completely taken aback at the vehemence of her anger. He had dared to hope over those past few hours that Emily of all people might see the funny side of the situation, that she might have been thrilled at his audacity, might have enjoyed the knowledge of his escapade. But she didn't.

"How could you do such a thing Eric, to such trusting, kind people. Do you have no shame, I think it was despicable of you?"

"Yes sweetheart," James tried to keep his voice down, a full-scale row in a railway carriage was likely to draw the attention of the guard and the last thing he needed was a showdown, "but Mrs Harrington is not herself, all good. She was prepared to blackmail my client over these letters. He needed to end the relationship."

"You mean he used dear Venetia and now that he is tired of her, thinks he can just abandon her like that?"

"She is a married woman Emily, she must have known the danger, if you play with fire you may well find your fingers burned."

"But from the goodness of their hearts, these people invited us to stay, they took us into their *home*, we enjoyed three days of their generous hospitality. This is how you choose to repay them? What if she finds the letters missing and realises it was you. It will be awful, no one will ever speak to me again."

"My love, I had no idea we would be asked to stay. I needed a hook for the Harringtons in order to carry out the job for my client and when I approached them, I thought they would suggest I visit one afternoon, and a steward would show me around the house and grounds. I had no idea they would ask us both to join them for a shooting party. But when they did, all I could think was how much you would love to come, I knew it would please you so much, and it did, I could see you have been so happy."

"That is what makes it so wrong, to betray them, they were so magnanimous to open their home to two strangers, and two strangers not from their world."

Emily was crying now and James wanting desperately to vindicate himself, ignored the hurt he was about to inflict, "Dearest, please don't delude yourself. Those people were not interested in us, they will not even remember our names in the morning.

They wanted only something for their own ends, they thought by entertaining us and making a good impression it was bound to secure their place, their name and Harrington Manor in Country Life. That is all they were interested in, being able to upstage their friends and neighbours who have had no such exposure. They want to feel better than the others. That is how their society works and why so much of it is, in my view, rotten. You are worth so much more than any one of those false women, Emily, but you just cannot see it."

"Well it is all spoiled now, thanks to you. I shall never be able to remember the time without the memory being tarnished. I just hope you write the best article you have ever written."

They sat in silence, James feeling more and more morose, Emily gazing out of the carriage window. Just before they reached Paddington, she turned to him, gave a glimmer of a smile and said, "I was pretty convincing though don't you think? I almost screamed when I saw you, you gave me such a fright and your face … well, I don't know who you looked like. Wide eyed and frantic! But I was always a good actress, wasn't I?"

Once home, Emily, memories tarnished or not, delighted in the attention from her friends, telling them all in minute detail of the house, the visit and the people. James, for his own peace of mind as well as hers, wrote a splendid, affirmative two thousand words which were published the following year. In return for the letters, he received a handsome fee from his client and in due course, when the article was published, a short note of thanks from Malcolm Harrington.

CHAPTER 33

1904
The New York City subway opens
Republican incumbent Theodore Roosevelt
is elected president

F rom time to time, James still undertook investigations for Paolo Bertini at the Cecil Hotel. In late January he had gone early one morning to discuss a case and agreed to meet Emily in the foyer later in the day. They were to have lunch and then make a rare visit to the theatre. He had persuaded her to attend the Wednesday matinée at the Lyric where his old friend Davy Mason was appearing in a musical.

Emily had arrived a little early and was standing, waiting in the lobby, holding Plum's hand. She'd had unkind words with Lizzie the nurse that morning and not for the first time and now was furious that the girl had packed her bags and left the house in floods of tears. The theatre visit would have to wait, she needed James to find a new nurse. She stood looking around, angry that she was having to wait for James, and barely noticed the woman next to her, also waiting alone, until she spoke.

"What a beautiful daughter you have," the woman, whom Emily guessed to be in her late fifties, said smiling, "I love them at that age, mine are all grown up."

The compliment jolted Emily out of her mood and looking at Plum, her blond curls now a little darker and more pronounced with red, cut short to frame her pretty little face, she had to agree. They were exchanging pleasantries. The lady gave her name as Elizabeth Thorne and that she and her husband had four children, two sons and two daughters. Emily was encouraging Plum to introduce herself when James walked up and instead, she said, "Marvellous Victoria, here's Papa, take his hand now."

Just at that moment, Elizabeth's husband arrived and looking at the group could not disguise his amazement, "James, I didn't expect to run into you." He looked at his wife, "This is my cousin James, Aunt Jane's son, the one who didn't want the wine merchants," and he added with a grin, "the black sheep of the family."

James looked blank until he heard, "It's me James. William, William Thorne."

"My dear, you must be Florence," exclaimed Elizabeth Thorne, "we've heard so much about you. Congratulations on your books, I have read two of them. *The Pillar House* and I particularly enjoyed *The Dowager's Determination*. How lovely it is to meet you. We had no idea you had a child."

"My dear man, I believe you have mistaken me for someone else," James said stiffly and turning away, took Emily's arm, "come my dear, I would not want to be late."

"Good heavens, James, I know we haven't seen

each other in what, twenty years, but I'd recognise you anywhere. Look at your hair," he laughed, his own, shorter and oiled back had the same pale red sheen on the dark blond, "The Severn red. I'm in touch with Tom, he said you'd disappeared."

Standing in stunned silence, James still pulling lightly on Emily's arm, they listened as William explained their presence in The Cecil, "Lizzie and I are here gathering the troops, we are off to Liverpool and from there to Canada. You can thank your brother John for that," he said with obvious enjoyment, "we've written to each other ever since he went and when things went wrong for me at the inn, he said why not come out to Winnipeg, there's still many opportunities out there. I shall miss seeing your sisters to say goodbye, I've written of course, but it's not the same."

Emily tensed, James had told her of his brother who emigrated to Canada, but had also told her he had died, he had never made a mention of sisters and had given her the distinct impression that the brother Thomas, whom she had met, was his only living family. "Lies," she thought, "more and more lies."

She said, her voice icy, "Eric, Victoria needs a new nurse, that stupid girl has finally gone. I shall not be in for dinner." She turned on her heel, and her head held high, she stalked out of the hotel.

James, aware, but totally unconcerned that their behaviour was unacceptably rude, looked at his cousin and said, "You will excuse me, I have an appointment," tightened his grip on Plum and walked out of the hotel leaving the Thornes baffled, staring after them. Unsmiling, he requested the doorman to hail him a cab.

He felt anxious, he had never heard that hardness in Emily's voice before and to hear it directed at himself was torture. He went to his office and put Plum in the charge of Perry who was delighted to provide her with paper and pencils and praised her drawings and letters so much that it made her squeal with giggles. He requested Agnes to contact Norlands immediately to secure a new nanny and he sat down at his desk, staring into space, thinking of Emily. After a few minutes, he couldn't breathe, he was suffocating and needed air. He put a lead on Monty, a fleeting pang of fear and sorrow breaking through his dazed mind as he noticed the laboured way the poor old fellow got to his feet, and they went out into the street. He gave no thought to direction and his legs led him to Holborn. In the window of Gamages, he saw a flawless china doll dressed in sapphire blue, satin, taffeta and lace. Without thinking, he bought it for Plum and returned to the office, and from there, still feeling detached from the world around him, went home with his daughter to Foley Street.

The housemaid put Plum to bed clutching her new doll, she had not missed her mother and after her story, she kissed her Papa furiously, her little arms tight around his neck. James sat in the rocking chair, watching until his precious girl was sound asleep, going over and over in his mind what he could do to make amends for Emily. Eventually he went downstairs to the drawing room, poured himself a large whisky, put a dash of water in it and sat staring into his glass, sipping and staring in a trance until he heard Emily come home.

It was late, he had long ago told cook to go home and leave their dinner in the warming oven. He wasn't hungry. He couldn't know if Emily would want to be greeted or not, he wondered if she would retire immediately to bed or search him out, he agonised over what to do and decided to remain where he was, his doubts whirling in his mind. After a few minutes she came in, "I thought I'd find you here," she said calmly, "I think I'll go to bed, I really don't want to talk tonight."

Emily chose not to talk the next day, or the day after that either. Leaving all the words unspoken, she continued her life as if nothing had changed. Relieved at Emily's ostensible forgiveness, and not daring to question it, James poured his energy into expanding Justin Chevasse & Co. He took on an extra room adjacent to his own in York Buildings, he employed another investigator and a clerk who had mastered the intricacies of double entry bookkeeping. Within the year he also took on a young lady as a typewriter. He had bought a Remington machine on impulse, thinking he might learn to use it to write his articles for the papers, but it had proved beyond the skill of his soft, short fingers. He employed Ruth, trained also in Pitman's shorthand writing, to sit before the mystifying, black demon and produce with her rhythmic tapping, perfect documents with carbon papered copies. The second office rang with the sound of the keys, the ding of the bell heralding the end of the line and the whoosh as Ruth launched the carriage return. She presented legible papers far quicker than James could write by hand and even after several months, from time to time he and the other investigators would stand, unseen by her, watching Ruth perform this marvel!

Business was booming, Teddy and the new man were more than happy to deal with the mundane and

Agnes proved invaluable for impersonating a ladies' maid or a shop assistant, eliciting information from the unsuspecting. James, still disturbed at times by the dishonesty of his life, chose to concentrate on fraud. He, with Perry's help, enjoyed pitting his wits against the clever men who thought to embezzle from their own companies or those of their employers. He relished following the paper trails, at home and abroad, finding the discrepancies and exposing the culprits. He reaped the benefits from grateful boards of directors who paid handsomely to keep the scandals quiet. His newspaper advertisements added the words, "Offices Worldwide: Europe, New York, Sydney, Cairo."

Whilst nothing had been said and Emily carried on with her daily routines, she did however remain cool towards to James and this caused him untold anguish. She wasn't given to deep thinking or introspection but even she realised that her anger following the meeting with William Thorne and the uncovering of James's lies, was an over-reaction, more a symptom of her frustration of life with him in general. Although she knew she was being unfair, she could not shake herself out of the negative frame of mind until she was delighted when in an effort to appease her, James suggested they move to a new apartment in Cornwall Mansions. Once there, James's healthy funds provided her enjoyment as she pored over fabrics and furnishings, parcels and packages arriving daily. She had needed new mirrors, new side tables, new carpets, new curtains of course and her 'one extravagance' she had explained to James, a four-poster bed with chintz hangings. She had not forgotten Harrington Manor for one moment. Still spending her days searching for pleasure, she lunched with her crowd as often as she could, The Beach at the Cecil a favourite haunt second only to The Savoy. She applied herself to her piano lessons with Alice, she played bridge every day or evening and she pressured James into attending and holding dinners and parties whenever the invitations came.

Unlike Plum, who cried for hours, Emily hardly noticed and cared less when Monty, James's faithful companion and friend for fifteen years, curled up into his basket for the last time and died peacefully in his sleep. James was struck with grief. He felt an intense pain and emptiness, Monty had lived in his heart for so long and was a part of his family and his daily life. Morning and evening routines had been set by him and James would miss the soft, unconditional love. Emily thought him ridiculous, but he had read an article in *The Strand* about a small garden, tucked away in the corner of Hyde Park where the gatekeeper allowed much loved dogs to be buried. Emily refused to allow Plum to go with James, she felt the child was upset enough without the circus of a burial, so James took Monty alone. Through the gate into the secluded back yard of the garden, he stumbled into what he could only describe as a Lilliputian graveyard, with row upon row of tiny headstones stretching out into the undergrowth. Later that week he erected his own, "Monty. He asked for so little and gave so much."

It was James, rather than her mother, who wanted to spend time with Plum. He loved her company, she was a clever, charming little girl and when she had passed her fourth birthday, he thought it time to relinquish the poker faced, Norland nanny and find her a governess. As it seemed so often in his life, fate intervened. He was called on by an old client, Herr Gerber, from whose balcony he and Emily had watched the King's coronation parade. They had first met when James had been called to his house to investigate the theft of a diamond brooch from one of the Swiss couple's house guests. He had made extremely discrete enquiries as he was dealing with rich and influential people. The doors and windows having been locked at the time the lady had found the tear in her pin cushion where the brooch had been snatched off, James figured it had to be an inside job. He had quizzed the maids, the cook, the butler, the footmen and the coachman, all of whom had struck him as honest. Finally, he had reluctantly, turned his attention to the family themselves and in particular Rosa, the youngest daughter. She was sixteen, the youngest of six children and in spite of speaking fluent French, German and English, having a passable knowledge of mathematics, geography, history and even basic science, she was plain and charmless. Her singing voice was strident and off key, her piano playing pedestrian, her embroidery stitches, no matter how hard she tried, uneven, and she lacked in self-confidence. Because of these failings, her parents had decided she would never make a good marriage and they did not try to find her a match. James however had liked the girl. He could see that she was desperate for attention and that bad attention was better than none. He had found the brooch hidden under her mattress, a vulgar looking piece of jewellery, which they both thought ostentatious and repulsive. They had talked together and built a slight rapport during those few days and James hoped that his words might have made a difference, made her understand that in this new and exciting century she could make something of her life, she did not have to be a wife and mother.

Now it transpired, his words had been of no use and on this occasion, the matter was already in the hands of the police. Herr Gerber brought Rosa to James's office and she sat opposite him, her plain, pale face filled with misery.

She had been caught stealing a notepad and silver pencil from the Army & Navy store in Victoria Street, the police had charged her, and she was awaiting a date for the hearing. She told James she had been with an older woman whom she had met some weeks before in Foyles bookstore in Charing Cross road where they had struck up a conversation, both being interested in astrology. She had come to regard this woman as a friend, and they had made several outings together.

"I told you to stay away from her," her father said sadly, "I asked you why a woman of her age would want to befriend a young girl like you. I knew she was a bad influence, you told me she was egging you on to steal."

"Do you know her name and address?" James asked, "I could interview her, see what she has to say for herself."

"No, I only knew her as Ada, I have no idea where she lives, we always met at a shop," Rosa was close to tears, "will I go to prison Mr Chevasse?"

"Not if I have anything to do with it, and I have an idea. I can tell that you were easily influenced by this older person, she has a more powerful will than you and for whatever evil reason, took delight in forcing you to steal. I shall speak for you in court and make your defence that you were hypnotised by her."

He was met with blank faces, then Herr Gerber

spoke, "Genius my dear Chevasse, genius." He smiled broadly and got up to leave but James was not finished. He had noticed the girl's eyes looking around, taking in the books, the pens and papers on his desk and he saw her catch the sound of Ruth's typewriting. Just for a second, her vacant expression changed to one of interest as she had looked through the open door towards the woman sitting at her machine.

"Your daughter needs a job, something to give her a sense of self-worth," he said, "Miss Gerber, you are a well-educated young woman, I have a four year old daughter who needs a governess and companion. It might make your court case go better if we can say you are now in gainful employment?"

In due course Rosa appeared in court where the judge was amazed by James's evidence and persuaded to show compassion and dismiss the case.

CHAPTER 34

1905
Sir Henry Campbell-Bannerman becomes
the UK Liberal Prime Minister

Plum and Rosa were a perfect match and they loved each other from the very first moment when Rosa had asked to call the little girl, 'Mademoiselle Victoria'.

"Victoria is such a beautiful name, so regal, 'Plum' is 'prune' en Français, I cannot think of you that way," she had worried, "and you must call me Rosa, not Miss Gerber, I would like that."

They spent their days happily, the dressing room off Plum's bedroom had been made into a small school room and there they held lessons in reading, writing and numbers in the mornings and after lunch they might take a walk in the park, Plum loving to bowl her hoop along, laughing and laughing as Rosa ran to keep up with her. Sometimes they would stroll by the lake feeding the ducks with the left-over crusts of bread, and from time to time, make a visit to a museum. Painting and sewing, piano practice and singing came before teatime and, as often as he could, there was a bedtime story from Papa. Rarely was her favourite china doll out of her hand.

James continued to do his best to think up treats for Emily. They went to the races at Ascot with her crowd and to Brighton for a week, James hoping it would rekindle their passion. She agreed to go to the theatre again, music hall only, but it was a beginning and he was proud of her reputation as a sought-after hostess. He made a private vow to keep his jealousy hidden, his jealousy which often burned inside his chest like a furnace. But in spite of all his efforts, Emily was still restless, and she felt guilty. She knew she wanted Johnny Rollinson and, since one fateful night a few weeks ago, she was sure Johnny wanted her too.

The Savoy had hosted an incredible, extravagant party for an American millionaire. The old courtyard had been flooded with water three feet deep, painted scenery had been placed round the sides showing the beauty of Venetian buildings, and a huge, stationary, silk lined gondola, strewn with thousands of carnations, was placed in the centre and held a table and chairs for two dozen guests. Johnny had been working with his staff for weeks to make sure the evening was a success and his sister Alice and Emily had begged to be able to peep at the arrangements on the night. He had allowed them to stand, to the side of the little bridge built to link the gondola to the hotel and over which the twelve-course banquet would be served by waiters dressed as splendid gondoliers. Later, a baby elephant, resplendent in a bejewelled headdress, carried a five-foot high cake to the waiting guests whilst hundreds of paper lanterns were lit above them, white doves were released, and the great Caruso sang. Champagne flowed like water, gaiety girls drank to the health of King Edward and Emily thought she might have been in heaven.

Now the party was over, his adrenaline subsiding and fatigue almost overcoming him, Johnny had eventually found the girls in a quiet corner of the bar, "It all went without a hitch thank goodness," he called the waiter for a large brandy and slumped down in his seat, "I am so relieved. There have been dozens of us working on it, but I think I have felt every ounce of the responsibility on my shoulders. I'm glad it's over."

He drank his brandy, Alice excused herself to visit the cloakroom and suggested they meet her in the lobby, it was late, they must get home. Johnny stood, took Emily's hand as she too got up and as she started to thank him for the chance to witness such a spectacle, he bent his head to hers until he rested against her forehead and, hesitating only for a second, closed his eyes and kissed her, lovingly and gently.

"Thank you," he whispered, "thank you for being here."

They began to meet in secret and when they became lovers, Emily told him the truth. She told him she was not married and that her daughter was illegitimate. Johnny tried to blame James, he stormed up and down, denouncing him for taking advantage of her, swearing that years before, he would have challenged the bounder to a duel. Emily had calmed him and tried, although she would never be sure she had succeeded, in assuring him this was not the case, that she had been as willing an actor in the melodrama of her life as James. Johnny asked her, there and then to be his lawful wife, they would bring Plum up as their own. The child need never know her true status.

James would never forget the day, the date, the exact time that his already precarious world fell apart. Sunday the third of September 1905, at nine thirty in the evening. A spell of hot weather had just broken, and a storm was raging in London. The rain was gushing down so hard that the drainpipes were rattling and the windows shaking. He had taken a solitary dinner, Emily was out playing bridge that evening with Alice, dining with their opponents unknown to James. Afterwards, he had moved to his study to wait for her to come home. He heard the scrape of the door as she came in and his heart skipped a beat, she looked radiant. The tiny curls around her forehead were damp with the rain or, and it came to him like a thunderbolt from the blue, passion. She had come to him straight from her lover's bed, buoyed with the courage and conviction to devastate his life that came only from the certainty of her love for another.

It all came out. Emily's despair at all the lies they told, not just to other people but to each other, her unhappiness.

"Eric, you are not to blame. If anyone is, it is me, I was so insistent that we be together." She gave a wry smile, "I was always impulsive, I ran away from school and home to go on the stage in London, but it seems my impulses are not always wise. I was never going to make a good actress, not even before I got involved with Freddie Matravers. I was not good enough but more to the point, I was never prepared to try hard enough." She looked up, her eyes far away and then focussed on James, "I'd like a glass of whisky darling, would you get me one please?"

James handed her the crystal tumbler, she raised it to her lips and took a sip., His mind was numb, giddy he felt he was spinning out of control, but he kept silent as she continued.

"Ever since I was a little girl, I have wanted to live a life I wasn't born to," she sighed. "My family were comfortable enough, Dada is a solicitor, my brother now too. My sister has married a Belgian baron, but he's penniless and she has only a title and a broken down, draughty rambling house. Eric, I wanted the bright lights. I wanted the best in life, exotic places, restaurants and dancing. I wanted, no, I still want, to be seen in all the fashionable places. I know how I look, and I wanted rich and powerful men to admire and want me." She gave a scornful laugh, "But deep down I knew I would only be a mistress, they marry their own, not a provincial Irish girl like me. So, I became a mistress and look how that turned out." She drank more of her whisky and looked James in the eyes, "and then I met you. Dear, sweet, kind Eric and you fell in love with me so fast and so deeply you couldn't see how I would spoil your life too. I thought it would be exciting to live in sin, it would be fun to act your wife, and you were on the stage, I thought we might become famous together, but I wasn't prepared to work at it."

She paused for a while and James, a lump in his throat, choked out, "My love, what can I do to make things right, I am sorry I have failed you."

"Eric, I told you, you could do no more. We did have such fun those early days and whilst you were employed at the Hotel I was able to pretend I really belonged to the fast set who were there as guests, I thought I was the same and I cannot deny we had wonderful parties and dinners and I came to think I might be living my dream."

She held her glass towards James who poured another splash of whisky, his mind was now racing, what could he suggest, "I could speak with Paolo, I could go back to the Cecil."

"Eric, that would never work, one cannot go back. I am very fond of you and I love our daughter even if it does not always seem that way, but I was not made to live a domestic life. I have always railed at the thought that I must learn to sew, embroider and cook, play the piano and sing prettily. To be a dutiful wife and mother, it's not what I want, and it stifles me. I want parties and nightclubs and people around me. Yes," she grinned at James, "I am shallow. I do not want to *do good* in the world, I don't give two hoots about votes for women or saving the poor. I'm not about to crusade for women's suffrage, I'll leave that to the blue stockings. Eric, I just want to feel *alive*. I want to look at the pictures of the latest fashions in *The Lady*, and buy them, not read about hygiene, nutrition, and child-care."

James spoke about what had been on his mind for so long, "I don't understand why meeting my cousin William Thorne last year upset you so much my love? We are both ostracised from our families, I thought it was your choice. Did it remind you how ordinary I am after all, not the dashing actor but a rather dubious character who lies, who goes around spying on people finding out their dirty secrets. It is not an honourable existence, I can agree with you there, but I could concentrate more on writing. I have ideas and plans for journalism, but it does not pay, and I want you to have as much of the life you crave as possible and for that, we need money."

"I think I realised, after your words when we left the shooting party at the Harrington's, I shall always be on the outside looking in. I shall never belong in the world I imagine." And then she drove the sword straight through his heart. "Johnny Rollinson has asked to marry me. I love him and I have agreed. I know I won't have the life I craved, so I must have this love. Now that I have found it, I don't want to let it go."

"But I love you too, with all my soul and being and I love our daughter, I love you both more than life itself," he had tried to say but his sobs disguised the words, his lips moved in spasms. Emily took his hand, "I'm sorry Eric, my mind is made up, I shall leave tomorrow and send for my things later. Johnny has asked that we bring Victoria up together, but I cannot be so cruel as to take her with me when it is plain for all the world to see that she adores you far more than me, she would much prefer to stay with you and her governess."

She left the room. James reached for the whisky bottle and longed for oblivion. If he could just sleep, all would be well in the morning.

James did not see Emily leave. The next day he stayed in his room telling the maid that he was unwell and wished to see no one, he did not want any food brought to him and he instructed Rosa to keep Plum away. Early that morning Emily had gone to Plum's room, sat on the end of her little bed and told her daughter she was going to stay with a friend for a while. The child was not unduly concerned, her mother had sometimes been away for a few days and her absence had never been a problem. This time however, her mother held her just a little longer, a little tighter and kissed her face, her voice faltering, she whispered, "I will see you soon my dear, be a good girl for Daddy."

From that moment, Plum would always, throughout her life, associate the scent of Guerlain's Jicky with loss.

Monday evening James left his room and went to his study where Plum found him the next morning, slumped in his chair, his unshaven face slack and his mouth open. Shaking his arm and calling, "Papa, Papa, wake up Papa," brought no response and frightened, she called for Rosa who, taking one look, thought to call the cook.

"You'll know what to do Mrs Briggs," Rosa said, then lowered her voice, "could it be that he is drunk?"

"You take Miss Victoria to her lessons, or out into the Park," Mrs Briggs answered in her no-nonsense fashion, "I'll see to the Master. The child shouldn't see him like this." She was a stout, strong woman and she needed all her strength to pull James up out of the chair, his feet knocking the empty whisky bottle as she did, "Come on Mr Severne," she said loudly, "you wake up and get to your bed. It's a disgrace you sleeping here, being found by the bairn, what sort of father does that."

She put his arm around her neck and half dragged him up the stairs to his room where he fell, mumbling incoherently onto his bed. Mrs Briggs removed his shoes, pulled the eiderdown over him, closed his curtains and left. She determined to give him a piece of her mind later when he sobered up, "So, the Mistress has left," she thought to herself, "and good riddance if you ask me, but it's not right for you to behave like this in front of that darling daughter."

CHAPTER 35

1905
Henry Campbell-Bannerman becomes
the UK Liberal Prime Minister
Albert Einstein, a clerk in a patent office in Bern,
Switzerland, submits his paper to a physics
journal, which develops an argument for what
will be his famous equation E = mc2.

The Rollinsons set up home in a flat in Gloucester Street, a genteel neighbourhood that Emily approved of greatly. Johnny and an equally energetic and ambitious colleague from the Savoy had taken over as managers of the Avondale Hotel in Picadilly, intent on making this tired hotel one of the most fashionable in London. James could not bear to hear its name mentioned but it was difficult to avoid, the hotel was the talk of the town. He buried himself in work but would not travel to any part of the city where he thought he might run into Emily. He became boorish in his office, upsetting his staff and he ignored his friends. Only with Plum and her eagerness for her fifth birthday coming up on the twenty ninth, was he able to put his hurt aside and smile.

"Papa, am I to have a party? Rosa says she always had a party when she was young, she says her Nanny made a special tea," were Plum's first words as James came into her room one evening, "and they played games and once she had a magic show. Please say we can too."

James looked at his daughter's face shining with health. Her hair was brushed till it shone, her little cheeks were pink from Pears soap and excitement, and a line of freckles across her nose, brought out by the summer sun, made her all the more adorable to him. He'd caught sight of his own face earlier that day, grey and gaunt. He had brushed his hair but, repulsed by the realisation that it was thinning a little, he had swarmed the unruly curls back with no real care. He'd even thought, "I'll have the damn stuff cut off as short as possible, who am I trying to fool into thinking I am still a young man, I'm nearly forty, I should look my age."

He wanted to hold Plum tight, put his arms around her and bury his face in her baby softness but as he leant over, she put her little plump hand to his chin and giggled, "Papa, scratchy Papa, no ...don't come near me!" Almost helpless with giggles she pulled her coverlet up over her head and James was rocketed out of his melancholy, he tickled and hugged her, laughing just as loudly and answered her question, "Of course my little Plum shall have a party if strict Miss Gerber says that is 'comme il faut'.

Later he sought Rosa out and apologised, "I have no idea where to start, but I have promised Plum a party for her birthday and I fear I shall have to leave it up to you and Mrs Briggs to organise. She is quite taken with the idea of a magic show and, as it was you that put the idea into her head, it seems only proper that you should have the trouble of finding a magician with only ten days to make all the arrangements." He realised this was the first time he had smiled in over two weeks.

Charles Arrow heard on the grapevine that Emily had bolted and not getting word from James, decided to take matters into his own hands. He turned up unannounced at York Buildings.

"Heard the news old chap, I'm really sorry. If there's anything I can do to help you must say the word."

James cut him short, "There is actually, I need children, preferably girls, five years of age, but some of your boys will do too. Plum is to have a party and I want it to be a party she will remember for ever. Who else has appropriate young?"

Charles looked at his friend, although James had shaved properly that morning it was obvious that he was not sleeping, his face was etched with fatigue and sadness, "That will be the easy part, I'll instruct Fanny. Martin's still got a girl about five, I think. I haven't seen him in months, have you? It will do you good to get back in touch, and don't forget Davy's got quite a brood now, does Plum know any of them?"

"Only yours I think, her mother took charge of these matters and she preferred to mix with the fast set. I'll not be inviting any of her friends but I feel I should ask Alice Rollinson, she's been teaching Plum the piano for the past year and the child's very fond of her. She's not been since ... since last month but I'll have to face her soon."

"So that's the party planning over, now what

about you? Rumour has it that you need some distraction?"

"I can guess the source of that rumour," James said acerbically, "and when I speak with him, Mr Peregrine Danvers will wish he'd kept his own counsel."

"Well I'm glad he told me," Charles ignored him, "I've got wind of a rather interesting case which I'm hoping will be right up your street, embezzlement combined with the old game of setting up a long firm fraud. Will give you something to get your teeth into, take your mind off things.

It was never going to be easy for James as, the party being arranged for the Sunday after her birthday, Emily had arranged to see Plum on the day itself. She arrived at the house late morning with a beautifully wrapped present and went to join Plum in the drawing room. Plum carefully unwrapped the parcel and squealed with delight at the contents, a beautiful edition of *Alice in Wonderland*.

"Mama, I can read the title, 'Alice', I know that word it is Alice's name, 'in w-o-n-d-er'" she was sounding out the word and Emily interrupted immediately, "not 'wander' as if you were lost, it is pronounced like a 'u', wonderland."

Plum looked, frowning, at James who smiled broadly, "We shall be able to read it together later my little one, I think you will enjoy it very much."

"I thought I would take you to Madame Tussaud's," Emily pulled the little girl to her lap, "the figures are remarkably life-like. I have heard that people ask directions of the policeman standing near the door only to find that he is made of wax! The Hall of Tableaux will teach us history as well as being a pleasure and they have special designs for children. You know the story of Cinderella and the Babes in the Wood? Well you will be able to see them too."

When Plum ran off to find Rosa and get dressed to go out, James turned to Emily. Other than a polite 'good morning, how do you do?' They had not had a chance to speak alone.

"What arrangements did you have in mind for spending time with your daughter," he asked coldly, not trusting his voice, "today is a special day but it would be better perhaps to have a more formal schedule. That way we should always know where the child will be."

"James dear, please do not speak so harshly. I am so sorry I hurt you, but I thought you understood, I felt I had no alternative. And of course, I wish to see Victoria. You know I am very fond of her, but I will agree to whatever plans you wish to impose. I see you are preparing a party?"

He was dreading the question and found his mouth dry, he licked his lips and managed to mumble, "Sunday, with Charles's children, and Martin's."

"Don't worry my dear, I will not embarrass you by coming here. I cannot imagine anyone would want to see me just yet. Maybe another year, when the disapproval has abated somewhat?" She smiled and Rosa brought Plum back into the room.

"You look very pretty darling," Emily said and then stood, turned and held her hand out to James, "I will have her home by tea-time and await your instructions as to our next visit. I shall manage without you today Rosa, thank you."

James was relieved when they had left, but it had

spoiled his day, he couldn't get Emily out of his mind. The sight, the sound and the scent of her, he wondered if he would ever recover. He would ask Rosa to take Plum to Gloucester Street each week, he could not bear to have his wounds opened like this every time.

The party was a huge success even though the eight children were outnumbered by their parents and friends. Charles and Fanny had brought two daughters who were just a little older than Plum and who, in the way that young girls do, had taken it upon themselves to act as her mentors and guides. Their four-year old son busied himself with the toy soldiers bulging from his pockets whilst waiting impatiently, and with many enquiries as to its readiness, for the food. Martin had brought his youngest girl, quiet, she was content to play a supporting role for the Arrow sisters. Martin's wife had been unwell for some years and confined to her room with an unspecified illness, James guessed the child had learned her stillness at home. Davy and his exuberant wife's daughter had inherited her mother's nature and was doing her best to organise the gathering whilst desperately trying to prize Perry's baby girl from his wife Ida's arms, unnaturally strong arms for such a timid, mouse like creature. The adults were boosted by Gussie and Constance who had arrived laden with gifts for their adored god child, Teddy and his olive skinned, and therefore automatically exotic, friend Lucien, Alice Rollinson who justified her appearance as music maestro and piano player and of course James himself and Rosa.

It was difficult to say who enjoyed the games more. The adults joined in with gusto to Pin the tail on the Donkey, Gussie falling onto a small, carelessly placed walnut table and only just avoiding ending up-side down on the carpet as it slid slowly along on its casters. They vied with each other in the diablo com-petition, commandeering the toys from the children in their efforts to show off long ago learned skills. The table in the morning room had been cleared and vigor-ous games of ping pong threatened the Meissen on the sideboard. The children indulged their elders and en-joyed their own snakes and ladders, quoits, blind man's bluff and pass the parcel.

Tea was served, cold meat sandwiches and saus-age rolls. Small egg savoury tarts and slices of Mrs Brigg's homemade pork meat pies. Then came what the little ones were waiting for, jellies and blancmange, ice cream, fruit purées and lemonade. Everyone ate their fill, James and his friends washing the children's fare down with champagne or beer. The rule of silence at the table banished for one day only, a happy cacophony of laughter, giggles and chatter filled the room.

Mrs Briggs provided the finale, she came into the dining room proudly carrying before her a cake tower-ing with pink icing, topped with the figure of a deli-cate Dresden china ballerina. The children gasped with pleasure and Plum almost cried with joy when she was handed the little doll, "Papa, Papa, now that I'm five, can I be a ballerina too."

They were all offered a piece of this sponge cake, but James had requested a plum cake for choice, ac-companied by a glass of madeira it was perfect for toasting his daughter's future. When hands and faces were cleaned, it was time for the magician. Resplen-dent in his black cape, he wowed and bamboozled them with his sleight of hand. Pennies disappeared, never ending streams of coloured scarves were pulled from every pocket, and to the delight of all the ages gathered round, his magic wand produced a fluffy white rabbit out of his top hat. The afternoon ended with Alice playing the piano for the children to perform their party pieces and then tired, happy farewells were made and the rambunctious home returned to its normal tranquillity.

When James went to tuck Plum up in bed, she threw her arms around his neck, wet kisses covering his cheeks, "Thank you Papa, thank you for the best party in the world. I think my tummy is still full of ice cream!'

She was too excited to sleep, "White rabbit Papa, read me white rabbit, Alice has followed him down the hole and everything is tiny." Her hands scrabbled at James's waistcoat, "Where's Papa's pocket watch?" She found it, took it from the little pocket and held on tightly as James picked up the book.

CHAPTER 36

1906 – 1910
Herbert Henry Asquith becomes the last Liberal
Prime Minister
May 1910, King Edward VII dies at age 69
and George V takes the throne

W hen he looked back over the next five years
James was content. He had made it his pri-
ority to give Plum a happy, stable childhood and he thought he had succeeded. Emily had
often proved unreliable in her contact, the initial
meetings at Gloucester Street for tea after her lessons were finished and the occasional outings were
exchanged for more and more excuses. "Darling child,"
she would say, "Mama is just so very busy tomorrow,
perhaps we should wait until Saturday, I'm sure we
could go to the science museum or even the zoo. Mama
will have all the time in the world for you then." Sometimes they met, sometimes, "Mama had this extraor-
dinary opportunity come up, and I couldn't possibly
miss it. I will make it up to you I promise." It wasn't
that Emily did not love her daughter, it was just Plum
did not take precedence over the rest of her life and she

was safe in the knowledge that the girl was more than cared for at home.

In contrast, James put her before anything. He delegated as much investigative work needed away from London, even in Europe, as he could, to Perry, Teddy and Agnes. He had complete faith in their abilities, after all, he had trained them well. whilst There were of course some evenings when he could not get home before her bedtime, he did his best to spend time with Plum before she went to sleep. Each morning before he left for the office, he would write a new word for her to learn on a slip of paper and leave it by her breakfast plate. In the evening he would be greeted with often bizarre statements, "Papa, it is my prerogative to leave my cabbage. I do not like it therefore it is my right or privilege not to eat it!" "Papa, today I was ecstatic to hear Rosa tell me I have a fine hand in writing." "Papa, I am aspiring to visit the fairground. Please tell Rosa I may go, I want to go on the rides, they have galloping horses that go around and around. Rosa says no, fairs are full of the wrong type of people but please Papa, may I, please?" James would hug her close to him and praise the use of the word and offer advice in response. He soon learned that she would incorporate the daily word to put forward any request of a debatable nature and, quietly proud of her canny ways, he would never say no without a considered discussion!

His whole life revolved around the office or home with his daughter and with Emily's resistance to the idea gone, he and Plum went one day to choose a new puppy. 'Wellington', 'Welly' to his friends, was a good natured, yellow Labrador who quickly became part of the family. He reintroduced a morning and evening stroll into James's routine and he became Plum's greatest ally. Having no great discernment in his taste for food and working on the basis that whatever was on offer was delicious, he surreptitiously ate her cabbage!

James avoided meeting Emily if at all possible and it was Plum who told him that she and Johnny had married that spring. The girl had been a little confused, "Mama tells me she is now Mrs Rollinson, does that mean that I am Victoria Rollinson now?"

"No" he had answered more harshly than he intended, "you are Victoria Severne. You are *my* daughter, you are mine. Victoria Irene Mary Severne," and he had hugged her so tightly that she gasped for breath, "Yes Papa, I understand, but can I like Johnny? He is very nice and he makes me laugh like you do."

Hiding his pain, James answered, "Of course my little Plum, of course, and you must always love your Mama too."

With Emily gone, James found it hard to shake off the feeling of emptiness he held inside but he gradually sought out company, people to spend time with, to ease the loneliness. He had his handful of real friends from his early years but perhaps it was the nature of his business, his need to be secretive and untrusting, traits which did not make easy bedfellows with open friendliness, which had stopped him forming new friendships. Now he began to seek out convivial fellows to talk, and more importantly, to drink with and, as long as they did not interfere with his time with Plum, he accepted the few invitations to socialise that arrived.

It was on a November evening a year after Emily had left that he made his way through the streets, thick with an almost impenetrable fog, to dinner with an acquaintance made through Gussie. Another of the dozen guests that night was a divorced lady of a similar age and an extrovert nature who made it perfectly plain that she was attracted to the handsome, sultry looking man sitting opposite her. She overlooked the slight greying and thinning of his dark blond hair and the minor thickening of his waist which was heralding a portliness to come. She was drawn to the sadness beneath the long lashes in his deep set, blue eyes. Sadness that did not dissipate entirely even when his head was thrown back with laughter. However, in spite of the sadness, he was charming, and he was intriguing. She became the first of many liaisons James was to have over the next few years, often with divorcees, but from time to time with ladies still married. He sometimes had occasion to wonder if one day, one of his own detectives might be watching outside a splendid house in Mayfair, or a grand apartment in Belgravia, waiting for him to arrive or leave!

Thus, his life became moderately cheerful. Business was steady if not booming, Plum was growing up to be clever and charming and he had bodily comforts enough. In March of 1910 he took on, what he did not know at the time, was a case that was to precipitate the end of his life as a private investigator.

"There's a lady in the outer office to see you Sir," Ruth, now stationed with her typewriter by the main door to act as guardian of the inner offices, had come into James's room and pushed the door shut behind her, "says she'll only speak with you, won't give me her name even. She looks a bit, well, strange. She's extremely short and dressed all in black with a veil over her face. She just appeared, I didn't even see her open the door. Shall I send her away, say you're busy?"

"No, send her in Ruth," he smiled, "you've made me curious to meet her, very mysterious."

The visitor slipped into his office without a sound, "My name is Mrs Joseph," she said in a soft, cultured voice, "Mrs Lavinia Joseph. My husband was the late Horatio Joseph, you may have heard of him?"

"Good afternoon Mrs Joseph, please take a seat. No, I don't believe I know of your late husband."

"Well, never mind, suffice to say that he left me a very wealthy widow and it is my wealth that makes me so vulnerable and in need of your services." Her hands fluttered a little in her lap, toying with the clasp on her small, black velvet bag, "It is such a cruel world, full of dishonesty, people who would try to steal from me if they could."

"Quite so Mrs Joseph, what is it in particular that you require?"

"I have made enquiries into you and your methods Mr Chevasse and you are highly recommended, your reputation is exemplary. I am aware of your success in unmasking a gold digging, American woman masquerading as a wealthy heiress. You saved an eminent member of our land from a most unfortunate alliance. No please, do not worry, that information is most certainly not in the public arena and I too am in need of a similar high degree of discretion. I would like you to check the credentials of these three ladies," she handed over a note, "and in particular, their financial means. I have met them both and interviewed them at length in the quest to find myself a companion. I find my life so very lonely now without dear Horatio, and a gentlewoman to share my comfortable home and travel a little with me would be such a pleasure."

"That sounds a sensible idea, but what do you wish to learn from these investigations, what should I be looking for?"

"I must know if these ladies are honest. All three have assured me they are of more than reasonable means themselves. They have sworn that they wish to come to me truly as a companion and not to trick me out of my money but my husband told me quite categorically that when he was no longer around to protect me, I should put aside my natural, trusting nature. Hence, I would like you to ascertain their true position, in the greatest secrecy of course. I could not allow Horatio's abundance to be appropriated by others, he worked so hard to make sure I was provided for. In a nutshell, I need to know if they are as wealthy as they say." Mrs Joseph allowed herself a small chuckle, "That they are not in cahoots with unscrupulous companions waiting in the wings."

James took a folded card from his desk drawer, "These are my terms Mrs Joseph, should they be acceptable to you I would be happy to carry out this work for you."

By May, James had been furnished with details of five more ladies to scrutinise, all so far proving unsatisfactory to his client, and now he had the results of his sleuthing on a further two candidates. Mrs Joseph had materialised yet again in the offices and sat before him, eagerly taking the neatly typed reports he handed to her over the desk. She held them close to her eyes and he watched as her head moved from left to right, line after line as she peered to read them through her veil.

"Hmm. Yes, yes, thank you Mr Chevasse, I shall inspect these closer at my leisure, but I am pleased to think that this time I may have found my companion. She is such a delightful lady too, très gentille as they say on the 'continont'. I am so pleased she appears to be just as she represents herself, wealthy enough but alas poor soul, not a living relative, how sad. I am sure this will be a new beginning for her."

James presented the last of his fee notes and thought no more about the lady in black as his mind was elsewhere, he was under siege from Plum whose latest bedtime book had been *The Fortunes of Philippa* and who was now continually pleading with him to be allowed to go to school and in particular, a boarding school 'just like The Hollies'. He had finally capitulated - partially. She was nearly ten years old and satisfactory as Rosa had been in teaching her during those early years, he knew Plum would benefit from a little more formal education. She had a good start in English, geography, history, singing, piano, drawing and needlework. She was an excellent reader and thanks to Rosa she was quite the little chatter box in French and had learned the rudiments of German too. He contemplated employing a finishing governess but in light of the child's obvious desire and enthusiasm, he made enquiries for the autumn term at the Francis Holland school in Graham Street. She was most definitely not going away to board.

"Plum, it won't necessarily be as Miss Brazil writes, she needs to make it sound exciting and fun otherwise you girls wouldn't want to read the stories," James had tried to reason with her, "day school will be a good compromise. You will still be living at home but there will be lots for you to do after your lessons. Plum, I would miss you terribly if you were not here, and who would you torment if not your Papa with your questions," he had feigned exasperation, "questions, endless questions!"

"Well I'd have a best friend Papa, like Philippa has Cathy, I would have a real friend and I wouldn't have to bother you all the time, surely that would be good?"

James thought his heart would break again, "Dearest Plum, please promise you will never stop tormenting me," his voice husky with emotion, he pulled her close so she would not see his tears, "promise."

September came and James thought Plum might burst with excitement and his own anxiety for her happiness proved ill-founded as she loved the whole experience of school from the very moment she arrived. Leaving her in the hands of Miss Faithfull on that first morning, James was a bundle of nerves and had not known how he would cope. He had spent the day unable to settle to anything and eventually had taken Welly out, walking through St James's Park and the edge of Green Park to Graham Street, just to look up at the building where his precious daughter was locked away from him. He had met her himself when school finished that afternoon, in future it would be Rosa, and they had taken a cab home with Plum holding his hand, talking nineteen to the dozen, laughing and smiling.

"Papa I have my own peg in the cloakroom, it is number seven and I must hang my coat there in the morning and I have a little cupboard that they call a pigeon hole and I can put my outdoor shoes in there and we had a drink of milk and a bun in the morning and we weren't allowed to talk and we had dinner which was lumpy meat and cabbage, but I ate it all and we had lessons except we were told they were adventures and discoveries and we had callis... calins... well, something where we did exercises and had to whirl our arms around and jump like a star and I dropped my pencil box and it made such a clatter and the pens and nibs all fell out and my friend helped me pick them up and I said she could keep one of the rubbers because I have two and she didn't have one and her name is Lily Adams and she is my *best* friend and I shall see her tomorrow."

By the time they reached Cornwall Mansions James too was smiling and laughing. Rosa who had been just as fidgety all day as James, had come outside to wait for them and Plum skipped up and hugged her, "Rosa, Rosa, I have had such a lovely day, I hope you haven't been lonely without me, it was so much fun."

James saw a tear escaping from the corner of Rosa's eyes and put an arm round her shoulders, the other one finally taking Plum's satchel from her back, and Rosa held tightly to Plum's hand.

CHAPTER 37

1911
Coronation of George and Mary
First escalator on the London Underground system
opens to the public, at Earl's Court tube station

"Now you have to agree with me that having a telephone is a necessity. If you'd not had it installed, I would have sent a message across town to get hold of you and then you would have sent one back changing my plans and I would need to send a third, but instead, I could speak to you and sort it out there and then," Charles Arrow had met James outside the Trocadero restaurant and they were walking up the broad staircase together on their way to the Long Bar, "however, I was only thinking of a cup of tea, thick, white cups from Gladys at Lyons corner house, not this extravagance."

"Extravagance? The telephone is an extravagance, I didn't want one of the infernal things, I managed very well with telegrams and the telegraph, but Perry convinced me it would help bring in business, and it does. I just wonder how many people listen in, I won't say anything private on it. Anyway, we're here because you made out it was urgent to see me and as I'm meeting a friend here for luncheon, a drink in the bar makes sense. I'm a bit short of time. What will you have, a cocktail or a glass of beer?" James was in high spirits as he ordered.

"Another of your liaisons?" Charles raised his eyebrows, "you're a lucky man! I'd better stick to beer, I'm on duty this afternoon and I wanted to tell you about this case coming up before the beak in a couple of weeks. A woman called Mrs Leslie has defrauded two old dears out of a fortune and the local police in Newmarket, where she was picked up, found a bunch of bills from you, Justin Chevasse & Co. in her house. You're not needed for questioning or to appear in court, but I thought you'd like to know, and you might be able to help us with our enquiries as they say."

"I don't know a woman called Leslie, when were these bills? This year, last year? The name's not one I dealt with personally, but I write all the invoices so I'm sure I'd remember it. What did she pay us for?"

"Bit vague, they just said, 'information provided' and were dated earlier this year, April and May. All of them over a hundred pounds."

"There's a lot of clients who pay that much," James began to wonder, "Describe her to me, Mrs Leslie. What does she look like?"

"Best word is small. Very small. I've only ever seen her in black and at first, she was putting on a cultured voice, but when she knew we were onto her, she suddenly became like an east end fish wife, cussing and swearing. She swindled the old ladies out of thousands. Tricked them into handing it over to be invested in an American syndicate, run by none other than the famous Pierpont Morgan himself. He's summoned to the Old Bailey to swear he's never met the woman, let alone been her friend since childhood. She persuaded the women not to say a word to anyone, not even each other when they met, and in the end, when one of them finally caught on that things weren't quite right and told her bank manager, he called the police."

"You say Newmarket? Not London? But I have a very uneasy feeling I know who she is, she fooled me completely if it is who I think it is. Told me she was a wealthy widow looking for a companion and would I check the background on," he thought for a moment, "must have been half a dozen or more women. Said they had all applied for the job and she had to know that they were wealthy enough in their own right not to plan on stealing her money. She called herself something biblical, Joseph, that's it, Mrs Joseph, said her late husband had left her a fortune. Tiny, bird like woman, bit creepy and always wore a thick black veil, I never saw her face clearly."

"Must be one and the same. Her real name is Marie Leslie. Do you remember the names of the women you checked out?"

"I'd have to look them up in the office, but I remember one of the last ones, name was Blunt, she was a widow from Worcester and it made me wonder if she could have been married to Harry Blunt, a boy I knew at school there. You say she cheated her out of thousands. Can you recover it?"

"No, afraid not. Most of it has completely disappeared and the shrew has sworn she'll not tell us where, but a vast sum went into the coffers of one Edward Evans turf accountant and another great deal into Harrods. She's an evil woman that's for sure but, that said, her victims were particularly foolish, took no proper advice with the huge sums involved."

"Since when was stupidity a reason to be robbed?" James had become morose, "I can't believe she fooled me so completely. I was just as stupid as them, I'm not sure I should call myself a detective anymore. How could I have been so gullible, I should have checked her out first, I'm not fit for this work if I can be party to such deception. But Charles, it's not just this, I've been disillusioned for some time, it's hardly a principled occupation. It was that business I told you about at the shoot weekend that was the final straw for Emily, made her leave. I'm going to quit."

"Don't make any hasty decisions," Charles was worried for his friend, "there are more and more of us police going into the PI business when we retire, it won't always be disreputable."

"No, I've been thinking it over for a long time. I've wanted to go back to writing and I could be a good journalist if I concentrate on it and now that Plum's at school, I can set up my office at home and make a go of it. I don't need so much money anymore."

Charles left the bar and James went to meet his lady friend and take her to the restaurant. He was very subdued during the meal, aware that he appeared rude and taciturn, but he could not snap out of the melancholy that had settled over him. However, he was not about to explain himself and had to accept that this engaging divorcée, who had accepted the luncheon invitation from a handsome, charming detective, was going to leave the Trocadero with a very disappointed taste in her mouth.

James wavered in his decision to quit the business, but he was adamant he wanted to write, paint and draw again and he made one life changing decision immediately. He decided to live in his own house in Warwick Street. All these years it had never been possible to make his home there. At first, the rent he received more than covered the cost of more modest accommodation and during all those years of struggling to be an actor whilst living with Florence, he had needed the money to live on. Emily had turned her nose up at Pimlico saying there was absolutely no way she would live there although she did admit the property itself was handsome enough, but now he was determined to give the tenants notice and have the place for himself and Plum. He would be his own master in his own castle.

Hesitant to meet Emily and tell her of his decision to move, he thought he would put all the matters in hand so that he could give a definite date for the change. The truth was, he was reluctant to face her, nervous that she would be against him taking their daughter to Pimlico, she had been caustic enough about the location of the Francis Holland school and Warwick Street was only a half a mile or so away. He could hear her objections in his mind, 'so unfashionable, full of boarding houses, omnibuses past the door and penniless French counts and disguised dancing masters everywhere'! However he was sure it was the right thing to do and when he contacted his agent, was relieved to hear there was no need to give notice to his tenants as they had already written to say they wished to leave the following February.

Next he needed to speak with Perry. Now thirty-three years old, happy with his timid wife Ida and a brood of children he was wanting more responsibility. James had begun to wonder if he had his eye on running the agency, and if so, this would be a perfect opportunity.

"Do you really believe I could do it?" Perry's face belied his words, his eyes were lit with excitement, "I must admit, I've been thinking about it for a while but never thought I'd have the chance. I think I could make a success of it, do you?"

"I wouldn't ask if I didn't Perry and you already handle the accounts. I think you might want to slim down, keep Agnes and Teddy and we'll need Ruth too, but I would let one or even two of the others go. I'm going to dissolve the company, we've no debts so it can just close and we'll will go back to being 'Justin Chevasse' without the 'and Co.' It makes sense to keep the name we've spent so long building up." He walked over and sat behind his desk, stroking the worn leather he said, "I'm going to concentrate on writing and will take this to set up at home. It was my great, great uncle James's and is a fine example of Georgian mahogany. You can move desk here and find a table for me for when I do come in, you will have to involve me if any of our old clients insist," he saw a shadow cross Perry's face, got up and slapped him on the back, "I'm sure they won't though, they know you and know that you are just as capable."

"Will you tell everyone. I can't wait to let Ida know. She'll be so pleased I'm sure. Terrified," he laughed, "but pleased."

Before James had chance to be in touch with Emily, he received a telephone message asking rather mysteriously if he would join her and Johnny for dinner. He supposed she had heard of his plans and prepared to defend his decisions and Pimlico. However, when he presented himself at their home, his heart racing in spite of the small whisky he had downed beforehand to calm himself, he was completely taken aback with their own news. They were leaving the country. Johnny had accepted the position as manager of an hotel in Monaco and Emily was thrilled.

"It is a quiet but very distinguished hotel called the Metropole and built in the most divine Belle Époque style, surrounded by palm trees and very central, near to the casino and the Hôtel de Paris. Eric please be happy for us, it will be utterly marvellous to live in Monte Carlo, the weather is perfect and Victoria can come and stay in her school holidays. It will improve her French no end to be there and I'm sure she will love it too."

"So you are not asking to take Plum with you?" James could not keep the relief out of his voice, "She can live with me still?"

"Oh Eric, you know that's what she wants, she likes being at school and she would hate to have to live with me, I'm not blind to my faults you know. Johnny's very good with her though and she's very fond of him, isn't she?" She turned to regard her husband and his smile at Emily radiated through his warm, dark eyes.

They are really in love, thought James as Johnny looked away from his wife and spoke to him, "I want you to know Eric, that I should always take care of my wife's daughter and I hope you will allow her to stay with us, she is, as you well know, a delightful girl and a pleasure to be with."

James found his nerves had settled and his appetite aroused, whilst they ate, he told them unhesitatingly of his own new plans.

"Pimlico is coming up in the world," he argued as Emily's mouth dropped open, ready to berate him, "London is becoming more and more crowded, the great and good are moving outwards all the time and it is the southern end of Belgravia after all. Plum and I shall be very happy there." He carefully omitted to remind her that his property was immediately adjacent to the King's Head public house, quickly changing the subject, "and one more thing, I have already explained to Plum, other than for the detective business, I am going back to my given name, I'm to become James William again. Ernest was only ever meant to be my stage name, and Eric ... well, you are both aware of why I chose not to use my real name then. It will sound strange to be James again, but I think the time is right. The only exception, as I told Plum, is that for her I shall always be called Papa!"

CHAPTER 38

1911 - 1914
4 August 1914, Declaration of war by the
United Kingdom on the German Empire

A few months later, Emily and Johnny were settled in Monaco, Peregrine Danvers was established as Manager in the office and James and
Plum had moved from Cornwall Mansions to 174 Warwick Street. That first day, they had stood outside together on the pavement looking up at the Regency
brick house and James felt happier and more relaxed
than he remembered in years. He watched the brown
coated removal men file in with furniture and boxes,
all their worldly goods. The basement was to be rented
out, the income would be helpful, and the space was
not needed. On the first floor was a small but adequate
drawing room, dining room and kitchen. Mrs Briggs
had made her tearful goodbyes, Pimlico was too far for
her to travel each day, but they had found Mrs Plumridge who came highly recommended as cook and her
daughter Martha came too as their general maid. On
the second floor, there was a good master bedroom, a
smaller one for Plum and a third for Rosa. James had

plans for the attic, the space was large enough to be divided in two and become both his study and his studio. The door to the attic had been securely locked for years, keeping separate from his tenants, many of his own belongings which he had stored there since leaving Powick and which had been added to from time to time. After his years with Florence, all his art work, brushes, paints, easels and canvasses had been put away plus many of his books, some small tables and an old chair that Emily had thought 'not smart enough' but which he wanted to keep and now his desk sat there too, amongst the chaos and cobwebs.

The house soon became a comfortable home, no-one would use the word elegant or fashionable, but the three of them and Welly loved the easy warmth of it. Top of James's agenda was setting up his studio and then, inevitably, he could not resist spending time with his paintings and his books. After the first weeks when he'd only presented himself at the office for short periods of time when Perry needed his advice, he applied himself seriously to the matter of income and prepared his first submissions for his favoured magazines. He wrote all day, breaking only to eat and spend time with Plum when she arrived home from school and quite soon he amassed a small portfolio of articles which he presented to editors at *The Graphic*, *The Strand*, *The Stage* and *The Era*. If he had no luck here, he had resigned himself to move down his list of options, but he struck lucky. He had been in touch with an editor at *The Strand* a few years before and when he learned that James Severn and Justin Chevasse were one and the same, he was pleased to give him a chance. He dismissed James's short story, a detective tale, and asked instead, that he collate interviews with well known authors of mysteries, to bring them together as an article. His chagrin put to one side, James enjoyed the project and even offered his own pen and ink illustrations which he found, also, politely turned down, "Sorry old chap, we have our usual artists, but I like the article. I'll be in touch when we have something else for you."

In reality it was up to James to keep in touch with all the editors, but his persistence bore fruit and he found himself a periodic, if not regular, contributor of pieces, the odd short story and journalist services for these weekly magazines. When he wasn't writing, he painted. He had the small attic windows replaced with one larger expanse of glass, the light flooded into the room and he spent hours sorting through the many sketches he had made over the years, choosing one or two to work up into a canvas. Many evenings after Plum had gone to bed he would go back up to his desk, sit back in his chair and pour a whisky from the crystal decanter held in the silver tantalus and light a Gold Flake cigarette. Perfectly at ease with the world, he sat thinking, writing and drinking by moonlight.

Some afternoons and evenings he would visit one or other of his paramours although these had transpired to not always be the uncomplicated arrangements he desired. One lady in particular had been *too* free, no husband or children and a little too much in love with him. It had been a tearful, painful business finishing the dalliance and he would often think back to his uncomplicated days all those years ago with Lottie and wonder how she was, but for the first time in a long while, he did not have to convince himself he was content, he felt it, he felt it every day. His fiftieth birthday had come and gone, he had enough dealings with Perry to tax his brain and enough art to satisfy his creativity. He struggled only as all artists do, with his painting, and lived in an orderly, comfortable home. His greatest delight was his daughter, who loved him.

In a matter of a few short weeks in 1914, his contentment was completely overshadowed by the looming unrest in the world and the turbulent upheaval the war brought. He was fundamentally, a gentle man. His very person was described as soft and kind and he could not share the jubilation that so many of his fellow men felt at the outset of the hostilities. He shared their love of his country, their patriotism, but he could never share their enthusiasm to kill or for the country's young men to kill on their behalf. Plum saw the posters everywhere, propaganda encouraging everyone to help their nation in its time of need, and asked, "Papa, are you going to fight the Kaiser?" He had replied with a great sense of relief, "They'll not want an old Papa like me." If ever he had been glad to have a decision taken out of his hands it was now.

"Lily's brother is going," Plum told him, "he says he'll be back in time for Christmas. He's very excited and there's to be a party in her street to say goodbye to him and his friends."

James had watched the recruiting parties on the streets, the soldiers marching around in their red coats, the sergeants pointing at the men in the crowds telling them they were needed in France but he could not quieten his unease, his revulsion of war, affirmed by the last war in South Africa. The public outrage at the scorched earth and concentration camps so recent in his memory. He would not fight, he *was* too old, however, he wanted to do something, something useful.

It didn't take long for him to decide to approach the War Office in Whitehall which was rapidly adapting and expanding to cater for the needs of a country at war. They were recruiting civilians and he was given a position in the department of The Chief of the Imperial General Staff. His interviewer was a retired Major, a short, bull necked man with a bushy black moustache from the depths of which emerged a smouldering pipe. "You're a detective, so we'll start you off in intelligence," he said, the pipe gripped firmly between his teeth, "we've contacts all over the world sending in reports every minute, need them all collated. You're used to secrecy and discretion. You'll know how to keep all information confidential and we'll ask you to sign a chitty to that effect. Defence of the Realm Act and all that. You'll be based on the third floor, ask for Miss Chiesman, she'll sort you out and find you a desk."

Helen Chiesman was a tall, bony girl. Her thick, dark hair, parted on the side, upswept and fixed with combs into a loose bun at the back, failed to soften her angular cheekbones, high forehead and altogether masculine looking face. Her perfectly starched, high collared, white shirt and dark brown, tailored skirt reaching to her plain, brown, low heeled shoes, only added to her austere appearance and James made an unconscious decision that his charm offensive would be ignored. However, by the time they had walked the length of the already busy, noisy, crowded office to a small, shabby desk in the corner, she had completely won him over instead. Her voice boomed with joviality, she fielded the banter from the men they passed with abundant good nature and humour and she talked nineteen to the dozen with boisterous enthusiasm. Before she left him he was aware of the identity of several of his colleagues, he knew the tea lady's rounds were ten thirty and three thirty, that he should refer to her, Helen, in the first instance should he need one of the girls to do some typing for him, that he could find pencils and pads in a cupboard in the corridor he had already walked along and that, as today was her twenty-first birthday, he was welcome to join her and many of those present, at six o'clock in The Ritz for drinks.

"Daddy is in Saint Mary Axe and he's agreed to come along and buy us all a glass of champagne. I've got the obligatory party at home in Surrey on Saturday, so this is just to kick the celebrations off."

James got straight down to work. He answered to a Captain who was a down to earth, straight talking man who conveyed his instructions in the fewest words possible and on this first day, the piles of papers on his desk grew and grew, no matter how fast he read, noted, sorted and reported, the information flooded in.

He was assured that evening by the irrepressible Miss Chiesman as he toasted her health, drinking her father's champagne, that things were bound to get even more hectic, "After all," she said brightly, "Daddy says all the younger men will have to go off to war soon, he doesn't believe for one minute that it will all be over by Christmas. Then there'll just be women to do the work and so you're bound to be put in charge."

Frederic Chiesman was of course right, the recruitment became more and more persistent and insistent, the war had a boundless appetite for men.

At first, life at home for Rosa went on much as usual. Since Plum had started school, she had taken over the role of housekeeper and friend. For two summers she and Plum had gone to the Riviera to stay with Emily and Johnny where Rosa had disliked the heat, but Plum had relished it, she loved being at the hotel and the beach, playing tennis and seeing the sights. It was plain Johnny adored Plum and it was he, rather than Emily, who went out of his way to make sure she had a good holiday. That August, their trip was cancelled. Monaco, James explained was neutral in the war but travelling there through France was not, in his opinion, safe. Emily had telephoned to argue, but James had been adamant, he would not let them go. She, he had said, could come to London to see her daughter but so far, she had found a thousand and one excuses not to.

It was not to be long before things changed considerably and all their lives were totally dominated by the war. The school was only a short walk away and this was where Plum's head was filled with ideals of patriotism and a burning desire to help with the war effort. Their curriculum, already heavily weighted towards religion their founder having been a Canon of Canterbury Cathedral, had increased services praying for the brave boys overseas and victory for the allies, the righteous. On a more practical level, the girls spent their time knitting scarves, socks and balaclava helmets which they sent to the front as comforts for the 'Tommies' along with any chocolate or jam they could collect. They learned how to patch and alter their clothes when fabrics became more scarce; they gave up sugar, since it was all imported, eating sweets was seen as unpatriotic; they gave their pocket money to the war savings association and the Blue Cross for injured animals; they became expectant of the air raid warnings and they practiced diving under their desks in readiness for the reality of an air attack.

She joined the local Girl Guides who had formed an alliance with the school and proud to be in uniform at last, she learned first aid and was drilled in carrying stretchers in preparation for emergency work. Alice Rollinson stopped coming to teach the piano when she enrolled with the Volunteer Aid Detachment to help in the local hospitals and Plum, as a Guide, felt she was playing her part too when she was allowed to roll bandages and generally fetch and carry for the nurses. The Zeppelin raids in the spring of 1915 brought the war right to their doorstep and, thankfully untouched, they complied with the blackout and then breathed a little easier when autumn arrived, and the raids stopped. Their maid Martha left, the lure of money or patriotism prompting her to answer the government's call to become a munitions worker. She went to live with an aunt and joined the workforce at the huge factory in Silvertown, leaving Mrs Plumridge to 'tsk tsk' about her 'canary' daughter and to cope, aided by Rosa, with the challenges of a national, diminishing supply of food.

CHAPTER 39

1915 - 1917
May 1915, Bombing by German Zeppelins begins
November 1916, First bombing of central London
by a German fixed-wing aircraft
January 1917, Silvertown explosion at a munitions'
factory in east London

J ames was now finding it hard to accept the glori-
fication of the war as it unfolded, the sheer
blind nature of the propaganda. He understood, of
course, the necessity for self-imposed and government
legislated censorship of the Press but he learned the
realities at work. From as early as the first September
battles he knew hundreds of dreadfully injured soldiers
were being brought into the London railway stations
late at night but reports of the horrors they had seen
and suffered were to be kept quiet, only their bravery and steadfastness was to be spoken of. Only the
cheerful, unbreakable spirit of the Londoners, not the
misery and ruin of those who'd lost their homes to
the air raids, the pain and suffering of those who lost
their lives or the lives of their loved ones. The brave
reporters at the Front were denied the right to be truth-

ful, the government dictated what they could divulge. He agreed with heralding the heroism, trumpeting the courage at home and abroad, the endorsed belief that Britain had divine right on their side, but the compassion and gentleness he held inside railed against it all. His hours were long and as the war progressed, they became longer. He arrived at his desk before dawn and left late at night. With less personnel available, he took on more and more, somehow hoping desperately that the knowledge he was assembling might help end the war sooner. Would stop the killing.

"How?" He asked Charles one evening, a rare occasion when they sat in the blacked-out saloon of the King's Head, "how can this 'Great War', be 'the war that will end wars" if the facts are never known? Millions have been killed on the Somme, millions more injured or maimed, their lives destroyed. How many thousands have their minds so traumatised that they will never sleep again? It is not cowardice that makes them shake and stutter, to find they cannot talk or walk, it is the horrors they have seen."

"It is a just war James, we have right on our side, and we must fight the tyranny of the Kaiser, defend our freedom." Charles answered.

"It is unreal. London is crowded with people, most of them in uniform." James carried on as if he'd not heard, "Just about every British soldier on his way to and from service comes through here, our hotels are full, the bars and music halls too with their patriotic, optimistic songs. Hundreds of thousands come through from Australia, New Zealand and Canada and stop to see the sights, and they bring all the wounded, bleeding and dying from France and Belgium back here.

I'm glad we've opened our land and our hearts to refugees, allowed them to start a new life. I do understand this war Charles, I just don't like it. I had some good German friends before all this, now I'm expected to regard them as the Devil. Kroell, the manager of the Ritz, thrown out of work, you couldn't meet a nicer, more genuine man and I worry about Rosa, she's Swiss but there are so many prejudiced, ignorant people around, she is not really safe." James drained his glass of whisky, his face drained too of all emotion, "Can I get you another Charles?"

Charles nodded his response and handed his empty glass to his friend.

James came back from the bar with a bottle of Johnnie Walker and a new jug of water, "Don't worry, not expecting you to drink the lot," he smiled, "I'll take what's left next door when you go."

"How's Plum? Still raring to get to France?"

Plum's latest ambition was to train as a nurse and go to France with the VAD.   "She's still too young, not seventeen yet and I've put my foot down. She volunteers enough already, sees things no girl her age should. She's used mainly as domestic labour," seeing Charles's smile, he smiled too, "yes, after all her education! Cleaning floors, changing bed linen, swilling out bedpans but she can't help but see the terrible injuries and tells me she cries at the sound of the men crying for their mothers. Please God it's over before she's eighteen or decides to defy her old Papa and go anyway."

"I was over in Silvertown today. The place is devastated and not just from the explosion but all the surrounding fires. Did you hear it? It shook the windows out of the Savoy apparently and tipped a taxi over in Pall Mall. Goodness knows how many people were killed and injured. They're keeping a bit quiet about it all at the moment but the Super wanted a squad of us to attend that young Constable's funeral in Finchley and I thought I'd see where it all happened. He was a brave young man, quite the hero, stood and tried to turn back all the crowds who'd come to see the fire, warned them that the place was going to blow up. Saved a lot of lives but got crushed to death himself. The Super thinks there'll be an award for him, the family will be proud of that."

"No award for young Martha," James said sadly, "or her aunt. Mrs Plumridge is inconsolable, don't know if she'll want to come back to work again. Martha was her only daughter and she'd worried for so long that the chemicals would kill her, she'd turned bright yellow like all the girls, never in her wildest dreams did it occur to her that the factory would explode and her sister's house with it."

Charles changed the subject, "Sunday tomorrow, would you like to bring Plum and Rosa over for lunch with Fanny and the children, cheer you up a bit. I think she's managed to get hold of a decent piece of beef. One o'clock and I'll not take 'no' for an answer, you haven't seen my tribe for ages. Pity Welly's not here anymore, he was always welcome, and the children will miss him!"

Monday morning James awoke feeling rather more positive. He'd enjoyed his afternoon with the Arrow family, and he was meeting with the Major later that day to discuss a new position.

He was thoroughly engrossed and apart from his trip to the Major's office, did not leave his desk, not even for lunch. It wasn't until he was packing up ready to go home that he realised he had not seen the ebullient Miss Chiesman, nicknamed by all those in his office as the Head Girl, whose customary good spirits generally brightened up his day.

She was at her station, sat behind her typewriter at the entrance to the large office and he stopped, perched himself on the edge of her desk, "What's up Head Girl, you've not been over to tick me off once today. I can't be behaving myself more than usual, so something's wrong. Tell Uncle James, I'll see if I can make it better. Has the Boss been making life difficult for you?"

She looked up at him and he was shocked, her eyes were swollen and red rimmed, the ever cheerful, utterly optimistic young lady had been crying.

"My dear girl, you're upset, can I do anything to help?"

"No thank you, I'm just going to finish up here and get home," she sniffed and drew an embroidered handkerchief from her sleeve, "I'm just a bit down, will be back to normal tomorrow."

"Nonsense, you are not going home to that little flat of yours like this, put your stuff away, we'll go somewhere quiet and you can talk to me. Can't have you looking after all of us and then leave you to be unhappy on your own."

She didn't put up much of a resistance and James waited as she put on her hat and coat, struggled to pull her galoshes over her leather shoes, put her leather shoulder bag over her head, picked up her utilitarian black umbrella from the stand behind her and, looking up at him with watery eyes, announced, "Ready, where shall we go?"

They splashed their way along the street under the darkening sky to the Bell. The snowfall from earlier in the week had turned to unpleasant, insidious slush, worming its way over the top of James's shoes making him wish he too had some rubber over-boots. A cloying warmth greeted them as he pushed open the small, almost hidden, door and they went inside. It was an old public house, no brash lights or polished tables, just a snug bar with a cheerful fire protected by a large screen. They did not sit there as the landlord, who looked to Helen as old as the building itself, bustled out of the small door in the bar and ushered them into a back parlour. It had dark wood panels, a high mantelpiece and a sanded floor. Hanging on the walls were four old prints in black frames of naval battles, men of war firing away vigorously, the background was of ships sinking, the foregrounds of tangled masts and drowning men. One dim light was suspended from the centre of the ceiling and on three sides were three narrow tables with shiny looking wooden chairs behind them.

"I thought we would be comfortable here," James said watching Helen's face as she looked around, "you didn't seem to be in party mood today and I always find this step back into the past very soothing."

She smiled, "It's perfect, although perhaps these days a painting or two of a still life or flowers would be more cheering?"

"I'll bear that in mind Miss," the landlord chuckled and raised his bushy eyebrows, "your usual Mr Severne and what can I get the young lady?"

They sat opposite each other at one of the narrow tables, whisky and water before James and, after a good deal of deliberation on her part, a sherry in front of Helen. "I don't drink in public houses as a rule," she had explained, "but this evening this is perfect. I'm not sure what drink to have though, I have a glass of champagne on special occasions, but here," she looked up at the landlord, "what would be appropriate?" She chose the schooner of sherry, took off her coat and stood the umbrella up in the corner behind her, leaving her hat and galoshes on. "I'm sorry," she apologised, "I'm not sure of tavern etiquette."

James had laughed and when they were settled, he asked, "Now, Miss Chiesman, please tell me why you are so distressed. A trouble shared you know is a trouble halved."

"My brother, Reggie, he's only just eighteen and he's a second lieutenant in the Life Guards. He's finished his training and left this morning for France or Belgium. I don't know where. Mother and Daddy are fiercely proud of him, but I just have this awful feeling that we'll never see him again."

"Is he your only brother?" James asked kindly. He had been working alongside this woman for the best part of three years and he knew nothing about her.

She sipped her sherry and began to tell him all about herself and her family. She had two older sisters, one younger and two younger brothers. "Mother lost two baby boys at birth so I cannot understand how she has let Reggie go, thank goodness Freddie is still at school. Maud's married, to a captain in the army and Dolly's engaged to a Lieutenant. Linda's at home still." She was talking softly and slowly, nothing like the 'head girl', then she lifted up her face and he could see how tired she looked, "I am a great disappointment," she smiled ruefully, "especially to Mother. Two years at the top finishing school in Vienna and I've not managed to bag a suitable husband, Mother does not see any virtue in shorthand and typing I'm afraid."

"What do you think?"

"I'm not sorry," she answered defiantly, "I wanted to live a bit before I settled down to be a wife and mother, this is the twentieth century and there is a war on, things cannot possibly stay the same for women. I admire Mrs Pankhurst so much, and she believes all us women should be helping win the war, that's why I applied to the War Office, Mother would have had a fit if I'd gone off to be a munitions girl."

"We're definitely doing our bit," James consoled her, "and I think you're right to want your own life." Then, as if her sadness drew the confidences out of him, or maybe it was the cosy warmth and glasses of whisky, he told her, "My wife always wanted to have her own career and she's done very well. Florence Severne, she is an author, you may have heard of her she's had six books published. I never talk about her now, we parted many years ago and have lost touch, but I admired her very much."

"Does she not miss her daughter," Helen asked, everyone in the office knew of Plum and James's devotion to her, "does she see her? Oh, but she lives in France now, doesn't she?"

Once he'd let the genie out of the bottle, James found he could not put it back and his life story poured out. He gave, admittedly a somewhat censored, account of his life with Emily and that evening, in a shabby public house, in the middle of the Great War, Helen became one of the very few people who now knew the truth. She was not shocked, she felt compassion for him and, she realised, strangely proud that he had shared his secrets with her.

It was getting late when James accompanied the young woman back to her flat in Portland Place. The underground had been packed with laughing, joking men in uniform but the couple, taken for father and daughter, had remained subdued. At the door, he said goodbye and made his way home in the pitch black, across the crowded capital to Warwick Street, sad that he had missed his evening with Plum and Rosa, and aware that he was feeling unsettled. Talking that evening, it had dawned on him that he had unfinished business which should have been dealt with years before, he should give Florence back her freedom.

CHAPTER 40

1917–1918
David Lloyd George is now Prime Minister

A t the first opportunity, James went over to his offices to see Perry. After much back slapping and hearty greetings, he sat at a table running his finger down the entries in the latest London telephone directory, looking for the name Severne, F. No luck, he tried Quinn, S and finding two, one in Ladbroke Grove and the other in Maida Vale, he made a note of the numbers and addresses. Later that day he called on Gussie at her offices in Oxford Street.

"I'm sorry I didn't make an appointment," he apologised to Connie when she came to greet him in their reception room, "thought I'd drop by on the off chance."

"About time too, it is so long since we saw you we thought you had forgotten us," there was a note of accusation in her voice, "Gussie's not here, if you'd bothered to find out before, you'd know she's at home. She's not been at all well for weeks, but I expect she'll forgive you if you visit."

Gussie was lying in bed, propped up with three pillows

behind her head, complaining hoarsely to a middle-aged woman who was attempting to strap a flax seed poultice around her chest during the lull between her bouts of coughing. She screeched that the mixture was too hot! Hearing the unfamiliar footsteps coming up the stairs, she stopped and kept still, the nurse finished, closed her nightdress, replaced the woollen bed jacket and wrapped two shawls around her patient's shoulders just as the maid tapped at the door and announced that James was here.

"Come in stranger," Gussie croaked, "bronchitis. It's no fun, I can tell you. We thought you must have joined up or been hit by a Zeppelin it's been so long since we've heard a word from you?"

James made all the proper noises, there were no reasons why he'd ignored the ladies for so long, just lame excuses and he felt a little ashamed. They had been good friends, was he always going to lose people along the way, shouldn't he try harder to stay in touch. He was looking out of the bedroom window, chilly in spite of the roaring fire, he surveyed the depressing view outside. A vast wasteland of roofs covered in dirty snow and grimy smoke being belched into an already grey, leaden sky. From the street, he heard the sound of motor lorries and omnibuses thundering through the slush, horns blaring from time to time and he felt sure he could feel the house shaking.

It didn't help that he had come to see Gussie to ask her for information yet again, but she soon forgave him. "I haven't seen Sylvia for years, she's been abroad most of the time, but I did hear that she was home now and home for good. Tapping on a bit too much to be travelling in those wild and dangerous places I should think."

"Do you happen to know where she is and, more to the point, if Florence is with her?"

"I think she's in Ladbroke Grove but whether Florence is there too, I don't know." She broke off into a bout of coughing, "It's the talking brings it on," she wheezed, "you talk, I'll listen. Why do you want to know?"

"It's time I legalised our situation, I think Florence and I should be divorced," James who was now sitting at the bedside, patted Gussie's hand.

"Why now after all these years," she gasped, "why not when you met Emily or when Plum was born?"

"The law's changed and she can divorce me without any blame attached to herself so I thought I should go to see her and put the wheels in motion. It needs to come from her. I haven't seen her for so long, I'm not sure how she'll take it, I suppose if she'd been keen, she'd have sought me out."

"Hopefully you'll find Sylvia and she'll know where your wife is. Do you need any help?"

"I beg your pardon," James said with mock hubris, "who did Robert Baden Powell quote in his book as 'the well known private detective'? Was it Gussie Bourne? Oh no, it was Justin Chevasse!"

They laughed until Gussie's coughing brought the nurse running and she shooed James out of the room.

"I'll let you know how I get on," he called back over his shoulder, "hurry up and get well, the City is safer with you around!"

His recent meeting with the Major had resulted in him

moving office to the Post Office Depot, a huge, wooden, purpose-built structure set in Regent's Park. All mail destined for the armed forces was routed through here, sorted, censored and despatched by thousands of women who had replaced the tens of thousands of regular employees now called up to fight. The logistics of moving billions of items by post each year was immense but James was brought in to help with the training, monitoring and management of the four thousand censors who read and redacted nearly half a million letters each day. Not just personal correspondence but commercial mail for neutral countries, newspaper packets and parcels. It was directed from above that Miss Chiesman would move with him to help oversee the female workforce and they became part of the extensive management team, assured that their training and vigilance would help foil spies, uncover enemy-related trade deals and preserve military secrets. They also learned that vast sums of money were habitually sent abroad, destined for the enemy, and that this censorship department would uncover them. Consumed with the daily routine, work overtook him for the next few weeks and there were nights when he slept briefly on a camp bed set up in his tiny, untidy office.

He had not spent time alone with Helen since that evening when they had confided in each other and from that time, they had seemed a little awkward to be alone. When she stopped by his office at the beginning of May to tell him tearfully that her brother was being shipped home, injured at a place called Arras, he asked if she would like to go again to the Bell with him. At the end of the evening, he promised to go with her to visit when they found out where Reggie was to be taken, and once again he arrived home with a strange feeling of restlessness. He promised himself he would make time to ring 'S.Quinn' the next day. It *was* Sylvia, she *was* living with Florence and yes, he was most welcome to call.

Their drawing room might well have been comfortable, but it now held even more exotic paraphernalia than the Bayswater house all those years before. The samurai warrior had been retained to watch over them and in addition to the Buddhas, the oriental prints and the swords and pots, were silk hangings of beautifully embroidered flowers draped from every available piece of furniture. Silk fans lined the mantelpiece and, here James did a double take, near the window was a large metal cage containing, what at first, he took to be a stuffed parrot, but on hearing it squawk realised it was very much alive. He was later to wonder why, in the midst of this astonishment, he was able to notice the vases on the writing table and feel a pang of yearning for the fresh flowers Emily had always placed around their house.

Florence came into the room, her hand outstretched to take his in greeting. At first glance, it might James thought, have been only last week he'd seen her but on closer inspection he noticed the deep lines around her eyes and mouth and the bands of grey in her swept back hair. There was no alteration to her features, her cheek bones were still well defined, but her skin had a weathered look which James guessed was from too much sun. She moved towards him across the room, still slender and graceful.

"James my dear, how lovely to see you, what brings you here? Sylvia is just on her way. Will you join us with coffee?"

He relaxed a little, "That would be welcome, and I want to hear about your travels abroad, however, I also wish to speak on a more delicate and private matter which you may prefer to hear alone?"

"Oh, Sylvia and I have no secrets James, you should know that by now, whatever it is, just speak up."

Her friend arrived, as did the coffee, and they entertained James for over an hour with animated tales of their journeys together to India and Nepal. They had been away for over two years and had the war not broken out, would have been adventuring again. "It may just be too late when all this is over," Sylvia sighed, "I'm succumbing to arthritis, hobbling around like a broken old lady."

James asked Florence, "Have you stopped writing? I have copies of all your books so far, including the poetry. Is there more to come?"

"No, that part of my life is over, I help Sylvia with her travel books now. I did very well, although I do not have many sales now but many of the circulating libraries hold copies and from time to time I receive a very nice letter through the publishers from a happy reader. These make up for the occasional odious review I'd had from the critics in the past! So, James, what is it you really came to talk about?"

He wasn't sure what he felt, sorrow, embarrassment or cowardice as he suggested to her that they obtain a divorce. She would need to write to him he said, "I can provide the words" he assured her, "to request a Restitution of Conjugal Rights".

"It sounds frightful," Florence said, taken aback, "why would I do that?"

"So that the court will order me to concede to your request and return to live with you. I shall refuse and they will establish that I have legally deserted you, following which you will have the right to a decree of judicial separation, and, when you add in my adultery, you will have an immediate divorce. You need not engage a detective, I can arrange everything through my colleague Perry Danvers and all the necessary papers will go to your solicitor. I thought you might like to use Robert Bartlett, he knows the situation and I shall be liable for all your costs of course, it should not be too inconvenient for you."

"Sounds straight forward enough Florence," Sylvia looked at her friend with a questioning look, "although I'm not sure being a divorcée is any more respectable than being a deserted wife these days."

Florence raised her eyebrows, "Since when have we worried about respectability my dear, I'm sure we've set many tongues wagging over the years, but James, I think I can see that this is what you would like? Do you wish to marry again?"

"You are right, it *is* what I would like. I cannot explain why, there is no-one in my life whom I should wish to marry." He took a deep breath, "I have a daughter, but even should I be free to marry her mother, it is impossible now, she has married someone else. I worry constantly that Victoria is illegitimate, but she would not be legitimised in any case. She lives with me." Looking Florence in the eyes he continued, "I am sorry our marriage did not last, I know it was all my doing and I regret my treatment of you, I hope you will forgive me."

"James dear, there is nothing to forgive, it was

not only your wish to separate if you recall, I was quite intent on having an independent life, I made things impossible for you. I have no regrets, not even that I did not give you your daughter, my life has been," and she smiled at Sylvia, "I hope will continue to be, happy and fulfilled. I have been blessed. Of course, I shall write as you ask, and *you* shall have your freedom. I have never stopped regarding you as a dear friend, even though we had lost touch."

By the end of October James had received Florence's letter, had responded negatively, the papers had gone to the court and the petition was filed. They would now have to await the slow workings of the legal system.

The new bombing raids on London started in June and James agreed with his tenants in the basement at Warwick Street that he, Plum and Rosa would take refuge down there during any night-time attacks. However, the German planes appeared brazenly in broad daylight and like most people, they were quite unprepared for this. On a hazy, summer's morning James was at work when they heard the immense noise of aircraft in the distance and he and his colleagues stepped out into the street. They gazed upwards, some mistaking the spectacular formation of planes as British until they heard the anti-aircraft guns opening fire to the east and then watched as the planes flew over, heading west and suddenly turned to bear down on the City of London itself. Isolated in the Park he was unaware that the streets emptied as people rushed to take cover. James stayed still, anxious, where was Plum? Was she safe at school? It was before midday so she should be indoors, under her desk, but what if they were out delivering their food parcels or going to the hospital to wind bandages. Would she know where to go? They'd talked ceaselessly about the drill. She was to go to the nearest underground station but would the teachers or the other girls remember this too. He thought he must go and look for her, but the bombers were almost overhead, the explosions were thundering so close, plumes of smoke and fire were rising up a few miles away, the noise was deafening.

He felt someone pulling his sleeve and turned to see Helen, her mouth shouting the words for him to follow her, to take cover. He stood one moment longer, the planes were targeting the city, Plum's school was further west, he prayed there would be no stray bombs, that his daughter was out of danger, and he let himself be pulled down the steps to his shelter. Thankfully they were all safe that day, but hundreds had lost their lives and property and that the enemy was prepared to attack during the day caused James to be on permanent tenterhooks. He tried harder to get home before Plum went to sleep on at least a couple of days a week, he quizzed her on the safety drills, he badgered her to promise over and over that she would run to the nearest shelter if she saw a policeman cycling along wearing a sign saying take cover and shouting warnings, or blowing his whistle. She swore to him she would not emerge from safety until she heard the bugles heralding that all was clear again. Still he could never relax, he slept only with the aid of his nightly whisky, more and more, and even then, his ears remained alert, straining to hear a night raid. These started in September and the three of them crowded with Mr Mossman the undertaker's coachman, his wife and four children in their tiny, basement parlour, Plum holding at least two of the little ones on her lap under the table.

The late September weather was fine and clear, the raids came night after night for over a week, James's nerves were shattered, he was stressed and scared for his daughter and for Rosa. The new attacks with incendiary bombs and the German plan to set London alight started in November and were terrifying. By then Plum had left school, she and Lily were volunteering with the VAD and he worried about her even more.

"Papa," she told him again and again, "you must not worry about me so much. I am an adult now and I am needed. Lily and I want to go to France, we're well trained auxiliaries and Alice is already out there. Lily says she can go but it won't be for a few weeks yet, so please Papa, will you give me your blessing? I want to help our boys where they need it."

"They need help in London too," James had answered, his whole being wracked with alarm at the thought of his precious Plum putting herself deliberately in even more danger, "the hospitals here are full of dreadfully wounded men, the effect of the mustard gas is devastating on the poor creatures who have survived it. They are being brought back to England and need you here."

In November he heard from his solicitor that the first stage of Florence's petition for divorce, the desertion claim, had been determined and he was required to pay her some thirty-five pounds for legal costs. He paid up quickly and waited again, the system slower than ever whilst the war in the air was raging. With parental consent not being forthcoming for Plum nor indeed it transpired, for Lily either, the girls had been seconded to a military VAD hospital in Hampstead and were sharing a house locally with four other nurses. Much as he missed her being at home, he thanked the Lord each night she was not in France. He looked for a way to get her safely out of the country to her mother in Monaco but she was adamant she would not go and he welcomed, with huge relief, the thick, suffocating fog and smog that fell and blanketed the capital at the end of the year. This would stop the air raids and he relaxed a little.

CHAPTER 41

1918
*January 28th, Night of unusually heavy bombing
in London and south-east England*

"Ouch!" Helen exclaimed, "I've just stubbed my toe on something huge." She hopped, wobbled and grabbed James's arm, "it didn't move, so I think it's only me that's hurt." Her throaty laugh echoed eerily in the murky darkness, "we must be almost there by now, I cannot see a thing."

The fog had been unrelenting during January and after three weeks of carefully feeling her way home early from the depot and spending the evening alone, Helen had suggested that they might go the Bell. "I shall go mad without an evening of good conversation soon," she had announced theatrically, "man was not designed for this miasmic hibernation. Do say you will brave the streets and come?"

The tavern was warm and welcoming, they coughed to clear their lungs and went straight to the same table in the parlour they had sat at on their first visit. The landlord, after a handful of visits over the year, now regarded Helen as a regular and emerged from behind the bar with drinks before they had time to take off their hats and coats.

"Evening Mr Severne, Miss, it's a real pea souper out tonight again, but whilst it's making life difficult for us, it keeps the Hun away. You can put the bombing to the back of your mind tonight, Miss. Enjoy the peace and quiet whilst you can."

Cosy and relaxed, they talked of their families. Plum had written several letters to James and he told Helen proudly of her work with the soldiers at the hospital, some harrowing tales of the young men damaged in body and mind and some uplifting stories of the bravery, humour and fortitude of men blinded and disfigured by the gas attacks.

"I'm so pleased Reggie was only wounded in the arm," Helen said, "although it was jolly bad, they thought he might lose it for a while. I'm pleased to report that he is out of hospital now, down in Thames Ditton with Mother, recovering, but that just means I worry he'll be sent back to the front again soon," her voice faltered, "he's frightfully good about it, doesn't talk about what happened out there at all, just worries for his men and his horse, says he can't wait to get back to them. I'm not sure I could ever be so brave."

"I don't think we know what we might be or do until we are put to the test," James said quietly, his thoughts not on war but on his own life, "sometimes it can surprise us for good," he looked up, sensing her familiar, awkward face, watching him intently, "or bad."

"Golly James, that sounds awfully profound. I can't imagine you doing anything bad in your life. You are such a kind man, I've told Daddy, the perfect gentleman."

"Sorry," he said guiltily, "I didn't mean to depress you. It's foolish to stay out too late in weather like this, they might stop the trains. I'll have one more whisky and then I should get you home."

"You see James, you are the perfect gentleman, coming with me all that way to make sure I am safe!"

The block where she rented a small flat was in Portland Place, "Please, come up and have a nightcap," Helen suggested when they arrived, "you've not seen inside, it's really quite satisfactory for a working girl," her laugh turned to a kind of snort and, as James had not declined, she held the front door open for him.

"I'm going to make a cup of cocoa for me," James had followed her through the parlour to the tiny kitchen, "but would you prefer a Johnny Walker? Daddy stocked my cabinet for me obviously thinking I'd be entertaining rather than living the life of a hermit here in the big city. Go and sit in front of the fire, thank goodness it hasn't gone out, I insisted my girl left early because of the fog. I'll bring your drink."

Stretched out on the small, upholstered sofa, he felt the heat from the fire begin to thaw out his frozen toes and spread up to his knees. He watched the flames spring through the new layer of coal Helen had quickly shovelled into the grate when they came in and rubbed his hands together to bring back the blood. After a few minutes she came in, put the drinks on a low table to the side of the sofa, handed James a crystal tumbler of amber liquid and offered him a tiny, china jug of water. That done, she flopped down next to him, "Dreadful sofa I know, bit threadbare and all the stuffing seems to have gone out of it. A bit like how I feel these days." Her laugh seemed forced and she went quiet, looking down into her cup, eyeing the steam rising from the dark brown brew, "When will it end? I read the news, but I can't make head nor tail if we are winning or not and I'm afraid the bombers will be back as soon as the weather clears, we're none of us safe." She raised her head and James could see tears welling, blurring the deep brown eyes, the colour of her cocoa, "I worry what will become of me. I'm not really that self-assured head girl you all see at the office, I'm a rather sad and lonely twenty-four-year old woman frightened that her life will end before she's had time to live it."

James reached for her hand and opted for platitudes, "I know it's hard to stay positive, but it's important work that we do, the public has a right to be protected and because of our efforts, the war will be over sooner."

"Do you really believe that? About the job I mean, not that the war will be over. Heavens, it cannot go on for ever, but the work we do. I often see that look on your face when you are gazing at the window and I see such sadness. I wonder if it's deeper than just the war though, it's not your life's dream to be crossing out badly spelled place names, is it?"

"I want to spend my time painting," he stared, unseeing, into the flames, "I know it's not practical, oh and I know I'm not good enough to sell and make a living, I have no illusions there. I just know that I am truly happy when I'm out with a sketch pad or even more so, with my easel and water colours."

"You should do it James, you told me before that you more or less stopped being an investigator when you could no longer accept the nature of the job so now, you need to stop this too."

He gave half a laugh, "I should like to try writing fiction too, I have a drawer full of half-finished manuscripts. I think I always felt that my wife had precedent in that regard but there is no real reason I have not written since we went our own ways." He let out a deep sigh, "It's impossible to think of resigning until the war is over but I do need to get out of London for a short while. I miss Plum dreadfully and whilst she is away, this would be a good time to take my paints to the country for a few days. I've not had real time off in these four years and nor have you. I shall do my best to arrange it very soon."

Hearing Helen's murmured assent, he realised he was still holding her hand. Patting it, he put it back down on the cushion next to him, raised his scotch and before he took a sip, ill at ease, he shook his head, smiled apologetically and asked brightly, "Where are all your young suitors then? Why are you spending time with an old fellow like me?"

"Poppycock, you're not old, just *older*! As for a line of eligible bachelors queuing up for my hand, that's not likely to happen. When I came back from Austria Mother and Daddy arranged dinners and parties for me - another of Mother's greatest sorrows in life is that none of us girls could come out, be presented at court. Not quite top drawer enough, don't you know, Daddy being *in trade*" she mocked, "but I was introduced to various weak chinned wonders and I regret to say I was utterly beastly to them all. I was less than interested in them and I'm not a half-wit, I know that Daddy's money was the bigger attraction for them."

"Don't put yourself down like that," James picked up her hand again and held it between both of his, "you would be a very good catch, whether your father had money or not," James surprised himself as he realised he meant it, "you put the usual birdbrained girls to shame, my suspicion is that you are just too fussy when it comes to potential husbands!"

James's laughter was cut short, Helen leant over to him and kissed his cheek. "What's that for," he asked in astonishment, and seeing her flustered look, added quickly, "not that it was not very sweet of you."

She picked up a loose cushion and hugging it tight to her body, picked at the already frayed piping and spoke softly, "I told you I was frightened that my life would end before I have had time to live and I meant it. I have never made love James, never even kissed a man I really want to kiss, just fended off the slobbery overtures from those unwelcome suitors. I've never held a man in my arms. Never been naked with him, never known the pleasure of love." She lifted her head to him slowly, "James, will you make love to me? We could all be killed tonight and I don't want to die a virgin and you are the only man I have ever cared enough for to make such a bold proposition."

His mouth dropped open and she leapt up from the sofa, "I'm sorry James, I'm so sorry. Please, I have embarrassed you, please forget I ever spoke, it is this wretched war, it makes one's brain addled, I am so sorry."

He saw the deep red blush spreading over her face and felt a real tenderness for this troubled young woman. "Calm down my dear, I am not upset," he too stood up, turned her to face him and rested his hands lightly on her shoulders, "I just wonder why me? I am thirty years older than you and rather, I'm afraid the word is, portly! Why would you want to experience such a special moment with me?"

"Because I have admired you since the first day we met, I have loved to secretly watch you," she said, shyly, "that little curl that sits over your ear makes me smile every time I see it and I have watched your mouth when you are talking, wanting to kiss your lips." She hurried on, "I don't see you as being so much older and anyway, I'm not drawn to men of my own age. I am much more attracted by your extra years, to me you are a man of experience, you have done so much in your life, you are my ideal."

"I am also married."

She shrugged her shoulders but did not pull away and he drew her to him, placed his lips on hers and kissed her, gently but passionately, then took her hand and walked with her into the bedroom.

The next day James found himself in a quandary. He had found the events of the previous night far more pleasurable than he would ever have anticipated before that moment, but he realised he needed to decide how to go forward from here. Helen was at great pains to assure him that he was under no obligation, that she by no means regarded him as, in her words, 'a cad or a bounder'. It had been she insisted, entirely her own wish and she would be grateful to him always. This assurance had been made by her when they were dressed ready for work, sitting at her little gate leg table, amongst her apologies for the coffee shortage and cups of milky tea provided instead. Earlier she had confessed, this time whilst stretching luxuriously under the covers, feeling the strangeness and excitement of James's body next to her, that it had been the single most important night of her life, she had never known such bliss, had never imagined that making love could be so wonderful and that she had always known James was to be the most important man in her life.

He was not naturally ungentlemanly, and, in spite of her words, he thought to ignore the situation would indeed be disrespectful and hurtful to Helen. He took the decision to use the excuse of his divorce, which was now approaching the climax, as a reason not to risk any further compromising situation at this time. He needed to provide his wife with evidence of his adultery and previous cohabitation. There was never any question of Florence naming Emily as the correspondent and James would certainly not allow Helen's identity to be known either. Aware they were forbidden from collusion, his wife was however, prepared to bend the rules, and agreed to cite, 'a woman unknown to her'. Florence was, James realised, a very dear friend. Nonetheless, the courts would need the proof and James not only needed a holiday, he realised it would be very useful for him to leave London for a while. His superior having agreed that he could take the whole month of March away, he booked a room at The Ferry Hotel in Cookham and told Helen that at least until this awkward business was over, it would be for the best if they refrained from any closer liaison.

"When it's done and dusted, we can see," he had told her, "and maybe you should take time off too, go to stay with your mother, you tell me your father badgers you to get out of town whilst this bombing is on."

When the time came for James to leave, so did she and they both left the capital on the same day. A cheerful James to a village by the river in Berkshire and a secretly tearful, gloomy Helen, to a village, also on the Thames, but in Surrey. James was to be joined overnight at the end of the month by an 'employee' of Peregrine Danvers to provide the necessary evidence for his divorce. Perry himself was to come down and document it.

CHAPTER 42

1918

By May, a virulent flu appears among French soldiers and spreads to nearly all European countries. Spain is not in the war and without press censorship, reports on it. Hence the name, Spanish flu. Death often comes within two days

Raising his eyes to the sky, James watched a dark cloud moving inevitably towards the already veiled sun and he packed his sketch pad and pencils away into his shoulder bag. He collapsed his folding stool and made his way back up the slope to the track at the top of Winter Hill where he stopped to look back once more at the view he had been absorbed in all morning. The river meandered in the valley below and he took in the meadows leading down to the water's edge, watching for a moment the cattle grazing and a few early spring calves butting at their mother's udders. It was a world away from the grime and terror of London. Closing his eyes, he breathed in deeply filling his lungs with the clean, bright air and set off back towards the village. The first spots of rain were beginning to wet his head and shoulders when he heard a sharp 'parp' and the brightest, buttercup yellow Rolls Royce motor car drew alongside him.

"Fancy a lift old chap? I'm heading for Cookham, hop in." The voice emanated from beneath a huge, white, handlebar moustache which itself was surrounded by goggles and a close, scalp hugging leather helmet fastened under the driver's chin. James knew immediately who his benefactor was, the legend went before him.

"That is very kind of you Colonel, I should be most grateful to ride with you. I miscalculated the weather today." He climbed onto the seat and settled his bag by his feet, "Splendid Rolls Royce Sir, splendid colour." The car gave a violent lurch and they set off down the narrow lane, "I'm staying at the Ferry Inn. Here for a few weeks to enjoy the countryside and paint. Been in London till now so I can't tell you how welcome it is to have this isolation."

"Understand, understand - out of the way blockhead," his saviour shouted at a hapless labourer walking with his dog at the side of the road, "make way or you'll be run down. Painter you say. You captured my house yet? 'Formosa', over on the island, often see you chaps sitting on the bank daubing away. Can't see the attraction myself, I've got one of these new cameras which takes an exact likeness. Marvellous, marvellous."

James found it difficult to get a word in and Colonel Ricardo's conversation, peppered from time to time with his vivid warnings shouted to men, carts and cattle alike, entertained him immensely such that the journey back to The Ferry was over all too soon. The whole of his left side was soaked where the rain had flurried in under the car's open sided hood, and he stepped down, repeated his effusive thanks and hurried into the Inn.

Still smiling he asked for his room key, told the landlord of his epic ride back and was not in the least surprised to be told that the Colonel, now acting as the Chief Constable for Berkshire whilst the war was on, had been the inspiration for Mr Grahame's 'toad' of Toad Hall. A boy was summoned to whisk away James's coat and hat for drying, he was instructed to leave his boots outside his door for cleaning, and then the landlord, his immediate duties completed, announced, "There's a lady waiting for you Sir, she's in the parlour, said she'd wait for tea until you arrived."

"A day early," James thought, "damn, I hope Perry is here too. I'm sure the woman wasn't supposed to arrive until tomorrow, this is a bally nuisance."

His surprise at seeing Helen sitting in the wing back chair in front of the window, still wearing her hat and coat, her gloved hands holding an open book on her lap, made him exclaim sharply, "What in the name of God are you doing here?"

"It's lovely to see you too James," she laughed nervously, "I realised my appearance here would be a surprise, but I hadn't reckoned on it being such a shock!"

"Forgive my rudeness Helen, I forget myself, but how and what brought you to Cookham. I thought you were safely at home."

"I came to see you James of course. Not to rebuke you for not answering even one of my letters to you," she'd found her spirit again, "but because I had some news for you."

"It seems a bit extreme to travel all this way, we

will be back in London in a few days. Or you could have written again? I'm sorry I haven't replied, up till today the weather has been so glorious that I have been out all day every day. Wait, shall we have tea and you can tell me all, in the meantime, give the boy your coat it's like a furnace in here." He came closer, "Is that your portmanteau there too? Were you intending staying?"

Whilst the maid brought the tea to them and fussed over placing the tray exactly, wanting to pour but being dismissed instead, they spoke of Helen's train journey and the turn in the weather. The moment they were alone, she flushed and unsure again, said, "I thought it would be huge fun to surprise you - and I really wanted to see you. It's so lovely to be here in Cookham, Mother is often quite demanding at home and I needed to escape."

James couldn't think what the urgency was, why she needed to track him down here to speak with him. He thought back to her letters, two in the three weeks he'd been at The Ferry, he'd read them only briefly, but he could not recall any matters of great importance, certainly nothing that had struck him as needing a speedy response. James said impatiently, "So, what is so important?"

She blurted it out, "James, I don't know how to tell you this, I am expecting your baby!"

He said nothing, numb with shock, just stared at her. Filling the awful silence, Helen gabbled on, "I've been bilious in the mornings these last few weeks and Mother heard and she just came right out with it, asked me if I was pregnant. Honestly James, you could have knocked me down with a feather, it hadn't occurred to me, I thought the sickness was just the strain of being in London and the bombing and what not, that it had all made me terribly tired too. You have to believe me, I did not plan this, I never thought it would happen and I want you to know, I shall not ask you for anything, no money, nothing. I can handle it on my own. Mother says she is not at all surprised, she feels I have been a lost cause for years and I'm beginning to believe her I'm afraid, but she is not unkind and has said she and Daddy will support me. I'm sure they'll tell all their friends that I married an officer and he has been tragically killed at the front, leaving me a widow with child. Daddy doesn't know yet, nor my sisters, but I'm sure they'll all rally round and everything will be for the best." She stopped to take a deep breath, "I thought of course I should tell you, after all you are the father and you might in all the circumstances want to know. You love your daughter so very much it would have been cruel of me not to give you the opportunity to love another," she was by now so agitated she rushed on, "not of course that you love me as you loved *her* mother and I am so well aware that you have just been being kind to me and that I am nothing to you and ..."

"Stop, for goodness sake, stop talking, I cannot think straight with you prattling on." James eased himself out of his chair, still in a trance, and stood up, "stay here, do not move. Do not even get out of your seat, and try to breathe, to calm down. I shall be two minutes, no more."

He went in search of the landlord and returned with a tumbler of whisky in his hand, "It's not every day I have news like this," he tried to smile but was aware it may have been more of a grimace, "I have ordered you a sherry, we need to gather our wits."

He felt the scotch work it's warming way down through his body and soothe his mind, he began to compose his thoughts and Helen sat, without saying a word, repeatedly tucking the same strand of loosened hair behind her ear, over and over again. After what seemed an age but could not have been more than a minute or two, James leaned across to her and picked up her hand from her lap. "You know my dear, I think this is excellent news. We have more than a few logistical problems to overcome, but mostly, I truly believe it is a welcome prospect."

Helen's relief was so great she did not hear how flat and unemotional his voice sounded, she burst into tears, scrabbled in her handbag to find a handkerchief, sniffed and mumbled and then gazed up at James with such adoration in her eyes that he was taken aback. Yet again his life was turning along a pathway not of his own, deliberate, making. This - he didn't even know what to call it, intimacy, dalliance, affair? - with Helen had never meant to be, as she had agreed, a 'big thing', but now, whatever its name, it had become another of the most significant events of his life.

His immediate problem however was Peregrine Danvers and Mrs Angel, even in his turmoil he had time to contemplate the irony of the working woman's assumed name, who would be arriving at Maidenhead station late the next morning. He must make sure Helen left The Ferry, but he did not want to explain the reasons why. He settled on overplaying the necessity not to besmirch her reputation and with a great deal of blustering and badgering on his part and a firm promise to not only telephone her at home but to arrange a visit too, she was persuaded to take her own room for the night and eat alone from a tray. Early the next morning she was carried off in the only transport to be found in the village at that time of the day, an old governess cart driven by the Colonel's retained batman, to Maidenhead station and thence back to Thames Ditton.

James was accustomed to an unconventional way of life, but even so, this morning seemed bizarre as he sat, not two hours later, in the parlour of The Ferry telling Perry the whole tale and awaiting the return of Mrs Angel who had stepped out for a moment 'to powder her nose'.

"To hell with this coffee Perry," he finished, "I need a whisky. One for you too?"

"No thank you Mr Chevasse, I'm working, and we need to go over the details for today."

"Aw, how lovely, I'll have a drink, a port and lemonade Ducks, it'll give me strength to get through my performance." Mrs Angel, James thought, must have ears as sensitive as a bat, she was still several yards from their table, "You was on the stage too, wasn't you?"

James looked accusingly at Perry and she said quickly, "No Ducks, it wasn't him what told me, was the young *laidee* in his office. No matter, I don't tell no-one who I'm wiv or where I am, your secret's safe wiv me."

It was arranged that James and the woman would stand obligingly close to the bedroom window in order for Perry to take a photograph. "I've only had the camera a few days and I'm not quite used to it yet, so can you stand still till you see me raise my hand Sir. Then I'll be sure I've got the image."

Then he would make a note of the times he witnessed the couple going to the dining room together, climbing the stairs together and entering the same bedroom together. They were compelled to stay the night in the room such that, in the unlikely event the landlord was questioned, he could honestly report that the lady had not booked a separate room. Perry would stay at the Bel and Dragon along the High Street.

"Then I just need details of you coming into breakfast together in the morning and I think that'll be enough. It's not as if you are going to contest the petition Sir are you."

It was an ordeal for James, even with the help of Johnny Walker, he dozed fitfully all night in the small, uncomfortable chair, pressed up against the bedroom door and rebuffing or ignoring all calls from Mrs Angel to "come on Ducks, lie down here next to me, no need to have any *convivial society*, it'll just be much more comfortable here for you to sleep."

He was never more glad to see the back of anyone as he was when she left in the morning and he headed straight to the bar where he learned of his new, and rather unwelcome, notoriety, the landlord having deduced wrongly that both Helen and Mrs Angel were in fact, his amours!

James stayed on in Cookham until the end of March, but the feeling of idyll had deserted him. Whilst he used the last few days to paint and write, above all else he thought of nothing other than Helen and the prospect of another child. With a sense of resignation, he packed up his artists box, tied the canvasses into a bundle, loaded his sketch books, note-books, pens and pencils into his case and prepared to return to real life. The Colonel with whom he had met up on several occasions was sad to see him go, extended an open-ended invitation to visit at any time, any time at all, and drove him in the Silver Ghost to the station.

CHAPTER 43

1918
July, Tsar Nicholas and his family are assassinated

The day after James arrived back at Warwick Street, a letter was hand delivered.

City of London Club,
19, Old Broad Street.
29th. May 1918

Dear Sir
I should be obliged if you would meet me at the above address at 12 noon on Monday 3rd April.

Respectfully.

Frederic Chiesman

No matter how many times he told himself this was to be a candid conversation with a gentleman of exactly the same age as himself, with all the shared life experiences that might entail, the churning in his stomach was the same as when, as a boy at Malvern College, he had been sent to the formidable headmaster for failing to submit his prep and was anticipating a resounding 'six of the best'. The rapid beating of his heart was start-lingly similar to that day the housemaid had shown him up to Henry Oatway's private study where he was to ask for Florence's hand in marriage. Now, he stood outside the Club willing his heart to slow down and his breathing to settle.

"Good heavens, pull yourself together," he said to himself sternly, "you are fifty-five years old and, just remember, his daughter is well past the age of majority, quite old enough to make her own decisions."

He was not entirely successful in quietening his nerves but had the presence of mind to understand that a confident overture was needed to wrong foot his opponent, should Frederic be assuming some moral or other high ground. The Club steward showed him to the library where he saw a gentleman, at least a head taller than himself, distinguished looking with a full head of swept back, steel grey hair. He had equally grey, professionally trimmed, eyebrows sheltering pale grey, piercing eyes and a matching neat grey mous-tache edging a long, upper lip. Frederic Chiesman was immaculately dressed in business attire, dark grey, pin stripe suit, white shirt and a maroon silk tie and was standing in front of the shelf of books beginning with 'C', he looked every inch the master of his own world.

James had a split second to consider his own, ra-ther more casual appearance. He was, naturally, wear-ing a suit, but for the warmth of the summer months it was in a lighter wool fabric and a less austere, mid blue. He had wisely chosen a single-breasted jacket to min-imise the look of his ever expanding girth and above his waistcoat his shirt sported a fashionable round col-lar and showed off the knot of an electric blue tie and pearl tie pin. His trousers revealed just a hint of equally bright blue socks above his black leather shoes and his final, flamboyant touch, was a deep blue cornflower in his lapel. "I am master of my own universe too," he thought, "actor, artist and author. Temporary government official," and holding his head high, he took a deep breath and strode directly across the room, smiling, with his hand held out in greeting. "James Severne," he announced, "we met very briefly at the Ritz on Helen's twenty first birthday."

If Frederic's aplomb was shaken, he did very well to disguise it and shook James's hand as if it would never have occurred to him to have refused, saying, "I shall get straight to the point. I'm very fond of my wife and daughter and they have begged me to be civil to you but for the record, had I my own way, I should have sought you out and had you horse whipped. A man your age carrying on with a woman thirty years younger, it's a disgrace."

James kept his thought, "But not in the least unusual!" to himself and allowed the aggrieved father the opportunity to vent his anger on him.

"Well now there is a child involved and my daughter's reputation is in danger of being ruined. Are you intending doing the honourable thing by her? Marriage?"

They were still standing, facing each other like medieval warriors and James, longing for a whisky, breathed a huge sigh of relief when the steward sidled up and asked if he could bring the gentlemen anything to drink. Frederic declined, saying he would wait until he went to the restaurant but James, emboldened by his craving, asked for a large Johnny Walker and water.

His opponent's eyes almost popped out on stalks and James, thinking he had gone too far, quickly tried to mollify him.

"I regret my divorce is not yet through, but rest assured that in any event, I shall support my child financially and play as big a part in his or her life as I am able."

Frederic seemed to run out of steam very quickly, his righteous indignation slipping away he satisfied himself by expressing his opinion that Helen would be safer living at home whilst the war was on than in Pimlico and that in any case, she was not too well from time to time and it was good for her to have her mother with her. James agreed completely and assured her father that he would not encourage Helen to return to London. He then accepted gracefully the invitation that Mrs Chiesman had extended to visit Beverley Dene for the weekend of June the fifteenth. James drank his whisky as slowly as he dared and an awkward silence fell, he was sure Frederic would have liked to dismiss him, but in fact he drew the meeting to a close himself. An uneasy truce had been negotiated between the two men.

Thus, it was the middle of June when James made his first visit to Helen's relatives and it was a baptism of fire. The entire family, except for Dolly's fiancée who was in France, had been invited. Not, he was assured by Helen, for his benefit, but because it was the first time they had the opportunity to get together in two years. Reggie was not shipping out again until the following Monday and Maud's husband had just been granted a week's furlough.

Helen was waiting at the station on the Friday

afternoon to meet his train from Waterloo. She had refused the offer of the dog cart, opting to walk, the sun shone from a clear blue sky and she was looking forward to having this short time alone with James. She had ignored her mother's reproach for leaving home in her dark blue gingham, loose fitting, house frock and as a result had managed to stay cool and composed in the heat. Watching a family with four very excited and chattering children waiting for the train to London on the far platform, she passed the time of day idly with the station master as he watered the thirsty geraniums in his beautifully regimented flower beds. When the train puffed slowly into the station and the doors opened, she saw James step down and her heart gave a jolt at the sight of his dear, familiar face.

Gripping his father's very battered, monogrammed, brown leather suitcase, James looked down the platform and felt an unexpected warmth spread through his chest as he saw Helen waving to him. He walked hurriedly towards her. He was dressed for the country, a loose, light coloured, linen jacket over his shirt and tie and a Panama hat. His darker trousers were also of a lighter weight and his brogues were polished to a high gloss. They shook hands and then, roaring with husky laughter, she put her arm through his and they set off home.

"It's been such a hive of activity, James, I think Mother has been reading too much Mrs Beeton. Everyone has been marshalled to help with vases of flowers in the bedrooms, little boxes with almond biscuits and bottles of Malvern water on the bedside tables and we had to check there were enough coat hangers. Oh, you are in what Mother now calls the blue room rather than the back, spare room, and how propitious, you have your cornflower boutonnière, you will match it perfectly!" Her laughter rang out over the sound of the horses, carriages and carts as they began their walk along the High Street, "We've all helped poor Reynolds pick enough broad beans, tomatoes and peas to feed an army whilst he's been trying to make sure the tennis court is in tip top condition and, in between that, dig up the early potatoes. You're bound to be given a bowl to fill with raspberries later on and I don't seem to be able to clean the earth out from under my finger-nails, I've been pulling up so many lettuces!"

"Sounds as if we shall be eating well this weekend," James said, "the shortages in London are so bad I believe they will introduce ration books next month."

"I've read that too and our local butcher has delivered so much meat that I'm embarrassed we are having more than our fair share, but it's just this once, and we are all together."

They passed the general store and Helen pulled on his arm, "Mother asked me to pop in, she forgot to order bacon, I need to tell Mr Strike. Watch out for the fly papers in here, they are usually completely revolting."

This done they carried on talking comfortably. James omitted telling of his conversation with her father and looking at her, was pleased to see her face had filled out a little, no sign of her pregnancy yet, but an overall plumpness that he thought suited her. He learned that her sisters and brothers knew she was expecting his baby, they had also been told quite emphatically by Helen, that no mention of marriage was to be made by any of them. "I told them all, this war has changed the plight of women for ever. No longer are we beholden to men for our livelihood, we can do what we want, when we want and if I want a baby without a husband, then I shall have a baby without a husband. We've come so far already, and I shall be able to vote in five years' time when I'm thirty and then I shall be voting for the voting age to be reduced to twenty-one in line with men."

James did not respond other than to squeeze her hand on his arm. He worried he had not yet found the right time to tell Plum that he was to become a father again. During a quick visit home with Lily, she had been exhausted, her work at the hospital physically hard and mentally draining and he had not wanted to risk giving her news that might prevent her from enjoying a total rest. He wanted her to relax completely away from the demands of her other life and so he had kept the revelation to himself, still not knowing how or when to tell her. As for marriage to Helen, he really did not want to approach the subject whilst he was here.

They arrived home at the same time as Frederic's newly acquired Wolsely motor car came noisily up the gravel drive and skidded to a halt outside the large, white, solid house. There were beautiful bay windows on the ground floor and twin gables reaching up to the steeply pitched roof which, it seemed, held a forest of chimneys.

Reggie leapt out of the driver's seat and shouted, "Am I the last? I went to collect Maud and Sheila, but it seems Herbert brought them over after all. I thought he wasn't going to be here till tomorrow. Thank you, Edmund," he slapped the chauffeur on the shoulder, "don't you think I did jolly well, it's only the second time I've driven. I want you teach me properly as soon as I get back next time, I don't intend having a gammy arm then." He swooped down on Helen, put his arms around her, hugged and kissed her cheek, then shook hands vigorously with James, good to see you again, I'm not doped up on morphine this time, but I do remember you. Come on, let's go and find the others." Helen and James followed him through the elaborately carved stone porch and Art Nouveau stained glass, panelled door into the long, airy hall. His suitcase was taken by a maid and he followed her, thankful for the temporary respite, to his room.

Helen was sitting on a wooden settle placed to the side of the staircase, when he came down and taking his hand, they walked together through to the back of the house. The others had all assembled under a fine horse chestnut tree on the beautifully manicured lawn where several small, white clothed tables, wrought iron garden chairs and brightly coloured deck chairs had been set ready for afternoon tea and cakes. Apart from Reggie who was completely friendly, the family were cordial enough, but James could certainly sense the initial frisson of coolness towards him and deciding quickly whether to accept this or challenge it, determined to engage every ounce of his native charm in an effort to win them over. At first however it seemed they were all so busy catching up with each other that he had time to observe and make lightning assessments of them all.

Nellie, Helen's mother, had a rather arresting appearance and was the obvious source of her three daughters' angular looks and high brows. She was, James guessed, the 'general' in charge of the home, authoritarian but content with the frequent, jocular insubordination of her troops. Frederic, in high command in his own work place was happy to play the part of willing 'second in command' until such time as his own matters of state took him away to the sanctity of his study. Reggie was charismatic and engaging, but, James thought, his ever-ready smile and amusing demeanour hid the occasional haunted look of anguish in his eyes when you could tell he was thinking about France. Maud felt her position as the eldest of the siblings quite keenly. Now mother to four-year old Sheila, she took pride in revealing her superior knowledge of life to her younger sisters and even to her husband Herbert, who she sometimes seemed to forget was a successful Captain, also in the War Office. Young Freddie was just seventeen and as uninterested in his family as any normal boy of that age, having four older sisters, could be. His sole concerns were that the war would be over before he had time to join up and whether anyone was going to play tennis later that day. Dolly was vivacious, slightly less lanky than her sisters and missing her Welsh Lieutenant. She acted as her mother's 'sergeant major' with gusto, which only left Linda, the youngest and the only girl to have inherited their father's paler colouring but not his height. She was a good deal shorter than her sisters and gave indications of a petulance simmering below the surface and a half-hearted performance as a 'regular foot soldier'.

When his moment arrived, James discharged every weapon in his armoury of good humour, wit, intelligence and magic with uncanny accuracy and by the end of the afternoon, if not completely forgotten, it seemed to be of no great importance that he was bordering on his dotage and yet the father of their very much younger, unmarried sister's, unborn child.

CHAPTER 44

1918

*July, Chilwell Shell Filling Factory Explosion in
which 134 Nottingham workers were killed*

E n masse they proved a jolly, happy family. The weekend passed in a surge of eating and drinking. Roast lamb and rice puddings. Poached salmon and summer pudding. Willow patterned cups of tea, madeira cake and flap jacks. He helped pick the fruit and shell the peas. He and Helen strolled along the lavender lined, terrazzo tiled paths, almost drugged with the heady perfume and the sound of the bees busy collecting the nectar. Secateurs in hand, they dead-headed roses as they passed by and they went to the stables. Taking an apple from her dress pocket, Helen put it on the palm of her hand and held it out to an elderly white pony who took it delicately and munched noisily. "Daisy has been my pony since I was little," she told James, stroking the horse's nose, "did you know that before the war the government made a census of all the horses in the country? Hundreds of thousands were requisitioned, and I was so scared they would take her. Daddy helped many other owners of ponies write and object to their children's pets being sent off to war and they eventually agreed a minimum height. I couldn't bear the thought of Daisy going. Reggie doesn't talk about it, but he did let slip that thousands and thousands of horses have been killed in battle or by disease or some just starve to death, it is so difficult to get them any fodder. I know he worries dreadfully about his horse out there, just as much as his men."

They sat side by side on the loggia in the evenings until the gnats and midges forced them inside, on guard for any baby rabbit brave enough to make a dash for Nellie's flower garden, ready to chase them away. He played chess with Frederic after dinner, smoking Havana cigars and drinking Chivas Regal whilst Freddie and Reggie argued over which music to play on the phonograph and the ladies sat sewing or reading.

On Sunday, after church, he had time to get out his sketch book and pencils and went quietly to the back door of the scullery and kitchen. He wanted to sketch the cook and her maid, both in a frenzy, stirring, popping things in and out of ovens, lifting wooden spoons and dipping fingers into the sauces checking the seasoning. The huge, scrubbed pine, kitchen table was covered with basins, jugs and saucepans. That afternoon after a long lunch, as the family sat indolent and drowsy in the shade, even little Sheila sitting still and quiet, he fetched his pad and taking up a position a little way away, up higher on a bank, with his back to the sun, he made his drawings of them. Especially Helen.

After a while he stopped to push back a lock of hair that had fallen over his forehead and a melancholy overcame him. The banter and fun, the closeness and love, "This is what my own family could have been like," he thought, "if Father had not died. If Mother had not married George. How different our lives would have been."

The peace was shattered by a piercing scream, Sheila had run full pelt into an urn of pelargoniums, chased by Freddie. There was no real cause for concern but by the time the little girl had been calmed and Freddie chastised, the serenity of the afternoon was broken. Games before tea was suggested and they scattered to collect quoits, balls, bats and blindfolds.

James was to leave late evening and he knew he must speak with Helen. She went with him to pack his few belongings before dinner. He had brought with him a ring, not at all ostentatious, a simple cluster of garnets in a gold setting, it was one of the very few mementos he had of his mother.

"Helen, I'm not yet free to marry, but will you wear my ring?"

Tears began to form in her eyes and she said again she could not bear him to think she had trapped him into marriage, that she would be content to have him remain her good friend and to be as involved with the child only as much as he would like. James felt ashamed that he agreed so readily, it was, he knew, a cowardly act on his behalf, but he insisted that she wear his ring and he promised not to mention marriage again until after their baby arrived.

"But I would so like to come back to London. It is peaceful here but I miss being in the city, I miss being able to see you more often," she sniffled, "Daddy is so against it but if you asked, I'm sure I could work for a few more weeks at least."

"Your father is right," James said seriously, "It's

being censored out of our newspapers in case it lowers morale, and I really shouldn't be telling you, but the Spanish are reporting daily on this worldwide flu epidemic. It's becoming rife in London."

"That's what Daddy said, that you can be well at breakfast and dead by teatime and that I will be far safer here in the country air. Do you know he said, if you're not bothered for yourself, think of the child and that was the single mention he had made the entire weekend to my 'condition'."

James could tell that it would have cost Frederic dearly to admit the facts. It was only his concern for her welfare that had induced him to and for that, James admired him. He backed him up one hundred percent.

Their son was born at Beverley Dene on the eighteenth of October. When James arrived, at Nellie's summons, two days later, mother and baby were 'doing as well as expected' but neither were thriving. Helen had been moved to what was previously known as the Peony room as this connected directly to a small nursery where Nanny had continued to reside even though the youngest of her charges, Freddie, was now long past needing her. She had been delighted that her recent role of laundress, seamstress and occasional cook had reverted to Nannying and was quickly resuming her officious but firm demeanour. The doctor was coming each day to treat Helen following her long, tiring labour and to check on the boy who, it appeared, was a 'sickly little thing'.

"It's nothing serious James, the doctor thinks he will get stronger quickly and Nanny says he takes his milk eagerly enough, just not enough of it. He tires and goes to sleep. Just like me," she gave a weak laugh, "I'm not sure I wasn't run over by a steamroller rather than give birth."

"Well, he may be small and weak at the moment, but my word, he's a handsome boy," James smiled down at mother and child in the bed, "what thoughts do you have on his name?"

"I should like to call him Reave if you agree. My second name is Vera and if you put an extra 'e' in, it makes what I think is a rather distinguished name. Maybe Reave James?"

He did his best not to raise an eyebrow at the novelty of it and ventured, "Of course, he must have the name you choose, but could his other name to be 'Justin' if you don't object. I'm very fond of that name."

"Perfect," Helen said sleepily, "Reave Justin Chiesman Severn. Perfect."

James did not return to Warwick Street immediately, he sent a message to New End Hospital in Hampstead, his son was now a reality and he could not put off telling Plum any longer. It had been tricky for her, asking to leave the hospital by five in the afternoon but Plum managed to get permission and rushed home to change out of her uniform and tidy herself up. She grabbed Lily's cup of tea from the kitchen table, laughing, "I don't have time to make one, I'm in such a rush it would never have time to cool. Wish me luck, Papa was so insistent I meet him I'm sure he's going to try to get me to give up nursing," and snatching the handbag Lily was holding out to her, she rushed off in the evening dusk to the Holly Bush.

"They've got their own vegetable garden here," James said when he had kissed and hugged her, "but it's not going to stop you wasting away. You are so thin

Plum. You must try to look after yourself better."

"Don't worry Papa, I'm fine. I like to be thin anyway. We should be able to eat well tonight. I think I'll
have pea soup and the cheese and lentil savoury. Sounds
very exotic," she smiled up at the barman who, having
told them they were only just in time to eat, had re-
cited the only food left, "you could have the Indian rabbit Papa and hope it's not too hot."

They ordered and sat, James with whisky and
Plum with another cup of tea, "I can't get hold of tea
leaves at the moment and I miss it so," she said pouring
it out and adding the milk, "I stole a mouthful of Lily's
as I was leaving the house, it's really given me a taste for
it."

"Victoria, I have something to tell you."

Just the use of her name made Plum realise this
was something out of the ordinary. She put the milk
jug down and, ignoring her cup, looked closely at her
father.

"Are you ill? *You* look thinner than when I saw
you when you got back from Cookham too? Have you
seen a doctor? Do they know what the matter is?"

"No, no, my dear I am fine," he took a deep
breath, "more than fine in fact, there is nothing to
worry about. I want to tell you that earlier this week
my son was born."

"Your what?" A line formed between Plum's
brows, "I don't understand, you have a son? I didn't
know you had married again, in fact, I didn't know you
and Mummy had divorced? What do you mean a son?
Does Mummy know?"

He did his best to explain, leaving out any mention of a divorce from her mother but saying he had

not, as yet, remarried. Plum was not sure what to think, she could not understand why this was the first she had heard of Helen let alone a baby sibling and James found it difficult to justify his position, he had to admit to himself, he too was a little perplexed. In the end, erroneously but he did not contradict her, she put his silence down to concern that as his daughter, she would be upset at the disparity in his and Helen's ages.

"Will you be living together at Warwick Street?" She had asked and he had answered that certainly in the short term, with the war and the influenza going around, Helen and the baby would stay with her family in the country. Plum suggested that she wait to meet her brother until such time as they came to London, "I'm not sure I'm ready for this Papa," she had said, tears brimming from her eyes, "it will change everything won't it? Will I be able to live at home too when the war is over? What about Rosa? What will Mummy think?"

It was a tearful, emotional night, James tried to console Plum, he told her that she would always be the most important person in his life, that she and Rosa would always have their home but that he must do right by Helen and the boy. He admitted he wanted to be part of his son's life. When they'd eaten, James hated leaving her, but he needed to get the train back into the city and walking together back to her digs Plum tried hard to hide her upset. James could only hope that in time his precious daughter would be able to forgive him. It was late when he got back to Warwick Street and he had few words left for Rosa who had waited up for him. He went straight to his study for a nightcap.

CHAPTER 45

1918 - 1919
November 11th 1918, World War I ends
with the signing of the Armistice

All their personal strife was completely forgotten for a while on Monday eleventh of November when the news came that the Armistice was signed and peace would come into effect later that morning. The streets were thronged with people cheering, waving flags, dancing, kissing friends and strangers alike, all celebrating the end of this Great War. Hanging out of their windows or riding on top of vehicles, hundreds shouted, laughed and cried as a cacophony of maroons, sirens, factory hooters, train whistles and car horns erupted at eleven o'clock. The war was over and all day and night, there would be rockets soaring into the sky, bonfires, street parties and church bells ringing. James pushed his way through the crowds to the underground station and boarded a packed train to Hampstead. He found Plum and Lily with friends on the main steps of the hospital, watching the merrymakers in the street outside. They had brought out with them many of the wounded soldiers, those able to dress were wearing their uniforms of sax blue suits and bright red ties. On crutches or in wheelchairs, these heroes forgot their pain for a few precious moments as they mingled, shouting, with the jubilant Londoners. When she spotted her father, Plum and James embraced, they thanked God it was all over and they were safe.

The nurses were eventually called back to their duties and James fought through the hordes again to the post office where he waited in the queue to telephone Helen. He was alarmed to hear she was still confined to her bed but was reassured that the doctor was satisfied there was no major cause for concern, she needed only rest to regain her strength. She promised that Reave too, although the doctor had said he was delicate, was perfectly stable and James therefore decided to delay visiting them until the following week. He would meet up with his friends that evening to celebrate, the Capital was an exciting place to be.

Whilst life for many began to return to a semblance of pre-war normality, it was never to be so for James. Everything was different, his daughter had her new-found adult freedom and he had the responsibility of a new family. Plum had volunteered to stay on duty in Hampstead over Christmas rather than return home and it was after the holiday that she told James of her decision to resign from nursing and go to live with her mother and Johnny in Monaco for a while. "I'm not cross with you Papa," she had said, "it's just that now I can travel freely, and I haven't seen Mummy for ages, five years. I thought it would be nice to stay long enough to really get to know her again and maybe to travel a little in Italy. Lily is going to join us out there in the summer and I thought I would go in June."

Before then, in April 1919, after a huge amount of soul searching, James asked Helen to marry him and applied for a licence. The baby was left with Nanny and they travelled up together to London and quietly, Helen thought almost secretively, married at the Register office in Pimlico. Their witnesses were Robert Bartlett, James's solicitor friend and a friend of Helen's from childhood. There was no party, no celebration and Plum had been told but not invited, she had no wish to meet Helen yet. "A purely contractual matter," James explained to her, "I cannot have the boy growing up without a father." In law however, he acknowledged that both his children were illegitimate, both born out of wedlock and it was a fact which constantly disturbed him.

Helen stayed on in Thames Ditton. She was back to her robust health but Reave was a sickly child given to frequent tummy upsets and when James heard that the doctor had worried about his wheezy lungs, he had insisted they keep away from London, "Stay in the country Helen, the smogs here are terrible still, it's hard for any of us to breathe. I shall come to see you both often, he is a splendid little chap, he reminds me of my father, he is a real Severn. We must make sure he stays healthy."

There was another concern for James, he was suffering increasingly with bouts of his own digestive problems. For months he had suffered the occasional bilious attack, thinking nothing of them but now he was very aware of a constant, general feeling of malaise. Rosa, who had transformed into James's 'keeper' since Plum had left home, nagged him unmercifully to consult the doctor. Dr. Seymour Taylor had long been a good friend, rarely consulted professionally, and surprised that James had admitted to feeling unwell had to confess the best treatment he could come up with for such vague symptoms was a complete change of scenery. "Get out of this infernal city my friend, what you need is to be by the coast, you'll be right as rain in no time. We've all suffered during these war years, you need better food and bracing sea air, marvellous restorative powers in the ozone. You could take that lovely daughter of yours with you if she wasn't already going off to the sun, last time I saw her she was looking peaky too."

James had gladly given up his position with the War Office, it was not a case of making way for the men returning from the war, he realised if he was to enjoy writing and painting, it had to be done now. Even if Seymour didn't know why, James knew in his heart that he was ill. Perry was keeping the detective agency ticking over and he took a small income from that plus the rent from the basement flat, and he hoped he would sell his articles and short stories to the magazines again. Plum had already left for Monaco and he wrote to make an open-ended booking for a room at the Wentworth Hotel in Brighton, packed his pens, pads and paints and set off for the summer.

Brighton was not much changed since his holiday with Emily and when he arrived a nostalgia settled over him as he remembered how happy he had been, how much in love and believing the feeling would last forever. Now he thought of what a strange turn his life had taken. He worried that revisiting the places he'd gone with Emily would bring up all his painful memories, but he was sanguine about it. All he'd ever wanted was for her to be happy and, sad as he was that he was not the one she was happy with, Rollinson was a good man, she was well looked after.

He forged a satisfactory routine for most days, early breakfast and if the light was good, sketching or painting, the sea, the beach, the Pavilion, the hotels, the promenade. Luncheon followed by a nap and writing. Dinner followed by coffee, whisky and cigars in the hotel lounge, enjoying friendly conversation with fellow guests. Each Tuesday he took the train to Thames Ditton to see his son, each Wednesday he sent Reave a postcard to say he would see him soon and entreating his baby to 'look after Mummy.' When it came to the end of September, he opted to stay a while longer, he had days when he felt his malaise more strongly and could not find the energy to paint or write and he preferred the view from this window, of the waves, the boats and the seagulls, to the soot and dreariness of London.

He returned to Warwick Street in February 1920 and Seymour Taylor confirmed that he had liver disease. Most likely cirrhosis, and the prognosis was not positive. "I suggest if you've things to do and places to go, you do them now old friend, I cannot cheer you by saying things will get better. I very much fear they will get worse."

James went to Robert and made his Will, directing that everything he owned, which, he acknowledged was little enough, went to Plum with the exception of his gold watch and tie pin which he left directly to Rosa. He also instructed that the sixteen years left on the lease at Warwick Street be assigned to Plum and Rosa jointly, both would have the house to live in, together or singly, until then. Painfully he then addressed the matter he'd pushed to the back of his mind for many years. Plum's legal status and the blackmail attempts by the Maddocks. Retrieving the packet of papers from the safe which was now in Perry's office, he marked them for the attention of Robert Bartlett, instructing that they were not to be destroyed along with all his other papers on his death, and then replaced them, securely sealed. He wrote a long letter for Plum, in which he told her that he and her mother had never married, that he had not been free to do so. He told her that he loved her mother very much and that he loved her, Victoria, more than life itself. He put the letter into an envelope and took his stick of sealing wax, lit a match and watched as the molten, scarlet wax dropped onto the back. He took the signet ring from his little finger and used it to press down firmly as the wax dried. With a deep sigh of relief mixed with sadness, he put the letter in the safe for her attention after his death. He appointed Robert and Plum as his executors and then he turned his attention to a final journey abroad, he had one more legal matter to attend to and he intended combining it with a final holiday with his daughter.

James took the boat to France in May and travelled to Monaco where he dealt with the last legal matter. Plum was not yet of age and he asked Johnny Rollinson to be her lawful guardian in the event that he died before she attained the age of twenty-one. He was proud to be asked and accepted readily. Plum was excited for the second of his final matters and in June she left to travel with him to Nice and thence to Paris where he could show her the places he knew and loved. He relived his first stay in Nice, he showed Plum the places she had seen over the years in his sketches and paintings. She wanted to see the site of his favourite picture, the washer women on the banks of the river Paillon, but the whole area was now covered by the Place Massena. They laughed and he tried to paint a mental picture for her, but it was impossible to imagine the river running underneath. They went to the Opera and the theatre, they dined at Le Chantecler in the Negresco, they walked along the Promenade and they lingered with croissants, coffee and Pastis in the cool shade of the Old Town. They took day trips to the medieval town of Eze, perched high on the rocks overlooking the sea and the beach at Beaulieu sur Mer. They took boat trips to St Jean Cap Ferat and Cannes and most importantly, they talked and mended the bridges Reave's birth had built.

In July they took the sleeper train to Paris, armed with the article he had written so many years ago for the *Saturday Review*. They laughed when he told her how his first impressions of Paris had been forged when he acted in the *Crimes of Paris*, how he had thought for a while the sets and scenery had portrayed the beautiful city realistically. Some days they ventured into the narrow streets where he had reported on the slums and the underworld, but mainly they went to the tourist sites. Nôtre Dame, the Champs Elysées, the Eiffel Tower and the Arc de Triomphe. They saw the Mona Lisa in the Louvre museum. They took a boat trip down the Seine and a day trip to the Palace of Versailles. They lingered with croissants, coffees and Pastis, this time in Montmartre, James talking with the artists, Plum helping with his rudimentary French. They dined at the Georges V and they went to the theatre and the Opera and they talked. James told her of his early life, he told her what he knew of his family, of his struggle to become an actor and of his downfall as a manager and his decision to become Justin Chevasse. He spoke of the friends he had made along the way and the friends he had lost but the story of Florence and the omissions in the tale of her own birth were left sealed in the envelope in the safe back in London.

Plum worried about her father, she worried that he was tiring himself too much. She worried on the days he could not find the energy. She worried and called the doctor when he had the first of his bouts of jaundice. James assured her all the time she was not to fret, that he was able to continue, that he didn't feel as bad as he looked. He wanted desperately to finish the trip and take her back to Monaco at the end of August. They both knew these travels and his conversations were his legacy to her.

When they finally arrived back in Monte Carlo, Plum begged to be allowed to come back to London with her father to look after him, but he refused. He promised that Rosa would send word when the end came, in time for her to travel to say goodbye, but until then she was to stay with her mother as he could not bear the thought that she would see him as his health deteriorated. Rosa was perfectly capable of looking after the house and him. Emily tried not to cry when she said her goodbyes, her emotions were confused. James was glad she had such a good husband.

CHAPTER 46

JAMES WILLIAM SEVERN
5th March 1863 - 1st April 1921

The journey home from France was exhausting and Rosa, so pleased to see him back, was shocked at his appearance, "Mr Severne, you look like death, you must let me look after you." She fussed like a mother hen and when he refused to take to his bed to recover, she climbed the stairs to his attic study dozens of times each day. She brought hot beverages, tucked his blanket round his legs, emptied the piss pot she insisted he use to save traipsing all the way down to the privy in the back yard. She banked up the fire which burned day and night and asked always what she could do to make him more comfortable.

After a couple of weeks James felt rested enough to tackle his next task. He slowly sorted through his paintings and drawings and withdrew all those of the south of France. On a crisp, cold day in December, he took a cab to Ladbroke Grove where he said his final goodbye to Florence and gave her the memories of their holiday. She was moved and promised to hang the 'Washer women of the Paillon' on her wall in pride of place. He asked his friends to drop by one by one for a final time, Charles, Gussie and Perry, all called, shocked to see him wasting away and bid him adieu.

Helen had begun the habit of bringing Reave to visit James in London once he was home. He was entranced with the little boy, bright as a button with a sweet and gentle nature, gingery, golden curls and bright blue eyes that reminded him so much of Plum as a baby. The sad difference was that Reave was a feeble child, always pale and often sickly enough to be confined to the nursery at home. When they were together, James loved to sit him on his lap and read to him, sometimes his eyes clouding over with sadness as his son fingered the gold watch and chain in his waistcoat pocket. At the beginning of January 1921, he instructed Helen not to visit again. She had quite understood when he told her that his meagre estate would go to Victoria on his death and she agreed wholeheartedly with the decision, her family had means enough to ensure Reave's future. She made her agonised farewells, James insisted on taking them to the door, kissed her and his son goodbye and watched them walk together away down the road.

That afternoon, tired and emotional from his exertions he was climbing the stairs slowly back to his study when Rosa ran up the steps behind him, "Mr James, you have forgotten your post today, no, no," she said as he reached behind him to take it, "I shall bring it all the way, I need to check your fire and settle you down."

Once at his desk, his swollen feet and legs warming under the blanket, he noticed an unusual envelope amongst his mail. He picked it up first, Jubb & Larkin was printed on the top corner. "Well I'm damned," he thought, "haven't heard from them in a long, long time." He slit the letter open and grinned as he read.

Dear Mr Severne,

I have no idea if this address for you is extant but in the absence of any better information, I can only hope that this letter finds its way to you.

Please accept my most sincere apologies for a rather unfortunate oversight on my Company's part. It has come to our attention during a reorganisation of our cellars, pending a move from Mark Lane, that we still hold six bottles of wine in your name. Wine deposited in our care in April 1887 as part of a consignment of fifty cases from Messrs. Severn & Co, Nottingham. I cannot excuse our culpability in this unfortunate mistake but since the death of Mr Henry Jubb who oversaw your account, I can only assume that you yourself had overlooked the possession of these final bottles too.

I regret to inform you that five of the wines, what would have been a very satisfactory Chateau Lagrange, will most certainly be undrinkable and I am therefore taking the liberty of substituting a very fine Claret that I hope you will find more than acceptable.

The last bottle however is very exciting, an 1883 Chateau Lafite - Rothschild, which in our opinion will be absolutely superb to drink after all these years. This wine has a most excellent reputation of quality and I know personally of a very recent occasion when this vintage was enjoyed immensely. These vintages seem to be able to defy the decades and never die.

I await your acknowledgement of this letter at which time I shall arrange for a timely delivery to an establishment of your deciding.

I remain your most obedient servant.
Jeremy Larkin-Green
Messrs. Jubb & Larkin

The irony was not lost on him but there was one thing for sure, dying or not, he was going to drink that Chateau Lafite.

He now had only one last mission and needed his final days or weeks to be uninterrupted. He wanted his son to know where he came from, he needed to leave Reave an account of his own life and the lives of their ancestors. Each morning Rosa helped settle him behind his desk, Livy Martin's desk, a tangible link to the past. Putting aside his modern fountain pen, he took from the tray, his silver pen and dipped the nib into the ink well. His neat, precise writing had become erratic, the tremor in his hands forming spidery, uneven letters, but he wrote until his eyes drooped and he slept, his chin sagging to his chest. On waking, he carried on, slowly producing page after page. With Rosa's help he searched painstakingly through the boxes in his studio, retrieving the letter his own father had written to him before his death with the story of the Severn ancestors. William born in 1723, the penniless boy whose legacy of a modest vintners led to his son James founding the wine merchants and restaurant, Severns. Of old James's nephew, John, and his son James Barratt who was to become Reave's grandfather. All these generations had cherished and grown the family business, they had left a legacy that provided the privileges they had all enjoyed. Until, that is, he, James William, had let it go. He wrote of his decision, his desire to forge his own life, independent of his family.

He found letters he'd forgotten he had kept from his mother Jane. Reave would know he had aunts and uncles, in England and in Canada. Rosa pinned and stacked the pages together. They found old theatre programmes with 'Ernest Severne' printed in black and white and he wrote to Reave of how much he loved acting, how walking out onto a major London stage for the first time in *The Crimes of Paris* was a realisation of one of those moments in life, so special and so transient that could never be repeated. He included his reviews from the newspapers, programmes from shows he had enjoyed and a theatre bill or two signed by the star of the performance. He compiled the newspaper accounts of the debacle of *The Oath* and the dismal proof even of his bankruptcy.

He wrote truthfully of his marriage to Florence, her success as an author and his failure as a husband leading to their separation. Rosa stacked the press reports of the Justin Chevasse investigations that had gone to court and caused publicity and James wrote about others for whom he had worked, either for Reave's future amusement or because of their importance.

He included copies of his published articles. 'The Slums of Paris' with the cover of the *Boston Sunday Post* and his favourite piece, an article about Monty with a photograph of his beloved collie. He told at length of his love for Emily and the existence of his daughter Victoria, the sister whom he hoped Reave would get to know and love. He made no mention of the blackmail, he felt it was for Plum alone to decide on that. He wrote what he could of his life and work during the Great War and of his admiration and affection for

Helen, his mother.

He wrote how much he now regretted being estranged from his family and how he wished he had tried harder with his step -father. He knew now how it must have hurt his mother and how he mourned that it was too late for any death bed reconciliations. He wanted his son to know it had taken him all these years to recognise he had never been the governor of his own emotions and had allowed his mind and body to be so easily seduced. He had acquiesced to the three main women in his life, Florence, Emily and Helen when each one had wanted something from him. He had obliged willingly and unquestioning but, in the end, he wanted Reave to know he was glad of them, without all three he might have sailed rudderless through his life. Finally, he recognised it had taken him his whole lifetime and the birth of a son to understand the importance, the significance, of heritage. Tradition, a history and understanding for future generations. A continuity. For his ancestors, the legacy had been Severns, for him, his legacy could only be his children.

These last weeks he had taken to staying in his attic, it was too difficult to negotiate the stairs and, besides, he often could not sleep at night. He would continue to write and, on moonlit nights, sit and watch the stars. Rosa had brought a chaise up and fashioned him a bed. She put the commode in the corner, and he dozed and woke, dozed and woke. He had no appetite, his body was swollen, and his sickness ever present, but she did her best to tempt him with delicacies and helped his pain with tiny doses of laudanum, his nausea with tiny sips of whisky.

By the end of February James had finished writing. Rosa bound the hefty bundle of papers into a large parcel and labelled it. She found James Barratt's beautiful silk waistcoat, wrapped it in fine paper and put it in his leather, monogrammed case. She picked out James's mother of pearl tie pin and silver backed hairbrush and put them in it too.

On the evening of the third of March, James called Rosa and asked her to decant the bottle of Chateau Lafite. He watched as she poured the wine carefully, anxious that she stop the moment she detected any sediment rising. She placed the wine and a little dish of salted biscuits to the side of his desk and left the room. James sat deep in thought for a while, then carefully poured himself a glass of the deep red liquid. He picked up his pen, took a sheet of Basildon Bond notepaper and wrote his final words to Reave Justin Severn, to be opened on the occasion of his attaining twenty-one years, 16th October, 1939.

174, Warwick Street,
London.
3rd March, 1921

My dear son, Reave,

As I write this letter you are not yet three years old and my time on this earth has come to an end.

These papers will tell you of the man I was and the man I might have been. My hopes and dreams, my successes and my failures.

My one and only regret in life is that I did not have the chance to know you nor you to know me.

Make of my memories what you will, but remember always, I loved you.

Papa.

Done, he sat back and asked himself, "If I had my time over again, would I do things differently? No," he answered, smiling inwardly, "I would do it all this way again".

He picked up his glass and savoured the complex flavours of the aromatic wine. The merchant was right, it radiated finesse. Severns had been masters of their trade and this was indeed their truly exceptional, "Last Vintage".

§

Thank you for reading this book. If you enjoyed it, please return to Amazon and leave a few words as a Review. I'd really appreciate it.

https://www.amazon.co.uk/dp/B07Z55KX3Q

ABOUT THE AUTHOR

I'm in my third age and I've been a wife, mother and homemaker, a divorcee and career woman, a second wife and widow and now I'm retired, with a new partner, and indulging my love of books and writing. I have two homes, my house in Berkshire and my partner's apartment, over-looking the bay, in Villefranche sur Mer on the Cote d'Azur. How lucky am I.

When I reached seventy, I thought, "What shall I do now? I know, I'll write the book I have always thought I could."

My characters were waiting for me in my head as over the years I had spent many happy hours researching the Severn family who became wine merchants and restaurateurs in Nottingham and whose legacy to the town is the medieval, timber framed Severns building, carefully removed, restored and repositioned from Middle Pavement to opposite Nottingham Castle. I have thoroughly enjoyed letting my imagination run wild with how so much of their day to day lives might have been lived.

Books By This Author

Grapes of Fortune In the 18th century, William Severn strives to rise out of poverty and make a better life for his children but their ambitions, devotion and determination give rise to heartache, jealousy and death until disaster strikes which could bring it all crashing down around them.

Vines of Promise January 1900 and James Severn awakes on the first morning of a brand new century, facing ruin. Set against the backdrop of the industrial revolution in Nottingham and London, the Peninsular Wars and the vineyards of Burgundy, James and his family strive to fulfil their legacy and give the next generations the promise of a future.

Lisa Absalom

I'm in my third age and I've been a wife, mother and homemaker, a divorcee and career woman, a second wife and widow. Now I'm retired, with a new partner, and indulging my love of books and writing. I have two homes, my house in Berkshire and my partner's apartment, over-looking the bay, in Villefranche sur Mer on the Cote d'Azur.

When I reached seventy, I thought, "What shall I do now? I know, I'll write the book I have always thought I could."

My characters were waiting for me in my head as over the years I had spent many happy hours researching the Severn family who became wine merchants and restaurateurs in Nottingham and whose legacy to the town is the medieval, timber framed Severns building, carefully removed, restored and repositioned from Middle Pavement to opposite Nottingham Castle. I have thoroughly enjoyed letting my imagination run wild with how so much of their day to day lives might have been lived.

Printed in Great Britain
by Amazon